Nichole Severn writes explosi⸻ strong heroines, heroes who dare challenge them and a hell of a lot of guns. She resides with her very supportive and patient husband, as well as her demon spawn, in Utah. When she's not writing, she's constantly injuring herself running, rock climbing, practicing yoga and snowboarding. She loves hearing from readers through her website, nicholesevern.com and on Facebook at nicholesevern.

Sandra Owens lives in the beautiful Blue Ridge Mountains of North Carolina. Her family and friends have ceased being surprised by what she might get up to next. She's jumped out of a plane, flown in an aerobatic plane while the pilot performed death-defying stunts, and has ridden a Harley motorcycle for years. She regrets nothing. Sandra is a Romance Writers of America Honor Roll member and a 2013 Golden Heart Finalist. Her books have won many awards and she is an Amazon bestselling author.

Discover more at millsandboon.co.uk

MANHUNT IN THE NARROWS

NICHOLE SEVERN

DANGEROUS AFFAIR

SANDRA OWENS

MILLS & BOON

First Published in Great Britain 2025
by Mills & Boon, an imprint of HarperCollins*Publishers* Ltd
1 London Bridge Street, London, SE1 9GF

www.harpercollins.co.uk

HarperCollins*Publishers*
Macken House, 39/40 Mayor Street Upper,
Dublin 1, D01 C9W8, Ireland

Manhunt in the Narrows © 2025 Natascha Jaffa
Dangerous Affair © 2025 Sandra Owens

ISBN: 978-0-263-39725-3

0825

MIX
Paper | Supporting
responsible forestry
FSC
www.fsc.org
FSC™ C007454

This book contains FSC™ certified paper and other controlled sources to ensure responsible forest management.

For more information visit: www.harpercollins.co.uk/green

Printed and Bound in the UK using 100% Renewable Electricity at CPI Group (UK) Ltd, Croydon, CR0 4YY

MANHUNT IN THE NARROWS

NICHOLE SEVERN

To Sara A.

Couldn't have written this one without you.

Chapter One

There were human remains all over the park.

National park ranger Sayles Green leaned into the familiar burn at the back of her quads as she descended past the Emerald Pools trailhead and into the main vein of the park.

Zion National Park could've been considered a wonder of the world with its sheer rock faces and plummeting gorges. Plant life thrived in the middle of the desert where temperatures reached over 110 degrees multiple times throughout the year. It wasn't just cacti and dead things that kept her eyes from itching and her nose from spreading her DNA over every trail and tourist but maple trees, horsetail that looked like failing bamboo, and fuzzy great mullein. Rare. Exquisite. Isolated.

The park was no Grand Canyon, at least not in the sense of how many bodies she and her fellow rangers pulled through the front entrance, but she liked to think that was due to her dedication to protect the park from the people and the people from the park.

Still, there was an off chance the report she'd gotten less than an hour ago from a frantic, glassy-eyed tourist—most likely a victim of the alcohol she'd smelled on his breath—held some weight. Of all the national parks in the

United States, Zion had its own reputation for falls from its 5,000-plus-foot cliff faces, for drownings and hypothermia thanks to the 1,000-foot depth of the Virgin River, and for its sheer ability to attract the most egotistical and arrogant hikers on the planet. Because they certainly couldn't die on a simple hike, right?

Sayles followed the man-made bridge over the tail end of the river and into the parking lot on the other side of the main artery that shuttled hikers to any one of eight current open trailheads. The truth was, anyone could die out here. A teen stepping off a cliff edge in the middle of the night looking for a restroom. A child who'd gotten too close to the river's spring rapids and fallen in. A grown man trying to get the perfect angle for a selfie along the park's most dangerous ascent with nothing but a chain handrail between him and a 5,000-foot drop.

She'd seen it all. Grieved it all.

And yet this park—with its dangers and fair share of overpacked trails and stupid mistakes—was all she had left. All she wanted. She protected woods and wildlife from hunters, destructive tourists and the occasional fire. She brought bad guys to justice while maybe even saving a few lives in the process. She'd carried scorpions and rattlesnakes out of campgrounds and her own personal trailer, transported a bighorn sheep to a rehab center, and convinced a bear to get out of a dumpster near the visitors' center. She'd changed flat tires, helped resolve marital disputes, provided directions and managed to extricate dozens of keys locked in cars. Her life as a ranger was as multifaceted as it could get. Freeing. Hers.

Sayles stood in line with the rest of the group waiting for the next shuttle. A couple of kids on leashes dared to strain against their parents' hold under and around the flimsy barriers meant to corral tourists into single-file lines, and she had to check herself from asking whether they'd come with their shots or if that'd been a separate appointment. The sun's heat worked its way beneath her uniform. The button-up short-sleeve shirt and shorts weren't fashionable in any sense of the word, but they got the job done. And that was what she was here to do. A job. The buses came every ten minutes. She didn't have to wait long before the newly christened electric shuttle pulled to the curb.

The driver's radio crackled with a request from the other end as she ascended the two steps at the front of the bus with a nod in greeting. The cell coverage in the canyons was nonexistent most days and unreliable on others. Couldn't take the chance of dropping calls during an emergency evac. She didn't know the shuttle driver's name. Hell, she could barely remember her own most nights as she fell into a dreamless sleep of exhaustion after her shift. That was how she liked it. Drivers, rangers—and their perspective cohorts—maintenance personnel and scientists tended to keep to their own pacts.

Sayles took her seat across from the family with the two children feral enough to require leashes, and the shuttle kicked into gear with a jolt. It didn't take long to hit the next stop. Two minutes, maybe three, before she was descending the bus stairs and dropping onto the sidewalk in front of the Temple of Sinawava trailhead.

Into a land of fishermen.

Hikers trudged across the open grass as though they were wading through several feet of water, sleeved in thick waterproof overalls, heavy rain boots and jackets. Because that was what was required to gain access to the Narrows—a sixteen-mile combination of rapids, unclimbable sandstone gorges and a maze of death traps. Sayles walked the one mile to the end of the paved riverside walk and was confronted with a crowd gathering at the edge of the Virgin River.

Right where the inebriated tourist had told her to look.

"Park ranger, step aside." She forced her way through a crowd of sweating red faces and odor-heavy shirts. To find a body half submerged in the river's clutches.

Holy hell. Sayles lunged for the man's side and pressed two fingers to his neck. No pulse. She grabbed the radio on her hip and pressed the push-to-talk button. "Risner, come in." It took a few seconds, but the radio gods were looking down on them today, and she managed to get through. Her skin heated underneath her ponytail and iconic ranger hat as she studied the face staring back at her. There was still some color in his cheeks, a touch of warmth despite the freezing temperatures of the river. But he was undeniably dead.

"Go ahead, Green." The district ranger's voice broke on her name. Risner wasn't anything spectacular when it came to the job. By the book, a little bit sexist and a whole lot of bland. But she couldn't do this without him. He'd come on a decade before she'd been hired, but they'd been up for the same promotion a few months ago. She'd gladly passed on rising to district ranger to him. Too much paperwork. He'd have a lot more today.

She surveyed the cluster of onlookers around her and gauged her chances of being able to control them on her own. It wasn't looking good as another shuttle full of hikers ambled down the paved path right toward them. "I need one of the law enforcement rangers. We've got a body. We have to close access to the Narrows and get everyone off the trail. And you're going to want to get up here. Now."

"What the hell is going on out there?" Risner asked.

"We've got a body." She managed to branch one arm out to keep tourists from getting too close to the scene, but she couldn't do anything to stop them from getting photos and taking video.

Whispers breathed through the mass.

Is he dead?

Wait. Was he killed?

Did he drown?

The same questions tried to break through the barrier of detachment she'd constructed the moment she'd set eyes on the body, but she couldn't give them weight.

"Everyone, please. I'm going to need you to take a step back." Sayles tried to herd them toward the paved path, but it was just like any other day when dealing with people who thought they knew better than a trained professional in the middle of the most dangerous environment on the planet. Negotiating with wild cats. The whispers grew louder. Full panic was about to take hold. Question after question vaulted through the crowd at her, as though she knew all the details of how a body had ended up on her trail. But she'd dealt with far more terrifying circumstances than this. She set her fingers between her lips and whistled above the increasing assault of questions. "Everyone, look here. I'm Ranger Green, and I need you to do exactly as I instruct to ensure you all make it out of the park tonight. Is there anyone who saw what happened?"

Nobody raised their hand.

"Has anyone seen this man before? Maybe on one of the trails or at the visitors' center?" A hand went up in the back. "Great. Come stand by me. Did anyone see or hear anything unusual here on the trailhead or on the trail?"

"I heard a scream. I… I turned around and there he was. Just lying there," a woman said. Her voice betrayed the realization sinking in minute by minute. She'd wrapped her arms around herself as though she were guilty of killing the man herself. A tremor shuttered through her. Shock. She was going into shock. "I didn't know what to do."

"All right. Stand next to me, your arm touching mine. Don't break the contact, understand?" It wasn't much, but it would give the woman something to focus on over the next few minutes. Sayles tried to keep her own voice even and raised it over the nervous and shifting crowd. She'd volunteered for short-haul operations, dangled at the end of a rope from a helicopter during rescues and climbed these cliffs with minimal support. But she'd never faced a body on her own. There had always been another ranger to walk her through the protocols. "Ladies and gentlemen, law enforcement rangers are on their way. We will be closing the Narrows trailhead. I need you all to gather your parties and belongings and make your way to the shuttles where you will be taken to the visitor center and asked for statements."

In her peripheral vision she saw another group had moved up the Riverside path, headed straight for her. Every muscle in her body was prepared to force them to turn around, until she spotted District Ranger Risner in the middle of the group, his gaze locked on her. Then the body. He'd brought the cavalry, and a rush of release coasted through her. It didn't last long. Because along with two other rangers—law enforcement rangers from the look of it—a fourth person compressed the air from her lungs. He stood out, a misfit among the rangers. Taller, more muscular, even outfitted in jeans, boots and a T-shirt. She didn't recognize him. Only men like him. Far too aware of their surroundings. Controlled. On alert for the slightest threat. And if he and any of his partners were in the park...

Sayles's breath lodged in her throat.

"Listen up, folks." Risner's voice rose over the murmurs and complaints. "The shuttles are waiting to take you back to the visitors' center. I apologize for the inconvenience, but please, we need you to leave this area as soon as possible."

Yes, a dead body was certainly an inconvenience.

The man Risner had brought centered his attention on the body at her feet. Barely sparing her a glance. All about the job. Principled and disciplined. Unwavering. She guessed she should be thankful for that focus. Because experience taught her that having that kind of intensity on her would be a very bad thing.

Sayles sidestepped, moving both potential witnesses away from the remains for the law enforcement rangers to do their job. Hopefully she'd be forgotten once she handed them off. "I asked these two hikers to remain behind to give statements."

"Agent Broyles of the FBI, this is Ranger Green." Risner pointed a strong finger toward her. The district ranger's thin, ratlike face contorted into something like a smile. A mask for those who didn't have to deal with his underhanded comments and criticism on a daily basis. "She's going to be the one you want."

That all-too-trustworthy gaze tore from the body at their feet and landed on Sayles. "I hear you're the one who can get me through the Narrows in one piece."

She'd hiked in and out of the Narrows and everything in between every weekend since she'd been hired four years ago. Rain, shine, snow, flood. That last one was far more likely this time of year when the winter snow was melting at an alarming rate. She knew the trail better than anyone else in the park, but panic flared hot in her chest. What the hell was the FBI doing in her park? "Why would you want to do that?"

"Because we have a killer on the loose, Ranger Green." Agent Broyles straightened to his full height, a full head above her. "And I need your help to find him."

Chapter Two

Ranger Green didn't like him one bit.

Elias Broyles faced a collection of national park rangers in Zion's visitors' center of all places, very aware of Green's desire to make him all but invisible. She'd kept her gaze solely honed out the shuttle window the entire ride back. Going out of her way to avoid him, it seemed.

Hikers of all types, from toddlers to overpacked amateurs to leathery, sunbaked mountaineers, had been escorted away a little less than thirty minutes ago. It would take a few hours to ensure visitors cleared out of the nearly 150,000-acre national park, but this couldn't wait.

Despite floor-to-ceiling windows punctured throughout the single-story structure, the scuffed brown cement and exposed support beams urged him to seek out more light. As if the natural woods and tones could close in on him at any time. The half walls showcasing things like Zion's geological layers and something called Weeping Rock didn't help with the open concept his body craved. A ceiling fan over the information desk failed to cool the space, but that was what he got for overdressing.

"Rangers, the FBI is in need of our expertise." Risner hiked his thumbs into his belt and puffed out his chest like one of those birds Elias had seen on the Animal Channel. Except the man had the uncanny resemblance to a rat with beady dark eyes and a thin face. His skin wasn't as deeply tanned as the rest of his rangers, but the man worked hard to give the impression he'd serve right alongside them in any situation. Truthfully, Elias wasn't sure the man had walked these trails in months. Risner rocked up onto the toes of his boots. "As you know by now, a body was reported by a hiker about an hour ago. Ranger Green responded and called me for assistance. From the look of things it seems to be a case of foul play. Agent Broyles, tell us what you need."

Foul play? Did people still talk like that?

Elias caught sight of Ranger Green's focus from the back row of wooden benches meant for visitors to sit and watch an introductory movie about the park. As far from him as she could get. Captivating, ethereal eyes—the color of rare jade and just as cold—centered on him beneath that iconic ranger hat. She hadn't said a word since his request for assistance back at the death scene. That distance was still firmly between them now, though he couldn't imagine what he'd done to earn her dislike in the hour since he'd stepped into the park. She'd kept a level head after confronting the body. Something he certainly hadn't been able to do his first time in the field. But maybe this wasn't her first time. Or maybe she just didn't like his face. He couldn't do anything about that. Besides, he wasn't here to make friends. He'd come for redemption.

"Rangers, our victim has been identified thanks to the ID in his jacket pocket. As far as we can tell, he was in the wrong place at the wrong time and not specifically targeted by his killer. His remains are now in the possession of your law enforcement unit and are being escorted to the Kane County medical examiner to determine how long ago and how he was killed, but we need more information. That's where you come in. There was a witness at the scene, but we need to know if our victim was traveling or hiking with anyone else in his party and what drew the attention of our killer."

"You just said he wasn't targeted." Ranger Green notched her chin higher, almost daring him to contradict himself to a room full of her colleagues. He had a feeling this wasn't the kind of woman who would back down. "Wouldn't your time be better spent focusing on the person who killed him?"

"You're right. I did say that, but that doesn't mean the killer didn't get something he needed from his victim. Supplies, cell phone, cash—killers need resources to survive here just as much as the rest of us." And they would take advantage of anyone who got in their way. "I want to know why the killer chose this victim over the dozens of others on that trail. As for the person who killed your hiker, my partner and I have been hunting a suspect who has left two bodies in California and one in Nevada. The unsub seems to be sticking to the main freeways, targeting drivers who travel alone, then stealing their vehicles until he runs out of gas before moving on to his next victim. We don't know where he is headed, only that the three victims' cell phone GPS indicates they all stopped on the freeway for a brief time. Most likely to pick up the killer. A vehicle belonging to his last victim was reported parked here at the visitors' center early this morning. My partner is searching the van now."

Risner raised his hand as if they were in the middle of a complicated psych lesson. "Unsub?"

"Unidentified subject." Ranger Green leveled that compelling gaze back on Elias, and his body tightened in all the wrong places. "It means they have no idea who they're looking for. Just that he's leaving a trail of bodies behind him. And now he's somewhere in the park."

It seemed Ranger Green had educated herself in homicide investigations. Interesting. That didn't help keep the atmosphere in the visitors' center from growing frenzied. Rangers looked to one another and kept to low whispers. "While we may not know the killer's identity, Ranger Green managed to secure a witness at the base of the trail who reported seeing the killer shortly after the victim's body was discovered. We've got a basic description of his appearance, but nothing more. It's possible our unsub will try to secure another vehicle, but we have Springdale police and your law enforcement rangers at every entrance to keep him from escaping."

"He went up the Narrows." Confidence bled into Ranger Green's assessment. That kind of intensity was hard to ignore, but he imagined it had caused her a lot of problems here in the park considering how many rangers had put physical distance between themselves and her position in the back row. Not a team player.

"We believe so, yes. A killer's number one priority is survival. He will do whatever it takes to avoid capture and arrest and try to wait us out. Lucky for us, adrenaline tends to make suspects very, very stupid, and I intend to take advantage." Elias folded his arms over his chest. "Problem is we aren't trained for this terrain. I'm going to need a guide to get me up the Narrows safely while my partner takes point here to prevent the killer from leaving the park."

Risner clapped his hands, facing the dozen or so rangers. "I've got the best rangers in the service willing to do whatever it takes to help. Apart from Ranger Green, I'm your best bet, Agent Broyles. Been protecting these trails for over a decade and assisted in a number of rescues. There isn't a single mile of park I haven't hiked."

Ranger Green gathered a khaki-colored pack from near her feet and stood to leave. Slinging it over her shoulder, she didn't bother glancing back as she extricated herself from the group. Making a quick exit for the front of the building when no one else bothered to move.

"I need someone who specifically knows the ins and outs of the Narrows." His brain latched on to the woman who'd extracted herself in a rush. He was trained to assess human behavior, and Ranger Green was trying to take herself out of the equation. Elias forced his attention back to the park's division ranger. "When was the last time you were on the trail?"

"Oh, uh. Well, it's been a while." Risner's nerves got the better of him, sucking the vibrato right from his voice. Yeah, no. Elias couldn't rely on someone who cowered at a hint of "I've been managing my team more these past couple of years."

They'd wasted enough time. Every minute he wasn't on that trail was another opportunity their killer would slip away. Again. Elias faced off with the remaining rangers. "Who here has the most experience in the Narrows?"

"Sayles does," one of the other rangers offered. "She hikes it every weekend like clockwork."

Risner ducked his chin. "Unfortunately, Ranger Green doesn't quite have the experience you'd need for your search, Agent Broyles. She's only been working here a few months."

"I thought you prided yourself on training the best rangers in the National Park Service," Elias said. "If Ranger Green has the most experience on the trail, she's the one I want guiding me during this manhunt."

Risner's jaw worked back and forth before he raised his hands in surrender. "Of course. Whatever the FBI needs. I'll get her for you."

"Not necessary. She just left. I'm sure I can find my way around a parking lot." His words sounded a lot more defensive than he'd meant, but there was something about the district ranger Elias didn't like. He shoved through the visitors' center doors and sucked in a breath at the view. Grand red rock cliffs stood sentinel from every direction, bright orange as midday sun arced overhead. It was enough to remind him how inconsequential a single human was on this planet.

Movement through the half-empty lot caught his eye. There one moment. Gone the next. Elias picked up his pace, ignoring the commotion around a built-out van two rows over as his partner ripped the vehicle apart for evidence. It took less than two minutes to catch up with the woman determined to get as far from him as possible. "Ranger Green, hold up."

She slowed her escape but didn't bother turning to face him. Head tipped back onto her shoulder, she'd obviously hoped to get out of the lot unscathed. Ebony hair cascaded across lean shoulders uniformed in a gray button-up before she confronted him. "Agent Broyles."

The defensiveness in those two words shook him to his core. "Word is you have the most experience in the Narrows. I'd like you to assist me during this investigation."

She paled at the statement. According to her expression, it most definitely was not a compliment. "There are far more qualified rangers I'm sure are happy to tag along during your search."

"No. There aren't. I need to get up that trail fast without dying, and according to your colleagues, you hike the trail every weekend." He wasn't going to budge. It would be her, or he'd have to hike with Risner. Not exactly his idea of a good time. "You have up-to-date experience I could use to find the man who killed a hiker in your park this morning."

Ranger Green stepped into him, all fury and barely leashed control pinching her eyes at the corners. Even a whole head shorter than him, she stood there as a one-woman army. "Did Risner put you up to this?"

"Excuse me?" He had the urge to step back to avoid whatever hell was about to rain down on him, but he was an FBI agent, for crying out loud. He could handle one little ranger.

"Is this another one of his pranks?" she asked. "To see how far he can push me before I quit? Because I'm telling you right now, it won't work. I'm not going anywhere."

"I have no idea what you're talking about." Though he wanted to know exactly what the district ranger had done to get a rise out of her like this. "I really just don't want to die on that trail, and you seem like the kind of person who can make sure that doesn't happen. Please."

The heat in her expression drained, but Ranger Green didn't add that distance back between them. She looked him up and down, taking in his jeans and T-shirt and tennis shoes. "You're going to need gear and supplies. We'll leave as soon as you're ready."

"You don't like me very much, do you?" His question had nothing to do with this investigation and everything to do with his own curiosity for a woman who clearly anticipated a battle from everyone around her.

"I don't have to like you during your manhunt." Ranger Green headed for a beat-up four-door sedan and tossed her pack inside. "I just have to keep you alive."

Chapter Three

Closing down the park took an act of God.

Or a serial killer on the loose.

Sayles clipped into her custom hydro bib. The waterproof material resembled a pair of overalls apart from one key difference: it added at least ten pounds to her already heavy gear. Worth it. The Narrows was one of the least forgiving trails in Zion. If you could call it a trail at all. Entry started at the bottom and forced hikers to travel upstream directly in the Virgin River anywhere from ankle-deep waters to full-blown you're-going-to-have-to-swim-from-here-on-out. And considering April marked that time of year when the snowbanks started melting, she and Agent Broyles were in for a treat. They could look forward to freezing temperatures and loss of more favorable camping locations ahead.

They had to do this fast.

Speak of the devil himself. She watched as Agent Broyles hauled a backpack over one muscled shoulder, those dark eyes locked on her as he approached from the visitors' center. It was cute the way he thought he'd get through this in jeans and T-shirt. This wasn't one of the park's amateur hikes where parents could carry their toddlers on their shoulders or stop to have a snack.

"Did you get everything on the list?" The answer was plain as day in his chosen outfit. Jeans would soak up river water and weigh him down. Not to mention they wouldn't do a whole lot of good against hypothermia. She could just imagine the blisters from the seams now. She'd left the suggestions for gear and supply with one of the information rangers in the visitors' center. He'd clearly chosen to ignore some of the key components. Probably thought he knew best, but nature didn't work that way, and people had died in the park for that same arrogance.

Agent Broyles unshouldered his bag, setting it down in front of him in the lot. They'd have to take the shuttle back to Temple of Sinawava to access the trailhead, then go on foot from there. And the sooner they got going, the better. She'd caught word of a storm about forty miles out that looked like it had its sights on the park. While she was sure the rest of Springdale police and whoever Agent Broyles had brought along on this hunt could manage their respective search grids in the rain, the Narrows would kill them if it flooded. "Think so. First aid kit, matches and a lighter, water, map, sunscreen, flashlight, knife, some food."

It was a good start. Between the two of them, they could make up the lack wherever needed, but there was one key item missing off that list. "What about a tent?"

She wasn't the sharing type.

"Worried you'll have to bunk with me, Ranger Green?" Amusement lit up his face and corrupted the whole emotionally unavailable law enforcement officer persona he'd had going on in the visitors' center. She wasn't dead. Agent Broyles was more than handsome with high cheekbones, a strong jawline with the barest hint of facial hair, a straight nose with a bump between his eyes that said he'd broken it at least once and a body that would put any Greek god to shame. None of which would be getting within twelve inches of her if she could manage.

Sayles shut down the urge to roll her eyes into the back of her head. Wasn't worth the sparring energy. Not for what they would face ahead. While she could easily traverse the Narrows alone, she wasn't just responsible for herself on this one. If she got a federal agent killed, even as a by-product of his own stupidity, she'd lose…everything. "There are no fires allowed in the park. A tent is the only way you'll keep from freezing when the sun goes down."

Agent Broyles unzipped his pack, showing off the single-person tent crammed inside. Brand new. They were about to find out just how experienced the federal agent was out here in the big wild. She had her bets with the other rangers. They weren't great odds. "This good enough?"

"It'll do." Twisting toward the trunk of her sedan, she pulled another hydro bib—maybe a little too small and definitely not custom-made for his frame—from the confines and tossed it at his feet. "Put this on."

Agent Broyles rolled the hydro bib out, then glanced up at her as she offered a pair of waterproof boots. She'd had to guess his size to borrow them from another ranger. They weren't perfect, but they would work for what they needed. "We going fishing?"

"The Narrows is an upstream hike. There are only a few areas dry enough to camp. Otherwise, we'll be in the river the entire time." She nodded to the gear. "These will keep you dry for the most part and protect you against water toxins."

He fumbled into the waterproof gear and tried to straighten fully, but the hydro bib was obviously cutting into some very vital organs below the waist. "Is this how it's supposed to fit?" His voice had climbed almost an octave.

"Not so much." Her laugh escaped without permission. "Here. Let me help." She stepped into him. Well, damn. She'd already broken her twelve-inch rule. Working the adjustable straps on his chest, she loosened the gear's hold on his manhood. "How's that?"

"I can breathe again." Agent Broyles shot her that crooked smile again. Wasted on her of all people. He grabbed for the rest of his gear after shoving his feet into the boots. "You just happened to have these lying around?"

"Not for you, Agent Broyles." Her ex had been a few inches shorter than Agent Broyles's six four, but there were a few similarities she didn't want to acknowledge between the two of them.

"Elias," he said. "If we're going to be spending the next few hours, possibly days, together, you might as well call me by my first name."

She didn't agree. Naming something humanized it, and she wasn't interested in getting to know him. "Let's get moving. The shuttle is waiting on us."

She didn't bother to check to see if he'd followed. This was his manhunt. She was just the guide, but Sayles couldn't ignore the permanent goose pimples along her neck and arms. The man they were after had already killed five people, including a hiker in this very park. What was to stop him from turning on a park ranger? It was her job to protect Agent Broyles from the park. What guarantee did she have Agent Broyles would protect her apart from his duty?

Sayles boarded the shuttle, one of the new electric ones the park had invested in over the past couple of years. The engine barely grumbled as she took her seat behind the driver and tugged her pack to her chest. A barrier between her and the man sitting across the too-slim aisle from her.

The ride wasn't more than twenty minutes, but those

minutes seemed to drag on forever as she focused every ounce of attention out the elongated windows over Agent Broyles's shoulders. Her body swayed as the shuttle's transmission shifted, making her overly aware of his attention centered on her.

"Risner said you were one of his newest rangers." He had to raise his voice over the shuttle's engine despite them being the only passengers on board. "How long have you been at Zion?"

"Five months." Her inexperience wasn't a secret. She was sure the FBI could unearth her personnel files with the snap of a finger.

"Did you always want to become a ranger?" he asked.

What was with the third degree? Narrowing her gaze on him, Sayles worked to shut down whatever expression on her face was telling him she was up for small talk. "Did you always want to be an FBI agent?"

"Ever since I was a kid." Broyles reached overhead to grab on to one of the many stand bars installed throughout the shuttle bus for balance. "But that was probably because I watched too many true-crime shows. You know, like *Dateline*."

"Your parents let you watch *Dateline*?" Damn it. She wasn't supposed to encourage conversation. There was a reason she didn't trust federal types like him. She had to remember that.

"Let me? No." His gaze cut to the driver as he shook his head. "Did I sneak into the living room in the middle of the night and watch TV after they fell asleep to watch that and *Tales from the Crypt*? Absolutely."

"That show gave me nightmares." As a kid, she'd believed that was the worst that could scare her. Then she'd gotten older and seen what real evil looked like. "My degree is in art history. I wanted to work for a museum, curating artwork and building collections, overseeing preservations, that kind of stuff."

She didn't know why she'd told him that. Wasn't even sure if she'd ever told her fellow rangers about that dead dream. Then again, they'd never asked. Not even her roommate, Lila, who everyone accurately nicknamed Ranger Barbie. But working in a national park came with a lot of transition. Rangers moved across the country to get coveted positions and full-time work, which was a lot harder than it looked. The big parks were where everyone wanted to be. Yellowstone. Yosemite. The Grand Canyon. Otherwise known as the crown jewels of the National Park Service, those were the ones that came with bigger animals to protect, more scenery to guard and bad guys waiting to get busted. Rangers had sabotaged, lied and manipulated their way into those assignments. Rangers like Risner. What was the point of getting to know your coworkers who would stab you in your gray-colored back for the opportunity to patrol Denali?

"Why the national park rangers then?" Broyles asked.

To hide. To escape. To finally have the chance to make her own decisions. Zion wasn't just a place for her to work. It was freedom in every sense of the word. Something she'd never had before and certainly not in her marriage. Sayles gripped her pack a bit too tight. "I needed a change."

The driver maneuvered into the semicircle meant to corral shuttles at each trailhead, and Sayles practically bolted for the door. Not like she could escape the federal agent on her heels, but she could sure as hell put more distance between them. She shouldered her pack and headed straight for the asphalt trail she'd hiked this morning.

Only there wouldn't be a body waiting for her on the other side.

At least, she hoped they didn't come across any more. She sensed she'd already be seeing that hiker's face when she closed her eyes tonight. They were well into the afternoon at this point. Shadows seemed to drip down the cliff walls waiting to consume them whole.

Sayles stepped off the asphalt path and headed straight for the canyon mouth towering over 2,000 feet above them with a mere sliver of eight feet of ankle-rolling, algae-covered rocks between them. "The canyon will block the sun for the rest of the day, but we've got about six hours before sunset hits. At that point, we'll need to make camp."

The slosh of water at her back told her he was sticking close. "Think we can make it to a spot and set up for the night in that time?"

"The driest location to camp is two miles in. About an hour and twenty minutes if we stay consistent." Her feet immediately became sluggish in the mere six inches of water fighting them at every chance. They had to move slow to avoid burning out before reaching a sufficient campground. "Problem is we're right in the middle of snowmelt season. The waters here are much deeper than any other time of the year. Your killer picked a hell of a time to flee."

"I'll be sure to mention that when we catch up with him." Broyles's words echoed off the canyon walls. "Back at the visitors' center, you knew what unsub stood for. I take it I'm not the only fan of *Dateline*."

Knowledge of law enforcement protocols and terminology wasn't something she'd ever been interested in. But that was the cost of escaping a murder charge. "Something like that."

Chapter Four

He wasn't sure how far they'd hiked. But his legs felt as though they were on fire.

Up ahead, Ranger Green made the trek look easy, but he'd already tripped, slipped and face-planted over the slimy rocks determined to stop him from going any farther. What the hell kind of nightmare was this? The getup she'd dressed him in hadn't done a damn bit of good on that last fall. Frigid water had worked down the collar and soaked his T-shirt straight through. His fingers had lost feeling a few minutes ago while she navigated him deeper into hell itself. "You really hike this thing every weekend?"

There was a certain confidence she carried he couldn't ignore. Like she'd been made for this place. Otherworldly and stronger than he'd estimated. Wilder than she wanted to admit. Definitely formidable and guarded. "When I'm not on shift."

His boot slipped off another of the small-ass boulders threatening his every step. Water splashed up to his knee that time, and a growl charged through him. What was he doing here? Oh, right. His last case had gone to hell, and his only witness hadn't survived. His supervisory agent had determined Elias could no longer be trusted and sent him on a wild-goose chase. Someone killing travelers along I-15. But damn. He wasn't an outdoorsman. The farthest he'd ever hiked was to the G laid out in white rocks on the mountain edging his hometown in sixth grade. Before everything had fallen apart two months ago, he and his partner, Grant, upended entire weapons dealing organizations, pulled women and children out of sex-trafficking rings and ran cartels into the ground. Now they were chasing a ghost. Because he'd screwed up both of their careers and any chance for promotion.

Couldn't argue with the view, though.

Sayles slowed her pace, then came to a stop atop an oversize flat rock at the river's edge. For him or for herself, he didn't care. He needed a break. The sun barely reached the tips of the canyon walls high above him, and a chill settled across his shoulders. Or maybe it was those intense green eyes assessing him from a few feet away. "You look like you could use a few minutes."

His lungs agreed. He was in shape. Part of the job. But this… This was something else. Muscles he wasn't aware existed protested every step. "How far until the first campsite?"

She swung her pack forward from one shoulder and extracted a metal water bottle. He'd expect nothing less from a national park ranger concerned with keeping her park garbage-free. Taking a swig, she threw him an unexpected smile. "We've only been hiking for twenty minutes."

Elias nearly doubled over at the realization. He checked his watch. Yep. Sure enough. Twenty minutes since they'd entered the trail. "I'm going to die out here, aren't I?"

"Don't worry. There wouldn't be any need for a manhunt. Given these currents, your body would turn up in a few hours." She repackaged her water bottle and zipped up the bag.

Was that a joke? Elias couldn't help but laugh as he dug around for his water bottle, which was plastic and not nearly as large as the one she'd brought, though he'd made sure he'd grabbed the water purification tablets she'd recommended. "Dark humor is your thing. I'll try to remember that."

With all the death and violence he and Grant had seen over the years they'd been partnered together, humor under pressure was something he understood well. It was a way to not let the bad things follow you home at the end of the day. Though you had to play it right. That meant no jokes around superiors or grieving family members. Both rules his partner had ignored a time or two. Maybe their current assignment wasn't Elias's fault after all.

"We've got to keep moving. Radar picked up a storm moving this way." She shrugged back into her pack but waited for him to catch up. "Flash floods are the biggest danger on this trail. The rating was low this morning, but there is a long section of the Narrows we won't be able to escape if we get caught in the rain."

"Good chance of dying. Noted." Elias tried for a thumbs-up. Damn it all to hell, his entire body hurt at this point. "So who'd you have to kill to get gear that fit me? Because I have a feeling you're not the kind to go out of your way to make sure I was prepared today."

"The boots are Risner's," she said. "What he doesn't know won't kill him."

He had to bury the hot thread of annoyance at hearing she had access to the district ranger's personal effects. Wait. "You stole them?"

"Borrowed." She angled her chin over one shoulder, putting him in her peripheral vision. Keeping tabs on him. "Don't worry. He'll get them back after they recover your body."

A seam rubbed the wrong way on the inside of his jeans. Taking off the first few layers of skin. Damn it. Water had made its way to his jeans. This was not going to be pleasant. "And the hydro bib?"

She faced forward, shoulders going tight. "My ex was really into fishing. I took that and the rest of his stuff out of spite."

Okay. So he could add vengeful to the growing list of attributes. A lot like the muscles in his legs screaming at him to go to hell if he took one more step. "I take it the relationship didn't end well."

"Most divorces don't end on good terms." The inflection had drained from her voice.

She'd been married. Why did that fact heat feeling back into his fingertips? Elias followed in her steps, kept to the same slimy rocks, spotted the steady gaps between. There was a method to her madness. As if she was following a map laid out by Indiana Jones himself. Or maybe he wanted to have more confidence in her so they got out of this alive. "I'm sorry. I didn't mean to pry."

"You didn't." An energy he couldn't put his finger on stiffened her movements. "I haven't seen anything to suggest your killer came this way, but we have miles ahead of us, and he has a good hour head start. He could already be at Orderville Canyon Junction. It's where we want to camp tonight."

He didn't miss the change in subject. All right. Back to the reason they were here. He could do that. Elias forced himself back into the right headspace, one focused on the potential of them coming into contact with a serial killer. Rangers had federal jurisdiction, but there was very different training involved between the NPS and the FBI. He was accustomed to violence. Sayles was accustomed to scolding hikers for relieving themselves off cliffsides. "Guys like this will do whatever it takes to escape arrest. Once we find him, I'm going to need you to stay behind me. Use me as a shield if you have to. I go down, you run like hell. Got it?"

"Got it," she said.

No argument. Interesting. He'd expected more of a fight, but he'd give her credit for self-preservation. A lot of people—especially civilians—fantasized about playing hero in situations like theirs. Though rangers weren't civilians in the least. They were federal agents only on a much grander scale. Some, like Risner, let their ego lead the charge, but Elias didn't get that feel from her. She wanted to be small and stay out of the way. Hidden.

They moved a few more yards upstream with nothing but the white noise of the river filling the silence, and damn it, the seam in his jeans cut through the first few layers of skin as easily as a blade at this point. He'd survived far more violent injuries since signing on with the Bureau, but this was a slow death. Heat charged into his face as he realized Sayles had stopped ahead, that intense green gaze on him.

Her eyes pinched at the corners. Assessing him from head to toe. "What's wrong with you?"

"Who says anything is wrong?" He hopped to the next rock and landed without tripping over his own two feet. Hell, maybe he was getting the hang of this trail after all.

"Your face. You keep wincing." She worked her way downstream, closing the distance between them.

"It's nothing." He was a federal agent, for crying out loud. A wet jean seam shouldn't make him feel as though his thigh had caught fire.

Sayles tipped her head back. Clouds rolled above the sliver of canyon overhead. Thick and darker than they should be. She'd mentioned a storm caught on radar before they'd left. Looked like they hadn't managed to outrun it. "We need to pick up the pace. The storm is almost here, and we need to be on higher ground by the time it hits."

Was that him groaning or the river? Elias wasn't sure.

She didn't wait for him to answer, heading back upstream.

Suck it up, Broyles. Wet jeans would not be the reason he met his maker. Every muscle in his legs protested against deepening waters. He wasn't sure he could feel his toes anymore, even with the waterproof boots. The water's temperature rated below freezing, all that snowpack melting off the mountains to the north and into the Virgin River.

A rumble of thunder seemed to shake the canyon around them.

Sayles pulled up short, attention to the sky. Her gaze then locked on him. If he hadn't studied human behavior his entire career, he might've missed the note of panic in her face. She scanned the waters around them, going from clear to muddy in a matter of seconds. What the hell? "Run!"

He didn't need to be told twice. The pain along the inside of his thigh shifted to the back of his mind. Elias forced his body to comply, tucking his thumbs around his pack straps to avoid the bounce. The water fought his every step, working to drag him downstream. He replicated Sayles's footsteps, the areas she steered clear of and her change in direction. Straight ahead to diagonal. To the right.

"Move!" Her warning was drowned out by an angry roar ahead.

His muscles burned harder as the waters seemed to rise several inches in a matter of seconds. Flash flood. The storm must've dumped rain higher up the trail, and now they were going to pay for it.

Panic ticked up his heart rate. At least they'd find his body in a few hours. That was what she'd said, right? It wasn't until Sayles cut down a smaller canyon to the right that hope dared show its ugly face.

She scrambled out of the river's grip and almost straight up a streaked, slippery rock face. Elias couldn't keep up, and she reached back for him as if expecting him to suddenly become a mountaineer. "Come on!"

The roar was growing louder. Closer.

The river water churned around his legs and rose impossibly higher.

Elias latched on to her hand, surprised by the strength behind the tug. He dug his toes into the slick rock and grabbed for the nearest shrub to get hold. His feet left the river a split second before the waters consumed the very rocks he'd been balanced on. But it wasn't enough. The Virgin River was going to eat them alive.

"Climb!" Sayles shouted over the thundering scream of the flood. Pointing to the next hold, she directed him to an outcropping of rocks overhead. His foot slipped. Her hand slapped across the back of his thigh as she took position behind him. Putting herself between him and the river. The waterproof boots weren't meant to be utilized as hiking gear. One wrong move and he'd take her down with him. He had to keep moving.

They'd reached the outcropping, and the ground evened out enough to provide a ledge overlooking the flood. Elias landed on his back, out of breath, staring up at the darkening sky.

The first drops of rain pattered against his face as Sayles centered herself in his vision. "And that's why we don't wear jeans hiking."

Chapter Five

They'd barely managed to escape.

And now she was stuck on a collection of boulders no more than five feet in diameter, marooned over the gushing waters of the Virgin River with a man she didn't know. They'd been lucky. If she and Elias had been even ten feet behind, they wouldn't have survived the crush of the flood.

Agent Broyles, she told herself. Using his first name humanized him.

Rain pelted her ranger's hat and fell in heavy drips from the brim. Her button-up uniform shirt had soaked through, leaking into her hydro bib, and she couldn't stop the chill skating across her shoulders. The sky unloaded its fury straight overhead, but this outcropping had been the only option to stay alive.

Mystery Falls sat off to their right, heavier than usual with the rain. The 110-foot angled rock face wasn't a waterfall in a straightforward sense but smoothed red rock forged over years of drainage. Like the stones peppering the bottom of the river. Thick green trees jutted out from the rock walls in random patterns, but none of them would provide any protection.

Sayles swept her hair out of her face, coming away with

a handful of rainwater as she took a seat. Closer than she wanted to be to Agent Broyles, but there was nowhere else to go, and they were in for the long haul as of right now. "Are you injured?"

"No." He shook his head, droplets flinging every which way, and threaded his hands into his hair. The action took some of the intimidation right out of him. Though he hadn't given her reason to doubt his agenda on this little assignment of theirs, she'd been fooled by a pretty face before.

"Good." She scanned the floodwaters. Dead wood, mud and leaves clustered and broke apart below. The only good to come out of this was knowing the man they were chasing would have to stop his escape to survive these waters, too. If he hadn't already been caught in them. "Because I'm not sure how long we're going to have to stay here. At least a couple hours, I'm guessing."

"Great." Agent Broyles dragged his pack around to his front. "The inside of my thighs could use the break."

She couldn't help but drop her gaze to the topic of this new conversation. Even through the hydro bib, she couldn't deny the strength and muscle encased in waterproof material. She'd gotten only a glimpse while he'd geared up in the visitors' center parking lot, and the image of his toned frame hadn't slipped from her mind since. "What do you mean?"

"About a half a mile back, I tripped. Water got into my gear and soaked a section of my jeans." Agent Broyles ripped his pack open and started searching for something. "The seam feels like it's trying to gnaw through my thigh."

Oh. Okay. A flush heated across her collarbones. Temperatures wouldn't significantly dip until the sun went completely down. They weren't at risk for exposure. Yet. But those chances went up every hour they were stuck. They had to make the most of it now. "That's quite a visual."

Sayles unzipped the top of her backpack and collected the packable first aid kit. "Take off your pants."

A stillness she didn't know was possible rippled through him. "I'm sorry. I don't think I heard you right. Did you just tell me to take off my pants?"

"Yes." She'd performed first aid on every manner of visitor to the park from extreme sunburns to overhydration and broken bones. Her training focused more on survival rather than medical, but a few bandages weren't anything she wasn't willing to donate to a good cause. And the way he'd started slowing the last quarter mile or so told her the seams of his jeans were at fault. "I can't bandage your thigh while you're still in your gear, and leaving it to get worse will only slow us down."

"I think I can manage on my own." Was that a matching rush of heat in his neck, or had she imagined it?

Honestly, she wasn't sure why she'd offered to bandage him up in the first place. They weren't friends. They were barely acquaintances, and as soon as this manhunt was finished, they'd never see each other again. She handed off her first aid kit. He had his own, but hers had been customized based on her experience in the park. Larger bandages, for one. His would most likely include the bare minimum and a few Band-Aids. "All right."

Agent Broyles stood, his head instantly connecting with a tree branch. He wasn't able to straighten to his full height. He'd be better off taking off his gear sitting to avoid falling into the river below, but she wasn't about to offer that tidbit of information unless asked.

"There's a tree there." Okay. She was being petty and couldn't hide the smile tugging at the corners of her mouth while she unpacked a deck of waterproof playing cards. She didn't know how long they'd be here. Might as well keep themselves entertained.

"I figured that out. Thank you." He shucked the hydro bib around his ankles. Then went for his jeans. He'd taken the smarter route in keeping his boots on. The second his socks got soaked, he'd be miserable and risk chance of infection. Hesitation slowed him down. "Could you turn around? I wasn't planning on putting myself on display for this field trip."

"No need to be embarrassed about your choice in underwear. We've all been there." Looking up at his lack of answer, she spread the cards in her hand. At a loss of where she was supposed to go. "There's not really any place for me to go on this rock, but if it makes you feel better, I won't look. Believe me, I'd rather be anywhere else."

Sayles angled her head down, but she could just make out his movements in her peripheral vision. First discarding his jeans around his calves, then the shift of muscle higher up. Her heart rate picked up. Breathing becoming shallower. You'd think she was being chased by a bear the way her body heated. If it was possible, she was sure steam would be drifting off her exposed skin at the thought of getting a glimpse of the FBI agent towering over her. Okay. It hadn't been that long since she'd been with a man. Come on.

"Damn it. I can't… I can't get a good look at the damage." Defeat tainted his voice. "I might need your help."

"Might?" Subtext turned out to be the killer of happiness, and she'd given up trying to read between the lines the moment she'd left her marriage. Trying to decipher someone else's meaning, mood and hidden agenda no longer interested her in the least. If Agent Broyles wanted her help, he'd have to ask for it.

"I need your help." He stood strong, feet shoulder-width

apart, half-naked and exposed to the rain. She imagined this was not an everyday occurrence, but she couldn't deny the view while she had it.

"Sure." Sayles shoved her playing cards back into the box and rocked forward to her knees. Facing off with the agent's lower body. And what a lower body it was. Tendons and muscle rippled as he was forced to keep his balance in a perfect display of power and strength. Dark hair jerked in place as rain hit the expanse of tan skin. Her mouth dried despite the humidity clinging to every inch of her body, but she somehow convinced her brain to focus on the task at hand.

His tight boxer briefs provided little protection against the constant rubbing of the seam of his jeans between his legs, and the result had taken a few layers of skin off in the short amount of time they'd been hiking. It was one of the reasons she encouraged visitors to choose stretchy, light, soft pantwear, especially during the hotter months. Jeans trapped heat, came with too many seams and got heavier as they collected sweat.

"How bad is it?" Agent Broyles asked.

"Not the worst I've seen, but it's not great." It wasn't just the first few layers of skin that'd been rubbed raw. Blood pooled at the edges, leaving him open to infection if they weren't careful. His attention pressed into the back of her neck from above as she prodded around the four-inch-by-one-inch wound. She could practically feel his body heat radiating into the side of her face. "Oh, were you talking about the mess you made of your thigh or something else?"

His laugh reverberated straight from his mouth into her core. Not the best distraction when she was supposed to be patching him up. "My thigh."

Truth be told, from her current viewpoint, she had no

complaints about the status of other…body parts. Everything seemed…great. "I'm going to have to clean the wound and debride some of the skin, but we have to find a way to keep the area dry before I can bandage it."

"Damn," he said. "I forgot my umbrella."

Turning to her pack, she extracted the folded solar blanket and ripped through the bag with her teeth. "Hold this over me and try not to move. No matter how much it hurts."

He unfolded the cellophane, draping it above her head as she'd asked. "Well, you're just a ball of sunshine, aren't you?"

"Not everyone can hike with a wound like this." No. That was not admiration that he'd kept his mouth shut when he'd obviously been in a lot of pain. Injuries turned deadly faster out here than in the real world. But the fact that he'd managed to get as far as they had without slowing them down said something about his character. "You made a stupid decision not to tell me about it sooner. We might not be in this position now."

The solar blanket crinkled above her as he shifted his weight between both feet. "Just add it to the list of stupid decisions I've made lately."

She wasn't sure he'd meant to say that out loud. Sayles managed to get the wound and the surrounding skin dry despite the overbearing storm above. After snapping her hands into latex gloves, she extracted a small pair of scissors from her first aid kit and tweezers to debride the curled and folded skin around the affected site. There wasn't much she could do out here in the middle of nowhere, but it was better than letting it fester. "What other stupid decisions have you made recently? Apart from dragging a ranger with no experience into your federal investigation."

She'd meant it as a joke, but he answered anyway.

"That one I don't regret, considering you currently have the best access to whatever is happening below my belt, which we will never discuss ever again, right?" Agent Broyles didn't wait for her to agree. Good thing, too. She wasn't sure she could keep her end of that deal when it came to unloading crazy stories at the next ranger meeting. "As for the biggest stupid decision? I got myself sent here. Chasing some low-level killer instead of being out there saving the world against the cartels and weapons dealers I usually handle."

"Is that really such a bad thing?" Low-level killer? The man they were chasing had already murdered five people, including a victim in this very park. Didn't bringing him to justice count for something, or was it the power trip that got Agent Broyles's rocks off? A sour taste coated her tongue at the thought. She'd known too many agents like him. Ones who liked to hold that control over others, who served their own agendas despite the promises they'd made. Sayles cleaned his wound as best she could with the alcohol wipes from her kit. Maybe with a little too much force as irritation built behind her sternum.

Agent Broyles hissed at the burn. Good. She didn't know a whole lot about his personal case history, but she knew one thing. Stopping a killer—no matter the bastard's track record—was just as important as all those big fish he preferred. Didn't he see that?

His voice lowered, barely reaching her above the slap of rain against the rock they stood on and the solar blanket overhead. "I got a witness killed."

Chapter Six

The injury wasn't just trying to eat through his thigh anymore.

It'd caught fire.

Ranger Green slapped a clean bandage over the wound, following it up with a couple pats around the edges. Something told him she'd left the alcohol pads on a little too long for a reason. In punishment. "You're done."

"Thanks." Elias tried to fold the solar blanket back into the neat little square it had come in, but it was no use. So he crumpled it in one hand and made quick work of pulling his jeans back into place, then offered it to her.

"You keep it." She repacked her first aid kit and pocketed the latex gloves she'd donned. Pack it in, pack it out. The kit went in next. Seemed everything in her pack had a place, and she wasn't the type of woman to break that habit. "I have another."

Their hot and cold back-and-forth was giving him whiplash. One minute she offered to dress his wound, the next she couldn't even seem to look at him. Like he'd offended her.

The rain's assault had lightened up over the past few minutes, but the river was still too angry for them to get back in it. The only consolation in losing the limited time they had to catch up with their killer was the bastard was just as stuck as they were.

The bandage pulled at the hairs along his thigh as he took his seat again. His knee knocked into hers, and he couldn't help the change in her body language. Too rigid. It only lasted a second, but while his career had taken a nosedive the past couple of months, he hadn't lost his observational skills.

Pulling a yellow deck-size box from her pack, she thumbed through a stack of playing cards. But they didn't look like any normal playing cards he'd seen at the countless convenience stores he and Grant had visited over the past few weeks on the road. No face cards or icons but numbers, bullet points and short paragraphs instead. The pack was color-coded. Blue diamonds, purple spades, red hearts and green clubs with a few black edges for jokers. They each seemed to mean something significant. "What's your poison? I'm really good at go fish."

Elias grabbed the deck from her hands and shuffled through it over his crossed boots. "I tell you I got a witness killed, and you want to play cards?"

"I figured if you wanted to offer the information, you would." A slow rise and fall of her shoulders tried to convince him of her casualness. It was all a lie, though. This woman was anything but casual out here in her element. Constantly aware of her surroundings, scanning the river every few minutes as if looking for something specific. Maybe a body? Always on guard. Especially around him. "It's none of my business why you're here. Just my job to make sure you get out of this canyon."

He kind of liked that. Someone with enough self-awareness to know when to push and when to pull. Why exhaust yourself trying to decipher someone else's moods when putting the responsibility on them to communicate saved everyone time and frustration? He needed more of that in his life. "Fair point."

Elias studied the cards before handing off ten to her. Flipping over the bright yellow-and-orange box they'd come in—thicker than a normal deck—he absorbed the oversize lettering on the front. "The don't die out there deck. Survival tips? Figured you rangers were above resorting to tourist souvenirs for guidance."

"Funny." She took the cards with a little too much force. "I brought them for you, Agent Broyles."

Ouch. Well, he'd walked right into that one. He'd yet to deal his own set of ten for their game—because who the hell actually knew when they were getting off this rock?—and read the first card in his stack. "If you are lost. Keep your cool. Don't panic. Take a break for food and water. Use your map. That's some great advice. For a five-year-old."

"Why do you think I brought them for you?" Ranger Green reshuffled her cards with a wide sardonic smile. Hell, the look fit her perfectly. A little wild and a whole lot daring. Most people had a healthy avoidance of law enforcement. Not overly obvious. Just wary. Like when their nerves get the best of them during a routine traffic stop. She wasn't one of those people. No. Instead, she carried something heavier.

"I see how it is." Elias dealt the cards with the rest of the deck positioned between them. "All right. You want to play, Ranger Green, we'll play. Best of this hand, and when I win, you have to tell me why you don't like me."

Her smile slipped. Barely enough to convince him he hadn't really seen the change. "And if I win?"

"What do you want?" He was far more interested in her answer than he should be. What did a woman like Sayles Green want more than anything? And why the hell did he care?

"If I win, you aren't allowed to speak for the next hour." Those intense green eyes brightened at the idea.

"Wow," he said. "You could've asked for anything, and that's what you're going with?"

"I like my quiet time." She slipped one card free and slid it toward the back of her hand. "It's why I come out here so often, away from everybody else. When I'm not on the trails, it's easier to believe the world isn't as cruel as I remember it being."

The rush of the river filled the silence between them.

Elias shifted his position on the rock beneath them, a very sharp edge working its way into all the wrong places. "All right. Do you have any fives?"

She was forced to give up two cards. And over the next few minutes, his pile grew while hers dwindled. Until he'd collected everything he'd needed to win.

A hint of annoyance flashed in her expression as the outcome took shape. It was a good look on her. The doubt. He wouldn't mind seeing it a few more times before this manhunt was over.

Ranger Green tossed the rest of her cards onto the middle deck. "You cheated."

"I'm not sure it's possible to cheat at go fish." It was, but he wasn't going to tell her that. "Maybe you're just really bad at it. Either way, deal's a deal."

The hard set to her jaw warned him she might back out, but sooner or later, he would figure out why she'd rather throw herself into that raging river than sit here with him for one more minute. "My ex-husband is a federal agent. FBI, same as you. He worked mostly serial homicide cases. I told you before things didn't end well. It's childish and immature of me to assume you're like him, but I've spent the better part of the past five months avoiding anything and anyone who reminds me of him."

That, he hadn't expected. Elias busied his hands by re-shuffling the deck, processing what little she'd given him. He could let her offer more information—as she had concerning his latest admission—but curiosity got the better of him. "That's why you're familiar with case terminology and protocols?"

"No." Her voice shook on that single word. "That came later."

"What'd he do to make you want to divorce him?" he asked.

She didn't answer right away, but they had all the time in the world on this rock. "What makes you think he wasn't the one to leave me?"

"Because you're the one in hiding." He didn't miss the slight widening of her eyes. The mask she wore was good. Probably forged over the years she'd been married. But experience had given him the tools to break through the thickest of lies.

Her breath shook from her. If the temperature had been a few degrees cooler, he was sure he would see crystallized puffs around her mouth. "It doesn't matter. I'm not going to give him the chance to do it again."

That didn't sit well. Elias wasn't sure why, other than an undercurrent of blame that shadowed her words. In his career, he'd met a lot of bad guys. Except sometimes those bad guys convinced everyone around them they were actually good. Had badges and federal credentials and the respect of neighbors, partners and family. He dealt her another ten cards. He'd play as many rounds as it took to bring back that smile from earlier. "Whatever he did, it wasn't your fault."

"You don't know that." She ignored the hand he'd offered, those pretty eyes on him. "You don't know anything about me."

"I know you're running. I know while you do everything you can to convince people otherwise, you're probably scared." He'd seen it enough times during his tenure with the FBI. Hell, even before that. As much as he didn't like to think of his childhood, there'd been days he'd blamed himself for earning that disappointed look on his mother's face. It wasn't that he'd done anything wrong—he knew that now. He'd simply existed, and she couldn't find a way to get rid of him that didn't have her ending up behind bars. If he'd just been good enough, done his homework better, cleaned the house instead of going to his friend's house, maybe—maybe—she could've loved him. It'd taken years for him to realize he'd deserved more than that permanent scowl on her face any time she looked at him. "Anyone who uproots their lives to move to the middle of nowhere and tells themselves the world can't possibly be as cruel as they remember isn't to blame for what happened to them. They're a victim."

She didn't seem to have any response to that. At least not for a few minutes as they quietly exchanged cards in another round of go fish. "The witness you said you got killed. Do you blame yourself for that?"

"Yes." There was no point in denying it. He could practically feel the stain of guilt on his skin. Surprised she couldn't feel it, too, when she'd bandaged his thigh. Elias threw down a card to hand over. "She was a kid, really. No older than twenty-one. A corner boy got shot one night, had his whole stash stolen right out from under him. Problem was, it wasn't his stash. It belonged to the cartel he was running for. Girl had been at the bodega behind him, working the late shift so she could attend classes during the day. Saw the whole thing, could identify the car he drove off in. Smart girl. Had her whole life going for her. My superiors wanted me to let her go. Said we had better ways of getting to the cartel, but I had this feeling she could get us what we needed. She was scared. She was worried the shooter would come back and kill her if she said anything, but I kept pushing. Finally, she agreed. I got her to come in and identify the shooter. Next thing I know, she's the one laid out on the sidewalk. Bullet holes in her chest."

Talking about it didn't do a damn bit of good. No matter how many times he'd told this story, the nightmares wouldn't stop. His hand shook as he discarded the next card. "I pushed her into identifying the killer against my superiors' orders, and the bastard came back to make sure she'd never see court. My mistake lost the FBI the element of surprise. The cartel packed up and vanished, and the man who put a bullet in her disappeared with them. Along with my career."

A hand landed on top of his cards, pulling his attention to Ranger Green's softened expression. No longer guarded by the mask she worked to keep in place. "If you didn't feel guilty, you wouldn't be trying to be better. That's what mistakes are for. To show us what to do next."

His throat worked to argue, but there wasn't anything he could say now that would change the outcome.

The touch was too brief as she extracted her hand, taking the playing cards with her. She repacked and shoved to stand. "The flash flood is over. It's time to move."

Chapter Seven

No signs of their killer.

Sayles gauged her every step as they descended back into the Virgin River. Debris and muddy waters heightened the chances of losing their balance and being washed downstream, but they'd missed their opportunity to turn back. The river reached the middle of her thigh, pushing against the limited energy she had to spare. Clouds hovered over the slice of canyon above, cutting the temperatures even more. The flash flood warning was still too high for her comfort zone, but she'd managed to get them through. It was another mile to Orderville Canyon Junction—the location she intended they'd set up camp. Anything could happen between then and now.

Agent Broyles pushed through as the waters at her back kept rhythm with her steady heart rate. The bandages on his thigh were doing their job, making it easier for him to keep up while staving off infection. He'd surprised her back there. Admitting his mistake in costing a young woman her life. The federal agents she'd known—her husband, his friends and colleagues, all wrapped around her ex's manipulative finger—would've taken a bullet before accepting responsibility for their screwups. Guilt didn't exist in their worlds. But it did in Agent Broyles's. She hadn't expected that.

She supposed not all FBI agents were willing to give false statements, fabricate evidence and commit perjury in the court of law for a friend.

Sayles pushed ahead, maybe a bit too fast for this portion of the trail, as dark memories she'd ignored these past five months caught up with her. It was as if a dam had set up residence in her head. Building, poking, prodding. Every slip cost her a hold on her control, and the bet Agent Broyles had instigated only made it worse. Sooner or later, the dam would break altogether, and not even Zion National Park could save her. Until then, she had to keep it buried so deep she could convince herself that it had been someone else's life instead of hers. "Watch your footing up here. The rocks get smaller, and the flood is making everything else hard to see. Don't need you twisting an ankle."

"You sure you wouldn't want to see that?" He spread his arms wide to keep his balance.

She could hear the smile in his voice but forced herself to keep her attention up front. She had to hand it to him for making it this far. More people than she cared to count failed to survive flash floods. Elias Broyles had found himself three steps back on the ladder of his career, but he was still here. Chasing a killer neither of them was prepared to face at the moment thanks to the flash flood.

The river protested his quickening pace until he caught up with her. His breathing deepened, but he held his own against the current. There were a few rangers who couldn't handle these waters after a flash flood like that. "Kind of seems like you're secretly hoping I slip up."

"That would get you killed." She'd never had an issue keeping her emotions on lockdown around her fellow rangers. Not even Lila, her roommate. The less she revealed about herself, the less chance her ex could use it against her, but Agent Broyles seemed to make it his own personal mission to get under her skin. "Despite your lack of respect for boundaries, I don't want you dead. It's too much paperwork."

His laugh echoed off the red rock reaching for the thunderous sky. "Oh. Is *that* the only thing keeping you from letting me die? Here I thought I'd impressed you with my go fish skills."

How did this man have the ability to draw her away from those angry thoughts she hadn't been able to escape? She hardly knew him, and if she was being honest with herself, she didn't want to know him. It wasn't anything personal. Just the thought of what he represented. What she'd run from. "I'd hate to think of the kind of woman you attract after mentioning those skills on your online dating profile."

"Now, how did you know I have an online dating profile?" He was back to messing with her. Trying to get her to crack. It wouldn't work. It *wasn't* working.

"I didn't until you just confirmed it." Sayles put everything into keeping her attention on the river and not on seeing if his expression matched the amusement in his voice. "But you're the kind of guy who's married to his work. You travel a lot. Doesn't give you a whole lot of time to make personal connections, and the ones you have are short-lived. So you have to rely on online dating profiles or hitting on national park rangers you scam into helping you catch a killer so you aren't spending your nights alone with nobody but your partner and a cold shower. Either way, I can see how you might like the challenge, but I'm betting your online profile says something like: Reasons to date me. One, you'd be the better-looking one in the relationship. And, two, please."

There was that laugh again. Except instead of it bouncing off the red rock around them, it charged straight through her, chasing back the brittle cold sinking through her gear. "How long have you been waiting to use that on me?"

"Since the visitors' center." She kept her smile to herself. Her ability to make him laugh was…new. Though she'd been trying to insult him. She'd always had a sarcastic sense of humor, but it'd bled dry every year she'd stayed with her ex. Felt good to let it out again. And Agent Broyles certainly made the perfect target. "What does your profile actually say?"

"I don't have one. Well, not anymore." Agent Broyles kept his head down. The stain of red climbing his throat gave him away. "Last time I went on a date was around two years ago. We met online. Met up after a few messages. We'd both made it clear we weren't looking for anything serious, but I guess she forgot about that at dinner. She proposed to me in the middle of the restaurant. Had a ring and everything. Not sure how she managed to get my ring size right though."

"Wait. You tried on the ring?" she asked.

"I felt bad that she went through all that trouble." He wasn't laughing anymore. If anything his expression turned outright ashamed. "But, little tip, it turns out, if you accept the ring, you're agreeing to get married. It was all very confusing."

"How did she take it when you told her you didn't want to get married?" Sayles carved through the next section of trail, the water coming nearly to her waist. The muscles in her legs burned from exertion, but it was one of the best feelings she'd learned to fall in love with since coming to Zion.

"Not well." He shook his head. "Apparently, my behavior wasn't becoming of a federal agent. She called my supervisor and filed a citizen's complaint against me. I still get shit for it."

She couldn't stop the laugh vaulting up her throat. "Serves you right for accepting the ring. You're lucky she didn't follow you home and suffocate you in your sleep."

"I'm aware. Watch out." Agent Broyles latched on to her arm, dragging her against his side as a branch raced straight for her. Automatic and under control, he dropped his hold and pushed forward. "Now I meet women the old-fashioned way. Through thorough background checks and face-to-face interactions on the job."

Her heart hiccupped in her chest. Too distracted by their easygoing banter, she hadn't seen the branch coming for her. The tip of the branch scratched against her hydro bib as it passed, straight across her thigh. Probably wouldn't have done any damage to her gear considering its size, but she had to protect herself and her survival supplies with her life. Only he'd just done it for her. "Thanks."

"Don't mention it," he said. "This is when you try to make me feel better by revealing a far more embarrassing dating story."

Sayles searched the river ahead. No discarded food wrappers or water bottles. No dead bodies or supplies. Seemed their killer was covering his tracks. Had he prepared for this trek before killing his latest victim? "I've only ever dated one person. I ended up marrying him, then I divorced him. Not sure which part is more embarrassing. That I didn't see him for who he really was before I legally tied myself to him, or the fact it took me six years to figure it out."

Agent Broyles seemed to close the distance between them by a few inches. As though she might need his support. "Who was he really?"

"A liar. Manipulative and vengeful." Her throat dried. "I caught him cheating on me. I don't know for how long, but it took me weeks to confront him. I wanted proof, and when I got it, he found out a way to use it against me."

"What do you mean?" he asked.

Exhaustion pulled at her legs. Real or imagined, Sayles didn't know, but she could feel the defeat that came with reliving the past. Its heaviness threatened to pull her under the water's surface, and she was just straight up tired of carrying it around. "I followed him to several locations. Hotels for the most part. At least four of them with four different women over the course of two weeks, but I was too angry to get photos. Every time I saw him it was like he'd stabbed me. I thought we'd had a good life. One we'd built together. I thought we were happy."

He allowed her the space to cut their conversation short or to go on. Sayles wasn't sure she could tell him the rest, but he'd asked for an embarrassing story. This was probably one of the greatest. Nothing but the roar of the river and the colliding debris filled her ears, taking her out of her own head. Distancing herself from those hard-to-manage emotions that came with vulnerability and shame.

"He denied everything. Said I didn't have any proof, and he was right. I didn't. After I confronted him, he left. He was going to stay with a friend for a couple days until I apologized." She should've known then how much worse it would get. That she was expected to apologize for daring to call him on his adultery. "Two days later, police were at my door. And I was put under arrest."

His hand was on her again, pulling her to a stop. Except she didn't want to look at him. She didn't want him to see her as anything…less. "Under what charges?"

Tremors that had nothing to do with the frigid water

temperatures racked her. This was a mistake. She shouldn't have said anything. He'd just made her...feel. It'd been so long since she'd let herself step outside the rules she'd mentally put in place to survive, but she'd been fooled before. He was a federal agent, for crying out loud. She shouldn't trust him, but she had no one else. None of her colleagues, sure as hell not Risner—none of them understood what she'd been through. Sayles brought her gaze to his, expecting the same look she'd witnessed on all of her family's and friend faces when they'd gotten the news. Disappointment. Resentment.

His expression softened. He lightened his grip on her arm. "Sayles."

It was the first time he'd called her by her first name. The shock ricocheted through her chest as if she'd been struck. That single inflection of her name, wrapped in invisible silk and warmth, loosened the death grip her brain had on her. It was almost enough to convince her Agent Broyles was exactly what he seemed. Then again, she'd fallen for that knight-in-shining-armor act once before. She wasn't sure she could survive a second time. "Murder."

A cracking sound split the air. She didn't have time to act as a thick log slammed into her torso.

Then dragged her under the river's surface.

Chapter Eight

It happened so fast.

Elias clawed for something to stop the spinning, but his hands only caught smaller debris as the current tossed him like a dead fish. He had no control. His lungs burned. Freezing water charged up his nose. Mud and cloudy river water kept him from determining which way was up.

It shouldn't be this hard. The water's depth had reached his waist. He should be able to kick to the surface—or at least just stand up—but agonizing seconds stretched as he remained clutched in the river's grasp. His pack worked against him, pulling and keeping him down.

Sayles. Where was Sayles?

She'd been standing right next to him. Elias twisted his torso, tried to pinpoint the sun above him. Only to remember the clouds had rolled in, blocking out the sun and turning the Virgin River into a raging beast.

Pain ignited along one forearm and pulled a silent scream from his chest. Water replaced the last few remnants of oxygen in a rush. But then his boot hit something solid. Dirt kicked up around him. The river bottom. He shoved everything he had into breaking the surface.

The cold burned down his throat as he inhaled greedy

gasps. Once. Twice. River water beat against his chest, so much deeper here than when they'd come through the first time. Hell, he didn't recognize this section of the Narrows. He wasn't sure if he was even still on the trail. "Sayles!"

Her name scraped up his throat as a plea. She had to be here. The current would've swept her downstream with him, right? They should be in the same location. "Sayles!"

No answer.

It took more time than it should have to get his feet under him. Stinging pain rippled down his forearm. Damn it. Blood combined with river water and ran in rivulets around his protruding veins and muscles, then dripped into the current. The gash had cut deep, past several layers of skin and into muscle. He'd need stitches, but he couldn't think about that right now. Sayles was out here somewhere. Still under the surface.

Elias shucked his pack free of his shoulders. He couldn't maneuver these waters with it adding to his weight. Hanging it on a thick branch of a tree that looked as though it'd given up the ghost years ago, he faced the river. Searching for something—anything—that gave away her position. "Sayles!"

An average swimmer could hold their breath for a couple minutes. How long had she been underwater? Panic swept away his control as easily as that log that'd pummeled them. His heart rate skyrocketed, breathing going shallow. He could do this. He had to do this. For Sayles.

He dived. The rush of water shocked his nerve endings and nearly stole the breath he'd taken. Leaves and stringy plants clung to his neck and face as he battled the current upstream and blocked his vision. Clouded water strained his eyes, but he wasn't giving up the search. Not until he knew she was safe.

Her uniform and pack blended into the black-and-white world beneath the surface. Nothing to help her stand out against the very forces she'd sworn to protect. Elias surfaced as the burn in his chest became too much. His vision darkened at the edges, and he shook his head back and forth to get a grip. Damn it. Where was she? "Sayles!"

Then he saw it.

The iconic Stetson all national park rangers were required to wear as part of their uniform. It dipped and rose as it came closer. He jumped for it, not daring to let it get away from him as easily as she had. She must've gone under farther upstream. Too far from his current location. Grabbing for his pack, he put what energy he had left into hauling his overworked and tired legs to the edge of the river. His brain told him it'd be faster to get to her in the shallower depths, but he quickly learned there was no shallow portion in this section of the Narrows. "I'm coming. Just hang on."

He hadn't made it more than a few hundred feet before his heart bottomed out. There. A hand shot out to grasp on to the side an oversize log pinning her smaller body under the water's surface. Elias didn't question his instincts, launching himself back into the current. "Sayles!"

Her attempts to pull herself free were slowing every second it took him to get to her in the middle of the river. She couldn't raise her head above the surface. She was drowning right in front of him. "I'm coming!"

He wasn't sure if she could hear him over the rush of her own pulse or the Virgin River's constant roar. Elias buried the urge to throw himself across the log trying to get to her on the other side and rounded the closest end instead. The log had to measure more than twenty feet in height and at least three feet in diameter. It'd lodged itself in a collection of rocks jutting from the river's edge, most of it free of the water. It would take everything he had to lift it, but he didn't have a choice.

Sayles's free hand slapped against the bark. Too slow. She had a minute, maybe less. He widened his stance at the opposite end of the log, secured his hands underneath and lifted as if his life depended on it. The downed tree rolled in his grip and slipped free. Pain stung across his palms, but he'd have to worry about that later. Her hand had stopped moving. He was going to lose her.

He tried again. The log protested as he hefted it off the rocks and let the current take control. The heavy weight rolled straight over her torso before moving onto its initial course downstream, but Sayles didn't surface. His entire body screamed for release as he hiked straight through the current to get to her. "Come on. Come on."

Elias drove his hands beneath the surface, fisting her uniform collar and dragged her up. Her head fell back on her shoulders, skin paler than he remembered. A quick scan of their surroundings didn't give him many options to get her out of the river's grasp apart from the same collection of rocks that'd caught the log. He hauled her frame against his. "Stay with me, Sayles. Almost there."

As gently as he could, he laid her across the rocks and pressed his ear to her chest. She was still alive. Angling her chin into position, he set his interlaced palms over her sternum and administered compressions just as he'd been taught before being allowed to work in the field. Water dripped from the edges of her mouth, but her eyes remained closed. "Breathe. You can do it."

Coughs jerked her torso upward, water spewing across his chest and face. Green eyes peeled open and scanned the sky before landing on him. Elias turned her onto her side to let gravity do its work on her lungs.

"There you go. Take it easy." Smoothing small circles into her back, he let her take as much time as she needed before sitting up.

"What…happened?" Sayles grabbed for her throat. Most likely to counter the burn clawing up. From what he'd read, the Virgin River was categorized as fresh water, but all the mud and water toxins held opportunity for bacterial infection. She needed medical attention.

"We got railed by a tree." The bruising pain in his ribs told him there'd be marks within the next couple of hours.

"I got stuck." Her memory was intact. Good. They might not have to worry about brain damage, though more than three minutes without oxygen could have lasting effects they couldn't assess here in the middle of the damn park. "My boot…"

"Shhh." He couldn't seem to stop himself from touching her, from making sure she was real, that she'd survived. "You don't have to talk. Just rest. All right? Here." Pulling the metal water bottle from his pack, he offered it. She had water of her own, but his was more accessible.

She took it without hesitation and guzzled a few mouthfuls. Wiping her mouth with the back of her hand—despite her entire body being soaked—she handed it back. Her uniform clung to her in every way, showcasing lean muscle honed from countless hours on these trails. She seemed smaller all of a sudden, that mask of confidence dripping away with the water from her clothing. "You saved me."

"That's what partners are for." He took a few swigs of his own water. "Was I just supposed to watch you drown?"

A shiver rocked through her shoulders. "We need to get dry. The sun will be going down soon, and the longer we're stuck in these clothes, the higher chances we'll start feeling the symptoms of hypothermia."

Another tremor shifted down her back. Could the symptoms already be settling in? Elias didn't want to find out. "Yeah. Okay. Where are we?"

Sayles seemed to realize they'd ended up in a completely different section of the trail than when they'd been hit by that log. Craning her head back, she pointed to the crest of a red rock cliff southeast of their position. Her hand shook, and she quickly brought it back down. She checked her smartwatch. "That's Mountain of Mystery. We passed it about thirty minutes ago. We haven't lost much ground, but almost dying set us back. At this pace, we won't make it to Orderville Canyon Junction before the sun sets."

"That's not good." Trying to navigate these waters when he could see was challenging enough. But losing their limited light? Not to mention dredging through this river without the benefit of the sun's warmth would kill them. At this point their mission to catch up with the Hitchhiker Killer was on hold. All they could think about was survival. Elias scanned the canyon walls on either side of them. "Is there anywhere else we can set up camp for the night?"

She nodded. Nothing more than a couple jerks of her chin. "There's an outcropping of rocks near where we went under, but it's not large enough for two tents, and if there's another flash flood, we'll be caught in the current."

"I trust you, Ranger Green." And for some reason, he meant it. He offered her a hand, noting the cool paleness of her fingers as he helped her to her feet. Her leg shot out to catch her balance, and Elias was right there. First chance he got, he'd take a look at those playing cards of hers and see what the deck said about hypothermia. Because right now, he was pretty sure Sayles was trying to hide the impact of drowning on her body.

"I think we're past formalities, Agent Broyles. You know,

considering you saved my life and all. You can call me Sayles." Stepping down off the collection of rocks he'd brought her to, she locked her attention onto her hand. Onto the blood coating it.

"Does that mean you're going to call me Elias?" Damn. He'd forgotten about his arm in the chaos of trying to make sure he didn't have to carry her out of this canyon. Blood seeped into the crevices of his palm and between his fingers.

She didn't answer, closing the distance between the, and grabbed for his arm. Her thumb slipped over his pulse point before she angled one arm free from her pack. Keeping her fingers wrapped around his wrist, she unpacked her first aid kit one-handed. "This is going to need stitches, but we don't have long before we lose the small amount of light left. I'm going to wrap it for now. Once we reach the outcropping, I can put you back together."

"Like Humpty Dumpty?" His attempt to lighten the mood was lost in the glazed film overtaking the green in her eyes.

She circled long strips of medical gauze around his forearm before repacking her kit and heading back upstream. Minutes—was it an hour?—passed in silence as before as they charged for a dry section of rock a mere few feet above the river's surface. "This is where we'll camp tonight."

"Looks like you got your wish." Elias sized up the slightly uneven elongated rectangle of rock two of them were meant to sleep on tonight. "We're going to be sharing."

Chapter Nine

She couldn't stop shaking.

Sayles had changed out of her wet clothing with her back
to the FBI agent invading her one-person tent, but she'd lost
all sense of embarrassment as she'd forgotten how to ask
him for the hand warmers she'd packed. Dry gear hadn't
made a difference. Her head felt as though it'd been split
down the middle with the effort of trying to keep her teeth
from chattering. She was getting worse. Her joints ached,
not just stiff from the impact of the log that'd tried to kill
her but from the uncontrollable shivers racking her. The
pulse at the base of her neck wasn't normal. Too elevated.
Breathing too shallow.

And Elias… Concern had etched into his expression a
long time ago and hadn't slipped since. He'd taken the lead
in getting the tent set up and unrolling their sleeping bags.
There was barely enough space for the Mylar material let
alone two bodies, but what annoyed her more was the fact
that she'd missed the log's approach at all. She'd put them
in this situation, and she didn't want his concern. She'd put
their lives at risk, but she would be the only one to pay the
price. She'd make sure of it.

"Are…you shivering, too?" Hell. She sounded out of it

even to her own ears. She just wanted to sleep but knew how slim the chances were of waking up in the morning if she closed her eyes now. "Or dizzy?"

"No." He'd changed into dry gear after helping her out of her wet clothes and boots. The sun had gone down over an hour ago, leaving them with nothing but a single flashlight beam. They'd save the batteries of the second by limiting their resources for now. "You gotta tell me what to do, Sayles. Please."

"I'm...fine." She wasn't fine. Her desperation to take care of herself—to make her own choices and be in control of her own body—was winning out over simple survival. Stupid. She was being stupid risking her lift like this. For what? So another man didn't have leverage to use against her? How would that happen if she was dead? Sayles's let her eyes drift closed. She was so tired. "I'm already...warming up. I just need...to rest."

"All right. If you're not going to tell me how to help, I'll figure it out myself." He dragged her pack into his lap and started removing everything she'd meticulously organized.

She forced her eyes open. "What...are you...doing?"

"Looking for those cards. The ones with survival tips on them." Pulling the slim yellow box free of her pack, he shuffled through the contents until he landed on the red heart cards. "Seek shelter. Done. Replace wet clothing, especially socks. Did that. Insulate from the ground. Sleeping bag takes care of that. Eat carbohydrates and drink an electrolyte solution. Great."

He didn't wait for her permission to dig through the rest of her gear. In seconds, he produced a peanut butter and jelly sandwich she'd made before leaving the visitors' center and an electrolyte mix. "Eat."

Nausea twisted in her gut. "I'm not...hungry."

"Card says you have to eat carbs. Bread is carbs. Eat."
He wiggled the sandwich in front of her until she grabbed
for it just to get it out of her face.

The first two bites sank to the pit of her stomach and remained there. The next few went down a little easier as he
handed off her metal water bottle with the electrolyte mix.
Within minutes, the fog in her brain started dissipating.
Okay. Maybe there was something to those cards after all.

Elias went back to reading off steps to treat hypothermia. "Use chemical hot pads in armpits and sides of chest."
More of her supplies hit the bottom of her sleeping bag as
he dug for the hand and foot warmers she'd stashed.

"Between…the thighs." The cards gave good advice, but
she was a ranger. In the past five months, she'd seen more
people die than on the news from small mistakes rather than
big ones. Not utilizing the femoral artery to reverse hypothermia was one of them. "Bigger arteries…pump faster."

"Okay. Let's do both." He cracked the hand and foot
warmers and shook them to ignite the heat inside. Like a
glow stick. Only this was one that could save her life. "For
the record, I'm only feeling you up to save your life."

Her smile pulled at chapped lips. "I won't file…charges."

"Glad we're on the same page." Elias tugged her the
sleeping bag she'd cocooned herself inside and slipped calloused hands along the front of her body.

She parted her knees for him and pinched the warmer
between her legs as he got it into position. Her heart did
the rest, pumping the new source of heat into her veins and
throughout her body. Elias kept to the plan and positioned
two more hand warmers in both of her armpits. Immediate
warmth cascaded through her. And not just from the addition of the warmers. "Thank you."

"Hey, you're not slurring your words together. Progress."

His thumbs-up broke the tension. "Looks like I'm better at this survival stuff than I thought."

"I wouldn't go that far." She snuggled deeper into the sleeping bag. The heaviness of the day—and nearly meeting her creator—pinned her in place, but she couldn't deny the sense of…safety she felt having Elias here. He'd pulled her from the river. Had administered CPR. He'd bulldozed through her pride to save her life, and she wouldn't be here without him. Despite his chosen profession and the air of superiority she'd assigned him when they'd first met, he'd done nothing but ensure the success of this assignment. "Don't forget. I was the one to patch up your thigh because you wore jeans on an in-stream hike."

His laugh was softer than the times she'd heard it before. Soothing. "How are you feeling now?"

"Mmmm?" She must've drifted off for a second because she was peeling her eyes open to look at him. The shivers had settled. Her fingers and toes would take longer to recover feeling, but she could finally think clearly. "Better. The warmers are doing a marvelous job."

"Good." Elias grabbed her gear, repacking everything he'd extracted from her pack. She couldn't even get her ex-husband to pick up his dirty socks off the floor. No matter how many times she'd asked.

"Why aren't you feeling symptoms?" It wasn't fair. They'd both gone under. Though she might've been exposed to the frigid waters longer. "Shouldn't you be wrapped up shivering your ass off, too?"

"I have more insulation." He slapped his stomach twice. Followed by that brilliant smile that didn't see the light of day—or flashlight—often.

"Now you're just complimenting yourself. There isn't a single ounce of fat on you." She liked this. The ease between them. In the few short hours they'd been partnered together, she'd dropped the mask she'd donned to stay small and unnoticeable to everyone around her. It felt…good. Freeing. The truth was she didn't have the energy to put it back in place, and wasn't that why she'd come all the way to southern Utah? For the freedom it provided? Only now, she realized, she'd done exactly as she always had. Becoming the person she thought she needed to be to accommodate others. For Risner, her fellow rangers, for Elias. It was all so exhausting.

There was that laugh again, and her body temperature rose another degree from the effect. "You say that now. Wait until you're sweating from sleeping next to me."

After setting their packs at one end of the tent, he secured the front zipper of the enclosure before positioning himself along her back. Hints of his natural scent—mixed with river water—tickled her nose. Something earthy. Then again, she smelled like mud and water, too. There was no escape out here in the middle of the desert. Her breath shuddered out of her as Elias shifted his hips against hers.

"What are you doing?" Panic spiked her voice.

"Those hand and foot warmers aren't going to last more than an hour, and you're still suffering from hypothermia symptoms." He dragged the edge of her sleeping bags higher, under her neck. "I'm here to make sure you stay warm."

"By crawling into my sleeping bag?" Okay. Yes. Sharing body heat was shown to drastically help with regulating body temperature, but the last time she'd let someone get this close, it was her ex. Heat that had nothing to do with the warmers or his body stirred low in her belly.

"You got a better idea?" He shook against her. And not in laughter.

Had he lied about feeling the effects of the freezing temps? Sayles craned her head over her shoulder, putting him in her line of sight. His gauzed forearm threaded over her rib cage and pulled her closer, cutting off her inhale. "Your arm needs stitches."

"Go to sleep, Sayles." Elias set his head against his biceps. Completely at peace while she was anything but. "We can deal with it in the morning."

He was putting her need for rest above his need for medical attention, and she didn't know what to do with that information. If she was being honest with herself, she wasn't sure she could sew in a straight line right now. She'd probably end up butchering any chance of a neat scar. He probably knew that. Knew she wasn't at 100 percent and didn't want to risk his annoyingly good looks on a hack job. "Don't bleed on me."

"I'll try to keep my blood where it belongs." His chest rumbled through her back. The soft rocking helped release the tension in her aching joints, and she felt herself relax against him.

His arm secured around her, as if Elias couldn't stand any sort of distance between them. She didn't have the energy to fight for those precious few inches of air, but that didn't mean she trusted him. "Did you know him?"

"Who?" His voice graveled this close to sleep. The effect did something to her insides.

"My ex-husband." Her pulse slowly receded from the rafters. The few things he'd done—making her eat, drink and warm up—were doing the job. Five months of hiding—of healing—she'd kept herself in check. Wouldn't let herself think of the pain and betrayal and *rage* that came with reliving the past. But in a matter of hours, Elias had pulled it all to the surface.

His arm tightened around her middle. "No."

She hadn't realized she'd been holding her breath for his answer. Sweat beaded at the base of her neck. Within minutes, he'd managed to chase back the cold, and she found herself wanting to lean more into it. Into him. "Oh."

"We didn't finish our conversation from earlier." His whisper sent tendrils of breath across the back of her neck.

"You mean when we were plowed over by a log?" Her ribs still hurt. She wouldn't be surprised to find her body covered with bruises in the morning. If they made it until the sun rose. Another freak storm and they'd be washed down this river all over again. Only with no escape from the tent and nothing to hold on to but each other.

"He had you arrested for murder." Hints of anger stained his voice. Or had she imagined it? "Whose?"

She could still feel the pinch of the cuffs as two officers had placed her under arrest. Sayles stopped herself from rubbing at the healed skin, afraid to lose herself to the fear all over again. But that didn't happen. The heat at her back refused to let her slip from this moment, and she clung to it with everything she had left as she lost the battle to her exhaustion. "His."

Chapter Ten

He breathed through a face full of hair.

The weight crushing his chest wasn't normal, and Elias blinked against the soft light coming through the canvas protecting them from the outside elements. He blew long dark hair off his mouth, realizing the weight belonged to the woman passed out on top of him. She'd escaped her sleeping bag sometime in the middle of the night and invited herself into his.

The hand and foot warmers lay around them. Discarded in favor of his body heat. Elias settled onto his back, not sure what to do next. The sun was up, and if they had light, so did the killer. They had to get moving. "Sayles."

A moan slipped free of her throat, and she buried her face deeper against his chest. Wetness pooled against his shirt directly beneath her mouth. How long ago had she climbed on top of him? And why wasn't he inclined to maneuver her back to her side of the tent?

Oh. Maybe because the last time he'd considered getting close to a woman, she'd asked him to marry her on the first date. But this one was off-limits. While they didn't work for the same agency, they were partners. And he had no inclination to climb into a single-person tent with Grant. As soon as they caught up with the Hitchhiker Killer, he and Sayles would part ways. She'd stay here in Zion, and he'd get sent back into the field on a new assignment. Apart from that, she had a deep-seated hatred of the FBI thanks to her bastard of an ex, and he wasn't excited about the possibility of being suffocated in his sleep.

Who the hell ever thought the woman in his arms was capable of murder? Elias shook her small frame gently. "Sayles."

Another moan—more frustrated—filled the tent. "Five more minutes."

Yep. She wasn't aware she'd climbed him like a tree. "Sayles."

Her head shot off his chest. It took a moment for her gaze to clear enough to recognize the position she'd put them in. Swiping at her mouth, she shoved against his chest to put as much distance between them as possible. Except there really wasn't anywhere else for her to go. The tent had been made for a single person. It was a miracle they hadn't tipped it moving around in the middle of the night. "This is your fault."

"Oh? I'm pretty sure I wasn't the one playing musical sleeping bags in the middle of the night." The instant loss of her heat gutted him, and he wanted nothing more than to drag her back. But they had a job to do. "Though I can't say I didn't enjoy it."

Her face heated, which was a vast improvement over the blue tint it'd taken on after he'd pulled her from the river yesterday afternoon. Sayles extracted herself from his sleeping bag and shoved to stand. Her head hit the top of the tent. "Pig."

"Blanket hog." He swallowed the laugh aching for release as she shot him a look that would certainly put a less confident man in the grave. Elias didn't waste time waiting for her instructions and slipped free of the too-hot cocoon. Grabbing for his pack, he pulled his water bottle free and finished off the contents, then shoved two protein bars down his throat. They were already trying to make up for lost time to catch up to the killer. Any more mistakes and the bastard would escape. "Does the end of this trail lead anywhere else?"

Sayles bit down on the toothbrush in her mouth as she pulled her slightly curly and frizzed hair into a ponytail between her shoulder blades. The shirt she'd changed into last night engulfed her from shoulder to mid-thigh, her sweats at least one size too big. Choosing comfort over style. He liked that. "The Narrows trail officially ends at Big Spring, about three miles from here."

"And unofficially?" Elias folded his sleeping bag in half and rolled it as tight as his Boy Scout leaders had taught him as a kid. It'd been a pain in the ass then, and it was sure as hell a pain in the ass now, but he saw the merit in keeping his gear accessible and organized after nearly getting washed downriver.

Sayles dropped to her knees, dragging her pack closer. She went for the front pocket and pulled a thin brochure from inside. A detailed map of the Narrows. Leaning into him, she ran her finger along the switchback-like trail. "This is us at Mountain of Mystery." She pointed to a section that looked more like a contorted *S* than a trail, then slid upward to the top of the foldable map. "The river continues north with several branches leading west."

Elias made a mental note of each landmark and the *No Flash Flood Escape* warnings peppered up its length. "All right. Is it possible the guy we're hunting can escape the trail off the beaten path?"

"If he knows the area." Handing off the map, she pulled a couple more supplies from her pack, including a fresh uniform. She scrubbed at her teeth as though punishing them for making the decision to crawl into his sleeping bag. "If he doesn't, I can't imagine he'll last long in the backcountry on his own. Some people spend years training to survive out there, rangers included, but most have no clue what kinds of threats are out there. It's one of the reasons all national parks require permits and gear lists. People have died from exposure, animal attacks, starvation. You name it."

The Hitchhiker Killer—it was just easier to give him a moniker than keep referring to him as their killer or the guy they were hunting—had murdered a hiker at the base of the trail. But why? What had made him a target? He could only think of one motive: supplies. Which could mean they'd underestimated his knowledge of the park and the killer's experience. "Can I borrow your radio? I need to get in touch with my partner."

"The canyon blocks radio signals." She swallowed the toothpaste in her mouth, washing it down with water from her bottle. "We'd have to hike pretty high to get through."

"Are there any open areas a signal might reach the visitors' center?" They had to know what they were dealing with. A man relying on his survival brain or a methodical killer who'd chosen this trail for a reason. Time could tell them, but Elias was never one to jump without a plan. And he had Sayles to worry about. If anything happened to her... No. He couldn't let himself get worked up about nonexistent scenarios. That was how mistakes were made.

"Not for another couple of miles. The trail reaches around

5,600 feet in elevation once we hit Wynopits Mountain." Storing her toothbrush, she closed the distance between them, crouching at his side. Her hair slid over her shoulder and brushed against his arm. Raising goose bumps in its wake. She turned the map in his lap, fingers grazing his sweats, and he was instantly reminded of her body pressed up against his chest when he woke. Craving shot through him. Want. "There's a chance we may be able to get something if he hikes high enough there, but it's two miles north. It'll take time."

Time they didn't have for a detour.

"We need to assume whatever reason the killer targeted your hiker was to get extra supplies." Elias refolded her map and took the liberty of reaching around her to slip it back into the same pocket she'd found it. "I'm starting to think Zion was his escape plan all along."

Confusion drew her eyebrows over the bridge of her nose. Over her map or their proximity, he wasn't sure. "What makes you say that?"

"How many people would you say can survive a surprise flash flood and live to tell the tale?" he asked. "I'm pretty sure we would've seen a body by now if he'd gotten caught in that storm."

"Very few. Especially if they've never experienced one before or know the signs on an impending flood." Sayles stared at him, her eyes widening slightly. "You think he's using the park to stop you and your partner from catching him."

"It's not the dumbest idea." Though the Hitchhiker Killer had already killed four motorists and a hiker. What was a couple FBI agents added to the tally? "I'm sure you can tell I have no idea what I'm doing out here."

She shoved to stand, turning her back to him as she

stripped out of her oversize shirt. Muscle flexed around her bare rib cage and between her shoulders. Flawless skin, peppered with just a few moles here and there, surged a wave of heat through his chest, and Elias turned away to give her some semblance of privacy. A good amount of color had come back into her skin. No signs of hypothermia hanging around her face and lips. "But he had to have known NPS would get involved, and we *do* know what we're doing."

He'd been lucky. If he'd found her a mere minute later... He swallowed that thought with a tendril of acid.

"Good point." So where did that leave them? Pursuing an amateur or a far more dangerous criminal? What were they headed into? Elias made quick work of changing his shirt, back facing Sayles, and repacking his gear. His head brushed the top of the tent for the hundredth time. He'd forgo the jeans today, opting for the sweats he'd slept in last night. They didn't have time for him to hold them back. Clawing from the almost claustrophobic one-person tent, he grabbed for the clothing he'd hung to dry outside while Sayles had changed out of her wet uniform and rolled them into manageable pieces. His boots had dried. Less chance of more blisters.

Sayles pulled her first aid kit from her pack as she stepped onto the thin, rectangular rock that'd kept them dry last night. "I need to change your bandage before we go."

He had an argument ready but remembered he hadn't been able to get a good visual of the wound along his inner thigh. Which meant exposing himself—boxer briefs and all—to her again. "Yeah, sure."

The ranger seemed to make an effort to avoid looking at him directly, focusing instead on a fresh section of gauze and medical tape. The hairs on his thigh protested as she pulled at the tape already in place, but her touch soothed the stinging almost as quickly as it'd arrived. Despite the hard exterior she presented to the world, she swapped out his bandage with consideration and a care he hadn't expected. "I'm done."

Her coyness was cute but unnecessary. He wanted that fire back, the one that gave him reason to laugh and kept him guessing what she'd do next.

"Stop looking at me like anything has changed between us. It hasn't." She broke down the tent in a matter of seconds, wrangling it back into its packable form. Practiced, with a swiftness he couldn't help but admire.

"If you say so." Elias hauled his pack over his shoulders.

In less than ten minutes, they'd cleared their impromptu campsite and geared up. Sayles took the lead stepping back into the Virgin River's depths. "Mystery Corridor is around this next bend. There won't be any flash flood escape for about a quarter mile. I'm not seeing any incoming storms that would put us in danger for now, but we need to keep the possibility in mind at all times."

Cold worked through his boots and hydro bib—colder than yesterday's temperatures—but he remained dry thanks to Sayles's gear recommendations. "Would you tell me if you did?"

"I'd consider it, but only after reminding myself the paperwork wasn't worth it." There she was. The woman who fought like hell to hold her ground and remind people what she was capable of. Her attention locked on something ahead. A flash of red in a brown, green and white landscape. "You see that?"

Elias didn't hesitate, hauling himself to the center of the river to grab whatever'd escaped downstream. He caught it at the last second and brought the lightweight material back to her position. "What is it?"

"It's a dry sack. Something campers use to keep their gear waterproof." She took it from him, turning it over, then raised her gaze upstream. "This river moves around seven miles an hour, which means someone dropped this recently. Looks like your killer might be alive, after all."

Chapter Eleven

The killer couldn't be that far ahead.

Sayles ignored the exhausted burn in her legs, pushing one foot in front of the other. They hadn't made it far but already she could feel the intensity of Elias's attention between her shoulder blades. The same sensation she'd experienced when she'd woken on his chest this morning.

Her body had absorbed his warmth more efficiently than that of the hand and toe warmers, and for the first time in…a long time she'd slept through the night. No panicking sense of survival. No urge to reach for the multipurpose tool she kept stashed under her pillow. She didn't even remember dreaming. The same sense of freedom she found on the trails these past few months had filled the tent last night. And she was already craving more. Stupid. Stupid. Stupid.

It wasn't because of him. No. It'd been the stress of chasing after a killer. That was all this was. She'd been exhausted. She'd survived drowning, and her body had crashed the moment she'd let it. Elias Broyles had nothing to do with it. Well, except for the fact that he'd kept her from drowning and the effects of hypothermia.

"So are we going to be completely awkward around each other now, or are you just not a morning person?" Elias's shift through the water hadn't stumbled or slowed in the past thirty minutes since they'd left their small island of rock. The gauze and medical tape was doing its job.

Sayles closed her eyes against that calming balm of his voice. How did he do that? What the hell kind of witchcraft convinced her nervous system he was safe? Nobody else had managed to get under her skin since she'd escaped to Zion, especially not Risner. Not that she was interested in him or any other man, but a woman couldn't isolate herself—or her libido—forever. Her heart rate descended as though she'd sunk into a hot bath, and she gripped her pack straps tighter. "I'm usually on the trails when the sun comes up."

"Awkward it is." His laugh surrounded her, closed in by the canyon walls until there was no escape for its effects. Damn him and his voodoo. "You don't have anything to be embarrassed about. So you cuddled your sworn enemy in the tent last night. I'm sure you were just looking for a heat source last night when the warmers stopped working."

A flare of prickling cascaded across the back of her neck, almost pulling her to a stop. If she turned around, she might shove him into the river, and that was not very ranger-like. "It's awfully presumptuous of you to believe you made the list of people I consider enemies."

"There's a list?" His resulting smile bled into his voice. Detach. Detach. Detach. She didn't like him—didn't like what he stood for—and had no reason to trust him. No reason to smile back. But her mind supplied the retort and made the decision for her. Traitor. "There is. And you're slowly working your way to the top."

"Who do I have to beat out on this list?" This was a game to him, and she couldn't help but fall right into Elias's hands. It was the distraction she hadn't expected to enjoy.

"Ex-husband? Wait, no. That's a hard position to hold on to if you're dead."

Sayles craned her head over one shoulder to put the agent in her sights. "Who says he's dead?"

"I imagine a lot of people, considering you were arrested for his murder." He picked up his pace to keep in stride with her, slightly deeper into the river at her right. "Unless… He faked his murder just to have you arrested. How?"

Was she really doing this? Trusting a man like Elias with the secrets she'd held on to all this time. For what? Because he made her laugh? Because her body was convinced of the safety he radiated? She'd fallen for that once before.

Her ex had been everything she'd ever wanted. They'd dated for years during high school and college. He'd convinced her and her family he'd love and take care of her forever. But the moment she'd said "I do," everything had changed. The man behind the mask had started appearing in small ways at first. Commenting on her clothing choices, suggesting she avoid that second lemon bar. Bypassing her password on her phone to look something up when he had a perfectly good device provided by the government. The control had only tightened from there. Banning her from reaching out to her parents to apologize after a particularly hateful fight at the last family dinner ended in tears. Detailing who she was allowed to text, what she was allowed to wear, portioning meals, watching what she spent. No more coffee dates with friends. No more movie nights with her sisters. No more going to school. Sure as hell no more contact with male colleagues or friends. She didn't need to finish her art history degree when he was more than capable of providing for their every need.

For years, the noose tightened around her neck. Inch by inch, and she hadn't even noticed. At least, not until it'd been too late. That was when the calls started. The ones he answered in the middle of the night and left their bed to take. When he started coming home later and later. Working a case, he'd told her. He couldn't talk about it. Lies. All of it had been a lie she'd voluntarily swallowed to avoid facing the hard truth.

In the end, she'd been the one to pay the price for his crimes. Still was.

"He had help." Sayles diverted her gaze above, distracting herself from the tightness in her chest, to the dark cloud that'd slipped overhead without her notice. It was heavy and gray. Full of dangerous potential that could force them to go back. "Friends he recruited from his office."

"You mean federal agents." Elias's words barely registered over the lighter crash of falling water as they approached one of the seasonal waterfalls—in full effect—ahead.

The 200-foot cascade was tucked in a small branching canyon off the main trail and created a trail in its wake, silencing the torturous memories in her head. This. This was why she'd fallen in love with Zion, why she'd applied to become a ranger with no experience, no outdoor skills and meager survival know-how. But she'd been a fast learner. From the very first time she'd stepped into the Narrows, she was reminded of the woman she used to be. The one who trusted herself, who had goals and dreams, who'd figured out the solution to any problem. Staring at this waterfall, she'd remembered who she'd been before her ex had taken over. Strong but a little bit wild. Carefree yet caring for those who deserved her love. From mere minutes of studying this exact waterfall, something had clicked into place. She'd become obsessed, learned everything she could about the park and the skills needed to become a ranger in a matter of weeks. She still wasn't sure why Risner had offered her the job based off her nonexistent résumé, but she would always be thankful he'd given her the opportunity. Even if it meant suffering through his pitiful attempts to raise the bar on sexist pigs.

"We can rest here for a couple minutes." Her body relaxed into that space where the past didn't exist and all that mattered was the next step forward as she splayed her hand into the waterfall. Cold water slapped into her palm, kept her from disappearing completely. "My ex was very good at reading people. Always seemed to know the exact right thing to say. He could win any argument, despite evidence contrary to his perspective. If he hadn't made a career with the FBI, I think he might've been a great lawyer in another life. I think it's how he was able to convince so many people that he was the victim in our relationship. That he was being emotionally abused and isolated and controlled. Not the other way around."

Elias stepped up into her, unaware or unconcerned with the spray of water coming off the rocks. "The police had to have something on you to show a history of abuse."

"They did. Turns out those friends I thought could see what he was doing to me—people I'd invited into our home for dinners and holidays and barbecues—had provided testimony on my ex's behalf." Her stomach soured. They'd been her friends, too. Once. Only now she realized just how deep her ex had his claws in them. "The GPS in my car told police I'd been following him to those motels where he met up with women, keeping track of who he was with. There were texts sent from my phone to his colleagues but later deleted showing how much control I had over his life. He lied to his partner about arguments and punishments and financial abuse I held over him. But it was all a lie."

"But you were the one being abused," he said.

"Not physically. He never hit me, but some scars aren't visible." Sayles pulled her hand free from the crashing water. Back to reality. Back to chasing a ghost in hopes of keeping him from hurting anyone else. "I'd wanted out. A few days before I was arrested, I asked for a divorce, and in return, he faked his death."

"That kind of planning takes time." Elias didn't retreat from the waterfall, squinting up at the source 200 feet up. His expression relaxed as if he were soaking up every moment, memorizing it, enjoying it. In the short amount of time they'd been partnered, she hadn't seen him look so... free. Very unlike an FBI agent who might turn on her, and something released from around her rib cage. "You can't just frame someone in a day. Or without a body."

She'd figured that out while sitting in a jail cell. Somehow her husband had known her intentions. Or maybe he'd just always had an escape plan designed for moments he didn't get what he wanted. She'd never know. Sayles directed her attention back to the main part of the river. "No. You can't. Somehow, my ex had gotten a hold of a body roughly the same size and weight as him. It'd been...burned beyond recognition, but his wedding ring, the one I'd had engraved for him, was recovered with the remains. Neither fingerprints nor DNA could be recovered to make a positive identification, and the teeth had been damaged. Based on his wedding ring and his friends' testimonies, police arrested me."

Elias unwrapped a banana that wouldn't last him an hour calorically considering his size and muscle. "How'd you find out he was still alive?"

"One of the friends he'd asked to perjure himself had a change of heart." It was the first domino to fall in a long line of lies unraveled over several months. Months wasted in a prison cell that she'd never get back. "He came forward and gave up my ex's plan. Texts and voicemails he'd kept just in case. After some dealing with the DA's office, he gave up my ex's location. My darling husband had paid for a death certificate, bought a new identity, became someone else—all while I rotted away behind bars. I was released after eight months."

"I'm sorry. I can't begin to imagine what you've been through." Those dark eyes pinned her in place. Held her up with invisible arms like nothing else had since her release. "But I give you my word, I will not fake my death and frame you for my murder as long as we're partners."

Maybe Elias Broyles wasn't so bad for an FBI agent, after all.

"That would be greatly appreciated." Spatters of rain hit the brim of her hat, and she turned her face up to the sky. The cloud had taken over the thin sliver of blue in the past few minutes, and her stomach lurched. The chances of surviving—outrunning—another flash flood were slim. They had to go back. "Another storm is moving in. Come on. We have to get out of here."

Sayles didn't wait for his response as she headed downstream. Back toward that sliver of rock they'd taken solace on last night. There was no telling if it would be enough, but there was no flash flood escape in this corridor. They would die if they pushed through.

"What are you doing? Our killer is this way." Elias pointed upstream. "He's close, Sayles. The bag he dropped is proof. We can catch him. We can stop him."

"Not if we're dead." The rain picked up, stinging her face as the winds barreled down the canyon as though in warning. She studied the rapids. Waited for the debris and the mud and the roar she couldn't forget. "There's nowhere to run—"

A loud boom filled her head.

Elias's mountainous body collided with hers.

Dragging her beneath the river's surface.

Chapter Twelve

He slammed into Sayles.

Elias caught the slight exhale of air crushed from her chest a split second before the river consumed them with cold, watery teeth as sharp as knives. Using his full weight against her, he held them beneath its surface.

Sayles dragged her nails down his arms, over his face. Drawing blood. Fighting against his hold. Fighting for her life. Her kicks missed their targets and failed to dissuade his hold around her.

Someone had shot at them.

Pressure built in his chest as oxygen burned out of his system. He couldn't give the shooter a second chance of hitting his mark, but they wouldn't last long in the river, either. He had to make a choice.

Elias fisted her uniform collar and hauled her above the surface. Water dripped into his eyes, compromised his vision. Her gasp infiltrated his concentration a split second before strong hands shoved against his chest.

Sayles's hat was gone. Lost to the river. She didn't seem to notice as he hauled her behind his back, corralling her into the branching slot canyon they'd stopped in a minute before, his front to hers. Dark hair streaked down her face in rivulets of water. "Get off me—"

"Someone just shot at us." He pressed his hand against her mouth. Pain sliced through the numbness brought on by their swim. Despite the frigid temperatures of the river, her warmth seeped past his soaked clothing and gear. His heart thundered hard, loud enough to drown out the clapping of the waterfall at her back and the roar of the river at his. They were at a disadvantage here. He couldn't hear a damn thing as thunder rumbled overhead. The slot canyon they'd taken shelter in seemed to vibrate along with the storm. Rain only added to his distress. Could they survive another flash flood? Did they have a choice? His training clicked into place, and he ran through their options. None of them great. "Where does this waterfall trail lead?"

"West for about three-quarters of a mile, but it's a dead end and difficult to navigate in places." She shook her head. "There's no way you'd be able to fit through the slots, even if you took off your gear."

They were cornered. Damn it. Elias risked getting a visual of the shooter, but where he'd caught movement on a ledge above the river a few minutes ago, there was nothing but a flash of lightning. The killer was on the move. Aware he wasn't alone. They'd lost the element of surprise, and Elias wouldn't risk Sayles's life to get it back. He spun her around, shoving her down that too-small branch off the main trail. Water kicked up as she stumbled forward. "Then that's where we hide."

"No, it's not." She turned back into him. "The Narrows feeds this slot canyon, and there's no drainage at the end of this branch. If we're on it much longer, it'll flood with no way for us to escape. We have to go back to the main trail. We have to go back downstream."

Where the water had barely crested his ankles while they'd taken a break, it'd climbed to the middle of his shins.

One of the first signs of danger. Soon that roar would fill his head, and they'd be right back where they didn't want to be. In the middle of a flash flood. Except this time, they might not make it out alive. "How long does it take for this branch to flood?"

Elias unholstered his weapon from the small of his back.

"You can't be serious." Sayles shifted her weight between her feet, swiping hair out of her face as the rains intensified. They were protected from the gusts whistling down the canyon, but there was no escaping what came next.

"When did I give you the impression I don't take my job seriously?" Disengaging the magazine, he counted the number of bullets in his weapon, then slammed it back into place with the butt of his palm. "How long, Sayles?"

"If a flood hits, five, maybe ten minutes," she said. "But I've never been dumb enough to test that theory for myself."

"Well, today you get to find out the answer. Let's go." He secured his hand in hers, pulling her past the waterfall and deeper into the unknown. Smooth rock scraped against his shoulders within the first twenty feet as they navigated over rock and gravel-size obstacles. Debris laced the edges of the canyon and added to the suffocation factor.

"This is a mistake." Pulling her hand from his, she surged ahead to take the lead. Always on alert. Always in control. It was what he'd asked of her, and if they were going to make it out of this alive, it would be because of her. "We tell hikers to avoid this section of the trail for a reason."

Elias checked over his shoulder, weapon in hand as they retreated. As much as he wanted to charge back onto the main trail to confront the son of a bitch who'd taken a shot at them, he wasn't going to lose another innocent life. Never again. "Would you rather get shot?"

He imagined it took everything she had not to respond with whatever retort she'd come up with. Now wasn't the time. They had to move as a team, make decisions as a team. Partners in the purest sense.

Ripples of rock—so much like cresting waves—jutted out and scratched at his arm as he passed. The scratches Sayles had inflicted in the river hadn't broken skin, but he couldn't ignore the sting as adrenaline drained, either. He couldn't blame her in her panic. And, hell, it wasn't the only way she'd left her mark on him these past days. The walls closed in on them, leaving no more than two feet to pass through. Water surged from the direction of the main trail at their back, climbing up his pant legs.

"It's starting. This canyon is going to flood. We need to hurry." Sayles picked up the pace, charging at a blockade of smooth stone that looked as though it'd been set directly in their path. They'd have to climb over to keep going. "Come on."

A second bullet sprayed dust and chunks of rock into Elias's face. Mere inches away.

"Watch out!" He launched forward, using his body to shield Sayles as much as possible. Pain ignited along his arm as fractures of rock rained down from above. Elias spun. And caught the dark shape using the canyon as cover. He pulled the trigger. Enough times to ensure she had a lead. "Go, go, go!"

He couldn't tell if she'd followed his order but trusted Sayles to take care of herself. His pack snagged between the two walls as he retreated backward toward that rock obstacle blocking their path. Elias tried to push through, but his upper body refused to fit.

Then he heard it. The roar.

Water bubbled and turned white as it assaulted the thin

slot canyon as violently as a pack of wolves closing in on their prey. He'd lost sight of the killer.

"Elias, take my hand!" Sayles's warning barely registered over the thud of his heartbeat thundering in his ears.

The shooter had disappeared, presumably to find higher ground, but had robbed him and Sayles of their escape. He couldn't fit through the slot, just as she had warned. His pack had caught on one of the rocks. Elias grabbed on to her, his grip slipping through hers. Once. Twice. She climbed back down. Giving up her own escape. In an instant, she'd sliced through the straps of his pack with one of those multi-tools and pulled him through the gap. Her hand was in his before she maneuvered him ahead. Water lapped at their heels, rising faster than he expected. It was different here than on the main trail where the flood could spread out. "Move it!"

They had mere minutes before this canyon was underwater. They'd be lucky if they managed to escape at all, and noting fresh water lines ten, even fifteen feet up the red rock walls, he wasn't sure the chances were good.

Cold seeped around his feet as he climbed higher. They couldn't keep up this pace. His lungs were on fire, his heart ready to beat straight out of his chest. But Sayles remained a constant presence at his back. A comfort in the storm. He reached the top of the incline, ready to sink to his knees in relief.

Sayles's boots slipped against wet stone. Over and over. The water level was catching up. Going to take her from him. Her eyes widened in realization, and unfiltered fear iced out the confidence he'd become accustomed to over the past two days. Rain plastered her hair against her face, her uniform clinging to her frame. She couldn't get a good grip.

"I've got you." He grabbed for the nearest handhold in

the rock with one hand and stretched for her. They weren't going to die today. He wasn't going to lose another innocent life. A foot separated their hands with no way to make up for the difference. "You can do it. Just a little farther."

Her hand trembled as she reached up the ninety-degree incline toward him above. They were going to make it. They had to make it. He couldn't do this without her. The muscles in his jaw ached under the pressure of his teeth. Water climbed to her waist, sucking her into its icy depths, robbing her of any leverage. The rock walls seemed to close in, squeezing the air from his chest as he tried to face her fully. It was impossible with the limited space. Acceptance smoothed fear from her expression. She lowered her hand a fraction of an inch.

And everything in Elias went cold. He shook his head. "Don't you dare. Don't you dare give up. Grab my hand."

"I can't." Weathered red rock betrayed one of the very rangers fighting day in and day out to protect it. River water infiltrated her mouth as she clawed to keep her head above water. Her pack. Her pack would drag her down.

"Come on! You didn't give up on proving you didn't kill your ex. Don't give up now, damn it." Pain flared through his shoulders as he forced his body into the unnatural position on his stomach. Rock bit into his ribs, but he pushed it aside. It didn't matter. He just needed to close that distance between them. It wasn't going to end like this. Not after everything they'd already survived. Not after what she'd been through. This park had become a safe haven when she'd needed it the most. He wouldn't let it kill her. "Now, reach for me!"

Rain splattered against her face as she tried one more time. Her fingertips slipped against his. A last bite of warmth shot through his system. Her boots couldn't get the right angle against the stone. Water churned around her—angry and chaotic—as the river started draining back onto the main trail. Taking her farther from him. Sayles slapped her hands out to grab on to something, anything, to fight against that tide. But it was no use. The walls were too weathered and smooth from centuries of storms just like this one. That foot between them turned into two. Three. The storm hadn't let up. She would die if she got sucked beneath the surface again. "Elias!"

He didn't know what to do. That sour rise of helplessness burned in his throat. Elias abandoned his pack and gauged the drop. Mud and debris made it impossible to measure the depth of the river. He couldn't risk diving. He'd have to jump straight in, and he inhaled a deep breath. His boots took the brunt of the impact as he hit the water's surface. The river swallowed him whole, and it took everything he had to get free of the crushing current working to keep him under. Tumbling end over end. "Sayles!"

No answer. She was already gone.

Chapter Thirteen

Her head throbbed as though her sinuses were infected.

Pressure built in her face, down the back of her neck. Behind her eyes.

Sayles couldn't help the groan of pain as she turned her neck to the side. Liquid drained down the back of her throat, and she turned to cough it up. Something sharp bit into her palms as her stomach heaved.

"Oh, good. You're alive." Footsteps skidded to a halt close by, but it was hard to tell with the cast of shadows. "I wasn't so sure there for a while."

That voice. She didn't recognize it. It seemed to echo, surround her, suffocate her. Jutted rock pressed into her hands as she got her bearings. Alive. She was alive. And wet. "Where am I?"

"Thought you ranger types knew every inch of this park?" His laugh wasn't anything like the warmth she'd wrapped herself in from Elias's. "Guess that saying is true. You learn something new every day."

The park. She was still in Zion. In a…cave? Dark walls had been stained black with minerals and drainage, curving up and over her head. It wasn't a cave per se. Didn't go deep enough, with an oversize opening. An outcropping in the rock. Her heart beat too hard behind her ears to pick up signs of the river. She worked to come up with an answer of how the hell that was possible. She did know every inch of this park, and the last thing she remembered... Cold. Falling. Fear.

Her senses adjusted enough to outline the man in front of her. The one sitting on a flat rock, knees hiked a bit higher, with a spoon in one hand and a bowl of something in the other. A backpack—similar to hers—rested against his thigh. Wait. That *was* her pack.

"Hungry? It's not great straight out of the can, but there's still some left." His features remained in shadow as clouds continued their rampage across the sky through the opening. Rain pummeled and slapped against wet rock a few feet away, tricking her brain into thinking the threat had passed.

The park had been cleared of visitors once word got out there was a killer on the loose. Which meant... Sayles shoved to sit, putting as much distance between them as the outcropping allowed. Her shoulders hit solid wall within a couple of feet. "You."

He offered her a spoonful of whatever he'd been eating, and her stomach rolled with ingested river water. "You look like you could use this more than I do."

She couldn't keep herself together any longer. Curling to one side, she let her stomach have its moment. Water and the small bit of food she'd eaten after waking this morning charged free of her mouth. The small hit of adrenaline dissipated as memories assaulted over and over. Elias. She scanned the half cave. The last image of him—reaching for her from above—intensified the trembling quaking through her. She locked her hands into fists to try to control it, but there was no fighting nature. Her throat burned as she swallowed around bile and river water. "What...happened?"

"You almost died." The killer set his meal aside, brushing both hands together as though discarding a thick layer of dirt. "I saved you."

That didn't make sense. Sayles searched the half-cave-like structure. For what, she had no idea. An escape. A sign of Elias. A general location of where she'd ended up. Her teeth chattered. The thin cotton uniform she'd worn these past few months only managed to hold on to the chill that refused to leave. "Why?"

Her captor—the killer Elias had been searching the interstate for—shoved to stand. He towered over her. Massive. Intimidating. The kind of man who was fully aware of his size and used it as a weapon against anyone in his way. Probably the same way he'd used it against those motorists he'd murdered. He closed the distance between them, crouching in front of her. Shadows blurred his features, but she could make out a pair of extremely arched eyes. Beard growth aged his face and accentuated the puffy skin beneath those eyes. He wasn't lean. Not in the way Elias had honed layer upon layer of muscle through training and hard work, but the bulk was there. Less defined but just as deadly. Short hair curled over his forehead. Almost boyish apart from the predatory smile splitting his mouth. "You're going to help me."

"I'm not available." Rock cut into her scalp as she tried—and failed—to add just a few more inches of space between them. Reminded all too easily of the way her ex had used his size and strength to get her to comply. But she wasn't that woman anymore. She'd survived his manipulations. And she'd survive this man, too. "Ever."

"But you were all too willing to assist Agent Broyles." He set his arms against his knees. Blocking her escape. Ready to strike at a moment's notice. "Isn't that why you're out here, Ranger Green? To help the FBI catch me."

The shock of her name on his lips must've registered on her face before she had a chance to shut it down. Her name tag. She closed her eyes against the stupidity of that realization. Of course he knew her name. She was still wearing her name tag. Sayles tried to swallow down the uncertainty in her voice. "I go where I'm told."

"That's good." An unnatural stillness seized the killer in front of her. "Because right now I need you to get me out of this park without the police or your agent following. Understand?"

She shook her head as best she could, every cell in her body focused on the wide opening at his back. No recognition of their surroundings, but she hadn't been unconscious that long. Right? He had to have brought her somewhere off the Narrows trail, which meant she could find Elias. They could stop this killer from hurting anyone else. "I can't do that."

"Of course you can." He stood, once again towering over her, using his size to force her compliance. "Otherwise, I have no need for you."

She locked her gaze on his face. Trying to memorize every detail, every scar, or tattoo or identifying characteristic. In case she got out of this alive. "Are you going to kill me?"

"Only if I have to." He shrugged as if the idea of murder was nothing more than a passing inconvenience.

"You make it sound like I have a choice." Despite her two-day trek in the middle of a river, her mouth had gone dry. She gauged her chances of running for the entrance and getting a head start before he caught up with her. They weren't looking good from her current position. "Did all your other victims get the same choice or did you make the decision for them?"

Elias would find her. She didn't know how. She didn't know if he'd managed to escape that slot canyon, and she didn't want to think about the possibility he hadn't. But she had to believe in something. The agent she'd agreed to guide through the park yesterday afternoon wasn't the man she'd come to know in the hours since. He was better. Understanding. Protective. The kind of man who believed evil should never go unpunished. So unlike the other federal agents she'd known throughout her life and her marriage. No matter what happened, she knew Elias would fight for her.

"Someone's been talking about me." That smile was back. Slick and oily with a hint of violence. "Tell me, Ranger Green, if you agree to get me out of this park unnoticed, will you share a tent with me, too?"

Nausea charged through her. He'd been watching them. Studying them. How close had he gotten without them noticing? She and Elias had assumed he'd been ahead of them on the trail, but what if he'd just been biding his time? A small piece of the courage it'd taken to stand up to her ex electrified her nerves. She raised her chin. She wouldn't cower. She wouldn't beg. If anything that would give this man exactly what he wanted—what her ex had wanted—and she'd grown tired of making herself smaller for other's comfort. "Sure. As long as you're not scared I'll kill you in your sleep."

His laugh rippled through her, raising warning in its wake. He crouched in front of her again, consuming her focus. Then gripped her chin harder than necessary to force her attention. "Hold on to that fight. You're going to need it."

Sayles ripped from his grasp and managed to summon enough saliva to spit at his face. Stars exploded as his hand connected to her jaw. Her body hit the unforgiving cave floor against her will. Pain unlike anything she'd experienced cocooned her in a never-ending echo. Tears sprang to her eyes. She couldn't fight them. Couldn't swallow the sob escaping her chest. Of all the manipulation, the abuse and the danger she'd survived, a single strike was the catalyst that would unravel her. She held her face as she righted herself, breaking off a piece of rock about as big as her hand.

"We leave in ten minutes. I suggest you eat something and get some fluids in you." The killer retraced his steps back to that rock she'd found him on upon waking and tossed her backpack at her. The bag landed at her feet, supplies shifting out of order. He'd gone through it. Most likely took her multi-tool to keep her from attacking him. "We're not stopping until you get me out of this hellhole."

She closed her hand around the sharpened rock. From the looks of the cave, he'd gone out of his way to ensure there wouldn't be anything she could use against him. But he hadn't planned for her fall to break off a chunk. Rangers fought against damaging the park's natural features, but she couldn't miss this opportunity, either. Her gaze cut to the entrance. She just needed to buy herself more time. Think this through while keeping her makeshift weapon to herself. "It's still raining. The trail is flooded. It's too dangerous—"

"Then what good are you?" Collecting his own supplies, he slung his pack over his shoulders and stared her down. Daring her to disobey.

Sayles shifted the rock behind her, pinning it between her low back and the cave wall. "You won't get far with a captive in tow. The FBI is going to catch up to you."

"Maybe." Another shrug. "Or maybe I leave your body

for him to find. That would slow your agent down, don't you think?"

Elias wasn't hers. She was fairly certain he didn't even like her, which fit her plans to avoid federal agents and men in general as long as she lived. But that lonely part of her—the one who'd always wanted and believed in happily-ever-afters—protested at her decision to isolate herself in the middle of a national park in the name of freedom. And it'd certainly enjoyed waking up plastered against his chest this morning.

"Seven minutes." He set himself against the arched entrance, arms folded across that massive chest. Waiting. "You're wasting time, Ranger Green. I will drag you out of this cave if I have to because I know you can still navigate while bleeding."

"Fine." Did she have any other choice in her current circumstances? He had a point. She wouldn't get far on an empty stomach and dehydration. Hikers had died in this very park with more in their stomachs than she had right now. After rummaging through her supply pack, Sayles discovered he had indeed taken her multi-tool. She extracted a bag of dried protein oatmeal and downed it as fast as she could, following it up with a couple swigs of water. Carefully repacking her bag with one hand, she shifted the severed rock into her pack without notice. And left something else behind. Elias had no idea what kind of monster they were hunting. This was her chance to find out. Sayles pushed herself to her feet and slung her drenched pack into place. "Let's go."

Chapter Fourteen

She was gone.

Elias blinked up into that dark, raging sky. Cliffs angled into his vision. Hell. His body ached. He couldn't feel his toes or fingers. Something was digging into his back. Rain pattered against his face as he raised his upper body off the ground. The river receded from the slot canyon a few feet away, its icy fingers trying to take him with it. Water sprayed into his face from above. That waterfall. The one they'd stopped under before the killer had tried to shoot them. At least he knew where he'd ended up.

He remembered jumping in after Sayles. And then... Nothing. He should've been swept downstream with her. Maybe if he'd spent the past few months in the gym instead of stalking convenience stores along the interstate for signs of their killer—and, let's be honest, road snacks—he might've been. Thank heaven for the extra few pounds he'd gained on this case.

"Damn it." Pain seared through his rib cage as he twisted. Blood. Debris. Elias sucked in a deep breath as he pulled at the stained edges of his shirt to get a better view. A twig, no more than six inches in length and about as round as his little finger, had embedded itself between two ribs. Thankfully not deep enough to deflate a lung. He set himself back down. Thought about what to do next.

Sayles was out here. Because of him. Because of his insistence of taking this trail to escape the shooter. It'd been a bad call that might cost the ranger her life.

He'd abandoned his pack in the slot canyon. The winding maze of rock and smooth lines kept him from spotting it from here, but he couldn't risk going back onto the main trail without it. Lifting his head again, he pinched the middle of the twig. And pulled.

Agony ripped through his torso. His scream bounced off the surrounding rock and shot it straight into the clouds above. Staring at the wound, he counted off the seconds. Waiting. It didn't seem to be—

Blood bubbled to fill the hole the twig had left behind, and he clamped a hand to apply pressure. Little humor coated the laugh rocking through him. "Well, now you're going to bleed to death. Great work, Broyles."

Damn it. He needed Sayles. Her know-how, her first aid kit. Elias hauled himself to his feet, stumbling as a rush of dizziness attacked. Pea-size rocks shifted beneath his feet. He spotted thousands of them between him and his pack now that the slot canyon had drained, each one working to slow him down. One hand pressed into his side, he followed the winding path to the area where he'd dropped his pack.

Memories of Sayles's scream, his name tearing from her throat, as she tried to reach for his hand threatened to convince him to turn around. Forget about the pack. Go after her. But he wouldn't make it far without addressing his wound. He needed that pack. Setting his foot against a blocklike section of stone, Elias tried to climb one-handed. Wouldn't work. The angles and the slick surface of rock worked against him, but taking pressure off his wound guaranteed he'd bleed out that much faster.

There was no other way.

The section of the trail where he'd left his pack was at least eight feet above. He'd have to two-hand it and pray the damn thing hadn't been washed away. He could do this. He had to do this. For Sayles. He wasn't going to lose another life on his watch. He'd promised to keep her alive. To make up for the past by protecting her throughout this manhunt. Nothing would stop him from finding her. Focused on how he'd get up the incline, he took short breaths, hyping himself up. "Come on."

He released the pressure on his wound. Blood instantly swarmed to the surface and spread through the soaked material of his shirt. Ignoring the bleeding, he shoved off the foothold and stretched one hand overhead, locking onto a handhold above. His other hand braced against the wall to his left. Now he just had to climb. The pain swelled. His heart rate skyrocketed. Warm liquid pooled along the waistband of his pants with every inch he climbed.

Seconds stretched into minutes. Minutes into an hour. His fingers ached as he tightened his hold against slick rock determined to buck him free. Finally, Elias threw himself over the lip of the incline, sprawling out across the cold stone with nothing left to give. And faced a miniature cliff off the other side. The world threatened to tear out from under him as he caught himself from going over the twenty-foot-plus drop.

His pack dug into his shoulder. Luck. Pure luck he hadn't kicked it over. Dragging himself back from the edge, he focused on stopping the leak from his side. Elias extracted his first aid kit and popped the lid. His vision wavered as he pressed his hand deeper into the wound. What had Sayles said about these waters being infested? Something about water toxins. He had to clean the wound first. Make sure it didn't get infected. That was what she'd done on his thigh. All right. He'd have to use his drinking water.

"Clean the wound." He could do that. Lifting his shirt, he pressed the hem beneath his chin to pinch it against his chest. Brown bits of dirt and crusted blood clung to the edges. He unscrewed the top to his water bottle and irrigated the hole as best as he could. The angle didn't give him complete visibility to ensure everything had been cleaned out, but it would have to work for now. Time was running out. No burn this time. He wasn't sure if that was a good thing or not. He used the gauze pads in the kit to dry around the twig hole, sprayed the blood-clotting spray and replaced the old gauze with a new layer before taping it down. "Okay. You might not die today."

He couldn't say the same for his partner.

Repacking everything as quickly as he could, Elias dragged his pack after him since Sayles had cut the straps in order to save his life. He descended the drop. The pain in his rib cage downgraded from a throb to an annoyance, but there was no telling if he'd done any of it right to avoid infection. He retraced his steps toward the main trail.

The river hadn't finished throwing its temper tantrum. Water levels were still much too high to navigate it safely, but the time for hesitation had passed. He had to find Sayles. Had to avoid getting shot, too. He patted the holster at his back. Hell. His gun. Scanning the area in tight circles, he couldn't see where the weapon had gone. Which created a whole lot of problems in and of itself. He couldn't risk hunting the Hitchhiker Killer without some form of protection or having some kid find a gun along a very public and popular trail when the park reopened. "Now's not the time."

Elias dove straight back into the river's grip, taking it downstream. Sayles had known. She'd told him the risks of getting caught in the slot canyon during a flash flood, and he hadn't listened. Now she was the one paying the price. That pressure kept him moving. Kept him angry. "Sayles!"

No sign of her natural-colored uniform or pack. No body caught on one of the many logs stretching across the trail or rocks. The current forced him to pick up his pace when his body wanted nothing more than to rest after being thrown around as much as he had been on this trail. One thing was for sure. Once he caught the killer, he'd never hike this trail again.

Sayles was smart. She knew this trail better than anyone. If there was a chance of survival, she would've taken it by getting to higher ground. He scanned the domineering cliffs watching over him and anyone else who came through this insane maze. From this position, there was no telling whether he could climb higher. Everything looked too smooth. He'd try farther downstream and hike back if needed, but his gut told him she'd gotten out. That she'd saved herself.

"I'm coming." He wasn't sure who he was trying to convince more, Sayles or himself, that he wasn't going to stand by and fight this alone. That he wasn't going to fail her like he'd failed the witness in his last investigation. Exhaustion slowed him down, but he wouldn't let it get the best of him. His partner needed him, and he'd be there for her the same way he'd be there for Grant if he were in this situation.

Water had long infiltrated his gear and pooled in his boots. He didn't want to imagine the blisters he'd leave this canyon with, but he was sure Sayles would help him with those as she'd helped him before. That was the kind of woman she was. She'd guarded that heart of hers against any threat thanks to her ex, but there were still pieces that couldn't be killed off. And for the first time since that disaster of a date two years ago, Elias found himself wanting one of those pieces. Wanting more of her smile. More of her determination and courage and intensity in his life. The backtalk and teasing and biting comments. He wanted it all. She'd lit something in him that'd been buried in him. Made him feel alive. He wasn't ready to give that up.

Every muscle in his legs protested the downstream descent, but he caught sight of a thin edge of rock that seemed to lead higher up the cliff face on the opposite side of the trail. If Sayles had escaped the flash flood, it seemed the perfect spot to gain the advantage until the storm died down. Rain kept pummeling down on top of him, weighing him down and increasing the risk of crossing, but there really wasn't any other choice. Not when it came to Sayles. He'd dragged her into this mess. He would be the one to get her out.

Elias charged through the raging currents, avoiding whitecaps and sticking to the boulders still peeking above the surface. It took longer than he wanted with the injury in his side, but within a few minutes, he'd reached the opposite riverbank. The edge of rock climbing overhead was nothing more than a thin, graveled trail rangers had likely advised hikers to avoid, but he'd take the chance. To find her.

His thighs screamed for relief as he ascended the incline, one foot after the other, until he'd reached a flatter section ending in nothing more than a half cave that provided little to no protection against the onslaught of rain and wind. Except there was something…functional about the small cavern. A flat rock took up residence in the center with fine grain sand kicked up around it. As if someone had indeed used this undersize barricade to escape the floods of the past two days. Heavier drops of water collected along the arched entrance and tapped against his shoulders and scalp as he moved inside. He barely managed to stand at his full height. Could stretch his arms out straight and brush both walls with his fingertips.

Someone had been here.

The footprints in the sand had gone undisturbed. And there. Against the wall. Elias crouched to a spread of tracks, picking up a tube of antibiotic ointment. The same brand she'd used to tend his thigh wound yesterday. Sayles. She'd been here. Right here. Had left this tube as a message, knowing he wouldn't stop the search, which meant she hadn't been alone.

He pocketed the ointment and turned to face the arched entrance. They had to be close. On the move. Stepping out into the storm, Elias hiked higher. "I'm coming for you, partner."

Chapter Fifteen

She was going to die.

Sayles fought to keep her balance as they hiked 2,000 feet above the Narrows on a goat trail no more than two feet in width. Park visitors and rangers alike were warned against setting foot on this path. With no handholds and the potential for falling rocks, no one had wanted to take the risk. Until now. A nudge from behind tightened the muscles in her jaw and neck. "Unless you want to take a dive headfirst off this trail, stop crowding me."

"Come on now, Ranger Green." Another brush of his hand against her waist. Purposeful. Meant to show domination. Show her who was in charge, even out here. "You and I have the same goal. To escape. That should make us friends."

"You don't know anything about me." The added weight to her pack threatened to pitch her backward into his frame. The rock she'd hidden wasn't much, but it might be the difference between escape or ending up dead whenever the bastard was done using her.

"Well, that's just not true." His voice took on a more distant tone, not quite directed at her. Like he was scanning their surroundings. She didn't dare to look back to confirm one way or another. "I know your name is Sayles. That you've been a ranger here in Zion for the past five months. Came all the way from Colorado, didn't you? Alone. With an art history degree of all things. Not a whole lot of work in that arena, but that's not why you ended up in one of the most isolated national parks in the west. Something must've scared you. Made you run from your hometown."

The ache in her jaw intensified. She wasn't going to give him the details. Wasn't going to give him anything other than a reason to regret forcing her help. "You read my résumé. Congratulations. You're officially a detective."

That oily laugh dredged through her and turned her stomach.

"Why try to escape through the park? It's all just wilderness at the end of this trail. There's nowhere for you to run." Gravel shifted under her weight. The storm hadn't let up, turning solid ground into inches of wet sand. She had to watch her footing. One wrong step and she'd end up a park statistic.

"That's not really any of your concern, is it?" He kept pace with her better than she expected, dashing her hopes of gaining distance in order to run. "Getting me through the park without being noticed by the backcountry patrols. That's what you should be focusing on."

It was getting harder to breathe at this elevation. The oatmeal she'd eaten dry was beginning to turn in her stomach. Her heart rate had risen into fleeting, shallow pulses. Every step higher brought on the risk of altitude sickness despite Zion's 4,000-foot dominance above sea level and her acclimation over these past few months. Turning her head slightly, she kept the killer at her back within sight. Searching for those telltale signs of slowing down, vomiting, dizziness. If she caught him off guard, she might be able to survive. "That hiker you killed at the bottom of the trail. Why him?"

"You're mighty curious, Ranger Green." He studied her as a scientist studied a bug he didn't like. "Could it be you're trying to pump me for information to hand over to the FBI in hopes of making it out of this alive?"

She locked down the shudder taking her by surprise. Sayles wouldn't let him see the effect of that thought. Of dying within the very park that'd gifted her a new life. One of freedom and choice. "If you plan on killing me once we get to the end of the trail, what's the harm of unburdening yourself along the way?"

"You think I feel guilty for killing those people?" Not with that smile she didn't. "You'd be barking up the wrong tree."

"So all of this is just some sick game to you?" Scanning the trail ahead, she tried to come to terms with her situation. Of being alone 2,000 feet up on a too-narrow trail with a man who could end her right here if the thought crossed his mind. She hadn't fought for this new life to end up dead now. Not without going out on her own terms. "You'll kill anyone who gets in your way without so much as thinking it through?"

"All I've been doing is thinking this through." The words were nothing more than a whisper nearly lost to the winds. Something maybe she wasn't supposed to hear.

Sayles didn't know what to say to that, what to think. It didn't matter. She'd never hiked this trail, wasn't sure where it led or if there was an end. For all she knew, she could be leading them straight over the edge of a cliff. Goats could jump up cliff faces. Humans not so much. Either way, she was running out of time before her usefulness was all used up. She had to act. To give Elias and his partner something if this ended poorly. She owed him that after he'd saved her life yesterday. "Do you at least have a name? Or should I just call you the Hitchhiker Killer?"

"It's got a certain ring to it, doesn't it?" He cocked his head as a predator might when confronted with prey. "But if that's too much of a mouthful for you, you can call me Patrick."

"Not your real name, I'm guessing." The trail crested the top of the north cliff overlooking the Narrows. She could see the river below, identify the curve leading into Wall Street Corridor. Most hikers turned around at this point where the river split into an upstream branch leading east into Orderville Canyon. Park visitors were prohibited from heading that way due to the canyon walls becoming so narrow they were virtually impassable and the clay soil making the trek too slippery. They were close to that junction. Right where she'd intended to lead Elias to set up camp before they'd had to stop to treat her hypothermia symptoms. Even now, that base chill refused to let up, and she wanted nothing more than to fall asleep beside Elias's heat. To inhale his earthy and masculine scent that clung to her hair and skin where she'd touched him.

"You'd be right." The killer didn't offer anything more.

Sayles caught the slight change in his step. A little too close to the edge. She'd picked up her pace, forcing him to keep up, to ascend several hundred feet too fast. Depending on his elevation experience, acute mountain sickness could set in as quickly as a few minutes. This was her shot. The one chance to get away. The goat trail they'd commandeered became even thinner ahead with a slight decline on the other side. She didn't want to be here. Didn't want Patrick—or whatever the hell his name was—to reach the end of the trail. Because who knew if the FBI would be able to catch up? Who knew how many more people would get hurt or killed if she helped him reach Big Spring? The lie slipped from her mouth with that in mind. "I need to stop. I'm getting lightheaded."

She didn't wait for an answer, pressing her back against the rock wall. Dark clouds kissed the peaks above, and that chill she couldn't get rid of only worsened as crystalized air brushed over the exposed skin of her face and neck. It was only then she realized she'd lost her hat to the river below. Risner would definitely be taking it out of her next paycheck, but she'd stomach the cost if it meant getting out of this alive.

"Fine." Patrick swung his pack to his front, his eyes a little more glazed than she remembered from the outcropping she'd woken up inside. Not as hard. "Two minutes, and don't even think about trying to run for it. I will catch you, and I will make you pay for trying."

"I wouldn't dream of it." She'd expected an argument, which meant he'd been experiencing lightheadedness and didn't want to admit he might not have been as prepared for this escape as he wanted to let on. One shot. That was all she had. Sayles maneuvered her own pack front-side and drove her hand inside. Around the rock she'd stashed at the bottom. She didn't know how to do this. Hurt someone. The inclination had come so easily to her ex. "It's called acute mountain sickness."

Patrick took a second too long to divert his attention from the opposite cliff face to her. "What?"

"That thing you're feeling right now." She gripped the rock tighter, still hidden by her pack. "The sluggishness, disorientation. Your brain isn't getting enough oxygen at these elevations. You've probably had a headache since yesterday, but the longer you're here, the worse your symptoms will get."

"I know what altitude sickness is." A hint of breathlessness softened his bite. "Start walking."

"Sure. But climbing higher isn't going to help you. At this point, nothing will." Sayles extracted the rock, sure to keep it hidden as she reset her pack on her back.

Then swung.

The impact of rock against skull reverberated through her hand. It hurt. A lot. The shock waves forced her to drop the weapon entirely. His groan punctured through the too-fast thud of her heart between her ears. She spun, launching herself ahead. Not looking back. She couldn't get enough air. While she'd acclimated to the park, adrenaline flooded her veins and took control.

"You b—" His rage seared down her back. Too close. Too close. The pounding of boots closed in.

Muscles she'd only recently developed protecting this park locked up at the sudden demand of exertion. A cramp skewed her calf as the trail dipped lower, and she nearly face-planted from the change in angle. Mud suctioned to her boots, providing a clear path straight to her. No matter where she went, he would find her. He would catch her. He would kill her. Faster. She had to run faster, but the unfamiliarity of the trail demanded caution she couldn't afford to spare. Aches screamed for attention. Her breathing too shallow. Black edged into her vision. No. She wasn't going to pass out. Not yet. Sayles searched for somewhere—anywhere—she could hide. To get her bearings. To gauge how close he'd gotten.

A quick check over her shoulder confirmed she'd added some distance between them. But was it enough? She turned face forward.

And caught sight of the sheer end of the goat trail.

Momentum threatened to throw her over the edge. Pulling back, she threw her hands out to grab on to anything that might keep her from going over. Her fingertips met nothing but smooth rock face, but she'd stopped just in time.

Giving Patrick a chance to catch up. She had to keep moving. Hide.

Except there was nowhere to go. Out of breath, Sayles gauged the distance between her side of the goat trail across the cavern of emptiness to the other. The rains surged down the slope between the two halves of the trail. Could she make it? Would the soggy ground support her weight? She didn't have a choice, did she? Not unless she wanted to end up as another notch in the Hitchhiker Killer's belt.

She backed up a couple feet. Determination similar to that she'd relied on to escape her ex surged. Shifting her weight into her toes, Sayles charged forward.

Searing pain rippled across her scalp.

Her back hit a wall of muscle, the growl in her ear pooling dread at the base of her spine. "Going somewhere, Ranger Green?"

"Please." She didn't know what she was begging for. He hadn't taken mercy on the five victims he'd slaughtered. Why would her pleas make any difference? She couldn't stop her whimper as desperation and survival won out.

"I warned you what would happen if you ran." Fisting her hair, he angled her head back into his shoulder. Exposing her throat. The tang of blood burned in her nostrils.

"You're going to want to take your hands off my partner." Elias's mass solidified in her vision, dangerous and formidable. "Right the hell now."

The world shifted as Patrick—the Hitchhiker Killer—swung her around. Using her as a shield.

Elias. He was alive. He'd come for her. The relief was temporary as she took in the bloodstain spread across his torso. His breathlessness.

"Agent Broyles, you made it just in time." Patrick released his hold on her hair.

Just before he shoved her over the cliff.

Chapter Sixteen

Her scream would follow him into his nightmares.

"Sayles!" Elias charged forward, hand outstretched as though there was a damn thing he could do to stop her from falling. Blood drained from his upper body in a rush. Dead. She was dead. Added to the growing list of victims in this bastard's wake. He couldn't breathe, couldn't think straight. How? How had this happened? How had it gone so horribly wrong so quickly?

The man in front of him peered over the edge where the ranger had gone over. Not an accident. Pushed off. Blood rippled down sharp features and caught in the killer's facial hair. A wicked, slithering smile spread the bastard's lips thin. "Well, will you look at that. Ranger Green has claws."

What?

Breath crushed from his chest as he caught movement at the end of the thin trail he'd followed her on. A boot swung into view, and the world stopped turning. She'd caught herself. Saved herself. Dangling 2,000 feet above the earth. One slip. That was all it would take to lose her, and Elias wasn't sure he could take it.

"Sayles." He took that step. The one that would get him closer to pulling her to safety. But was stopped by the killer standing between them. Elias's fingers tingled for the weight of his weapon lost to the river below, and he dropped his pack off to the side. Fisting his hands, he reminded himself of why he was here. To stop a killer. To keep the son of a bitch from escaping custody.

"I'm sorry, Agent Broyles. Did you really think it would be so easy?" The Hitchhiker Killer wasn't anything Elias had expected. Though the crazed look in his eye certainly fit the bill of a serial killer. The attacker cracked his neck to one side, taking his own step forward. "You've been hunting me these past few weeks. You had to have known I would've prepared for this, and I can't very well have you following me to my final destination."

Sayles's sob drove through him. The rains wouldn't make it easy to hold on for much longer, but he had to trust her to take care of herself for now as the threat edged closer. "You talk this much to those motorists you gutted, or am I special?"

That smile didn't falter as the killer pulled a gleaming blade from the back of his waistband. "Don't forget that hiker. He got an earful, too."

"You're going to pay for every one of them." Elias braced for the oncoming fight. Battle-ready tension taking over. "I don't care how long it takes me. I will have you in cuffs."

The killer lunged knife-first. His movement worked against him as Elias dodged the attack. The blade slipped along Elias's chest, a mere inch away from cutting through him. He latched on to the killer's wrist and turned the tip of the steel straight into the Hitchhiker Killer's face, shoving the bastard into the cliff, putting his own back to the 2,000-foot drop.

Surprise and something along the lines of humor laced the killer's expression as Elias struggled to inch that knife closer, but sheer strength fought back. A knee slammed into Elias's gut, and he lost his leverage on the killer's wrist. Pain sparked through his torso thanks to that damn twig that'd impaled between his ribs, and he doubled over to counter the effects. Soggy gravel bit into his knees as he hit the ground. The Hitchhiker Killer stepped free.

"Elias!" Sayles's pleas notched his blood pressure higher and called to something deeper. Had the witness he'd sent to her death begged for him to save her in her last moments? Would he have been able to save her if he'd been there?

"Hang on!" Elias blocked the arc of the blade aimed for his face. Striking as fast as possible, he launched his elbow into the killer's jaw. His attacker's head snapped back. Giving him the few seconds of disorientation he needed to get to Sayles. He jumped for the end of the trail, both hands curling over the edge.

Brazen and unfiltered fear contorted her beautiful face as she whipped her gaze to him. The knuckles of her fingers were white against red rock. She couldn't hang on for much longer. "Help me. Please. Help me."

He wrapped his hands around both of her wrists and pulled with everything he had. It wasn't enough. Memories of them in the same position, of her relying on him to protect her—to save her—from the river clawing through the canyon, had him screaming against the effort straining his injured ribs. He'd failed her then. He wouldn't fail her now. "I've got you. I won't let go."

She put her trust in him, loosening her hold on the rocks she clung to. Her eyes widened a split second later, cutting to something over his shoulder. "Look out!"

Agony ripped across his side, and he lost the grip on one of her wrists. Sayles's weight pulled her down. She swung, her pack skimming against the rock face. Another scream escaped her control as she twisted in his hold, dangling by his grip alone. The killer penetrated his peripheral vision. Elias braced for the second kick, and he nearly lost his hold on his partner altogether. "Reach!"

The order barely left his mouth before Sayles was clawing to regain her grip. Toes digging into the side of the drop-off, she scrambled for purchase, but the rock and mud simply crumbled under her weight. She dropped again. Lower. Water reduced the friction between his hands. He was losing his grip on her, and they both knew it.

A shadow slipped over him. Lightning sparked, solidifying the killer's proximity.

"I think this is one of those 'if I can't have her, no one will' situations, Agent Broyles." Heaving breaths reached his ears as the Hitchhiker Killer carved his blade downward. Directly for Elias's spine.

Sayles locked onto a rock and pulled her wrist from his hands. "Move!"

He rolled into the cliff face, putting solid rock at his back. He was at a disadvantage as steel cut across his face and imbedded into the shifting gravel above his shoulder. Stinging pain spread across his cheek, followed by a flood of warmth. Blood. The attacker had come close to sending that blade home. Shoving everything he had into his next attack, Elias kicked out and made contact with the killer's chest.

He didn't give his assailant time to regain his balance and surged to his feet. Catching the Hitchhiker Killer around the waist, Elias hauled the bastard up and back and slammed him into the ground. Except he hadn't accounted for the narrowness of the trail. His knee slipped off the edge, and it was only his hold around the suspect in his arm that kept him from going over completely.

The knife slipped through the small gap between their bodies, and Elias barely managed to avoid its tip sinking into his chest. He bent the killer's wrist at an unnatural angle, forcing the him to release the blade. A scream ripped from the man's throat as the knife plunged toward the Narrows below.

"Elias, I can't hold on!" Sayles needed him to finish this. To get them the hell off this trail.

He rocketed his fist into the Hitchhiker Killer's face. Once. Twice.

"Is that the best you've got, Agent Broyles?" That serpentine smile only spread wider as the bastard's head bounced off pea-size gravel underneath them. Blood dribbled from his mouth, lost to the biting rain slashing through the too-thin air.

Elias hit him again. Knocking the killer unconscious. Something released from around his rib cage, and he crawled off the suspect's body. "Sayles."

Diving for the end of the trail, he grabbed the collar of her uniform shirt. The cotton threatened to tear in his grasp, but it gave him some sense of friction compared to her bare skin. "Hold on to my neck."

The ranger stabbed her toes into the crumbling mountainside and hurled her weight upward. Her arms secured around his neck, and Elias dragged her over the lip. Holding her against him, unwilling or unable to let her go, he didn't know. She was alive. She was real. She was here. "It's okay. I've got you."

Sobs racked her upper body, and Elias held on to her tighter. The lip of the trail disappeared under his heels as he kicked them a few feet back from the edge. Threading his fingers into her hair, he buried his face in to her neck, letting her use him for however long she needed. "He was going to kill me if I didn't get him out of the park."

"I know." Elias framed her face, pulling her back to get a better look. He scanned the length of her body for any signs of blood or injury. "Are you okay? Are you hurt?"

She shook her head. "No. He didn't hurt me, but I can't say the same for him."

"Good." He wasn't sure what came over him, why every cell in his body urged him to close that short distance between them, but he had nothing left in his arsenal to avoid it. Elias crushed his mouth to hers. This beautiful, confident, inspiring woman who a mere twenty-four hours ago couldn't stand being in the same room as him. There was nothing sweet and romantic about the kiss. A frenzy had started the moment he'd realized she'd been taken and hadn't let up. Every second of concern and fear laced each stroke of his mouth against hers until he had to break to catch his breath. Setting his forehead against hers, Elias breathed her in. Tried to convince his nervous system the danger was over. "I'm sorry. I'm sorry I wasn't able to keep him from taking you."

Blood blended with water between her fingers. "It wasn't your fault. I knew you were coming for me." She interlaced her hands with his on either side of her face. "I knew you wouldn't give up."

"Never." Reality tendriled into his awareness. They weren't safe up here. At any moment, the trail could fail altogether, and he'd never forgive himself if something happened to Sayles because he couldn't keep his mouth to himself. "We need to get the hell out of here."

She nodded as if just realizing their situation. Water streaked down her face, and Sayles swiped it away to clear her vision. Most likely missing that iconic hat of hers.

"We're above Orderville Canyon Junction. We should be able to camp there until the storm passes."

"Good. Then let's get moving." Elias helped her maneuver off his lap, instantly missing the heat she'd generated. Then the pain moved in. Hell. He'd forgotten about the hole in his side. "I might also need you to patch me up again. Seems I got into a fight with a twig."

Sayles didn't answer. Didn't even seem to breathe.

He followed the direction of her gaze over his shoulder. And froze. "Damn it."

Surging to his feet, he searched for signs of movement. Of something to give them an idea of where the hell the killer had gone. He couldn't have just vanished. Had his unconscious body gone over the trail's edge, or had the Hitchhiker Killer managed to escape without notice? Elias couldn't see the bottom of the canyon clearly from here. Not with the storm attacking from every angle.

"Come on." He grabbed for his pack with one hand and for Sayles's hand with the other. He wasn't letting her out of his sight from here on out and headed along the trail he assumed was meant for pack horses rather than actual human beings. Toward that cave where he'd found her antibiotic ointment.

They'd barely managed to survive between two flash floods, hypothermia, a rogue twig and a killer determined to get away with murder, but one thing was for sure. "This isn't over."

Chapter Seventeen

It took longer to set up the tent than it should have.

Between the gashes on her palms and the wound in Elias's side, they were moving slower than either of them wanted, but the storm had given them a slight reprieve. In the end, neither of them had even bothered pretending to want to sleep in separate tents. They didn't have the energy by the time they'd collapsed onto their sleeping bags or to fight the incessant need for warmth. And connection, in her case.

Sayles stripped free of her wet uniform with sore muscles that fought her at every turn as Elias did the same on the other side of the tent. There really wasn't that much room between them. Her tent had been structured for one person, and she collided with his shoulder or arm more than once as the weight of this assignment pressed in. A single spear of sunlight reached the bottom of the canyon, but seemed to go out of its way to avoid them, and she couldn't fight the responding chill.

They hadn't spoken a word to each other since descending down that too-thin goat trail that'd nearly killed them. Didn't want to acknowledge the fact that the Hitchhiker Killer had gotten away, that he had won, leaving them to do nothing but lick their wounds. Elias had held her hand the entire time, as if he couldn't stand the thought of letting her out of his reach, and she'd been just as desperate. Her awareness of the federal agent prodding at the medical tape from his bare torso only grew through the unending exhaustion trying to drag her down. He'd come for her. Risked his life for her. Saved her. "Thank you" didn't feel like enough.

Elias flinched against some invisible pain as he lifted the tape and gauze to get a better view of his wound.

"Here. Let me." Relieved of her soaked uniform, she realized she should've been embarrassed about the fact there was nothing between them other than the thin material of her oversize T-shirt from her recovered pack. But she couldn't summon the internal argument. Sayles skimmed her fingers around the edge of the dressing, reveling in his instant body heat soothing the scrapes on her hands, and peeled the gauze away to get a better look. He'd done a good job cleaning the small hole. Managed to stop the bleeding. "It doesn't look so bad. What did you clean it with?"

"My drinking water." His voice sounded as though it'd been raked over gravel. From screaming, from tiredness, from debris in the water he'd swallowed. Almost…broken.

The effect chased back that relentless need to keep her mask in place, to be the woman he'd met in the visitors' center. The one who could keep herself together despite their circumstances. Maybe right now she could just…be. Acknowledge that they'd been through something terrible and leave expectations outside the tent. As rewarding as it'd been to disappear in Zion, to start making her own choices and discover who she was without a manipulative bastard calling the shots, wasn't letting go another kind of freedom? "Good choice."

"I learned from the best." The weight of his gaze burned her scalp, but Elias held utterly still as she inspected the wound. It wasn't deadly. However, infection took root in all kinds of circumstances, and they couldn't take the chance. Not with the killer still out there. Potentially watching them as he had these past two days.

Grabbing for her pack, she twisted to pull her first aid kit free and spread the supplies she'd need. "You mean my survival cards."

"No. Not the cards." The whisper contradicted the fierceness with which he'd kissed her on that trail. As though his entire being depended on consuming her from the inside out. He'd done a fantastic job. She could still feel the press of his mouth against hers, the heat they'd shared, the desperation. It'd awoken something in her she hadn't felt for a long time. Not just her physical desire but the desire to feel wanted, to no longer be ignored and small. In those rare seconds, Elias had eradicated her deep need to slide through life unnoticed and alone. He'd empowered her to make the next call. And she wanted more.

"I have more alcohol." Redressing his wound was all she could focus on to keep that crazed want in check. She wasn't sure she'd ever been kissed like that. From the beginning, her ex had made her feel owned, and there'd been a kind of safety that came with it. At first. Instead of choice, he'd taken the brunt of their decisions—her decisions—and convinced her it was for the best. The fewer decisions she had to make, the more energy she had to focus on him, his needs, their relationship. It'd somehow made sense, but over the years that ownership had turned to domination. To belittling and criticizing any attempts to take control of her own life. Questioning her loyalty and commitment to their marriage. A long con. That was what it'd felt like.

Like she'd signed up for one thing but had wound up with nothing in the end. Slowly and meticulously destroying everything that made her…her. Shaping her into someone she didn't recognize in the mirror, the damage irreparable.

Sayles dabbed a fresh pad of gauze with alcohol and pressed it against Elias's wound. He sucked in a deep breath through his teeth, and she pulled back. "Sorry. I know it stings, but it'll lower chances of infection."

"I trust you." Elias notched his head back on his shoulders, staring up at the top of the tent.

Her heart shuddered in her chest. Was that physically possible? Because it certainly felt like he'd just handed her the keys to the kingdom without so much as doing reconnaissance. Trust. Had her ex ever trusted her? Beyond believing his nightly dinners weren't poisoned, she wasn't sure. He hadn't trusted her to choose her own outfits or to lead in the bedroom. He hadn't trusted her to stay in touch with her friends and family. Or maybe he just hadn't trusted himself. But Elias… This was a man who earned respect and expected others to do the same. The idea that she'd met his qualifications added to the lightness of knowing they'd survived a killer. Though she wasn't sure what she'd done to join that small club.

The skin across his stomach was smooth and warm and urged her to linger. Muscle flexed and released under her ministrations, and she couldn't deny there was something wholly superficial in the heat clawing up her neck and into her face. He was attractive—no argument there—and Sayles almost didn't recognize that tug in her lower belly. It'd been so long since she'd let herself notice another man. And Elias was definitely hard to ignore. "Almost done. Just need to apply a new dressing. Does it hurt?"

"Not so much anymore." The gravel in his words eased. Softer.

She stretched one hand across his midsection to hold the new gauze in place and fought with the roll of medical tape. The burn of his attention spread lower, raising goose bumps along her arms and waking her nerves to the point she couldn't focus on what her hands were doing at all.

"I got it." Taking the roll from her, he sectioned out four pieces, handing them off one by one. They worked together to press the dressing into place.

"I'll take another look at it in a few hours to make sure there's no signs of infection. Until then, try to keep it dry and don't jar it." Repacking her supplies back into the kit, she swallowed the urge to close those inches between them. To lose herself in him all over again. That deep-rooted need would have to wait. The killer had been watching them since they'd stepped onto the trail. There was no telling if he'd attack again, and she wasn't going to distract Elias from doing his job. Sayles rushed through organizing her pack and inventorying what was left. Seemed the killer had only taken her multi-tool. Probably in case she decided to stab him with it while he forced her help. "We have a couple hours of until sunset, but I'm not in the right headspace to keep pushing. We'd be better served getting some rest until tomorrow morning."

Because Elias had been right. This wasn't over. Surviving a serial killer hadn't done a damn bit of good. He was still out there.

A calloused hand covered hers. Pinning her in place. Elias slipped a finger beneath her chin, directing her to meet his gaze. Understanding and a hint of concern etched his expression where she'd only been met with frustration and disappointment from her ex. She wasn't used to this.

This consideration. She didn't know what to do with it. "I'm not going to let him get to you again. I give you my word."

"I'm not sure that's something you can promise." Against her best defenses, her chin wobbled as the burn of tears crested, but she wouldn't break. Not because of the bastard who'd shoved her off the trail. She wouldn't let him haunt her. Ever. "You were right before. He wanted me to lead him to the end of the Narrows at Big Spring to cut west, but I don't think he's as experienced as we assumed. He'd started suffering from acute mountain sickness, getting dizzy the higher we climbed."

Elias let his hand drop away from her face, and she instantly regretted the loss of connection. "Did he say anything else?"

"Told me his name is Patrick, but I can't be sure he wasn't lying." A heaviness she'd refused to acknowledge seeped into her muscles, into her bones. The adrenaline brought on by sheer survival had left her raw and unstable. The crash was coming. It was only a matter of how long until she turned into a psychopath. "And he certainly liked the moniker you'd given him. Went straight to his head. But I didn't get the impression he's doing this for fun. He had a plan."

"What kind of plan?" He sat back on his heels, every inch of his muscled frame fighting against his sweats and T-shirt. So unlike the suits and ties and slacks she'd been expected to iron up until a few months ago. Her ex never would've felt comfortable in a tent this small. Or camping in general.

Sayles hauled her pack to the side of the tent, out of the way, and summoned everything she had left into crawling into her sleeping bag. The rough material aggravated the cuts across her hands, and she fisted them close to her chest.

"He wouldn't tell me. Said he had his reasons for killing those people. I tried…"

"You did good, Sayles." His voice sounded close. "I'm proud of how hard you fought today. Not everyone can say they survived like you did."

A swell of emotion worked to reinvigorate her mission, but her eyes slipped closed. Dragged into near unconsciousness within seconds. She couldn't get settled. Like there was something she was forgetting. She rolled onto her side, then onto her back and repeated the cycle all over again.

Movement registered behind her, the rustle of his sleeping bag as he climbed into it too loud despite the rush of the river mere feet from their position. It wasn't until Elias secured his arm around her waist and pulled her flush against his front that her nervous system released her from the fight. "Get some rest. I'll keep watch. I won't let him take you from me again."

The words carved through layered defensiveness and flipped some kind of switch in her brain that told her it was safe. That he would protect her. He would fight for her.

And she drifted off to sleep.

Chapter Eighteen

There was no going back.

Elias made quick work of packing their gear before setting onto the trail. Muscles he hadn't known existed ached as he grabbed for his pack and took that first step back onto the Narrows. They'd cleared the tent and set out in record time, barely saying more than a few words to each other. Working in comfortable silence. He'd learned Sayles's morning routine over the past couple of days, and she'd silently fixed his backpack Tetris game with a smile. Yeah. Nearly dying tended to bring people closer.

They'd reached a comfortable partnership. So different from the years he'd been assigned to work cases with Grant. This was…pleasant. And Sayles wasn't trying to suffocate him with too much body spray.

Sayles handed off one of her protein bars. They hadn't eaten nearly enough in the past two days compared to the effort it'd taken to come this far, and Elias shoved the bar down with a few swigs of water, then got into his own supplies for a sloppy peanut butter sandwich. The bread had been squished during moments of survival and panic, and condensation had built up in the baggie, but his stomach didn't care in the least. He caught Sayles going for seconds, too. As if she understood what lay ahead.

Blue sky touched with a hint of wispy clouds at the edges slowly flared to life as they traversed Wall Street Corridor. The morning crest of sun reflected off 1,500-foot walls closing in on either side of them, merely twenty-two feet across, and cast rays of purple down weather-worn rock. Evidence of drainage stained blinding red stone in white streaks and dark patches. The canyon itself curved, cutting off any chance of scouting the trail ahead of them. They were going into this section of the trail blind. At a disadvantage. The only comfort was their killer would be, too. There was no escaping this portion of the trail if another flash flood hit. The Hitchhiker Killer would be caught right along with them. Hell, a storm might even flush him out. But the weather seemed to be cooperating this morning.

Sayles arched her head back onto her shoulders, slowing a few feet ahead of him. A body-wide sigh released the tension in her neck. "This view never ceases to amaze me. There's just something about this specific spot before heading into Wall Street Corridor that gets to me."

He couldn't argue. While he'd never been an outdoor explorer, even when the other kids in his neighborhood growing up went out on hikes together and spent every minute figuring out how to, Elias felt a sense of…peace here. Of soul-deep quiet. He couldn't say he'd still feel that way if it weren't just him and Sayles on this trail, but something in his chest released as he took in the natural monument overhead. The rough edges of rock, the smoothness of where rain and a natural waterfall had rubbed away the harshness, the differing colors of wear and age. The river itself had quieted through this section and reflected that same blue of the sky above. He couldn't remember a time he'd allowed himself to slow down and just…be. He couldn't describe the beauty of this place. Made even more extravagant by the woman urging him to notice it. "I can see why you're out here as much as you are."

Though he wasn't sure he'd step foot on this trail again once the investigation was closed. In a little under two days, they'd nearly drowned—twice—been shot at, he'd been stabbed by a tree and watched Sayles go over the edge of a cliff. He'd just about soaked up all the nature he could handle. But turning back wasn't an option. Not with the killer still out there. With the improbability of getting a signal out of the canyon, NPS had no reason to believe they required assistance or rescue, which meant he and Sayles were on their own for now.

"At first it was a way to escape. To hide from the gossip that still followed me. To avoid any chance one of his friends may want to do him a favor, even from prison." Her smile didn't reach her eyes. As much as she wanted to play off the trauma she'd survived, Elias understood it would always be there. Always shape her choices, her relationships, her way of thinking. It would determine who she allowed to get close and bar anyone she deemed unsafe from experiencing the fighter beneath that guarded gaze, but damn, she was a sight. In her element. Worth every pain, every second of fear. "The more I came out here, the less it became about the hiding, and the more I found myself. Just hours in my own head, forcing myself to face what'd happened. And figuring out who I wanted to be next. It's probably weird to consider a trail like the Narrows capable of saving my life after everything we've been through these past couple of days, but that's what happened."

Sayles set that green gaze on him, and he could see it, feel it. The life and the brilliance bleeding to the surface, past her defenses. This wasn't the park ranger who'd built walls to avoid getting too close to her cohort or make herself small enough the FBI wouldn't notice. The mask had come off, leaving nothing but the woman who'd ensnared him from the beginning, and he didn't have the discipline to look away.

No. He wanted to stay right here. Just the two of them and these cliffs. Pretend nothing else existed outside of this perfect bubble they'd created together. In another life, he'd just be one of the millions of hikers who came here each year and she would be a ranger working to keep him from doing something stupid and dying on this trail. Because... paperwork. Of course, he'd notice her right away, and she'd politely stir conversation to the specifics of the park and her job. She might not be interested in him at all, but he'd keep trying. Ask her to take that leap of faith and trust in something again.

"Do you have something like that back home?" The spell broke as Sayles guided them farther upstream. Water rippled away from her charge forward and collided with the base of the cliffs on either side. "Something that makes you happy?"

Was it too cheesy to tell her that over these past couple days she'd made him happy? That their back-and-forth had kept him from ruminating on all the mistakes he'd made in the course of his last case? That she'd resurrected some part of him that wanted a partner in crime that didn't come with Cheetos fingers and burping the alphabet in a too-hot FBI-issued car? Yes. Too cheesy.

Elias gripped his pack tighter to counter the hole spreading through his chest. He'd managed to tie both straps together to make it easier to carry but still couldn't strap it to his back. "My job. Bringing killers to justice makes me pretty happy. Knowing that they won't hurt anyone else because I was able to put it to a stop."

"You don't sound happy about that." Her retort didn't come with the expected judgment or disappointment.

He couldn't stop his laugh at seeing the pinch between her brows. As if he'd personally given her reason to react on his behalf. "What do I sound like?"

Sayles slowed her pace. Seemingly giving herself time to form the words without offending him altogether. "Like you've accepted your fate, and there's nothing you can do to change it."

He pulled up short. A tug started in his gut. In a way, she was right. He'd never imagined another life for himself than the one he had now. Maybe a few changes in the details, but this—working for the FBI—was where he belonged. Where he felt his purpose. "My dad served as a highway patrol officer for thirty years. Everything I know about law enforcement came from him before I was fifteen years old. It's in my blood, and the second I turned eighteen, I applied to the local police academy looking to follow in his footsteps. I wanted to be just like him. Protecting people, making sure the bad guys didn't get away."

Guiding them deeper into the corridor, Sayles kept at his side instead of ahead. As though she knew the cost of giving up this small part of himself. As she had.

"He worked hard. Gone every week on shift, driving up and down the state, mostly pulling people over for speeding. My mom and I would see him on the weekends, and I looked forward to every Friday night when he walked through our front door with stories from his week. I'd wait in the kitchen with a chilled beer ready for him and a pizza on the way. After a while it just became our tradition." Elias remembered every single story. Held on to them as best he could. It was the only way he could think to honor his father's dedication to the job. To turning Elias into the man he was today, whether he'd been there or not. "Until one Friday he didn't come home."

Sayles's attention settled along his left side. "What happened?"

"He'd pulled over a suspected drunk driver on I-80, outside of a little nothing town you'd never heard of. Nothing but desert around. Multiple calls had been made about the truck hitting both lines, cutting people off, going slow, then speeding up. Typical driving under the influence." Except the stop had been anything but routine. "He was sideswiped by another vehicle. Killed instantly."

"I'm so sorry." Genuine regret laced her words and tunneled through him, straight through his skin, muscle and bone, and settled in his soul.

"It's one of the risks of being highway patrol. Motorists, no matter how much driving experience they have, aren't paying as much attention as they should. He knew that and wanted to do the job anyway. That was just the kind of man he was. Saw a need and worked to fill it, even if it meant putting himself in danger." Because who else would step up to do the right thing? His father had made sure Elias had absorbed that mentality from a young age. "We got the call he'd been in an accident, and the paramedics hadn't gotten to him in time. We found out later the driver who'd hit him hadn't bothered to stick around, and the one my dad had pulled over had taken off."

"They just left him there?" Her voice wobbled, and Elias couldn't hold himself back from looking at her anymore. His sorrow had become her own, as if she were trying to shoulder some of the weight.

"Another driver called it in a couple minutes later. Tried

to help him, but there was nothing they could do." Tension radiated from his shoulders down his spine. "Later on, we learned the truth of what'd happened. Once I was in the academy, I convinced my dad's former supervisor to show me the dashcam footage from his car that day. Turned out the driver he'd pulled over hadn't been drunk. He'd had a woman in the car with him. Someone he'd kidnapped. She'd been trying to fight him off while they barreled down the freeway, and the vehicle that'd hit him was his partner."

Sayles's jaw slackened. "Your dad was trying to help her?"

"He didn't get the chance, but I think he realized what was happening when he stepped up to the car. He was in a position to help, and he would've done anything to get her out of there safely.

"I'm not sure I had much of a choice about joining the academy after that. I wanted to keep him with me, help people, and falling into law enforcement seemed like the right way to do it. I worked for Las Vegas Metro police department for a few years before turning my sights on the FBI. So, yeah. Being an agent makes me happy. Gives me a reason to keep going."

"What happened to the drivers?" She didn't need to voice the rest of that question. Worried about what'd happened to the woman in the car.

"They were never found. The license plates on both vehicles had been stolen. A search of local auto body shops never turned up anything concrete. State police closed their investigation three months after the incident without any new leads. We were told to move on. That that's what my dad would've wanted." But he'd known better. He'd known his father never would've given up had Elias been in his position. His own regret soured at the back of his mouth. "But I'm still looking."

Her eyes widened at that. A secret he'd never told anyone but his mother before now. Not even Grant. "What will you do if you find them?"

He didn't bother lying. "I'll make them pay."

Chapter Nineteen

Her heart hurt.

Along with the rest of her.

She could feel the pain rippling off Elias as he'd relived the last few memories of his dad. It was a wonder he hadn't let that loss corrupt him. Turn him bitter and guarded. As she had. How had he done it? How had he managed to keep himself grounded when all she'd wanted to do was run, to hide and forget all those broken pieces of herself?

Flecks of water caressed her face as they passed beneath a tendril of water snaking down the rock canyon wall. He was going to make the people responsible for his father's death pay. Because Elias was the kind of man who never gave up on the ones he cared about. He'd proven that coming after her, hadn't he? Loyal. Warm. Dependable. She wasn't sure her ex had ever possessed those qualities, and maybe she'd blinded herself to the red flags. Maybe her standards for affection had been so low that the small amount she'd received from her ex had felt like a privilege instead of a given, but that wasn't the case anymore.

Elias had shown her that in the span of mere days as they'd worked together, survived together, saved each other. It was in the way he'd treated her as an equal and trusted her experience. How he'd let her take the lead and speak her mind. Respect. He respected her, and the realization imbued her with a sense of power. And desire. For possibility and change and…hope. It was an odd feeling. The shift that came with looking toward the future instead of living in the past.

Her ex was still out there, though she'd been granted a divorce by the state considering law enforcement couldn't find him. He would always shadow her every thought, every choice, but she was so tired of letting him win. And that was exactly what she'd done by running from Colorado after her release and the courts had settled on her wrongful imprisonment. She'd let him win by giving up contact with her family, by pushing her away from her friends and her home, by not fighting back.

"I hope you find them. The people who killed your dad." She meant it. Wanting that closure for Elias, even though she couldn't have it for herself. To see her ex pay for what he'd done to her. They were nearly through Wall Street Corridor. The sun's rays descended along rough outcroppings and sharp edges of the canyon wall. Her body temperature dropped as they crossed into the shade, then immediately spiked entering the sunlight. "I know what it's like to not have closure. To wish you could change things."

It wasn't a great feeling, succumbing to a feeling created solely by a man determined to give up her entire identity for him. For nothing in return.

"You'll get yours." Elias's confidence fought to soak into her, would if she let it, but she'd become all too accustomed to wearing a mask. A thick layer of protection against any and all feeling. It'd been the only way to get through those horrible months behind bars, to not hope. But the federal agent at her side had slowly started dismantling the darkness she'd lived in these past few months. Bringing with him a hint of light so small she hadn't recognized it for what it was. A raft. He winked at her. Still playful after everything they'd survived. She hoped he never lost that ability. "It might not be today or next week, but sooner or later, he's going to make a mistake. People like your ex think too highly of themselves. Think they're smarter than the rest of us. Most of the time to their own downfall."

Why did she get the feeling Elias would ensure her ex's arrest if given the opportunity? Sayles didn't let herself follow that thought down the rabbit hole too much further. If she was being honest with herself, the comparisons she'd drawn—between her ex and Elias—were another added layer of protection. Trying to find similarities. A reason to shut whatever this was between them down before it had a chance to get under her skin. But he'd saved her. When she'd had nothing more than a palm-size rock and a knowledge of the park to her advantage against the Hitchhiker Killer, he'd saved her where her ex had purposefully tried to destroy her. And fear that had nothing to do with the trail and everything to do with that distinction slithered into awareness.

"I think I would like to see that." Maybe she could somehow get a front-row seat in the courthouse. Just to watch her ex betray himself as effectively as he'd betrayed her. He deserved it. For what he'd done. For what he'd turned her into.

"Didn't take you for the vengeful type." Elias dragged his feet through the chilled waters rising to their calves, flashing her that smile quickly highlighting her days. "I like it."

"Thanks. I think." Her self-critic—moderately created by the man who'd framed her for murder—fought against that compliment. If that was what it was. Sayles shut down the inclination to shrink. Elias liked something about her, and the comment hadn't come with a hint of sarcasm. She... believed him. Maybe her willingness to watch her ex go down in flames of his own making wasn't the only thing, either. Wow. He'd really screwed her up, hadn't he? Convinced her she wasn't worth complimenting, that she was nothing without him. How was it even months later she was fighting against all these little mechanisms and habits she'd picked up to cope throughout her marriage? Why couldn't she just let it go? And why the hell couldn't she give herself a break and accept it would take time?

"You good?" Elias tapped the back of his hand against her arm. Bringing her back to the moment. Pulling her out of the spiral with mere touch. Just as he had in the tent, dragging her body against his. Giving her permission to use him in whatever capacity she'd needed to get through what they'd suffered.

It'd been enough. She'd dropped into unconsciousness within seconds with him pressed against her. That was all it'd taken. Because she'd felt...safe. For the first time in a long time, she hadn't even thought about putting a weapon beneath her pillow or triple-checking the zipper on her tent. She hadn't startled awake in the middle of the night at the slightest sound that didn't fit her surroundings. There'd only been Elias, who'd held her throughout the night as though he'd needed her as much as she'd needed him. And it'd felt right. Like a puzzle piece she'd been missing for months had finally clicked into place. "I'm good."

And it wasn't the same lie she'd been telling her fellow rangers or Risner or anyone else who'd bothered to check in out of a warped sense of obligation. The heaviness she'd adapted to since leaving Colorado didn't have the same hold on her as it had a few days ago. Because of him. "Thinking about what happens after you catch this killer."

"What do you mean?" Elias made a good effort to focus on the path he carved through the river.

"I mean you kissed me yesterday." Tightening her grip around her pack's straps, she tried to counter the ball of anxiety in the pit of her stomach. It was no use. "Do you normally go around kissing your partners during an investigation?"

"Grant hasn't complained." His laugh charged through her, sweeping the last remnants of apprehension from her veins. He shook his head. "No. I don't just go around kissing people on cases. Though, can you blame me for wanting to kiss you? You're freaking formidable hanging off the edge of a cliff. Anyone else in your position would've given up, but you fought."

She didn't have an answer for that, but the beaten-down ghost of her past self preened. Hell, she needed a life. Friends, hobbies, dreams—all the things her ex had systematically cut her off from. Lila, her roommate, didn't count, and could she really consider hiking the Narrows every weekend a hobby if it was technically her job? As for dreams... It'd been a long time since she'd considered what would come next. Since she'd allowed herself to hope it wouldn't be taken away. "Oh. Well, I haven't...um, kissed anyone since...before I was arrested. Or dated anyone. Or just generally given anyone the impression I am a nice person, but I want to know what you think it meant."

"You mean if I want to kiss you again." Elias halted right there in the middle of the river. The mere words out of his mouth—the idea of his mouth on hers again—coiled something low in her belly. "Yeah. I think I do."

"Why?" She hadn't meant to ask, but there it was. All of the doubt and self-hatred and disappointment in herself that'd built up since two officers had shown up at her door to arrest her for her ex's murder. Doubt that she'd make it through, self-hatred for staying with the bastard as long as she had and the disappointment for not seeing who he'd really been before it was too late. A rawness spread through her. Why? Why did a man like Elias—tough-minded, accomplished and honor-bound—want anything to do with the hot mess in front of him?

He closed that short distance between them, looking far too put together than he deserved after what they'd survived. "You want to know what I see in you?"

Did that make her needy? Wanting to know who in their right mind would look at her and see something other than a broken thing that had no chance of living a normal life again? Her mouth dried.

"I see a woman who isn't afraid to express her very strong opinions." His smile cracked another layer of armor she'd relied on over the past couple of years. "You never seem to run out of energy, which makes me think you're some kind of witch sent to put my outdoor skills to shame." Elias skimmed calloused fingertips along her forearm, then over the pulse in her wrist. The contact was enough to shove those fears back into the box at the back of her mind where they belonged. "Despite the front you put on, I think you feel more than anyone else I've ever met. You're the kind of person who will never forget or forgive the slights against her, and I admire that about you. I admire your outright determination to become someone you're proud of, who will never take abuse or manipulation again and who will put herself at risk to protect others from suffering what you went through."

Six years of marriage and her ex had never bothered to really get to know her, but this man had somehow worked past her defenses. She couldn't dislodge the swell of emotion in her throat. "You see all that after only two days to-gether?"

"I saw it the moment I met you." Dropping his hand from hers, Elias waited for her to make the next move. Choice. It was always a choice with him.

They were coming up on the four-mile point, a marker that should've taken no more than three and a half hours to reach on a good day, but the park itself seemed to be turning against them. Not to mention the killer determined to escape. Wynopits Mountain demanded attention over the wall of the canyon to the east. One mile more and they'd reach Big Spring, where the Narrows officially ended. Where the Hitchhiker Killer had wanted her to take him, but her instincts told her there was something more to his final destination. Not that he'd just wanted out of the park, but that there might be something there he needed.

"The killer—Patrick—wanted me to get him to Big Spring before the FBI could catch up with him." Sayles swiped at her face with a renewed energy singing through her. Of possibility and hope. "I think we should get there first."

Chapter Twenty

He could still taste her.

On his tongue, in his soul.

Sayles Green had barged into his life without mercy and taken him for everything he had. She'd picked up their pace after he'd agreed to her plan to head the Hitchhiker Killer off, but they still had to fight the river's current with every step. She never faltered. Each foot strike more sure than the last. It was a testament to her determination to prove she was more than the woman who'd been conned by someone she believed had loved her, and he couldn't help but follow in her footsteps. To think he had a chance of escaping the past as she had. Of fighting back.

His body ached, particularly the tops of his thighs as he battled against the upstream current. Floodwaters had spread out and down the trail, but the river still parted around his waist. It was a fight, plain and simple, and they had no idea how far ahead the killer had gotten in the time it'd taken him and Sayles to recover since yesterday. Every second counted. They couldn't waste a single one of them.

They'd navigated through Wall Street Corridor and lived to tell the tale on the other side. If another flash flood hit, they had an actual chance of making it out alive. It was the threats he couldn't predict that simmered beneath his skin now. His entire career centered on seeing all the ways an investigation could go south and giving himself the advantage in the end, but he couldn't discard the possibility he'd missed something here. Potentially putting Sayles back in the killer's sights. Not an option he could live with.

"You're awfully quiet for once." Sayles dared a glance back in his direction, her face slightly flushed, out of breath. She was exerting herself, burning through whatever energy she had left over after the attack from yesterday. While they'd both managed to get to sleep in that cramped tent last night, she'd tossed and tensed throughout the night. No matter how tightly he'd held her.

They'd packed supplies for three days, and neither of them wanted to acknowledge what would happen when they ran out, though he didn't doubt it was one of the main concerns on her mind. Always planning ahead. Always looking for the escape.

"Is that your way of telling me you don't enjoy my company?" The retort slipped from him easily enough, but he'd left his humor a few hundred yards back. "Something about this case isn't sitting right."

"What do you mean?" She'd turned forward again, never one to lead them off the path or put their safety at risk. He'd been the one to make that choice, to prioritize catching a killer above both of their lives. A mistake he wouldn't make again. If it came right down to it, he'd make sure Sayles got out. He owed her that.

"The killer's motive." It was the key to this entire case. He could feel it, but nothing they'd gathered so far during this investigation hinted as to what drove the Hitchhiker Killer. "He murdered four motorists between California and Utah. Then a random hiker here in the park. Nothing connects any of the victims. They're a mixture of male and female, married and single, with no common backgrounds. Not even the same makes or models of vehicles. He wipes down every car he's in to make sure he doesn't leave his prints behind. Our forensic techs haven't been able to collect any DNA to identify him. What's he running from?"

"What if he's not running from something?" Sayles chanced another glance over her shoulder, giving him a glimpse of brightness in her gaze. "What if he's trying to get somewhere?"

Elias had to focus on his next steps to keep himself from face-planting in the middle of the river. "What makes you say that?"

"Nothing. Never mind." She shook her head, pushing them forward. "It probably doesn't mean anything."

His heart jerked in his chest. Reaching out, he secured his fingers around her elbow and dragged her to a stop. He could see it then, the signs of a person who'd been convinced she'd meant nothing. That she wasn't important enough or deserving of someone's time, least of all when it came to matters of an investigation. Elias's teeth protested as a burn of rage at the bastard responsible for ever making this woman feel less than took over. "Of the two of us you're the only one who's had a real conversation with this guy. I want to know what you think."

"I just… I got the impression there's something waiting for him at the end of the trail." Her shoulder rose on a deep inhale, but Sayles refused to look at him. "Like he didn't so much want to escape, but rather get to something or someone waiting for him there. It's ridiculous, I know. I'm probably reading too deep into it. He'd threatened me, and I was scared—"

"No." Her body heat seeped into his hand, kept him

grounded and calm in the face of the chaos and confusion closing in around them. He wasn't sure he'd ever experienced that because of another person. At least not since his dad had been killed. "During my training, instructors and training officers would always encourage recruits to look at facts and evidence. They didn't want us making assumptions or taking an investigation off course because of our bias. Logically, it makes sense, but some of the best calls I've made in cases like this are from listening to my gut. That instinct has saved lives over the course of my career, and I trust yours. Especially out here."

She wanted to brush his reasoning off, to pretend that she was nothing and nobody to him and this investigation, but that just wasn't the truth. In a matter of days, she'd taken up more of his thoughts than he was willing to admit and sure as hell never would to Grant or his special agent in charge back at the home office. "I'm not in law enforcement. I'm not trained to theorize killers' motives."

"But you know people." That was how trauma worked. The terror of it could never be erased. Not from the victim's nervous system and not as the brain physically rewired itself to stay on alert and absorb the slightest shift or possibility of a threat. "You know what they're capable of and how to read the smallest signs that something isn't right. You've been doing it for years, and I trust you, Sayles."

His words hit a barrier in her emotions, as he'd expected. Her bastard of an ex had done a thorough job in tearing her down, but Elias wanted nothing more than to erase that pain. To show her how to believe in herself again. As she'd done for him without even realizing it. In the way she'd relaxed in his arms the two nights they'd camped in that too-small tent. In the way she'd challenged him to reconsider his priorities in life, to allow something other than his job to consume him. In the way she'd shown him what real strength looked like as she'd fought for her life instead of waiting for anyone else to save her. He shifted his weight between both legs, leveling his gaze with hers. "You talked with him. He told you things about himself, so what would a man like Patrick kill five people for if not to escape arrest?"

The muscles in her jaw ticked as she considered him for a few moments, unsure of herself and her own theory, but he noted the moment she decided to take a chance. "I think he's looking for someone."

Pride heated through him, and Elias stood a bit taller. There she was. The woman he imagined she'd been before her ex had gotten a hold of her. One forged of single-mindedness and mission, who wouldn't let anyone stop her from getting what she wanted. "Do you know who?"

"He didn't even tell me that much. I just…" Doubt bled from her gaze, leaving nothing behind but a flare of excitement. How long had she been waiting for someone to believe her? To take her word for it? To see her? "I have a feeling it's someone important."

"All right." Elias nodded once. It was a vague detail that could risk the investigation if she ended up being wrong, but one they didn't really have a choice other than to take. He'd meant what he'd said. He trusted her. He wasn't sure when it'd started. Maybe when she'd hauled him out of the raging river's path during that first flash flood. Maybe when she'd called his name from the edge of that cliff, telling him she trusted him to help. Maybe when he'd kissed her in the aftermath and something in him had snapped at coming so close to losing her. All it meant was she'd been right about him. There was more out there than his job and running himself into the ground case after case. More to live for than the mistakes he'd made and the people he'd let down, including his dad. "Then we proceed on that assumption."

"Why?" There was that question again. Her need to understand why he believed her above his own training, why he'd even consider trusting her when no one else had.

Elias didn't have an answer. At least not one that would satisfy the doubt she'd lived with for so long. Stepping into her personal space, he framed her chin with his thumb and index finger and pressed his mouth to hers. Not as he had on that trail they'd left behind, full of desperation for something real and solid to hold on to. But intentionally forcing himself to slow down, to feel every sensation and sweep of her lips against his. And his defenses crumbled. Desire, unlike anything he'd experienced with all those meaningless dates, surged through his veins. He wanted to be the one she trusted, the one who cracked that careful control she'd put into place to protect herself against any further hurt. Coaxing her lips apart with the tip of his tongue, Elias tightened his hold on her chin as she jerked against him. Then she softened into him, opened for him. Allowed him to take control, and his whole body shuddered in response.

Hell, it wasn't his first kiss, and it sure as hell wasn't hers considering she'd been married—it wasn't even their first kiss with each other—but it felt as though something new was building between them now. A bridge between damaged souls who'd gone through this life long enough without each other and had finally come home.

She'd fisted her cut and bruised hands in his shirt as though afraid the river would sweep him away, but he wasn't going anywhere. Not now and not after he closed this case. He wasn't sure how it would work between her here in Zion and him based out of Las Vegas, but a few hundred miles between them wasn't going to make a damn bit of difference. He'd make sure of it.

A screech echoed off the canyon walls, and Elias broke the kiss to assess the oncoming threat.

Spotting a lone turkey fanning his brown-gray wings in a sliver of sunshine upriver.

Elias blinked to clear his head. Hard to do when all he could think about was Sayles. "Either I'm severely malnourished and dehydrated, or there's a turkey sunbathing on that rock."

She craned her head over one shoulder but kept her hands locked in his shirt. "That's Frank. He lives in the park."

"You named it." Of course she had. His stomach growled, reminding him he hadn't eaten since they'd set out a couple hours ago. "I don't suppose we're allowed to eat him."

Sayles smacked her hand against his chest. Almost hard enough to knock him off-balance. Thankfully she wouldn't be witnessing that blunder. "You can't eat mascots, but if I'm being honest, turkey sounds really good right now."

"I'll get you some when we're back at the visitors' center." He just wouldn't tell Frank about that. "So tell me, Ranger Green, how do we get to Big Spring before the killer does?"

Chapter Twenty-One

She could've gone another lifetime without seeing this trail again.

They'd taken a gamble in hiking the 1,500-foot incline that crested the west canyon wall hiding the Narrows in its base. Her toes slipped on the next ascent, nearly launching her back into Elias. His hands framed her hips as she righted herself, keeping her from falling, but the rains from the past couple of days dissolved any sort of traction. One wrong move, and they'd lose the game the Hitchhiker Killer had set in motion. She had to be more careful. Breath crushed from her chest and aggravated the bruising along her ribs. "Thanks."

"I was hoping never to do this again." Elias struggled to even his breathing at her back, and she only hoped they hadn't ascended too fast and triggered altitude sickness. He was assigned out of the Las Vegas FBI office. Well below the park's elevation. "Can't promise I won't have a heart attack before we get to the top."

"Almost there." Using the goat trail gave them the slimmest chance of getting ahead of the killer by avoiding the river's current and any debris and obstacles in their way if he'd kept to the official Narrows trail. It was the only option they had despite the anxiety-tense muscle strain memories of yesterday tightening down her spine, but she'd never hiked the rim of the canyon. Her knowledge extended to the main trails in and around Zion. Elias had hired her as a guide, but this was foreign territory where any number of dangers could bite them in the ass.

Sun blinded her a split second before the ground under her feet evened out. Clear skies stretched as far as the eye could see. Miles and miles of barren red rock spread out before her in every direction, and a lightness she'd initially felt on the trails prickled the hair on the back of her neck. Wispy clouds played against the velvet of the sky, almost dancing on the breeze that untucked her hair from its crude braid. This. This was what she'd chased all those months after leaving Colorado. A fullness she couldn't find anywhere else. Except she'd felt it down in that canyon, with Elias's mouth pressed to hers. With every stroke of his tongue and shift of his hand on her face.

The kiss had been sweet and coaxing and freeing all in the same breath. Unlike anything she'd experienced before and a reminder of how little she'd been cared for in the past. But the anger—the disappointment—wasn't there anymore. She waited for the shame to rear its ugly head. It never showed, and Sayles didn't know what to think about that. What to do with that.

She explored that sensation, reveled in the emptiness the view and the man at her side provided. She'd survived the past couple of years off spite and anger alone, but now there was nothing but a hole where it'd slept. Because of Elias. No. Not emptiness. Something lighter that took her a few seconds to feel out. Brighter. Filling. It'd slipped in without her notice and meticulously replaced the hurt she held on to to keep everyone at arm's length.

Hope. That was what this was. So foreign and unusual but stronger than the remnants of a lost life she'd tried holding on to for herself. That pain and betrayal she'd believed protected her were nothing but scraps compared to the solid hold Elias had offered. A lifeline she hadn't seen until now. Where she didn't have to shoulder the past alone and could let herself imagine a future. Dream and plan and thrive. With him.

"Wow." Elias kept his distance, not willing to crowd her on the too-narrow trail though his massive frame threatened to tip her right over the edge.

"Yeah." They weren't shaken by the same view. His amazement came from their physical perspective. Hers from inside. She planted her boots. It'd be easy to let the lack of guardrails and the sheer elevation get to her, but right now, she felt as though she were flying. Free. The river tendrilled and curved below them, but she couldn't make out any distinguishing signs of the killer. He'd managed to escape them once. She couldn't let him get away again. Couldn't be responsible for the devastation he would cause if she failed.

Crackling reached her ears, raising her senses on to high alert. There. A voice? Broken but there if she listened hard enough. Understanding hit. Sayles wrenched her pack free and swung it around. Diving her hand inside, she hit the solid casing of her emergency radio. "We're out of the canyon. Radio waves can reach us here."

Pressing the push-to-talk button, she called into the visitors' center. They could reach Risner—or anyone else—from this elevation. "This is Ranger Green. Hello? Can you hear me?"

Stillness flooded through her and Elias as they waited, barely willing to make a noise that might drown out any response. She tried again. "Green to VC. Is anyone there? Risner? Hello?"

"Green? Copy." For perhaps the first time ever, Risner's nasally response flooded her with a sense of relief. "We've been trying to get to you for two days. We thought we'd lost you and Agent Broyles. Where the hell are you?"

Sayles closed her eyes against the drugging sensation of contact with the outside world. Nearly pressing the radio to her face, she leaned against its metal casing. "Four miles in the Narrows, closing in on Big Spring. Damn, it's good to hear your voice." She'd never admit that to anyone. Ever. Least of all Risner after today. "We're still in pursuit of the killer. Lucky to be alive after those flash floods."

Elias silently beckoned for the radio, and she handed it off. "Risner, this is Agent Broyles. I need to speak with the agent there with you at the visitors' center."

"Agent Marques is here. Hold on. I'll put you on." Static crackled over the airwaves for more than a minute before another voice broke through. "Elias, what the hell, man. Where have you been? I've been trying to get a hold of you since yesterday afternoon. We've got reports of flash floods in the Narrows. Search and rescue is waiting for the flooding to clear so they can come in and get you. Are you all right?"

His gaze locked on hers as he raised the radio to his mouth. "That doesn't matter. Listen, we're closing in on this guy. Do you have any updates from your end that can help us?"

"Yeah, yeah. Just a sec. Let me get my notes." Her partner looked as though he was about to crumple the radio's casing as they waited. The sun had already started making its afternoon arch across the sky. They would lose daylight in the next couple of hours, and there was nowhere to camp on this trail. Not to mention a single source of light to ensure they didn't step straight off the cliff face. "I searched the van our unsub stole from the last interstate victim, but the entire setup had been wiped down as we expected. I managed to contact the victim's family and send them photos of the van to see if they might notice anything missing or out of place."

Elias raised the radio again, quick and efficient before lowering it back between them. All the while refusing to take his attention off her. Sweat built at his temple, and it was then she realized how much protection the canyon had offered. Now? Now they were exposed. Vulnerable. Easy targets. "And?"

"Turns out she was an avid climber. Ropes, chalk, carabiners, the works. She was making the trip across the country to climb the national parks, including Zion." The radio cut out. "—must've taken all her gear."

Pinching the radio and raising it back to his mouth, Elias narrowed his gaze on her. "What would he want with climbing gear?"

"Zion has over two hundred and fifty documented free climbs, but none in the Narrows." This didn't make sense. Sayles mentally ran through the possibilities.

"There's more." Agent Marques—Grant—waited a beat, and Sayles's own impatience charged to the surface. "The victim discovered by your ranger lady at the bottom of the trail. He was traveling with a group of friends from Texas. Four of them, but two days ago they'd split up to take on the trails they personally wanted to hike. Our vic went straight for the Narrows that morning. The other three came to the visitors' center after the park had been emptied. No one had heard from him, you know, because he was dead, but what they really wanted to tell me was that our latest victim never went anywhere without his handgun."

Sayles shook her head. "There wasn't a handgun on the body when I found it."

Her partner straightened. Every inch the federal agent he was supposed to be. The one she'd feared would break the last dregs of her soul if she gave him the chance. Gone was the easy smile and the banter, the warmth he'd supplied in the middle of the night with her pressed against his chest. This was the trained agent who'd vowed to find his father's killer, and Sayles had the inclination to back away. And that lightness she'd felt a few minutes ago faltered. "Because the killer took it."

The Hitchhiker Killer—Patrick, or whoever he was— had a gun. She turned her attention back to the river below, somehow managing to take an even breath as her heart threatened to beat out of her chest.

Elias and his partner's conversation distorted into short commands and faded responses. She didn't have the energy to follow along as pieces of this messed-up puzzle started falling into place. A stolen handgun, climbing gear, a blurred target at the end of the trail. Each seemingly dangerous enough on its own, but together? Sayles shuddered as footsteps thundered through the slight ringing in her ears.

Elias. "Grant is going to go back and talk with our forensics teams to double-check all the other vehicles our unsub stole to see if anything is missing from the victim's bags or trunks."

"We should keep moving. We only have a few more hours of daylight and another mile to cover before we reach Big Spring." She didn't have the capacity for much else, dependent on the feel of the trail under her feet, the reliability of her balance. Connection to the very park she'd given herself over to these past few months. Sayles took that initial step, but Elias's hand threaded between her arm and rib cage.

"You good?" He studied her. His gaze raked her from head to toe. Too close. Too aware. Did he see the cracks breaking through her resolve? Or that she was on the verge of falling apart altogether? "Tell me what you need."

She fought for her next inhale, forcing a smile. Need? She needed this case to be over. She needed to collapse into bed for the next several days and sleep. She needed a shower and food and water that hadn't been cleaned by filtration tablets. She needed pain reliever for the aches in her body. All of it combined to tear her down to nothing, and she hated how…weak it made her feel. Useless. Her ex didn't have to be standing right here to tell her how pathetic and needy she was being. His voice had adapted into something familiar and terrifying, her own mental critic. But worst of all? She needed Elias right there with her through whatever came next. Which she hated most of all. "Nothing a bed and a hot meal can't fix."

He considered her for a moment, and she was ready for him to call bullshit. To read her thoughts on her face as he had so many times before. "You're still thinking about that turkey, aren't you?"

She couldn't stop her laugh.

"I can't stop. My mouth is still watering." Sayles didn't wait for his response, turning back to the trail. She didn't know what they would be facing up ahead. She just hoped she'd be enough.

Chapter Twenty-Two

Something was off.

Sayles forged ahead along the rim of the canyon, that impenetrable mask back in place, a few feet ahead. His feet ached. The blisters along the inside of his thigh screamed for new dressings as the weight of his gear wore him down. He'd lost his usual gait in the days they'd pushed themselves to the brink, overcompensating on his right foot and aggravating both injuries. It was harder to breathe up here. Took more effort to take that next step. None of it explained the change in his partner.

She'd lied to him. He'd read it in her face, but Elias wouldn't push. Not yet. Not while they were still on the verge of losing the Hitchhiker Killer to the backcountry spread out ahead. She was on the cusp of burning out. He could already see her instinct to shut down, shut him out, but they'd been through too much already. He couldn't lose any part of her, and that scared him the most. How thoroughly she'd pulled him in with that gut-wrenching smile, borderline rude retorts and sour attitude. How utterly dependent he'd become on her out here. And how quickly he'd given up on making up for his mistakes, for letting his dad down. Justice had always called to him, but with Sayles… It didn't have quite the same pull anymore.

The ground shifted underneath one boot, and Elias jerked to the right. To the edge of the goat trail. His arms went wide in a fight for balance, but he'd overcorrected. A hand shot out to stabilize him—strong and sure—pulling him back to safety. Her fingers dug into his wrist, and his pulse jumped against her touch. Out of control. Then again, when had he been in control around her? His heart had taken a beating over the past two days. Level for one moment and rocketing into the atmosphere the next. He wouldn't be surprised if he failed his next annual physical with the damage he'd done to his cardiovascular system. Not to mention the invisible scars. "Thanks."

A flush worked up her neck, her mouth parting on a strong exhale. "You're not getting out of here that easy."

"Wouldn't dream of it." While he had no intentions of hiking this particular trail again, Elias had already accepted that Zion National Park would be in his future. As many times as it took before she realized he wasn't her bastard of an ex. That she mattered. "You can let go now."

"What?" Sayles dropped her gaze to where her hand gripped his, then pulled away as if he'd burned her. Stepping back, she added a couple feet between them, but no more. Ready to grab him again, he imagined. "Sorry."

He managed not to go tumbling over the edge this time and closed the distance she'd added. Sliding his fingers into her ponytail, Elias tipped her head back, forced her to look up at him. An entire galaxy swirled in her green gaze as dark as any pine tree he'd caught on the way into the park, full of a combination of hesitation and brightness. "I'm not. That's the second time you've saved my life."

"It's a wonder you've gotten this far in life without me." Her hand found its way to his chest, to push him away or draw him closer, he wasn't sure yet. He didn't dare ask.

His smile tugged at the dry patches at the corners of his mouth. Damn, he hadn't expected this. Hadn't expected her. This case was supposed to be the next rung to getting his career back on track, but she'd solely knocked him down a couple of pegs. "What else does that mouth of yours do?"

"Probably hurt your feelings." There wasn't an inch of give in her position. No inclination to run. Or hide. She stood toe-to-toe, every inch his equal, and he couldn't get enough of the sight. Of the power she held over him.

He couldn't stop the laugh charging through his chest. Releasing his hold on her hair, Elias swiped at the dryness around his mouth. "Go out with me. After this case is finished and I've arrested this asshole we're hunting, go out with me."

"I've slept in your sleeping bag the past two nights, whether I realized it or not." Sayles swung around to face the goat trail, giving him her back. "Kind of feels like we've already missed our chance at a first date."

She wasn't going to make this easy, was she? And, hell, Elias wasn't sure what he would do if she had. He followed in her mud-stiff tracks. "All right. Then tell me what you see happening between us after this case is finished."

Sayles didn't answer for a breath. Two. And he realized he'd stopped breathing to avoid missing her answer. "Why can't we just appreciate what we have now?"

The sucker punch struck as a physical hit that nearly made him falter. "What does that mean?"

Turning her face toward the sun, she gripped her pack's straps. "It means I've lived through the mind games and the manipulation, the isolation and control, and come out on the other side worse for wear. I want to be able to make my own decisions and have a say in my life. For the first time in over a decade, I'm putting myself first, and I'm not sure going from one bad relationship into another is going to give me that freedom."

His hand found hers, and Elias pulled her to a stop. While they were headed for the same end point on this trail— aligned in their goals on this investigation—she'd donned those damn defenses again. He scanned her expression, looking for a way through, but she'd locked him out. "Have I given you any reason to believe I would try to control you like that?"

That intense gaze, highlighted by the sun's arc through the sky, bounced between his eyes. Her lips pursed at the edges. He could see the gutting response forming, but a rush of defeat smoothed her features. "Being thrown together on a death-defying assignment for a couple days doesn't amount to anything, Elias. I knew my ex for years before I married him. There weren't any red flags until it was too late, and I paid for it with eight months behind bars. I refuse to go into anything that blindly."

"You're serious." His fingers tingled to touch her. To pull her against him and remind her she had more instinct than she gave herself credit for. That she was the one who held all the power in this dynamic they'd forged over the course of the investigation. What would it take for her to see herself the way he saw her? "I'm not your ex, Sayles."

"I know that." She slipped her hand out of his, leaving him colder than he'd expected. "That's what makes this all the more terrifying."

Because for her it would be better to go back to that familiar misery than take a risk on something new. Tension radiated down his spine as he squared off with the meaning behind her words, and it wasn't until right then Elias realized how much he'd allowed himself to hope. For this. For her.

At some point since losing his father, he'd stopped working for anything other than justice. The next killer, the next victim, the next break in the case—they were all that mattered. He'd sacrificed friendships and what little family he'd had left. Nights out, vacations, sick days. Every waking minute had been filled with that unending craving for forgiveness. For not finding the people who'd killed his father, for costing his confidential informant her life. He'd thrown himself into the work until it'd consumed him and left nothing but a husk of the man he'd wanted to be in honor of his father.

Until her.

Over the course of the past two days, he'd felt like a new man. A better man. One who wasn't held back by everything bad that had ever happened to him. None of it had mattered. Because of her. She'd pulled on some internal string he hadn't known existed, hidden deep and out of reach, and had managed to unravel him in a matter of days. He'd had a lot of firsts, but Sayles was the first person to show him he was more than a man shaped by mistakes. That he could be anything he wanted if he just let himself, but that required letting go of that familiar misery, didn't it? He hadn't been prepared for the force of this attraction, and now it was going to cost him. Elias cleared his throat. A distraction. He needed a distraction. Mountains towering over 5,000 feet in elevation crowded around their position along the Narrows cliffs. No way to discern if the Hitchhiker Killer had come this way. "What are the chances the killer will take one of these smaller branches off the end of the trail to avoid us?"

"I don't know. Most of the smaller canyons are impassable after a few hundred feet, which is why park rangers made Big Spring the official end of the trail." Confusion deepened the lines between her brows, but she didn't call him out on the change of subject. "I think he's more likely to head into the backcountry along the east river that feeds into the Narrows. Hikers are required to apply for permits so we can keep track of who is out here and how many, but I doubt he filled out the paperwork. That would make finding him too easy."

"Then we head for the backcountry." Swiping the disappointment to the back of his mind where he would never unpack it again, Elias maneuvered ahead, taking the lead. "Can we access the east river from this trail—"

An explosion of pain ripped through his shoulder.

Sayles's scream echoed off the opposite canyon wall and seared into his brain as he fell back against her. They slammed into the rock face together, his feet hanging over the edge of the trail. Her breath crushed out of her beneath his weight. Long fingers clamped directly over the new hole he'd acquired, and Elias kicked against the dirt to make them as small as a target as possible. They were cornered. Unable to flee without putting them back in the shooter's path. "Stay down."

"You're bleeding." She scrambled to free herself of her pack's straps, but the movement only jarred the bullet lodged in his shoulder deeper.

Elias gritted against the pain.

"That's what happens when you get shot." Her heart thudded hard against her chest and down his spine. Out of control. Though she wouldn't admit it. Damn it. He had to get them out of here, but short of crawling on their hands and knees, the killer had every advantage. Where was the son of a bitch? He scanned their surroundings. He'd done this, let his personal agenda get in the way of this case. He'd made another mistake. "You need to run. Get out of here. I'll draw him off."

Sayles ripped the top of her pack open, the zipper protesting as she searched for something inside. In a matter of breaths, the first aid kit was balanced on her knee, and she popped the lid. "I'm not leaving you here to fight him alone. We barely survived the last time. We have better odds together."

"Well, isn't that romantic." The Hitchhiker Killer blocked the path ahead. Raising his weapon. And took aim at Sayles. "I hope I'm not interrupting, but as I said before I do have need of your assistance, Ranger Green, and I'm on a bit of a schedule." He motioned Sayles up with the wave of the gun. "So, if you don't mind, chop chop."

Positioning himself in front of her, Elias set himself up as a shield. Though he wasn't sure it would do a damn bit of good considering he already had two holes punctured in his torso. Her hands clamped over the wound in his shoulder. Even at gunpoint, she was trying to ensure he wouldn't bleed out in front of her. "She's not going anywhere with you."

Elias didn't give the bastard the chance to pull the trigger. He lunged. The collision knocked him off-balance.

With a single shove, Elias went over the cliff.

Chapter Twenty-Three

"No!" She dived for the spot where Elias had disappeared.

The ground rushed to meet her in a frenzy of dirt and lacerating gravel. Her chest threatened to cave under the impact as she reached for nothing but air.

He was gone. There one second and gone the next. Acidic loss burned up her throat. No. It wasn't possible. This was all some kind of nightmare. She was going to wake up. Any minute now they'd be in her one-person tent, her sprawled across his chest and him acting like he'd gotten the best night sleep of his life. They would have breakfast together and throw barbs at each other. He would flash her that smile that went straight to her insides and maybe kiss her again. "Elias!"

Only the Virgin River's roar answered. Tears burned in her eyes.

"Yes, very sad. Shall we go?" A strong hand wrapped around her biceps and hauled her to her feet. Her legs had turned to Jell-O. Her inability to get her feet underneath her—to comply—testified to his strength as an all-around psychopath. "As I said, I'm on a deadline, and I've already wasted enough time trying to get my hands on you for this little project."

They were moving. Along the trail. Away from where Elias had gone over the edge. She couldn't just leave him. There was still a chance he'd survived, right? Sayles ripped her arm out the killer's grasp. "I'm not going anywhere with you."

Stumbling back, she spun on her heel. Ready to launch down the trail. But she didn't make it far. She saw his shadow first. Then came the pain. Crushing weight tackled her into the ground. Her knee slipped over the edge of the two-foot-wide goat trail, but the killer's weight held her in place. Her forehead bounced off slick mud. White explosions danced behind her eyes. Air. She couldn't breathe. Excruciating agony threatened to snap her spine in half as she tried to suck in a breath.

"Unfortunately, Ranger Green, that's not your decision." He fisted his hand in her hair and pulled, forcing her back to compensate. The barrel of his gun cut into the side of her face. Somehow warm and cold at the same time. Mouth pressed against her ear, he exerted pure dominance over her. "Now, I've been patient up until now. Keep fighting me and I will burn this entire park to the ground before throwing you into the flames. Do you understand?"

The grip on her scalp tightened. Tears leaked from the corners of her eyes, quickly dying with the gust of wind over the top of the canyon. Not from the pain but the sudden gulf of darkness bleeding from her heart. Right where Elias had set up residence. She'd convinced herself she'd known emptiness and loss, but it was nothing compared to the void chipping away at her now. Dirt infiltrated her mouth and nose; thick layers of mud stuck to her uniform and face.

"Say the words." Another wave of pain punctuated the Hitchhiker Killer's point. "Say that you understand what's at stake."

Every cell in her body fought against agreeing to anything this man wanted. The fight might physically cost her, but inside, she knew Elias would expect nothing less. Her teeth locked. "Go to hell."

"Oh, Ranger Green, where do you think I came from?" The pressure against her spine vanished.

She managed to suck in a lungful of oxygen a split second before the killer wrenched her upward by her hair. Slapping both hands over his to ease the pain, she had little physical control facing him. Any second now, Elias would drag himself over the lip of the canyon. He would tell this bastard to let her go. He'd look like hell but throw her that crooked smile to ease the anxiety churning nausea in her gut. One second. Two. She waited. Ignored the Hitchhiker Killer's prompts for her attention. And waited. The hard pound of her heartbeat between her ears stretched seconds into minutes, into what felt like hours. But he never came, and her heart broke all over again. Gone. He was gone.

He'd been right there for the past two days. At her side. Keeping her from mentally breaking when all she'd wanted to do was curl into a ball and disappear. Elias had seen through the armor she'd built around herself and accepted every broken piece she'd tried to hide from the outside world, and she'd thrown it back in his face. Unwilling to give up a sliver of the hurt she'd survived in favor of the unknown. Because she'd been scared. Unfairly compared him to her ex when they couldn't be more different. She'd regret it for the rest of her life.

"Let's go, and if you try anything like that little rock-in-your-bag maneuver, I will shoot you in the arm. Then the other arm. And then I'll move on to your hands until there is nothing left of you." The killer shoved her forward, and it took everything in her not to hit the ground a second time. He collected her pack and tossed it at her chest with too much force. "You won't need them where we're going."

She faced off with golden-yellow sun making its way toward the horizon, brushing off layers of dirt from her uniform shirt. Sweat beaded at her temples despite the consistent breeze skirting the rim of the canyon. "Asshole."

His laugh hit wrong, disingenuous and sickly. He didn't answer, but she had a feeling he wasn't the first person people invited over to dinner.

"Where are we going?" Sayles kept awareness at her back while searching for a way to escape. Rocks shifted beneath her boots, the gravel much looser here than along other parts of the trail as they closed in on Big Spring. She could throw a handful in his face. Give herself a head start, but she wasn't sure her ribs could hold up against another tackle. Emerald-colored waters rippled 1,000 feet below under the onslaught of two medium-size waterfalls. The river was shallowest here, a hub that swelled only with the onslaught of storms. There was no surviving a jump from this distance. Elias had fallen at a deeper section. He could've survived. He could need help.

"If I told you that, I'd be ruining the surprise. All you need to worry about is helping me avoid any other ranger patrols." The killer's footsteps kept in time with hers. Deliberate. Intimidating. He wanted her to know he could strike out, that he was the one in control here.

Damn it. Why had Elias put himself between her and the man at her back? He had to have known he'd lose a fight against a gun, but he'd made the choice to protect her anyway. To give her a chance to run. Because that was the kind of man he was. A protector, through and through, with the weight of the entire world on his shoulders. No one else would've been good enough to do the job, but that relentlessness had forced him to sacrifice so much. And for a stupid minute, she'd convinced herself she could be the one to help him break free of those self-inflicted responsibilities. For a stupid minute, she'd considered saying yes. But handing her heart over to someone else—giving him the same power she'd granted her ex—scared her more than falling over the edge of this cliff. She couldn't do that. She couldn't go through that again,

Sayles glanced back, vying for a view of the river. For some sign Elias wasn't dead.

"I've never met someone who thinks so loudly before." A nudge in her lower spine forced her to look ahead. The gun took shape in her peripheral vision. "Whatever escape you're considering, Ranger Green, it won't work. I will find you, and you will wish you were dead."

She was out of options. No weapon. No escape from this trail. Her best chance was to get them to the backcountry and wait for the opportunity to run where she didn't have to fight the elevation, a too-narrow trail or the river itself. But biding her time could cost Elias precious minutes he didn't have. "What do you want from me?"

"Keep moving. Daylight's burning." Coldness—all too familiar and terrifying—solidified the killer's face as he guided her forward, and Sayles couldn't help but conclude this was going to end badly. For her. For Elias. For anyone else who came across this man's path.

She was the only one standing in his way of him getting what he wanted. Whatever that was.

They kept to the goat trail, bypassing the beauty of Big Spring below. This was the official end of the Narrows. That emerald pool below had changed her every time she'd hiked this trail. In small ways at first, then with life-altering clarity. Zion National Park held a magic to it she couldn't explain, one of possibility and healing and support. But she didn't feel it now. People liked to think time healed all wounds, but those people were idiots. Wounds like hers didn't heal. She'd just had to learn how to control the bleeding.

Gravel crunched under her weight as they hiked past the oasis 1,000 feet, down then shifted to fine-grained dirt and sand. Desert weeds clawed at her shins and caught on her bootlaces as they entered backcountry. Waves of mountains crested and dipped against the crystal-blue sky. The rock here took on more of a pale tan coloring compared with the red and orange along the Narrows, but it was still just as beautiful. Miles of unending desert, canyon and green trees stretched out before them, but Sayles didn't have the guts to stop to take it all in this time.

"Northeast." One word. That was all he gave her as they approached a lightning-struck tree, its black bark smooth where animals and weather had worn it down over the years.

Shards of wood warned her not to get too close, and she couldn't help compare herself to those broken pieces. Sharp. Burned. Exposed. At first glance, she would've assumed the tree had reached the end of its life, as she had. Under arrest for a murder she hadn't committed, imprisoned with no sign of release, captive by a man who'd promised her the world. She and this tree had a lot in common. Except, as the Hitchhiker Killer nudged her a second time, she caught sight of new growth. Dead center in the middle of the charred remains of the tree. Surrounded by all the bad, a wisp of life.

She'd had that these past couple of days. A glimpse of something alive and renewing. Made possible by the federal agent she was so determined to hate. Her past had lost its grip in his laugh, in the way he'd put her needs first. How he'd risked his life for hers. No one had done that before. Sayles slowed her descent down the rounded, cracked hill leading into unfamiliar territory of Zion's backcountry. No one was likely to do what he had for her again, and she'd wasted it. By letting fear win. By not telling Elias how he'd changed her, gifted her something no one else had. How he'd gotten her to dream again.

Unsure how long they traversed the desert in silence, Sayles was caught off guard by the bright spot of blue against the natural landscaping a few hundred yards ahead. Her heart shot into her throat. Hikers. Her skin turned clammy as she checked to see if the killer had noticed. The park was supposed to be evacuated, but it was impossible to hunt down every visitor in a short amount of time, especially those who came to the park to get off the grid. She made no assumptions that she'd make it out of this alive, but she could still save innocent bystanders.

She cut to the left, leading the Hitchhiker Killer more northeast. Hoping to bypass the tent altogether without drawing attention to it. But it was too late.

"It'd be awfully rude of us if we didn't say hello." Patrick dragged her back in front of him, the barrel of his weapon pressed into her ribs, and led her straight for the low voices coming from inside the blue canvas. "Don't you think?"

Chapter Twenty-Four

He was dead.

That was the only explanation for the white light taking up his vision.

Elias blinked to get a better sense of his surroundings. Walls of red, orange and green bled through the brightness and took shape in his peripheral vision. Was dying supposed to hurt this much? Hell. Every inch of his body screamed. Dragging his chin to his chest, he mentally cataloged which of his limbs worked and which he'd have to let go of. Where was the train that had hit him? Water beat against one side of his face and seeped past his lips. Gross.

Turning onto his side, he let the groan stuck in his throat free. Rock cut into his hip and rib cage. Damn it. That hurt. He pressed his hand to his side to somehow keep himself together. A barrage of memory slapped into place. The killer. The cliff. The fall. Holy hell. He'd gone over the edge. And survived. That had to qualify for the Guinness World Records. He craned his head up, where he imagined the spot from which he'd done a Peter Pan into the river below, but he was too far away to tell.

Elias struggled to get his feet under him, moving slower than he wanted to. A scream echoed through his head and sent his heart rate into overdrive. Sayles. She'd tried to grab on to him. She was still up there. Alone with a killer who wouldn't let her walk away unscathed. He had to move. If he started the climb now, he might reach the goat trail by sundown. Searching the top of the rock wall, he failed to see any sort of movement.

Moving his arm, he noted blood on his shirt. His abdominal wound had reopened. The fall must've torn it open. He'd lost his pack. His first aid kit. Sayles. There would be no cleaning or bandaging it this time. He stumbled as he straightened. Not good. "Damn."

The hydro bib's straps dug into his shoulders; his gear was full of water. It would only work to slow him down. Hauling himself to the edge of the river, he surveyed his current location. Oversize stair steps jutted out from the base of the canyon, overgrown with trees and shrubs. Okay. Not one of the corridors. He had to be close to the end of the trail then, to Big Spring. Elias cleared the river, collapsing on a rock lip double his height. He unlaced his boots and dumped water from each. The blisters would be a bitch with wet socks, but he didn't have time for his gear to dry. Sayles needed him now. Discarding the hydro bib, he left it behind as he scanned the canyon walls.

They'd accessed the goat trail around the four-mile marker. If the river had swept him downstream, he should be close enough to get back on. Except this time he wouldn't have any gear, he had a hole in his torso and the sun would give out in the next hour or so. Who wouldn't bet on him? Elias kept to the edge of the river, careful of every slippery, algae-covered rock threatening to bring him down. If he was being honest with himself, he might not get back up.

Attempting to hold his blood inside his body, he navigated the trail downstream. Every cell in his body begged him to give up now. To wait until Grant or another ranger could lead the manhunt, but Sayles didn't have that kind of time. And he wasn't going to be another person in her life to give up as her friends and family had when she'd gone to prison.

She deserved better. Deserved to be happy after everything she'd survived. Not just her emotionally abusive husband but the grief and loneliness that came with betrayal. But she couldn't see it. How ridiculously beautiful and strong she'd become in response to her circumstances. And his heart hurt at seeing her continually retreat into that shell of a survivor she'd come to rely on since her arrest. Because he'd been privileged enough to glimpse through that armor, to the woman underneath. The one who took risks in moving to a whole new state to find a new path, who put her life on the line for tourists and hikers every day, who gifted a nobody like him with new purpose. Showed him how to stop letting the bad things win. In a matter of days, she'd changed him. Reached deep into his soul and resurrected a piece of himself he hadn't realized he'd let die with every failed date and case gone wrong. She'd brought him back to life.

So, no. He wasn't giving up on her. He'd keep going until the killer finished the job, or Sayles told him to go to hell. Either way, he owed her that much.

Elias left the cold dependence of the river and braced himself to ascend the goat trail a second time. His legs protested each step, but he had to keep moving. He already carried the weight of one innocent life on his shoulder. He wasn't sure he could support another. Gravel shifted beneath his boots, and he had to use more of his upper body to stay balanced. Step after step, shallow breath after shallow breath. The pain in his side speared throughout the rest of his torso, as if a nerve ending had been struck.

He was going to make it. Because there wasn't any other option.

Sun penetrated his vision, blinding him and gold-washing the landscape ahead as he crested the lip of the canyon. Hand up to block the sun, Elias picked up the pace into a reckless jog. The pressure in his chest hadn't let up from the moment he'd gained consciousness on that canyon floor. Whatever plans the Hitchhiker Killer had for Sayles, it didn't include letting her walk away. Her clock had started the moment he'd gone over the edge of the trail, but he wouldn't leave her to fight this alone.

His lungs burned. From the elevation, exertion or dropping temperatures, he didn't know, and it sure as hell wasn't going to slow him down. Shallow footprints took shape in front of him, one set smaller than the others. Sayles. She'd been here. He was getting close. "Come on."

Utter exhaustion clawed beneath his skin, and a gush of blood filled his palm as he added pressure to the wound. The two were probably linked, but logic wasn't running this show. He was racing against the clock on pure need. Need to get to Sayles, to catch this killer, to make his father proud. All of it combined in a heavy dose of adrenaline that wouldn't last long if he pushed too hard. But what other choice did he have?

The trail flattened out in front of him. Mountains demanded attention from every angle with valleys hidden by an insurmountable amount of trees and brush. Sayles could be anywhere, and without her as a guide, all he could do was trust his instincts. "This isn't going to end well."

Elias stepped off the goat trail and into the unknown. Sweat won the battle against the sun, seeping through his

T-shirt despite the onslaught of drying heat. His ankles ached from uneven terrain, but he'd just add it to the long list of problems he'd have to deal with later. If he survived. Patches of snow highlighted the northern peaks of the cliffs staring down at him as he cut his own route into the first valley. Gravity added to the weight on his body, and it took everything he had left not to fall face-first into the dirt.

No signs of life. Of anyone else out here. The killer had to have brought her this way. There were no other branches to follow at the end of the Narrows, but the park itself stretched over two hundred square miles. A gust cut through the valley and whipped up the dirt under his feet, erasing any kind of tracks. Still, Elias's gut told him he was headed in the right direction, as if Sayles had connected that invisible internal string she'd discovered inside him to herself. To give him something to focus on. To follow.

And, hell, he'd follow her to the ends of the earth. He'd chase her forever if that was what she required of him, to show her she was worth every second, every mistake, everything he'd be required to give up for a single shot with her.

There were no paths out here in the backcountry, but he kept heading forward. Blood crusted in his palm and between his fingers though the pain remained consistent. Pulsing and unrelenting. It was too late to go back now. Backup wouldn't get here in time. Without Sayles, he was stranded in the middle of the desert without any idea where to go next, food, medical supplies or a way to contact the visitors' center. All he could hope for was that Grant had gotten enough information on their location to provide support, whatever that looked like.

He was on his own, but this was what he'd trained for. What he was good at. He'd studied the thinking patterns and motivations of killers for years, including the very people involved in his father's death. The Hitchhiker Killer wouldn't be any different. There was a reason he'd followed the interstate to Zion National Park. Elias had originally assumed it'd been to avoid arrest, but most criminals wouldn't trade a nine-by-nine cell and three meals a day for an early death in the middle of the desert. The closest thing to civilization outside the park was Springdale, a tourist town constructed and dependent on the lure of the park, but the town sat completely in the opposite direction. No. The killer wasn't looking to escape. Sayles had said he was looking for something. Someone. But who the hell would be out here?

The answer came as Elias rounded the next bend in the unofficial trail. In the form of a blue canvas tent. The entrance had been left unzipped, the makeshift door collapsing into the tent and exposing the window at the back. A white-and-red cooler lay discarded on its side, melted ice leaking into the dirt in a spreading dark patch.

More evidence of a struggle peppered the dead landscape. A paperback—tossed face down into the dirt—a shredded sleeping bag thrown over a cactus a few feet away.

And the foot peeking out from the corner of the tent.

Dread pooled at the base of his spine, pulling Elias to a stop. He studied the boot-clad foot, willed it to move. Compared it to the pair Sayles had been wearing these past two days, and the dread turned into something darker as he recognized the brand. No. No, no, no. It wasn't her. It couldn't be her. Then he was running. "Sayles."

Dirt kicked up under his shoes as he rounded the tent. And froze.

Chest heaving, wound bleeding, Elias studied the body, doubling over. Nausea churned in his gut, and he had to look away as horse flies started circling. He'd faced bodies before, but this one…

Not Sayles. The face he studied belonged to that of a stranger. Hispanic male dressed in a denim button-up shirt and shorts, full mustache with a peppering of beard growth. Maybe thirty, thirty-five years old. The park was supposed to be evacuated. What was he doing out here by himself? Blood clotted around the bullet wound between the victim's eyes. Fresh. Couldn't have been shot more than thirty minutes ago, which meant he still had a chance of catching up.

National park rangers would have to collect the body. For now, Elias grabbed a half-eaten bag of beef jerky, shoved a handful into his mouth and searched through the tent for something—anything—to help him find Sayles. No radio. No weapons. He tossed a second sleeping bag to the other side of the tent. And realized this victim hadn't been out here alone after all.

The Hitchhiker Killer had taken another hostage.

Chapter Twenty-Five

A scream seared her nervous system.

Not hers. Though Sayles was close to losing her mind as images of a bullet ripping through that man's head refused to dissipate. She'd been forced to leave him there next to his tent, his pleas for his wife's life still shredding through her.

But it'd just been a game. One the killer had already decided the winner. Empty promises of choosing one victim while the other would walk away unscathed replayed through her head as she'd just stood there, trying to make herself as small as possible so as not to regain the Hitchhiker Killer's attention. Except Patrick had never intended to let either of the campers go. Instead, he'd pulled the trigger and left an innocent man die at her feet. There hadn't been anything she could've done to stop him. Not without taking a bullet herself.

She stumbled forward as the toe of her boot caught on a rock and turned to see that gun still aimed at her back even as the man dragged the female camper across the desert floor by her pretty blond hair. Sayles didn't know where they were going, had no idea how to get out of this mess. They were at the mercy of a man who possessed no mercy. This… She wasn't trained for this. What happened now? "Please, you don't have to hurt her."

Another scream bounced off the mountains around them as the killer wrenched the woman's head back, and Sayles's heart squeezed too hard in her chest. The camper had dropped to her knees, trying to keep up with the killer's push forward. Dirt-crusted blood trickled down her shins and pooled along the tops of her white socks. "You're right. I don't have to hurt her, but it's been a long time coming. You deserve what's coming, don't you, Mae?"

Mae.

Shock slapped Sayles across the face with an invisible hand. Her legs threatened to collapsed right out from under her. How… How did he know her name? The hairs on the back of Sayles's neck stood on end, and she wanted nothing but to escape. Run as fast as she could and never look back as realization set in. She tried to pick up on details of the woman's face, to give herself something to keep her grounded. The soft curve of groomed eyebrows, the way her flannel shirt—much too big for her frame—hung off her shoulders and revealed the tank top underneath. None of it did a damn bit of good. "You…you know her?"

"Mae and I go a long way back, don't we?" The killer smoothed the pad of his thumb along the woman's cheek. "Years, in fact."

Tears streaked down the camper's—down Mae's—face as she latched both hands on to the killer's wrist for relief. But there was no escape as long as Patrick kept that gun on them. Sayles could try to run, but that would leave this woman, whoever she was, in the hands of a man who looked as though he was one wrong response away from putting a bullet in both of them. The sobs intensified, each striking Sayles harder than the one before. "He's my… He was my husband."

The world almost tipped on its axis. Sayles tried to focus

on something—anything—but the cavern tearing through her chest.

"*Was?* Are you kidding me, Mae?" The Hitchhiker Killer tugged Mae's head back against his abdomen with more force than necessary, earning a whimper that Sayles found all too familiar. She'd heard it before, coming from her own mouth as her ex stood above her screaming for an answer as to why she hadn't picked up the phone when he'd called. "I seem to recall you telling me it was death do us part. So, no, Ranger Green. I was not her husband. I *am* her husband, and it's time for Mae to come home."

The control, the domination and manipulation—it was all coming back in full force. Unfiltered terror surfaced. Sweat broke across her skin despite the dip of the sun behind the mountain to the west. The urge to shrink, to hide, wrestled with the new facets she'd forged since her release from prison. The ones that told her she was stronger than her abuser, that she'd survived, that she'd won. They felt like nothing more than the sand stuck between her fingers compared to the black hole dragging at her body, anything but solid.

She couldn't let it win. Couldn't let this man win. She'd stood up to this particular killer before, shown him she wouldn't be beaten down to that husk of a woman again. It hadn't been a conscious effort but created from choice. From Elias showing her exactly how much power she exerted. Her choice. It'd always been her choice when it came to him, and…and she loved him for it.

The solid wall of adamant she'd built between her and the rest of the world had crumbled in a matter of days because of him. Because he'd encouraged her to trust herself, to save herself while he'd stood nearby in case she needed help. And she'd used that agency to reject the idea there could ever be anything between them. She'd been wrong. So wrong. What she wouldn't give to wake up pressed against Elias's chest in a too-small tent again. To hear that laugh that physically brushed her insides and surged heat into her face. To feel his mouth on hers and forget all the hurt and the pain and the bitterness.

She'd started falling for him. And lost the chance to tell him.

Trusting Elias with her heart wasn't about giving up her freedom. He'd never take that from her. He'd never cage or isolate her as her ex had. It was about choosing him over that deep-rooted fear. And she wanted to choose him. More than anything. Regret fought to consume her whole, but she wouldn't give it leverage.

Squeezing her pack to her chest, Sayles understood in that moment what she had to do, what she wished someone else had done for her. She took that initial step to close the distance between her and Patrick, with Mae positioned between them.

Mae's cries shook through her. Blond hair fisted around the killer's hand, she couldn't budge an inch without his permission and the Hitchhiker Killer wasn't about to let her go again. Sayles could read it in the deadpan expression etched into his face. "How...how did you find me?"

"You didn't think I would let my favorite plaything off the leash without having a tracker to keep tabs on you, did you? It took some bribing, but your dentist left a few thousand dollars richer during your last cleaning. Unfortunately for him, he didn't live long enough to spend it." Zero remorse laced his words. As if violating his ex-wife had become an everyday occurrence, and Sayles had no doubt of the depths of his depravity to claim something that didn't belong to him. The killer hauled Mae up by her hair, pressing his mouth to her ear. "Time to go home, darling. Where you belong."

"Please, Patrick. Don't do this." Sayles took another step, grabbing on to that smallest bit of confidence Elias had praised her for so many times and holding on tight. The second the Hitchhiker Killer got his ex out of the park, Mae's chances of survival plummeted. She couldn't let that happen. Not now. Not ever again. "I can help you. Nobody has to get hurt."

"I'm not your wife anymore." Mae shook her head, seemingly running out of tears. She was losing energy. Burning through whatever remnants of adrenaline her body had produced upon seeing her partner killed in front of her, and Sayles needed her to keep fighting. "I left. I'm happy. Javier—"

"Is dead, Mae. What did you think would happen?" The killer stabbed the barrel of the gun into his ex-wife's temple, his index finger over the trigger. Her silent scream told Sayles how much pain he'd inflicted, that he wanted it to hurt. "That I would just let another man put his hands on you? Kiss you? Take you to bed and not pay for touching you?"

"Please." Defeat and grief battled across Mae's freckled face as she struggled to get free of her ex, and Sayles couldn't wait anymore.

"Please, what?" Patrick pressed his face against Mae's tears. "Let you go? I gave you everything. A house, a better life. I paid for your clothes, your food, anything you wanted. All I wanted in return was for you to love me as much as I loved you, but you just couldn't do that, could you?"

"You killed him." Mae was on the verge of losing herself to the anger, the grief.

Now. Sayles had to go now. "Hey, Patrick?"

His gaze locked on hers.

"Go to hell." Sayles threw her pack at the killer as hard she could. The weight slammed against his chest and knocked him back. The gun arced away from Mae's head. Just for a moment. Sayles grabbed for the woman's hand and tugged, forcing Mae to her feet. "Run!"

The desert stretched out in front of them.

The gun exploded from behind, and Sayles's instinct automatically had her ducking her head to avoid a bullet. She clutched on to Mae as hard as she dared so they wouldn't be separated, blocking her head with her other hand. As if it would be enough to stop dying as Javier had. "Come on!"

The last slivers of watery sunlight vanished from the horizon, leaving nothing but a warm orange glow in the sky. Within minutes, they'd have nothing but their pathetic human vision to navigate the wilderness, but it was enough. It would have to be enough. Weeds and cacti clawed at their exposed shins as they worked together to create as much distance between them and Patrick as possible.

"Mae!" Rage coated that one word, hiking Sayles's defenses into overdrive. A second gunshot ripped through the night, but they couldn't stop. Not yet. Not yet. "I will find you, Mae! I will make you pay for those ninety-two days you've been gone."

The air was thinner here at 5,500 feet. Dizziness swam through her head, but she only dragged Mae to her side, unwilling to let go as they confronted the base of the mountain to the east. Her boots caught on a rock she hadn't detected with her adjusting vision, and Sayles hit the ground. Cactus needles pierced the skin of her palms, and it took everything she had not to scream in pain. To give away their position.

"Are you okay?" Mae tried to help her to her feet.

"Keep going." Scanning the massive wall of rock in front of them, Sayles ignored the agony in her chest and knees.

She'd hit harder than she expected, but it wasn't enough to stop her from escaping. "We have to climb."

The mountain seemed to ignore their desperation, throwing obstacles in their path as they clawed upward. Patches of rock and weeds bled together in the lack of sunlight. Snakes and scorpions—along with much more dangerous wildlife—lived in these mountains, but Sayles couldn't think about any of them right now.

"You can't hide from me! I will find you both, and when I do I'll finish this, I swear. You'll never leave me again, Mae." Patrick's voice had gained some distance. "Shall we play a game of Marco Polo? Marco..."

Sayles's hand flattened on a length of rock that went deeper into the mountain. Cool air brushed across her face, almost begging her to get closer. She shoved Mae ahead of her, keeping her voice low. "In here."

"Marco!" That single word tensed the muscles down Sayles's spine.

The cave mouth wasn't large, but it would provide them a couple minutes of rest. That was all they could afford. Sayles scrambled across the dirt-covered floor, maneuvering Mae deeper, away from the entrance. A burning odor clogged the back of her throat, but they had no other choice.

"Behind me." She positioned Mae at her back as she faced off with the mouth of the cave. A shadow crossed at the entrance, and Sayles fought down a shiver.

His frame came into view, dark against the backdrop of the last glow of the day. "Marco..."

Chapter Twenty-Six

The sound of the gunshot drilled straight through him.

Elias picked up the pace, following the curve of the mountain. He was losing blood, losing energy, but every step got him that much closer to Sayles and whoever else the killer had taken hostage. It was harder to breathe now. If he hadn't been scheduled for a heart attack anytime soon, this manhunt would do the trick.

Forcing himself to slow, he tried to pick out evidence of movement or voices. The rustle of wind through scrub was all that responded. All right. He had to think despite his ability to grit through the pain; he was leaking. He wasn't sure how much blood he'd already lost while unconscious in the river, but he had to guess any amount would come back and bite him in the ass if he didn't get a handle on the situation. Damn it. He should've grabbed the campers' first aid kit, but in the moment, all he'd been able to think about was Sayles. Getting to her.

And it was too late to turn back now.

Those gunshots hadn't been for nothing. His partner could be out here hurt or worse. The Hitchhiker Killer would have a hard time controlling two hostages, no matter the circumstances. And he knew Sayles. She would take the first opportunity to escape, but that meant leaving an innocent in the killer's hands, which wouldn't even cross her mind. Even with the threat of death barreling down on her, she'd do whatever it took to protect someone else. It was one of the things he loved about her most, and hell, he wouldn't change it.

He loved her.

All the retorts she threw in his face, her rashness and impulsivity, the way she fought to keep her mouth closed when a thought was on her mind. The ranger advertised every emotion of her face and gave him a front-row seat to the whirlwind of danger flashing in her eyes when he'd gotten too close to a line she'd drawn between them. He loved how she unconsciously sought him out in the middle of the night and that his body melted against her when nothing but exhaustion and sleeping pills had done the trick in the past. He just…loved her.

All the bad dates, all the loneliness, the obsession with his work—he'd go through it all again if it meant he could keep Sayles in his life. He'd even hike the Narrows again if it gifted him with a glimpse of her in her element. Because here, in this park, she'd freed herself, and he couldn't help but be drawn in. To want that for himself. Without him even realizing it, she'd filled the hollow spaces in his chest, highlighting just how empty he'd been without her.

"Where would you go, Ranger Green?" Elias sucked in a deep breath, scanning the barren landscape. He wasn't familiar with these mountains. Well, hell, he wasn't familiar with any portion of this park, but Sayles was. If she had a chance to get away, she would take it, and she would take the second hostage with her. And hide. He'd noted enough half caves and outcroppings in the rock walls of the canyon to know these mountains most likely had similar structure.

Okay. She would head for a hiding spot. Wait the killer out until they could escape unnoticed or until help arrived. But they would've had to have moved fast. The Hitchhiker Killer had a gun, after all. He would've gone after them, desperate to keep what he thought he was owed.

Which begged the question, why take a random camper hostage alongside Sayles? Why increase the risk of one or both of them turning on him? Unless the killer had been looking for that specific camper. Sayles thought he might've been searching for someone the killer deemed important. Not something. Someone he knew. What if he'd been engaged in his own hunt? All the murders on the highway, the death of the hiker at the base of the Narrows—it hadn't been random at all. It'd led the Hitchhiker Killer to Zion's backcountry, to that tent and his latest victim.

Surveying the nearest mountain, Elias tried to discern any caves or outcroppings in the rock face, but it was far too dark for his pathetic vision to pick up. He'd have to get closer, risk heading in the wrong direction for the slightest chance of learning Sayles's location. But psychology and the body's automatic fight-or-flight response dictated humans as a whole sought immediate safety when threatened, which meant Sayles had most likely run to the mountain southeast of his position. Once she'd added some distance between her and the killer, she'd try to make her way back to civilization.

Jogging the few hundred yards to the base of the mountain, he sounded like an asthmatic pug. His atoms had started vibrating at dangerously high intensity, threatening to crack him open from the inside out. But he'd push through. Not because of some outdated need for justice but for Sayles. For their future. Because there would be one. He'd make sure of it.

Something solid and out of place took shape on the ground ahead, and Elias slowed his pace. Every sense on alert. The lump wasn't moving. Didn't hold any life. Not a person. A pack. Toeing the material, he flipped it face up. And froze.

Sayles's pack. She'd been here. But worse, a national park ranger had abandoned a mass of supplies she'd guarded more carefully than a dragon and its hoard. She wouldn't have given it up for anything, which meant it'd either been taken from her by the killer or she'd surrendered it to give herself a better chance at survival. Either way, she needed him now. Tipping the pack upside down, he crouched, emptying the contents into the dirt. He hit the power button for the flashlight and slipped the end between his teeth to get a better accounting of what was left. Bingo. The first aid kit. He didn't bother with cleaning the wound in his side this time around, drying the edges with one of her shirts and slapping a new section of gauze to hold him together. He could hear Sayles's criticism in the back of his head now. How she'd argue he was doing more harm than good in leaving the hole to fester. How he'd regret it and probably turn into a brain-craving zombie, but for now, it would be enough to get him to her.

He couldn't control a groan as he got to his feet. Elias braced himself against the mountain's wall, holding his side to keep the new gauze in place. Dirt shifted beneath his boots, and that damn blister between his thighs burned. His vision played tricks on him as stars began peppering the velvet night sky. There one second and gone the next. Or maybe he'd finally started losing his mind. Hard to tell when stranded out in the middle of desert, his drinking water had run out and he'd been surviving off adrenaline fumes for two days straight. "Keep it together, man."

The pep talk didn't hit as hard as he'd intended, but he pushed upward, legs protesting the slightest shift in his balance. Hard-to-see claws caught on his jeans and tore at his exposed arms. Stinging pain ripped at the side of his thigh. Damn cactus. The mountainside had gone from vivid red rock stained with water damage to nothing but a black landscape determined to tear him apart. The moon had yet to make an appearance in the east while the sun had already given up the ghost. He was in the dark. Thoroughly and completely surrounded by nothing but the unknown.

Except he knew Sayles was there. Waiting for him. Pulling him in, and he wouldn't fail her. Not as he'd failed the last innocent life entrusted to him. Trees rustled on either side of him, as if disturbed by something he couldn't see. The ground flattened out under his feet, and his lungs eased up on trying to kill him. Elias nearly fell to his knees as gravity lessened its mission to pull him back down the mountain.

The black hole staring back at him wasn't large by any means. At least nothing compared to the massive echoing caverns he'd explored as a kid. No. This cave hadn't wanted to be discovered, hidden back away from prying eyes, and he couldn't help but shiver at all the possibilities waiting inside. This. This was where Sayles would've taken cover if she'd managed to escape the Hitchhiker Killer. To buy herself enough time before going for help. Or fighting back.

No signs of life or death. Just a stillness that crept into Elias's bones and waited for him to make the next move. He scanned the stretch of black emptiness behind him, light outlines of mountains and deep valleys bleeding into his vision. Then stepped over the threshold of the cave.

The ceiling dipped down, scratching against his scalp. At over six feet, he had to watch his head. The walls themselves pressed in on him from every angle but led him deeper into the belly of the mountain. His footsteps and skids echoed around him, announcing his presence to anyone inside. Silence—deadly and expansive—took up residence in his head. He arced the flashlight beam toward his feet, careful of every step, with his free hand sliding against rough stone wall caked in dust. "Not creepy at all."

But he'd endure a thousand caves just like this if it meant finding Sayles at the end. He didn't know how they would make it work with him assigned out of Vegas and over state lines, but whatever happened in this park wouldn't be the end of them. Not as long as he had any say about it. He'd been an idiot to think he could come out here and fix his career—to pretend that working cases harder would make him happy, that it could fix the fact that he hadn't caught his father's killers—when all he really needed was a heavy dose of prickly national park ranger to set him straight. She hadn't meant to do it. He knew that. Neither of them had meant for any of this, but that didn't mean they got to turn their backs on it, either. Walk away as though they hadn't been altered on a cellular level just by being in the same proximity as each other. No. Elias had already lost too much. He wasn't going to lose Sayles, too.

She'd hate that he'd called her prickly, and he couldn't wait to test out his theory.

Elias navigated farther into the mountain. Then heard a voice. No. A whimper.

His rib cage suctioned tighter around his organs. He picked up the pace, pressing his back into the curve of wall ahead. Just beyond a pool of flashlight highlighting his park ranger. She'd taken a defensive stance in front of another woman he didn't recognize. He didn't have a weapon. He had nothing on his side but years of fieldwork and training burning to be let free at the sight of those women at the hands of a cold-blooded killer. And he'd make every move count. Elias slipped around the corner, closing the distance between him and the Hitchhiker Killer as quietly as possible.

"There's nowhere you can run that I won't find you." Raising his arm, the killer brandished the gun. Taking aim directly at Sayles's chest. "And you've both tested my patience beyond my usual limits."

Sayles shifted her weight between both feet, keeping the killer's attention locked on her and away from the sobbing woman clinging at her back.

The killer took a single step forward. "We always knew it would end like this, Ranger Green. Thank you for your help in locating my wife. I couldn't have done it without you."

Elias clenched the flashlight under his knuckles. "I think it's safe to say she quits."

Chapter Twenty-Seven

She was either going to have a heart attack or faint.

Sayles couldn't decide.

That voice. She knew that voice. The gravelly undertones urged her to breathe while delivering warning straight to her gut. Elias. He was alive, but she couldn't discern his condition as the federal agent who'd single-handedly upturned her life lunged.

Mae's fingernails dug into her arms a split second before the impact.

Elias collided with the Hitchhiker Killer. Flashlight beams scattered across the cave walls and blinded her. White lights danced across her vision. She pressed Mae into the dead end they'd reached a few minutes before, completely powerless as the sound of fists and groans and pain ricocheted around them.

"Sayles, go!"

Elias's command shoved her into action. She grabbed for the woman at her back, boot slipping across the cave floor.

Her escape instantly cut off by the killer. "You're not going anywhere." A flashlight beam launched directly for her, but it was Patrick's fist that slammed into her chest.

The impact crushed precious oxygen from her lungs,

and she collapsed back into Mae's arms. Sputtering coughs were all she could manage. She kicked against the floor to straighten her torso, to make it possible to breathe, but it was as though she'd gone into spasm. Her body didn't know what to do, how to get that next breath. Sayles grabbed for her throat, heart rate so high in the rafters she feared it would never come down.

Mae's sobs filled her ears.

And she was finally able to take a breath.

Elias's strike to the killer's throat turned the bastard's attention off her. The brutality of his attacks—precise and controlled in perfect sync—told of experience far beyond anything she'd ever seen. And gave her a glimpse of the violence that could've turned on her at any point during her marriage.

She scrambled onto all fours, still out of breath but able to move. "We have to get out of here. We have to go. Now."

"How?" Mae interlaced her hand with Sayles's. Desperation filtered in through the tight grip capable of blocking blood flow to her fingers. "They're blocking our escape."

She was right. And despite Elias's combat expertise, the Hitchhiker Killer was holding his own. Taking and delivering blows that would surely wear Elias down within minutes. He'd survived a fall from 1,000 feet. There was no telling what internal injuries he'd already sustained or if the next hit would kill him. She couldn't leave him here, but she couldn't ask Mae to stay. Her ex-husband had come for her, killed six people to find her and wouldn't hesitate to make her the seventh if she ran again. He'd never stop coming for her. Never stop hunting her.

"Run!" Elias struck with his left fist, then the right, grabbing the killer's wrist. He yanked the joint hard enough the cave filled with a pop and quickly launched his opposite hand into his opponent's chest.

The Hitchhiker Killer stumbled back. Rubbed at his chest as though he'd merely been inconvenienced. "No, Sayles. Stay. You know what happens if you run. What I'll do to you once I've finished off Agent Broyles. What I'll do to my darling Mae."

A whimper from behind chilled the blood in Sayles's veins. This. This was what she'd been afraid of all these months. Knowing her ex was still out there, wanting to hurt her, to make her pay for having the courage to leave. She'd broken his rules, after all, thought of herself for once and summoned the will to leave, and the possibility of him finding her had kept her in a permanent state of paranoia since. Numbness that'd taken months to shed infiltrated her nervous system and held her paralyzed. One breath. Two. Any minute now she'd lose all control, and there would be nothing she could do.

"Sayles!" Elias's demand barely reached through the white noise of blood rushing into her ears. The flashlight in his hand flickered as if traumatized by the violence, like the new light inside her chest. A light that a cocky, relentless, merciless federal agent had lit over the past two days. "Sayles, you can do this! Fight!"

Fight. Hadn't that been what she'd been doing for so long? Fighting to cope with the viciousness of a man who'd sworn to love her until death. Fighting for her life after her arrest for a murder she hadn't committed. Fighting to make it one day to the next while behind bars when it felt like the entire world had turned against her. Fighting. She was so…tired of fighting.

But that didn't make the war disappear.

And for the first time since she'd come to Zion, she

wasn't alone. Clarity sharpened as Elias clutched the flashlight and shot his fist into the killer's face. He'd been rooting for her the moment they'd been thrust together on this assignment. Empowering her to trust herself, to break free of the self-inflicted weight she insisted on carrying these past few months. Showing her what real power looked like.

And she could do the same for other womn who'd been in her position.

Mae had been living through hell. So thoroughly tortured without the man ever needing to lay a hand on her. But she and Mae could rewrite the narrative. They could take that first step together. Sayles strengthened her hold on the woman's hand and maneuvered Mae behind her, acting as a shield as Elias had done for her. "Stay behind me. No matter what happens, don't let go of my hand."

She felt more than saw Mae's agreement.

Her partner took the opportunity to lunge. He threw what looked like everything he had into rocketing his fist into the killer's face but missed. Bringing his elbow up, he blocked the next assault, but the one after landed its mark. Elias stumbled back into the wall, unable to get his balance as the Hitchhiker Killer attacked.

Now, Sayles kept to the wall, dragging Mae behind her. The killer's flashlight rolled closer as he and Elias battled for dominance with gut-wrenching violence, but the Hitchhiker Killer's attention remained solely on survival. On winning. That was the kind of man he was. The kind that needed to control, to dominate and come out on top, but Sayles wouldn't give up little pieces of herself to avoid the consequences of that rage anymore. She'd face them head-on and help Mae do the same by getting them out of this cave.

The killer pinned Elias against the far wall, both hands

around his neck. Her partner rained hits down on to the bastard's forearms, but the Hitchhiker Killer refused to loosen his grip. Elias's face seemed to swell in the dim light of the flashlight rocking back and forth across the rock floor from the commotion. Pinched in a way that told her he wasn't getting any oxygen. He was dying right in front of her, forcing her to choose between saving Mae or saving him.

There wasn't a choice. There never had been when it came to Elias.

Sayles grabbed for the flashlight and shoved it into Mae's hand. "Go. Get out of here. Run east as fast as you can. Don't stop. There's a trail there that will take you down in the Narrows. Find somewhere to hide, out of sight. National park rangers will find you in the morning."

"What about you?" Terror etched into Mae's face. The thought of being alone—of dying alone—clearly scared her and she gripped onto Sayles's forearm.

"Get to the Narrows. You can do this. I promise. Go." Maneuvering Mae ahead of her, she nodded. "It's all going to be okay."

It was a promise she'd needed to hear in the middle of the storm. She couldn't force Mae to believe her, but someday she could look back and see the rainbow peeking through the clouds.

The woman didn't have to be told twice, her outline blending in with shadow and darkness as she ran for the cave's entrance. Hiking through the backcountry without supplies brought its own set of complications. In the dark held more dangers, but Mae was strong. She just didn't know it yet.

Strength drained from Elias's attempts to get free. The weak beam coming off his discarded flashlight revealed he'd lost enough consciousness his eyes had fallen closed.

She was already moving. Jumping. She secured her arms around the killer's neck and pulled as hard as she could to break his grip on Elias. They fell as one. Then came the pain. Her head snapped back against the unforgiving cave floor. Another round of bright lights exploded behind her eyes. Weight vanished from her front.

"You just don't know when to give up, do you, Ranger Green?" The Hitchhiker Killer stood above her. How he'd moved so quickly when she was still reeling from the impact, she had no idea. "I guess now is as good a time as any to punish you for coming between me and my wife."

Coughing punctured through the high-pitched ringing in her ears. Elias. Was he hurt? She couldn't afford to take her eyes off the man in front of her.

"That's one decision I will never regret." Sayles scrambled to her feet, unsteady but determined to buy Mae as much time as possible. She was out of her depth, facing off with a man who'd killed multiple people, some full-grown men, but she wouldn't budge. Not because of him. "And she's not your wife. Men like you believe you're owed everything you set your sights on. I'm proof that we're strong enough to fight back."

She didn't give him the chance to respond, throwing her fist directly at his face.

He stepped out of her path, and her momentum carried her forward. Too far. Too close. Sayles braced for the attack, but it never came. Adjusting to put him front and center and block his path to the cave's entrance, she swung again. And missed. That crazed smile that didn't quite show his teeth and deepened the cracks around his eyes triggered a chill in her bones. He was toying with her. Making her believe she had a chance only to pull the rug out from underneath her when he got too impatient. A mouse trapped beneath a cat's paw.

"I must say, Ranger Green, I'm quite disappointed. Surely, NPS trained you better than to provoke a predator." The Hitchhiker Killer hauled his foot into her chest.

She was flying, her legs swinging out from under her. Slamming into the cold floor. Sayles rolled onto her side. Pain radiated from her shoulder to her hip and across her torso as she sucked in a shallow breath. It was all she could manage.

The second kick emptied her lungs and cracked something vital.

Her scream drilled through her head. The barest hint of moonlight filtered through the darkness ahead. The entrance. Escape. To lead the killer away from Elias. To put herself between him and Mae. She owed it to them both. Every cell in her body screamed for her to move, but all she could do was push off with her toes. Gaining nothing but a few inches of distance at a time. She felt more than saw the killer's presence at her back. Watching her suffer, enjoying the power it gave him.

"You can't protect her. No matter where she runs, I'll find her. I wasn't lying about the tracker in her mouth. Though now I suppose she'll try to have it removed." Weight stacked on top of her calf, halting her in place. "In the end, she'll still belong to me, and I will kill any man who dares put his hands on what's mine before I take it out on her."

Sayles had heard it all before—lived it. He wasn't anything special, but someone somewhere had taught him he didn't have to work for the things he wanted. Taught him he was owed. "Are you finished with your villain speech? I was promised turkey when this case was over, and I've got to tell you, I'm starving."

The third kick hiked her off the floor and upturned her entire world. Gravity shifted from the center of her body to the edges as the ground ripped out from underneath her. Needles of pain clawed across the exposed skin of her face and arms. She was in free fall, out of control and moving too fast to stop down the mountain face. Three times. Four. Her spine curved around a boulder, a cry spilling into the night.

The killer's outline crossed the path of moonlight staring down on her. This park had saved her life. She should've known it would require something in return. Sayles struggled to breathe around the jagged pain in her rib cage. "It's over, Ranger Green. Look at you. You can't save anyone. You can't even save yourself."

But she had. With Elias's help.

A second outline cleared through the shimmer of disorientation. Or was she seeing double? Movement slashed over the Hitchhiker Killer's shoulder. He jerked in place. Then dropped to his knees and onto his face. Elias tossed a rock at his feet, kneeling beside her to scoop her against his chest. "That guy talks too much."

Chapter Twenty-Eight

"Ow." The park medic prodded at the contusion bubbling from Elias's forehead with a little too much force. He tried to jerk back but didn't get far. The back of his head hit the ambulance door and triggered a whole new headache.

"Hold still or I'll sedate you, Agent Broyles." Okay. There was a witch underneath the expertly done makeup, platinum-blond hair and gum snapping. Ranger Barbie was actually a sadist. His investigative skills had failed him.

The first morning rays of a new day made him sick to his stomach. Then again, that could be the fact that he hadn't eaten anything substantial in three days, fought a killer determined to gut him and fallen from 1,000 feet off the side of a cliff. But what did he know? He narrowed his gaze on the ranger setting a butterfly bandage across his forehead. Honestly, he hadn't even known he'd hit his head while fighting the Hitchhiker Killer. At least, not until Sayles had winced looking at his face. "You're not as nice as you look."

"I get that a lot." Another snap of her gum. She set piercing blue eyes made for magazine covers on him with a slow spread of her lips. Demonic. That was the word that came to mind. "Comes in handy for one-night stands. They can't leave fast enough."

Shock caught in his throat. Elias had to swallow to keep himself from spitting all over her pressed uniform with laughter. "I'll warn whoever I can." At the moment, that included Grant, who'd interrupted Elias's physical exam twice now to ask Ranger Barbie about a mole on his back. Then his front.

Elias closed his eyes and set his head back against the ambulance bay door. He and Sayles had somehow dragged themselves back to Mae and Javier's tent after their face-off with the killer. The radio hidden inside had given them direct contact with Risner and search-and-rescue. Since the helicopter couldn't retrieve them at night, they'd had to settle in beside a dead man and wait until the sun crested the horizon in the east. Another team had been sent up the Narrows to retrieve Mae, who was currently wrapped in a solar blanket on one of the park benches with an oxygen mask strapped over her face. Alive. Traumatized, but alive. She and Javier had been on their honeymoon. Married just two months ago, they'd chosen to take a road trip across the country to start their new life off with adventure. Right around the time bodies had started turning up on the interstate.

The Hitchhiker Killer, identified as Patrick Corrl—yes, he'd actually given Sayles his real name—had been airlifted in a basket. And right into a body bag. Now that the case was concluded, each of the victims would be returned to their families for burial or cremation, including Javier and the hiker murdered at the base of the Narrows.

"You're good to go. Keep it clean and dry, and there will be minimal scarring." Ranger Barbie shucked the bright pink latex gloves she'd donned to examine and treat his injuries and tossed them into the biohazardous waste bin in the rig. "You know, I think my mom said the same thing about the first time I had sex. She wasn't wrong."

"Thank you for that visual, Ranger Jordan." Elias shoved to stand. Mistake. He'd made a mistake. His bones hurt. Was that possible? Hell, how they'd managed to escape with nothing more than a few bruises and cuts—well, apart from his broken nose and Sayles's cracked ribs—he didn't know. Some X-rays were in order.

"I can go all night." Was every word out of Ranger Barbie's mouth meant to be sexual?

Elias wasn't interested in finding out and left her to pack her supplies. There was only one woman on his mind. Searching the parking lot, he headed for the visitors' center. Away from the chaos of Risner giving the media snippets of the harrowing assignment his department had taken on, Grant's incessant attempt to get Ranger Barbie's attention and law enforcement rangers begging to confirm his statement for the fourth time. The tug he'd experienced while racing to find Sayles led him through the visitors' center's tinted glass doors and toward the theater seating set up for hikers heading out of the trails.

The exact location he'd first set eyes on her.

That intense green gaze snapped to him as he approached. He couldn't shut down the flinch as he took in the bruising across her face and a matching butterfly bandage on her chin. Taking a seat next to her on the bench, Elias fought against the pain in his torso. New dressings pulled at the skin across his side and along his inner thigh, but he'd yet to change into a fresh set of clothes. "To think just a few days ago you were trying to get out of this assignment. Look how far we've come."

"I'm still debating if I made the right choice." Sayles set her head against his shoulder, and the ricocheting pain vanished with her warmth. They stared at the dark theater screen, almost closed off from the rest of the world in this small corner of the building. "You owe me a turkey."

He couldn't contain his laugh. "I remember." And he had every intention of following through.

"How is she?" Sayles didn't have to specify who she meant. He could see Mae through the front doors from their position.

"Alive thanks to you." Angling his nose against her scalp, he kissed the top of her head. Not daring to pull away. Not wanting to be apart from her for a second longer. Neither of them had slept during the night—too keyed up, too desperate to prove they'd survived. He'd held her, but his brain still wasn't convinced this wasn't just some part of a nightmare he couldn't wake up from. "No one else with your past would've done what you did, putting yourself between her and her abuser. You saved her life."

"Did I?" The words were almost too soft for him to pick up, and if he hadn't been totally and completely tuned into every minor shift in this woman, he might've missed it. "Because from where I'm sitting, she's leaving this place a lot more traumatized than when she arrived. Not only did her ex try to kill her. but her new husband is dead. Shot right in front of her."

"You saved her life, Sayles. You gave her the gift of slaying her demons and moving on, of never having to look over her shoulder again." Securing his arm around her back, he hauled her against him. Putting them flush against each other shoulder to hip. Right where she belonged. "How many women in her position can say that? You made that happen. She owes you her life."

"She doesn't owe me anything. She's free. That's all I ever wanted for her. And for me." She straightened, notching her chin higher to look him dead in the eye. "And I got it. Thanks to you."

He didn't understand. "What do you mean?"

"These past few days, I was so determined to hate you. Not you specifically, but what you represented. I'd convinced myself all federal agents had to be like my ex-husband because why else wouldn't have anyone seen what was going on in my marriage? Why wouldn't they have said something unless there was this unspoken code to always have another agent's back?" Shrugging, she relaxed into him further. "I made you the enemy, and I'm sorry. When you asked what our future held, I got scared. I was afraid if I gave you a chance to show me that you weren't anything like him, I would be handing over my freedom to live life how I wanted all over again. I never meant for you to feel you weren't enough like I was made to feel, and I hate that your heart was the casualty. But more, I hated the fact that I didn't hate you. In a way, I was holding myself prisoner. You showed me how to free myself."

His heart shuddered in his very sore chest. "Does that mean you like me?"

"I'm saving my conclusions until after our first date." Slipping her palm against his chest, she smacked him lightly. That breathtaking smile lit up her whole face. "No, Agent Broyles, it means I'm falling for you. Of course, I didn't realize it until you went over the side of a cliff, and by then it was too late to tell you."

"Good thing I'm a lot harder to kill than I look." Elias tilted her head back with an index finger under her chin and pressed his mouth to hers. He kissed her until his mouth was swollen and his body tingled. Until every second of fear and desperation leaked from his nervous system and dissipated between them. "Will it make you feel better for almost letting me die without knowing how you felt if I tell you I'm falling for you, too?"

"Maybe." She traced a finger along his jaw, prickling the scruff on his face. Three days without shaving or a shower, but she didn't seem to mind. "But will you be taking those feelings back with you to Las Vegas now that the case is closed?"

Silence settled between them. Just for a moment as he considered the risk in admitting this thing between them had somehow grown to overshadow anything else in his life. "After I told you about my dad's death, you said it sounded as though I'd accepted my fate and that there was nothing I could do to change it. You weren't wrong. I've spent so long trying to live up to his legacy, to prove I could be good enough to catch the people who killed him, that it gradually became everything I am, and I let it. But I don't want that anymore."

Sayles pulled away. Not out of reach—because he wasn't sure either of them could handle that after everything they'd been through—but to get a better look at him. "What are you saying?"

"I'm saying…" He took a deep breath. Took the leap. "I'm saying I don't want my career to be all I am anymore. I want more out of life, and I want you in it. As much as possible. If that means quitting the FBI and signing on with Springdale's police department, I will. Because you're worth it."

Her mouth parted on a soft exhale. "Okay."

"Okay?" His laugh vibrated through him, and he rocked back in his seat, taking her with him. "I spill my guts, almost literally after losing that fight with a damn twig, and all you have to say is okay?"

"Am I supposed to put up more of a fight?" She smoothed

her fingers along the collar of his T-shirt with an answering smile of her own. "The truth is, I was thinking of making some changes, too."

Damn, he couldn't get enough of this woman. Would never let her go. "What kind of changes?"

"The moving on kind." She traced the length of his throat with one finger, and her smile slipped. "I can't forget what my ex did to me, but I think it's time to stop living in the past. To start making choices full of joy instead of fear. On my terms rather than out of a sense of survival."

Elias couldn't stop staring at this magnificent creature who'd been thrown in his path a mere three days ago. "Am I one of those choices?"

"That depends." Her smile was back in place, spreading slowly and revealing a playfulness he'd only glimpsed during their times in the Narrows. And, hell, he couldn't be more grateful she trusted him with the real her.

She had him hook, line and sinker. Or rather flash floods, death-defying falls and one-person tents. "On what?"

Her stomach growled, and Sayles kissed the corner of his mouth. "On how fast you can get me that turkey you promised."

* * * * *

DANGEROUS
AFFAIR

SANDRA OWENS

This book is dedicated to all the book lovers in the world. Y'all rock!

Prologue

"I have to go to work." Liam O'Rourke gave his new girl-friend a quick kiss as they stood on the school grounds after the final bell. He was going to be late, and his father wasn't going to be happy. When Patrick O'Rourke wasn't happy, no one was. Late to work at his father's Kansas City pub meant he was going to be put on dishwasher duty as punishment, the job he hated the most.

"You always have to work," Christina whined. "Can't you come with us just once?"

"I can't." She wasn't going to stay his girlfriend for long if he never got to spend time with her outside of school.

She and their group of friends were meeting up at Charlie's, their favorite after-school hangout. While he was buried up to his elbows in suds, they would be eating cheese fries, drinking milkshakes, and having a great time. Sometimes, he hated his father.

His senior year in high school should be all about having fun with his friends, having a girlfriend he could spend time with, and being a carefree kid. Instead, he was in training to learn all about the family business from the ground up so that someday he'd be qualified to take over Danny Boy's Irish Pubs International. Someday being in the far distant future because his father would have to be on his deathbed before he gave up control of his empire.

Liam left Christina and his friends and ran the one mile to work. It burned that he wasn't allowed the time to just be young. It also burned that as rich as his father was, he'd refused to give Liam a car so that he didn't have to run everywhere just to be on time when at his father's beck and call. A lot of the senior kids had cars, and Patrick O'Rourke could afford to buy Liam a fleet of them, but no…he couldn't even have one measly used car.

Resentment bubbled up in his chest as he raced for the pub. No matter what he might want to do with his life, the choice wasn't his to make. His resentment wasn't that, as the only child, he was being groomed to take over the business one day. He was good with that. He just wanted to be like his friends who were allowed to have fun the way teenagers were supposed to.

Two blocks from the pub, he glanced at his watch as he ran. He was only going to be five minutes late, but as far as his father was concerned, five minutes might as well be an hour. His backpack bounced against his spine as he picked up speed.

He was crossing the street at the last intersection before reaching the pub when a white van screeched to a halt in front of him, and unable to stop in time, he ran into the side of it. His head bounced against the van and, dazed, he stumbled back.

"Hey, watch where you're going," he yelled as white stars floated in front of his eyes. He rubbed his forehead, and already, a lump was forming. Great, he was going to have a big fat egg right between his eyes.

The side door of the van slid open, and before he could comprehend what was happening, he was yanked inside.

He was pushed face down on the floor, and a knit cap was pulled over his head and halfway down his face, covering his eyes. He'd been stunned, unable to comprehend what was happening, but when he realized someone was binding his hands behind his back with a plastic tie, the first wave of panic hit. He struggled to get his arms and hands away before they could be bound, making him helpless.

Something small, round, and cold was pressed into his cheek. "That's a gun, Mr. O'Rourke," a man with a gravelly smoker's voice said. "Unless you want to die right here, you'll stop fighting us."

Us? How many were there? Had anyone seen them abduct him? Was someone calling the police right now to report a kidnapping? He hadn't noticed anyone around, but he hadn't really been paying attention to his surroundings as he ran. His father was going to be so pissed when Liam didn't show up for work.

The van hit a bump in the road, and the rough metal of the floor scraped his chin and the tip of his nose. That hurt. Through the fear pounding in his chest, he tried to focus on the van's direction, but he didn't have a clue. He needed to calm the hell down and think.

Wait… They'd called him O'Rourke. They knew his name? This wasn't a random kidnapping. He'd been targeted. Was that a good thing or a bad thing? Danny Boy's Irish Pubs International was worldwide, consisting of over five hundred pubs. His father was a millionaire many times over, and that wasn't a secret. Was this a kidnapping for ransom? If so, that was good, right? They'd need him alive to collect any money.

"What are you going to do with me?"

Someone kicked his thigh. "Shut up."

"Ow." The plastic tie was too tight, making the tips of

his fingers tingle, but he didn't want to get kicked again, so he kept quiet.

He lost track of time as the engine droned on, and even though he was frightened out of his mind, he dozed off. He didn't know how long they traveled, but it had to be two or three days, and he mostly slept the miles away.

He never had a chance to escape because they never let him leave the van. The knit cap was kept over his eyes, and he was good with that. If he never saw his captors' faces, they'd have no reason to kill him.

The plastic ties had only been removed long enough for him to go to the bathroom in a bucket and to let him eat the hamburgers they'd gotten for him at fast-food drive-throughs as they traveled.

"If you try to yell or call for help, we'll shoot the worker," one of the men said the first time they got food.

Since that was something he couldn't live with on his conscience, he kept quiet.

Where were they taking him? Sometimes he heard the low murmur of voices from the front of the van, but he could never make out what they were saying. He thought there were only two men, but there could be three. If he tried to talk, he got kicked, so he stopped asking questions. On what was the second or third day, the van stopped, and he was roughly dragged out. Standing for the first time after so many hours of lying face down on the floor, his legs buckled when he tried to stand on them.

Rough hands grabbed his arms on both sides, and he stumbled along between two men as they dragged him into what he thought was a house because a door slammed behind them. After walking for a minute, he was pushed down onto a hard floor. It felt like wood under his face. The ties were cut off his wrists, and then he heard receding footsteps and a door closing. Afraid to move, he lay there for… he didn't know how long. He'd lost all sense of time.

He was hungry, his body was sore all over, and he was scared out of his mind. He'd give anything to be at his dad's pub washing dishes. If he ever got out of this, he'd never complain again.

His family would know by now that he was missing and would be searching for him. Would they even know where to look? He had no idea which direction they'd traveled, but he did know he was far from Kansas City. He tried not to cry, but tears welled up and spilled down his cheeks. He wanted to go home.

Suck it up, O'Rourke. Crying wasn't going to get him out of this, and he needed to figure out a way to escape. At least they'd untied his hands. It felt like he was alone, and he tentatively pushed the knit cap up, uncovering his eyes. When a kick to his body didn't come, he sat up.

The room was dark, and he crawled until he found a wall. On still shaky legs, he stood, leaned against the wall, and waited until his legs agreed to do their job of keeping him on his feet. Once he was steady, he circled the room, trailing his hands at the height that light switches were usually located.

He came to the door and tried the knob, unsurprised to find it locked. Switches were usually near the door, so he searched to the side of it. "Yes," he exclaimed when he found it, and a light came on. It was nothing more than a single light bulb hanging by a cord from the ceiling, but he could see.

There was nothing to see.

Other than a bucket in the corner, the room was empty. No bed, no chair, no blanket or pillow. Nothing, nothing,

nothing. The windows had thick boards nailed over them. How was he supposed to escape?

Fear and helplessness washed over him, and he slid down the wall. He cried, and he hated himself for being weak. He wanted to go home.

"Oomph!"

Liam startled awake when the silence of the room was broken. He'd left the light on, and he blinked to clear his eyes, doubting what he was seeing. A boy his age was sprawled on the floor, and another boy, also his age, was standing, glaring at the closed door.

"Am I dreaming?" He had no idea what day it was, how long he'd been asleep, or if he was even awake now. Maybe he was hallucinating.

The standing boy tore his attention from the door to Liam. "Who are you?"

"Liam." He pinched himself as he got to his feet. Okay, that hurt, so not dreaming. "Did they kidnap you, too?"

"Yeah, me and Cooper. I'm Grayson. Do you know who they are and what they plan?"

"I don't know. Where are we?"

"South Florida. It's spring break here."

"No shit? Florida?" He'd always wanted to go to spring break in Florida, but willingly. Not as a kidnap victim.

"Yeah," Grayson said. "You didn't know that?"

"They took me in Kansas City, where I'm from. I've been blindfolded and in the back of a van for two or three days."

Grayson frowned. "This all seems really odd. Why take you from Kansas and me from Florida. What's the connection?"

"Yeah, weird."

"They knew my name," Grayson said.

"They did mine, too. What do you think that means?"

Grayson shrugged. "Who knows, but I'm hoping it means that they kidnapped us for ransom. Is your father rich?"

"Very. Yours?"

"Same."

He studied the other boy. His clothes didn't seem to be as expensive as Liam's and Grayson's. Maybe he was from a rich family, too, and was just slumming? Cooper caught him staring, and Liam jerked his gaze away.

"He wasn't targeted," Grayson said. "He was with me when they took me, and they grabbed him, too. They didn't know who he was." He tapped Cooper's foot with his own. "Sorry for that."

"Not your fault." Cooper rolled over and sat up.

"Is your family rich?" Liam asked.

Cooper laughed as if that was the funniest thing in the world. "We don't even know what money looks like."

He and Grayson glanced at each other, and even though they'd just met, they both understood the message passed between them. If this was to get ransom from their rich families, what did that mean for Cooper if his family couldn't pay?

That was the moment Liam was more worried about someone other than himself. Somehow, he was going to get out of this and take his new friends with him.

Chapter One

"I got one for you," Cooper Devlin said.

Grayson Montana groaned. "Not another dad joke. I beg you."

"You might as well try to stop the tide," Liam said to his friend as they sat on the deck of Grayson's beach house. Cooper had an entire book of dad jokes in his head.

"What do you call a fake noodle?" Cooper grinned when no answer was forthcoming. "An impasta."

"Don't encourage him," Grayson said when Liam chuckled, but there was amusement in his eyes.

"Sorry, that laugh slipped out. Won't happen again."

Cooper clutched his chest. "Bro, you wound me. You love my dad jokes. Admit it."

What he loved were these two men. Getting kidnapped sucked, but he wouldn't change a thing. An act of violence had brought these men he considered his brothers into his life. Didn't matter they weren't of his blood, they were his family.

The three of them had started The Phoenix Three because of being kidnapped when they were teens. They'd bonded during their time in captivity and had become the best of friends. After graduating high school, each of them had enlisted in the military to learn the skills necessary to plan and complete missions.

The Phoenix Three's purpose was to save children who'd been kidnapped like they had been, to find runaway children and get them help before the streets ate them up, even to save children from the very people who were supposed to love and protect them. Really, just to save children whenever and wherever they could. It was a mission they each had dedicated their lives to and fervently believed in.

They'd dreamed up the idea of doing this work when they'd been young and idealistic…and very naive. But they'd made it happen, and Liam felt a sense of completion and satisfaction that he never would have achieved working for his father.

When he'd told his father he was enlisting in the Marines, they'd had a fierce argument, his father refusing to understand why Liam needed to do that. What his father didn't understand was that the kidnapping had changed Liam.

If there had been another son to groom for the business, maybe his father wouldn't have disowned him. He'd never know. How things had gone down between them was a hurt Liam kept buried and tried not to think about.

Tyler, the son of Grayson's fiancée, raced out the door with the energy only a five-year-old possessed. "I'm here! Let's go surfing."

Liam chuckled. The kid already had on his wet suit. Grayson had said Tyler took to surfing as if he'd been born on a surfboard.

"Do you have any homework you need to do first?" Grayson asked.

"Mama said I could do it after we surf."

"All right then. Let me put on my wet suit." Grayson eyed the ocean. "The waves are good today."

Five minutes later, man and boy were walking across the sand, Tyler's surfboard half the size of Grayson's. Of the three of them, Grayson had the best role model for a father, no doubt why he'd fallen into the role as a father to Tyler so easily.

"Grayson told me that Harlow's ex has been writing her, demanding she bring Tyler to see him," Cooper said.

"That bastard might as well wish for the moon to fall in his lap."

Cooper grunted his agreement.

Tyler's no-good father was in prison for murder. He didn't give two figs for his son. He was just trying to manipulate Harlow. Harlow had hired The Phoenix Three to help her get her son back. They had, and Grayson and Harlow had fallen in love.

It was a warm summer day, but there was a nice sea breeze and big fluffy white clouds floated by, blocking the sun about the time it started to feel too hot. Liam hadn't slept much the past few days, and his eyes slid closed.

"They're coming in."

He blinked awake and focused his gaze on Cooper. "What?"

"They've been surfing for an hour, and now they're coming in. Enjoy your nap?"

Actually, he had. He shifted his gaze to the ocean. Grayson rode the small wave next to the boy he planned to adopt. The two of them grinned at each other as they hit shallow water and hopped off their boards. Grayson held up his hand and they high-fived.

His friend lived on the beach, had found a wonderful woman, and had fallen in love with her and her son. His life was about perfect. Liam was happy for Grayson, and although he tried not to be envious, he was. He hadn't let himself be serious about a woman while he was in the military. As a Special Ops Marine Raider, he'd lived a dangerous life and was gone more than he was home. That wasn't conducive to having a relationship. Now that he was out of the military, he was ready to settle down and find his own happiness.

The dating scene—going out to clubs, one-night stands, and meeting women who were just out to have fun—wasn't his thing. Also, and surprisingly, he wanted kids, something he'd started thinking about after seeing how much Grayson enjoyed being around Tyler.

"Are they finally coming in?" Harlow said, joining them on the deck. She carried a bucket of beers on ice that she set on the table.

"Looks like." Liam grabbed a bottle and twisted off the cap. "I think they're going to turn into fish as much time as they spend in the ocean."

"But such cute fishies," Harlow said. She smiled fondly at the man and boy as they walked across the sand, carrying their boards.

Liam grinned. "Well, the little one, anyway."

"Yeah, the word *cute* just doesn't cut it with the big one," Cooper said.

"Hush, both of you. My boys are the cutest things ever." Harlow moved the beer bucket to the other side of the table, away from them. "No more beer for either of you until you take it back."

"Do I need to kill them for you, love?" Grayson said as he joined them on the deck.

Tyler raced up the stairs behind him. "Please don't kill them, Dad. I like Liam and Cooper."

"Hey, I was just kidding, okay?" He put his hand on top of Tyler's head. "Why don't you go change out of your wet suit?" After he ran inside, Grayson gave Harlow an embarrassed smile. "I need to remember that kids take things literally."

"Like when he asked what the brown things in his soup were and you told him monkey toes?" Harlow said. "He'll never eat cream of mushroom soup again."

A snort escaped from Liam. Although she was going for stern, he picked up on the amusement in her voice.

Grayson grimaced. "Uh…sorry?"

"Bro," Cooper said. "You gotta work on your jokes."

"Wait. Back up a minute." Liam pointed his bottle at Grayson. "Tyler calls you Dad?" That was big.

"Yeah. Started that a few days ago. Said he needs to practice getting used to it for when his mommy marries me. Kid owns my heart, man." He and Harlow shared an intimate smile.

That. That right there was what he wanted. A family of his own. A woman who looked at him like that. He just needed to find her.

Chapter Two

Quinn Sullivan hurriedly packed her suitcase. She wanted to be gone before Jasper returned. What she thought of as a temporary fling while they were both in California covering the wildfires differed from Jasper's growing possessiveness. When they'd first hooked up, he was fun, but now, if she even said hello to another man, he would get jealous and mentally abusive. That was shit she didn't put up with.

This morning he'd hurled insults at her after she'd told him she planned to leave soon. According to him, she was a cold bitch and only cared about herself.

"You'll leave with me, and I'm not ready yet," he'd said. He'd sneered at her then. "What's the big deal? There's no place important you need to be. You just take pictures of kids, no big deal."

Jasper hadn't been the first man to tell her that her work wasn't important, and that her priority should be him. He had no idea how much of a trigger hearing him say that was. She'd told him she was leaving, and he didn't want to hear her, so she wasn't waiting around to have another fight with him.

He was a photojournalist embedded with a team of hotshots, and she was covering the devastation left in the wake of the fires, especially the children who'd lost their homes. Also a photojournalist, children were her forte.

She'd documented the horrors of war on children, the gaunt faces of hungry children in Africa, the fragile bodies of abused children living on the streets of cities around the world. Wherever children were suffering, she went. Her hope was that her photos would make a difference in the lives of those lost souls. That people seeing them would feel compelled to reach out a helping hand however they could.

When Jasper had asked her to stay with him in the house he was renting, she'd first refused. She was a nomad and didn't do relationships. He'd convinced her that he didn't either, and when it was time to leave—a few weeks at the most—they'd go their separate ways. The icing on the cake, though, was the money she'd be saving on a hotel room. She should have listened to that little voice telling her staying with him was a mistake.

She carried her suitcase into the second bedroom. Jasper never went in there, so if he did come back before she could leave, he wouldn't see it. Her cameras and accessories were her life and needed to be packed carefully to prevent damage while traveling. Some of her accessories were on the dining room table along with Jasper's. She was almost finished packing everything up when she heard Jasper's car arrive. Panicked, she grabbed her thumb drives and stuffed them in her camera bag.

Her rental car was parked out front, so he would know she was here. She ran to the spare bedroom, put the bag in with her suitcase, then left the room, closing the door behind her. The last thing she wanted to do was talk to him right then, and the only thing she could think to do was take a shower. He never bothered her when she was in the bathroom.

She'd just locked herself in when she heard him come into the house. He was talking, and at first, she thought he'd brought someone home with him, but after a minute of listening, she realized he was on the phone. The bathroom door was thin plywood, and Jasper had a loud voice. She could hear his conversation.

"I told him I'd give him the photos for a million dollars," Jasper said.

Huh?

"Well, he's not happy, but what can he do? If he doesn't pay, I'll release the photos to the news outlets. See how he likes that. He sure as hell doesn't want the world to know kids are getting sick because of him."

Who wasn't happy, and why were children getting sick? She put her ear to the door to hear better.

"Yeah, it was pure luck that I stumbled on their dumping ground when I was in Hope Corner."

Dumping ground for what, and where was Hope Corner? He'd told her that he'd been in West Virginia before coming to California. Was that where it was?

"Million-dollar payday, dude."

Who was he talking to?

"No, just hang tight. I'll let you know when the meet is. I'll make sure it's in a public place where you can watch my back. Later, man."

Quinn took a second to panic that Jasper would be suspicious she'd heard the conversation. *Do something*, she screamed at herself. The shower! She hurried and turned it on. She had no intention of disrobing and getting in. If Jasper did suspect she heard him, she wasn't about to be naked if he forced his way into the bathroom.

"Quinn?" He knocked on the door.

"Oh, hey. You're back already? I'm in the shower. Be out in a few minutes." Or never.

"Walked out without my wallet. Why don't you put on something pretty tonight, and we'll go out to dinner."

"I'd love that." Not.

She left the shower running as she put her ear back to the door. After a good ten minutes of silence, she turned off the shower and ventured out. The relief that he wasn't tricking her and waiting for her to emerge was so great that she almost fell to her knees. But no time for that.

It was time to boogie.

QUINN WAS HOT, hungry, and tired. She'd been in Hope Corner for three days and had nothing to show for her efforts. She had found a lake and was working her way around it, looking for any sign of illegal dumping. She had also found a textile plant, a big one, but it wasn't on the lake. It was about a half mile from Black Bear Lake, and the plant would have barrels of dye and other chemicals, so it seemed possible it was the place Jasper was talking about.

She'd briefly stopped home to do some research after leaving California. Hope Corner was in the Appalachian Mountains in West Virginia. After deciding this had to be where Jasper was talking about, she'd made a reservation in a motel in the small town.

The people here were tight-lipped, and her inquiries about children getting sick were met with silence until this afternoon. A man who she wouldn't want to meet up with in a dark alley told her it was none of her business when she'd asked her questions and that she wasn't welcome in Hope Corner. She was getting a little scared to be here, but if Jasper was right, children were getting sick. What if they started dying? She couldn't turn her back on that.

The little that she'd learned while here was that the largest employer was the mill, Hanson Textiles, Inc. About 80 percent of the people in Hope Corner worked there. What she needed to do was go home and regroup. Take the time to research the mill, and if they were involved, how? Who owned it? What chemicals did they use and what illnesses would those chemicals cause? Then she'd call her friend Brett, a professor of environmental studies. Get his input on where to go with this.

First, she needed food, a shower, a glass of wine, and a good night's sleep. Oh, and she had to call her father. It was Wednesday. The deal she'd made with him when she'd told him at nineteen that she was going to be a photojournalist was that she'd call him every Wednesday and Sunday evening when she was traveling. Because she'd be traipsing the world, he needed to know she was safe. She hadn't missed one promised call.

Too tired and sweaty to eat at a restaurant, she went through a fast-food drive-through. Back at the motel, she grabbed her purse, her camera case, and the bag of food to take with her into the room. Food first, then a shower. After she ate and was clean and in her comfy clothes, she'd call her father, then pour a glass of wine from the bottle in her room to enjoy while she went through today's shots on her camera.

The motel still used actual keys to open the door. She should have thought to get it out while she was still in the car. With her camera bag strap over one shoulder and food in one hand, she fished around in her purse for the key with the other.

"There you are." She slid the key into the lock, and as she opened the door, something hit her from behind, pushing her into the room. "Umph." She tripped, and she dropped everything she was holding so she could put her hands down and catch herself to keep her face from hitting the floor.

Before she face-planted, an arm slid around her stomach and pulled her back against a body. "Hello, Quinn."

She stilled. "Jasper?" What the devil was he doing here? After leaving him in California, she'd hoped to never see him again.

"I came for you," he said, his breath hot on her neck.

"Let go of me." When she tried to step away from him, he tightened his hold.

"I don't think so. You left without a word. I have to wonder why."

She tried to elbow him in the stomach, and he only laughed. It never occurred to her that he'd follow her. Even more alarming, how did he know she'd be in Hope Corner? She pulled away from him again, and surprising her, he let go. She stumbled a few steps, her foot landing on the bag with the hamburger and fries she'd dropped, smashing them.

"Damn it. That was my dinner." She turned to face him and gasped at seeing him pointing a gun at her. "What the hell, Jasper? Put that thing away."

"This is how it's going to be. You're coming with me."

"I'm not going anywhere with you." He laughed, and the sound of it sent shivers snaking down her spine.

"You have a choice, darling. You come with me, or I shoot you." He picked up her camera bag. "All your equipment in here?"

"That I brought with me, yes. Why?"

"Let's go."

What was going on? This couldn't be because she'd left California without telling him. That wasn't a reason to threaten her with a gun. It had to be because, somehow, he'd found out she'd overheard his conversation. She glanced around the cheap motel room and decided it wasn't a place she was willing to die in. If she went with him, she could find a way to escape.

"I need my suitcase."

"No, you don't."

She looked into eyes that were flat and dead. Eyes that said he might just shoot her if she didn't do as he said. Her purse was at her feet, and she scooped it up. Her phone was in it, and somehow, she'd escape and call the police.

"You don't have to do this. We can talk here."

"Shut up." He pushed her toward the door. "You try anything when we walk out, and I'll shoot you and anyone you try to talk to."

When she left California early because he was raising all kinds of red flags, she'd instinctively known that he was a man who could be physically abusive. The kind of man who'd claim it was for her own good. What she hadn't anticipated was that he would hunt her down and threaten her with a gun.

As they walked out the door, he pressed the barrel of the gun against her hip. To anyone seeing them, it would just look like a couple checking out of their motel room. The one good thing was that she hadn't called her father yet, and when she missed her scheduled call, he would know something was wrong. Her father would move heaven and earth to find her.

"Remember what I said I'd do if you tried anything." He let go of her to open the back door of his car. After setting her camera bag on the back seat, he opened the driver's-side door. "Get in and slide over."

She glanced inside. "There's a console. Can't I just get in on the passenger side?"

"And have you try to run when I'm coming to this side to get in? Don't think so."

It was awkward, but she managed to climb over the console.

"Put your seat belt on," he said as he buckled his. "Can't have the cops stopping us because you're not belted."

Her mind was racing with a million thoughts, but there was one thing that was certain. She had to get away from him as soon as possible. As they drove through the dark, deserted mountain roads, she tried to come up with a plan. She could feel Jasper's eyes on her as he watched her every move. She had to be careful.

They drove for about an hour, and finally, they arrived at a secluded cabin in the woods. Jasper parked the car and got out. She opened her door and stepped out, her gaze stopping on the cabin. It was old and run-down, with weeds growing up around it.

He waved his gun toward the cabin. "Inside."

Should she make a run for it now? She glanced around. It was dark and the cabin was surrounded by forest. There were probably bears and mountain lions in those woods. And she didn't know where they were, so she had no idea which way to run. She'd be better off escaping when it was daylight.

She followed Jasper into the cabin. It was just as run-down on the inside as it was on the outside. It was clear that no one had lived in it for quite some time. It was small, with a living room, bedroom, and kitchen area combined. Next to the bed was a closed door, which she assumed was the bathroom.

The power must not be on because there were oil lamps scattered around. They were burning so that meant he'd already been in the cabin. "Who lives here?"

"No one." He motioned to the worn-out couch. "Sit."

A spider crawled up the wall behind the couch, and she shuddered. God only knew what all might be living in that couch. And she didn't even want to try to guess what the stains on the cushions were. "I think I'll stand."

"Suit yourself." He set his gun on the kitchen counter, went to the small table, and started removing the contents of her camera bag. When he got to the two thumb drives she'd brought with her, he stared at them and frowned.

"Leave my stuff alone." He knew better than anyone not to mess with a photographer's cameras.

He dropped the thumb drives as he faced her. "Where is it?"

"Where's what?" The rage in his eyes was scaring her. She eyed the gun. It was about halfway between them. Could she get to it before he did?

Thanks to her father, she knew how to shoot. It was one of the things he'd insisted she learn when he'd accepted that she was going to go after her dream and that meant she'd sometimes find herself in dangerous countries. She owned a gun, which unfortunately was in her gun safe at home. It hadn't occurred to her that she'd need it here. A mistake she wouldn't make again. From now on, wherever she went, her gun would go with her.

"Don't play games, Quinn. Where's my thumb drive?"

"Why would you think I'd have anything of yours?" Had she accidentally taken what he was looking for when she'd hurriedly packed up her camera bag? In her haste, she had scooped up several thumb drives that were on the table. During her brief stop at home, she'd sorted out her cameras and accessories and had only brought with her what she would need for a day or two of snooping. If she had his thumb drive, it was at home. Not something she was about to tell him.

"Because you're the only one who could have taken it." He glared at her. "If it's not here, I'll start shooting you in places that won't kill you but will hurt like hell until you tell me where it is."

"And here I thought you liked me." She didn't know where her bravado was coming from because she believed him. When he returned his attention to her camera bag, she took a deep breath. "I'm thirsty." The gun was her aim, not a glass of water. Just a few steps, and she would be closer to it than him.

As if he had eyes in the back of his head, he spun, going for the gun, too. Their hands reached it at the same time, and they wrestled for it. What she didn't see coming was his fist. It was hard to see anything when her world turned black.

Chapter Three

Liam answered the ringing phone. "The Phoenix Three. Liam O'Rourke speaking. How may I help you?"

"I need you to find my daughter," a man said, his voice urgent and tinged with fear.

"To whom am I speaking?"

"Robert Sullivan. My girl is missing. I was told that if anyone could find her, it was you people. I don't care what it costs, just find her for me."

"How old is she, and how long has she been missing, Mr. Sullivan?"

"Since at least yesterday, but the last time I talked to her was Sunday, so it could be since then. Something's wrong. She never misses our scheduled phone calls every Wednesday and Sunday."

Not a small child then. "And she's how old?"

"Twenty-eight. Quinn's a photojournalist. A damn good one, and she travels all over the world."

Liam frowned. "So, she's missing in a foreign country?" That was going to make it harder…if he accepted the case. The Phoenix Three's emphasis was on saving children, which Quinn Sullivan was not.

"I didn't say that. She's supposed to be in West Virginia."

More than likely, he would be wasting time on finding a woman who simply got busy and forgot to call her father. "Mr. Sullivan, I think you should give her a few more days to contact you, and if she doesn't, call the police. Our company focuses on finding missing children."

"She is a child, my damn child!"

Liam pulled the phone away from his ear. The man could shout. "Sir, I'm sorry, but—"

"Your father said you could find her."

Liam almost gasped. "My father?" That was not something he ever expected to hear. His father hadn't spoken to him in over ten years, not since the day Liam had told his dad that he had a higher purpose in life and was enlisting in the Marines. That was the day his father had disowned him. Said Liam was turning his back on family, on his inheritance.

"Yes, he gave me your name and number. Said if anyone could find her, it would be you. I don't care what it costs."

That his father even knew his phone number was shocking. "Has anyone been hassling her that you know of? An ex who might want to hurt her? Anything like that?"

"No, no one would want to hurt my Quinn, and she doesn't have a boyfriend."

That you know of. "Mr. Sullivan, send me everything you have on where your daughter is supposed to be, along with a photo of her and any other information you think will be helpful. Also, include her cell phone number. I'll find her for you." He gave the man his email address, then disconnected.

His father! Liam couldn't wrap his mind around that. The old man had disowned him, said he'd never utter Liam's name again. Yet, after ten years, he had, and apparently with praise. How was he supposed to feel about that?

It had taken years of not hearing from his father, but he'd finally accepted that his old man meant it when he said he no longer had a son.

Liam pulled open the bottom drawer of his desk. He stared at the folder for a moment before picking it up and setting it on his desktop. He hesitated before opening the folder and spreading out the contents.

His gaze roamed over the photos of his father and mother, the place that used to be his home. For the first time in what felt like forever, he let himself miss being a part of his family. He secretly talked to his mother once a month, but that only made him feel guilty because it meant that she had to lie to her husband. He picked up the photo of his father. What did it mean that he'd given Liam's name to Robert Sullivan? *Probably didn't mean a thing.* Liam closed the folder and slid it back into the drawer. He was dead to his father, and he wasn't going to wish for a change that would never happen.

A few minutes later, his computer dinged, signaling an incoming email. Mr. Sullivan hadn't wasted any time sending the information on his daughter. Included was a message saying that a deposit of ten thousand dollars would go in the mail tomorrow. Liam had been so gobsmacked by the mention of his father that he hadn't thought to discuss payment. He printed out the attachments then settled back to learn about the missing woman.

The first item he looked at was her photo, and it was the green eyes with laughter shining in them that caught his attention. She looked like a woman who would be fun to know. The most striking thing about her was her curly hair the color of copper. His gaze moved to her face. A phrase he'd heard somewhere came to mind. Peaches and cream perfectly described her complexion. Her smile was infectious, and he almost smiled back at the photo.

"Get a grip, O'Rourke," he muttered. She was a case, not a woman he needed to be lusting over. Even if there was something about her that had him wanting to meet her.

He set the photo aside and read her father's email. Quinn Sullivan wasn't just a photojournalist. She was an award-winning one. Her specialty was the children of the world. Her photos of children caught in the middle of war zones were heartbreaking.

There was a long list of links in the email, and by the time he reached the last one, he was impressed with not only her heart-wrenching photos posted online and in magazines and newspapers, but with the attention she brought to children who needed the world to save them. He had much in common with her.

Her father was adamant that his daughter wouldn't willingly miss their scheduled calls, and after reading about her and seeing through her lens the love she had for children, Liam believed that Quinn hadn't voluntarily gone radio silent. She wasn't a woman who'd worry her father like that.

According to her father, she was supposed to be in West Virginia, in a small Appalachian mountain town he'd never heard of. He did a search on Hope Corner and decided to drive, since there wasn't a flight out of Myrtle Beach until the following day. He could get there faster by driving, and that would give him the added benefit of being able to carry his weapons without having to declare them to the airline.

He called Grayson, got his voicemail, and left a message for his teammate to call him. Grayson was in town, searching for a fourteen-year-old boy who'd gotten in a fight with his father and had run away. Cooper was in Texas, tracking down a mother who'd kidnapped her two-year old daughter. He was on the woman's trail and should wrap the case up in a day or two, so Liam didn't call Cooper.

Next, he went to their weapons room, and after putting his palm against the reader to unlock the door, he went in. The three of them had a wide assortment of weapons, some they'd collected over their years in the military and some they'd bought after starting The Phoenix Three.

Not sure what he was walking into, he decided on two handguns and a long gun, along with plenty of ammo. He added a KA-BAR—his knife of choice—to his weapons, along with a handful of smoke grenades and night-vision goggles. Hopefully, he wouldn't need any of the items he was packing up, but it was always better to prepare for the worst.

On his way to his condo to pack, he stopped and topped off his gas tank. He was packing his duffel bag when Grayson returned his call.

"Hey, man," Liam said on answering. "Any luck finding the kid?"

"I got a tip that he's couch surfing among his friends. I'm sitting on a house that he's supposed to be sleeping at tonight."

"No doubt you're bored. Hope you can get the kid home to his family tonight."

"Tell me about it. What's up?"

"Got a job, and I'm heading out to West Virginia."

"Now?"

"Yup. Woman who her father swears is very reliable is missing."

"Thought we agreed we were only going to take on cases involving children."

Liam had expected that response. "I have to take this one. My father told the woman's father to call me, that I could find his daughter."

"That's unexpected."

"Understatement." Grayson and Cooper were aware that Liam's father had disowned him. "Not sure what the deal is, but I'll keep in touch. I'm leaving now, and I'm driving. I need you to track the cell phone number I'm going to send you and text me the coordinates."

"I'll do that, and, Liam, be safe."

"Back atcha."

He made coffee, filled a travel mug, then grabbed a box of power bars. In the car, he started the ignition. "All right, Miss Sullivan, let's find out what kind of trouble you've landed in."

LIAM ARRIVED IN ELKINS, West Virginia, at five in the morning. It was the closest good-sized town before Hope Corner. He found a decent-looking hotel, checked in, and in his room, he stripped down to his boxer briefs. A few hours' sleep, and he'd be ready to go.

Three hours later, he was up and in the shower. Twenty minutes later, he was dressed and ready to leave. He slipped his wallet and phone in the back pockets of his jeans, his duffel bag over his shoulder, and with his car keys and travel mug in hand, he went to the lobby. After dropping off his room key and getting a receipt, he went to the breakfast area.

"That's what I'm talking about," he said when he saw that the hotel served sausage, cheese, and egg biscuits at their free continental breakfast. After filling his travel mug with coffee, he stacked two of the sandwiches on a napkin, added an apple, and he was good to go.

He'd already programmed the Hope Corner motel where Quinn was supposed to be into his car's GPS, and he brought up the directions. According to the GPS, he had a two-hour drive before reaching the Sunset Motel.

The drive along the country road was beautiful, and he enjoyed the scenery as he ate his breakfast. Since Quinn hadn't been in contact with her father, Liam didn't expect to find her at the motel. His hope was that someone there might have seen something. Maybe she'd asked the desk clerk directions to somewhere or talked about places she wanted to go.

The Sunset Motel was appealing. The grounds were well-kept, bright flowers lined the entrance to the parking lot, and the yellow paint was cheery. He parked in front of the office and went in.

Mr. Sullivan had said that he'd called the motel several times when Quinn missed her scheduled check-in, and she hadn't answered the phone in her room. He'd left messages for her to call him, but she hadn't.

Liam expected to be told they couldn't give out her room number or any information on her, and he could respect that, especially if he just walked in, a stranger, and started asking questions. He'd considered his options before leaving Myrtle Beach, and he'd decided the best approach when asking anyone about her would be a brother looking for his sister. He'd created a fake license with his name as Liam Sullivan, and he'd photoshopped a picture of him with her to put in his wallet.

An older woman was at the counter, and he hoped she'd be willing to help after hearing his sob story. He smiled as he walked up to the counter.

"Good morning," she said. "Are you needing a room?"

"I'm not sure. I'm Liam Sullivan. My sister's supposed to be staying here. Quinn Sullivan. Can you tell me if she's still booked in a room? If she is, I'll want a room, too."

The woman narrowed her eyes. "How do I know you're

her brother? You could be one of those sex predators they talk about on the TV."

"It's smart of you to be suspicious, ma'am. It makes me feel better that my sister is staying in a place where you're looking out for her."

"Well, I got daughters, and I'd want someone to watch out for them if some stranger came looking for them. Your sister…if she really is your sister…is a pretty girl like them. Some men don't have good intentions, you know."

"I do know." He took out his wallet. "This is my driver's license with my name on it. As you can see, Quinn and I have the same last name. And this is a picture of my sister and I together, taken two years ago at our father's house." He'd given the photo a Christmas theme with him and Quinn supposedly standing in front of a decorated tree.

She took the picture and brought it close to her eyes. "I see the resemblance."

It had always fascinated him how you could lead someone to believe what you wanted them to with a few details, whether they were true or not. "You see, Miss…"

"Just call me Betta. Everyone does."

"Betta, my father and I are worried. Quinn was supposed to call him Wednesday night, and she didn't. She's not answering her cell phone, and he's called here several times, but she's not answering the room phone either. He's left messages, and—"

"Oh, I've taken those messages. They're right here." She turned and pulled several pink message sheets from a cubbyhole. "Your sister hasn't stopped by so I could give them to her."

"When was the last time you saw her?"

"Hmm. Not sure. Maybe two days ago. Her car's still here. Haven't seen it move for a few days now. It's the nice blue one parked in front of her room. She's booked for a week, so I just assumed I hadn't noticed her coming and going."

"Something's not right. I feel it in my bones. Will you let me see inside her room? Please, Betta. My father and I are so worried."

Betta's eyes widened. "You think she's dead in there?"

"No!" He sure hoped not. "But I think I need to see inside her room."

"I'll have to go with you."

"That's fine."

She picked up a key on a large ring and dangled it in front of him. "The master key."

"Do you have maid service?" he asked as they walked toward the room. If there was anything unusual—such as a dead body—in Quinn's room, housekeeping would have reported it.

"Yes, but Miss Sullivan asked that no one enter her room unless she was in it. She said she had some expensive cameras and stuff that she didn't want bothered. We've cleaned her room twice since she checked in, and she was there both times."

They stopped at the door to Quinn's room, and Betta inserted the key. He put his hand on her shoulder. "Let me go in first." He didn't know why, but he didn't expect to find Quinn Sullivan's body. There was the possibility that he was wrong, though, and if so, he didn't want Betta to see.

"Oh, Lord, please don't let her be dead," Betta said.

He stepped into the room. There was no body. *Thank you, Jesus.* "You can come in." He walked farther into the room.

"There's her suitcase," Betta said. "She must be around."

A small white bag on the floor caught his attention, and

he picked it up. The smell of rotten meat hit his nose as soon as he opened it.

Betta scrunched her nose. "Good Lord, what stinks?"

"I'm guessing this was going to be her lunch or dinner. It stinks because it's a day or two old." And smashed. Someone had stepped on it. His gaze shifted around the room. There wasn't any sign of a struggle, and her suitcase was still open on the suitcase rack. He glanced inside but didn't touch anything.

Quinn Sullivan was gone but had left her things behind. Because of the smashed meal and that her car was parked out front, his gut said someone had come to her room, and that she hadn't left willingly.

"How long is the room paid for?" he asked.

"Sunday. Do you think something happened to her?"

Yeah, he did. Today was Friday, so only a few more days on the room. It needed to stay untouched. If the worst had happened to Quinn, the police would need to send a crime scene tech to the room, where hopefully whoever took her had left fingerprints behind.

"Betta, I'm going to pay for another week on the room. I need you to keep it locked up and everyone out."

"You think something happened in here?"

"I hope not, but maybe." He lifted his chin toward the door. "Let's talk outside and not contaminate the room any more than we already have." As he followed her out, he grabbed the Do Not Disturb hanger and put it on the outside of the door.

"Should I call the police?"

"Not yet." He didn't want the police to hinder his search for Quinn. "I'm an investigator, so I know how to find people. Why our father sent me here. Did my sister have her camera bag with her, do you know?"

"She had a large purple backpack every time I saw her, so that could have been a camera bag. Like I told you, she said she had some expensive camera equipment, and nothing like that was in the room."

"Did she say why she was here? My sister's a photojournalist, and her specialty is children who need help of some kind or other."

"She did ask when she was checking in if there was an unusually high number of children getting sick in Hope Corner."

That was interesting. "And are there?"

"I don't know what a high number would be, but I know of three children who have leukemia."

If Quinn was asking that question, she had come to Hope Corner for a reason. As he stood by while Betta closed and locked the door, he glanced over, seeing a housekeeping cart outside of a room with an open door. He headed that way.

"Excuse me, miss." He dropped Quinn's food bag in the trash can on the cart.

A young woman carrying sheets out of the room froze at seeing him. "Yes?"

"I'm looking for my sister. She was staying in room nine. Have you seen her?"

The woman's gaze went past his shoulder.

"It's all right, Macy, you can answer him," Betta said, coming up next to him.

Macy's eyes shifted back to him. "The last time I saw her, she was leaving with a man."

Every bone in his body said she hadn't gone freely. "How long ago?"

"It was Wednesday."

That would fit the timeline. "What time did you see her?" Quinn had missed her Wednesday call. But the good news was that she hadn't been missing since her last phone call on Sunday to her father, so the trail wasn't all that cold.

"Around dinnertime. I was finished for the day and had gotten in my car to leave. She came out of her room with a man, and they got in a car and left. She didn't look exactly happy, but it wasn't my business."

"Macy, this is really important. I need you to describe the man and the car."

"Is something wrong?"

"Macy," Betta snapped. "Answer his question."

"Um, the man was a little taller than her, but not by much. He wasn't skinny, but he wasn't heavy. I guess I'd say he was lean. He had dirty blond hair, and he looked like he needed a haircut."

"How long was it?"

"Past his ears but not touching his shoulder. That's all I remember about him."

It was better than nothing. "What about his car? Make and color?"

She closed her eyes. "It was…um, dark green, but I don't know what kind."

"A sedan or an SUV?"

"Not an SUV. It had four doors because he opened the back door and tossed her backpack in. I know it was hers because it was purple, and she always had it with her. I'm sorry, but that's all I remember."

"You've been a big help. Thank you." He walked over to Quinn's car, tried the door, finding it locked. He peered through the window and didn't see anything inside. There was a sticker on the rear window for a rental car company. Betta had followed him, and he said, "Let's just leave the car here for now. I'll call the rental company if I need them to come pick it up."

"I'm so worried about her now, Mr. Sullivan."

He was concerned, too. "Let's go to the office so I can pay you for another week on the room. I also want to give you my phone number if Quinn should show up or you think of anything else you might remember."

"I hope you find her," Betta said after she took his credit card.

Oh, he was going to. The question was, what shape would she be in when he did?

Chapter Four

Quinn grimaced when she opened her eyes. The sunlight coming in the window hurt. Had she forgotten to close the curtains last night? And her head. A royally pissed off tiny drummer must have taken up residence in her brain. Had she drunk too much wine? That would explain forgetting to close the curtains. She really, really had to pee.

She frowned as she took in the room. Right, this was the cabin where Jasper had taken her. She remembered that he'd hit her when they'd fought for the gun. She wasn't nauseated and her vision wasn't blurry, so she didn't think she had a concussion.

She lifted her hand to see if she could feel a bump on her head. *What?* It took a moment to comprehend what she was seeing. *What the hell?* Manacles attached to heavy chains were fastened around both wrists. Her gaze followed the chains up to the wall where they were secured to one large hook over the bed.

The jackass had chained her up! Now she was furious with him. She stood and tried to yank the chains out of the hook. They wouldn't budge. When the door swung open, she backed up to the wall and pressed against it.

Jasper strode in, a smile on his face as if chaining her to a wall was normal. "You finally woke up. Good."

"What the hell, Jasper?"

"Tell me where my thumb drive is, and you can go home."

"I don't believe a word out of your lying mouth." Would he really let her leave if she gave him the thumb drive, which she might or might not have? She didn't think he was going to pat her on the shoulder if she did have it and gave it back. As long as she kept her mouth shut, she might find a way to get out of this still breathing.

"I have to wonder if you think you can steal my payday for yourself," Jasper said.

"What payday?" Maybe she could get him to tell her what this was all about. She wanted to ask about the children who were getting sick, but that would tell him she'd overheard his phone conversation.

He narrowed his eyes as he studied her. "Why'd you leave without a word, Quinn? Could it be that you had my thumb drive and wanted to leave before I found out?"

Should she tell him the truth or lie? "Take these things off, and I'll tell you."

He laughed. "Nice try. Tell me where my thumb drive is, and you'll be free to go."

"I don't have it. I swear I don't. What's on it that's so important that you'd…" She rattled the chains. "That you would do this to me."

"Don't you know? You looked at what was on it, didn't you?"

"How can I look at something I don't have?" Maybe she could convince him she was really hurt. "I don't feel so great. I think you gave me a concussion." For effect, she rubbed the side of her head. The chain banged against her face, which made her mad all over again. "Seriously, Jasper, I need a doctor. And take these damn chains off me."

He laughed. "Not happening. I have a question for you. If you don't have my thumb drive, and you haven't looked at it, why are you in Hope Corner?"

She couldn't answer that without admitting she'd overheard his phone conversation, so she just stared back at him and said, "You're a bastard. You know that?"

"I do know that, pretty girl." Something dark and dangerous was in his smile and his eyes. "I have to go out. While I'm gone, think real hard about telling me where my thumb drive is if you want to leave this cabin."

She'd told him more than once that she didn't like pet names, and that he'd ignored her and kept calling her things like *babe* and *pretty girl* had been a red flag she'd ignored. Any man who didn't respect a woman's wishes was a jerk.

"What about food and water? I'm hungry."

He walked out without responding.

"Bastard." Although relieved he was gone, what if he never came back? No one knew where she was, and she'd die here. She remembered reading that people died from lack of water before starvation.

How far did the chains reach? There must be water or at least ice in the cooler on the counter. Maybe even food. The chain wasn't long enough to get to it she learned when she reached the end and was a foot from being able to touch it.

She went back to the thick S-hook screwed into the wall, but as hard as she yanked on the chains, the hook wouldn't give. She tried to unscrew it, but that didn't work either. "Damn you, Jasper," she screamed.

Her gaze shifted around the room, landing on her camera bag. If she was able to escape, she'd grab the bag. She was able to reach it, and after putting everything back in it, she zipped it up. There, ready to go.

The closed door next to the bed caught her attention. It must be the bathroom, and she could reach it. Disappointment that the room was empty almost crushed her, but there was a hand pump over a basin. A well? Maybe water? She eagerly pumped the handle, and at first nothing happened. She almost gave up, then a trickle of rusty water dribbled out. It wasn't anything she wanted to drink, but as she kept pumping, the water cleared up.

Would it make her sick if she drank it? She cupped some in her hand and smelled it. It didn't have an odor so that was good. She stuck her tongue out and tasted it. It seemed fine. As thirsty as she was, she wanted to lap it up, but the last thing she needed was to get sick from drinking it. She'd test a tiny bit, see if she felt okay in an hour or two. Even the little she drank seemed like the best thing she'd ever had in her mouth.

Now for the other thing she needed. She eyed the toilet, recognizing the compost toilet. She'd used one before when she was overseas. "Desperate measures," she muttered as she lifted the lid. There wasn't any toilet paper, but that was the least of her problems. The last thing she wanted was for Jasper to return while she used it, so she made haste.

Better, now that her throat wasn't so dry and her bladder relieved, she left the bathroom and returned to the bed. Bored, she napped for a few hours. When he still wasn't back by dark, and since the water she'd drunk earlier hadn't made her sick, she returned to the bathroom and drank some more. The water in her stomach helped a little with the hunger pains.

How long had he been gone, anyway? Did he plan to starve her until she turned over the thumb drive? She could only assume that she did have it if he didn't. No one else had been in his rental house before she packed up and left.

If she trusted that he'd let her go, she would tell him she might have it at home, but she had a strong feeling that her life depended on denying she had the stupid thing. Or maybe she was being too dramatic, and she should just tell him. She didn't know, and the not knowing was what was going to keep her from saying anything. At least for now.

Movement outside the window caught her eye. A cardinal landed on a branch, a male. She could tell because he was a brighter red than female cardinals. She wished she had her camera in her hand. As she watched him, a female landed close to him. The male chirped his love song, and the female chirped back.

The female cardinal flew off, and Quinn wished for wings so she could do the same. The male continued his song, perhaps begging his lover to come back. After a few minutes, he flew away. Was he chasing his girl bird? Was he fighting off the attentions of other males who wanted her? Was he swooping in like a white knight in a fairy tale, saving her from the evil cardinal trying to steal her away?

She wanted a white knight for her own.

She wanted to be a cardinal and fly free.

Chapter Five

Liam hadn't learned anything helpful from Quinn's father. As far as Mr. Sullivan knew, she didn't have a boyfriend, and no one was stalking her that he was aware of. Grayson had texted Liam the coordinates Quinn's phone was pinging from. Hopefully, it was still with her.

Most people didn't know that you didn't have to have a tracker app on a phone to find it. He wouldn't be able to locate the precise location of her phone without an app, but he would be able to narrow down his search to a few miles in either direction.

The coordinates took him to a rural area of spread-out dirt driveways and KEEP OUT signs posted at their entrances. Unfortunately, whatever structures were at the end of those driveways were hidden by a thick forest of trees. These were the kinds of places where a shotgun awaited any strangers daring to trespass. He'd have to do reconnaissance when it got dark.

While he waited, he cruised around, watching for driveways with recent tire impressions. There were five that showed signs of activity. More than he wished for, but it could have been worse. He had six hours before dark, so he returned to the small town of Hope Corner that he'd passed through earlier. Not wanting to stay at Quinn's motel and face Betta's questions, he found another decent motel and a diner. A few hours' sleep and food in his belly, and he'd be good to go all night if necessary.

At midnight, when most people would be asleep, he did his reconnoitering. He left his BMW SUV at the entrance of the driveways at each location and walked in. The first three cabins were a bust. One was empty; at the second, a man with a white beard halfway down his chest sat on the porch smoking a pipe; and at the third, there were a half dozen junk cars in the yard, along with chickens and pigs. The pigs almost outed him with their squeals when they picked up his scent, and he quickly retreated.

At the fourth place on his list, he turned off his car's lights as he drove up the dirt lane, and as soon as he was no longer visible from the road, he pulled off the dirt driveway. He grabbed his night-vision goggles and exited the car. He made his way through the woods until he came to what looked like an abandoned small cabin. It wasn't abandoned, though. There was a green late model Toyota parked in front of it. Not the kind of vehicle he'd seen at the other places. The hair on the back of his neck tingled.

"This is it," he murmured.

The forest was thick around the cabin, the trees shutting out any moonlight to light his way. He slipped on the goggles, turning everything he was seeing green, yet distinct. There weren't any lights on, and no one was sitting on the porch smoking a pipe, no pigs waiting to squeal on him. He crouched low and ran up to the back of the car. A rental.

"Found you." The question, was she here willingly? He didn't believe so, but he wouldn't go storming in to rescue her until he got the lay of the land. On silent feet, he made a circle around the cabin, listening for voices as he searched for a window without a curtain blocking his view. There wasn't one, and there wasn't any sound until he got to what he thought was the bathroom based on the small, high window.

The cabin was old, the walls were thin, and soft crying had him stopping. That had to be Quinn. Even though she didn't know he was listening to her cry, he couldn't bring himself to leave her. As much as he wanted to rush in and rescue her, she wasn't alone. Until he assessed the situation, and especially learned how much of a danger the man who'd taken her was and if he was armed, he couldn't make a reckless move.

He pressed his palm to the wall. "I'm coming for you, sweetheart," he softly said. He circled the cabin again. There was only one door, so just one way in and one way out. That was unfortunate. He eased onto the stoop and gently tried the doorknob. Not a surprise that it was locked.

Time for a plan. He wished he knew if the man who'd taken her was asleep or awake and if he was armed. If asleep, Liam could easily take him by surprise. If he was awake and had a weapon, different story. That could put Quinn's life in danger. On a special ops team, there was a lot of hurry up and wait, so the military had taught him patience. He'd spent endless hours with his team while holed up near their target, waiting for go time.

As much as it went against his desire to storm in, he still needed intel, so he'd wait. But not too long. He made his way to the back of the house again, stopping where he'd heard her crying. All was quiet now. Unless he heard anything that told him she was being hurt, he'd wait for daylight. If he was lucky, the man would come out without her, and Liam could take him by surprise.

As he stepped to the right, a board creaked. He froze.

What was that? He pushed the night goggles to the top of his head, then took his penlight from his pocket and shined it on the ground at his feet. A thin slice of wood was visible through the pile of dead leaves. He crouched down and brushed the leaves away.

"How about that," he murmured at seeing it was a cellar door. Even better, there was no lock on it. He eased it open. His penlight revealed five steps leading down to a small root cellar. With luck, there would be a door giving him entrance into the cabin. He glanced at the sky before he descended. The gray light of dawn was on the horizon, and the sun would be up soon.

The best option would be to sneak Quinn out of the cabin before her captor woke up…assuming the man was asleep. Since he hadn't heard a male voice or footsteps walking around inside the cabin, he thought his chances of safely getting Quinn away were good. They needed to be gone before sunrise.

It was his lucky day. There was a door, and when he turned the knob, it opened. On silent feet, he stepped inside the cabin. Without any light to amplify, night-vision goggles might as well be a blindfold, so he left them off. Loud snores greeted him. Excellent. The man was asleep, and since he was, Liam risked clicking on his penlight. It was black as night in the cabin, and he didn't want to stumble over something and make any noise that would wake him up.

He shined the light at the floor, but it was enough to make out a bed with a man in it. Where was Quinn? She wasn't in the bed, so she must still be in the bathroom. A small kitchen with a cooler on the counter was to his right. A ratty couch was the only other furniture in the room besides the bed. He took a few more steps into the room.

To his left, past the bed, was a closed door. That had to

be the bathroom and where she was. The trick was going to be getting to her before she could scream at seeing a strange man. As he aimed for the door, his foot came down on something hard, and he looked down, frowning at what he saw.

Son of a bitch. Two heavy chains trailed along the floor, disappearing under the gap between the door and the floor. She was chained. His gaze followed the chains back to where they were locked to a hook in the wall. This complicated things.

As he quietly moved toward the bathroom, a SEAL saying he'd often heard from Grayson when things got complicated popped into his mind. *The only easy day was yesterday.* That was the damn truth.

When he reached the door, he paused. Should he try to talk to her before he opened it? He needed her to be quiet and not wake up the snoring man. Briefly, he considered returning to the bed and removing the threat of the man waking up by putting him out of commission. Knocking him out with a hit to the head with the barrel of his gun would do it, but again, risky. Sometimes, people didn't react the way you wanted them to, and he liked the idea of the man waking up and finding his captive gone. Vanished into thin air.

He'd leave the man to his snoring. His best bet was to get to Quinn, free her from the chain, and get the hell gone. After she was safe, he'd get her to tell him her story, and then he'd do what needed to be done.

Chapter Six

Jasper didn't return until the next night. Friday? She was pretty sure it was. He walked in the door and threw a white bag at her. Inside was one measly hamburger. Just a burger, bun, and ketchup. *Thanks for nothing, jerk.* But she was starving, and it was better than nothing. She had to force herself to slow down and chew. When she finished, her stomach didn't understand why there wasn't more.

Strangely, he didn't grill her about his stupid thumb drive. After she scarfed down the hamburger, he closed all the curtains, then ordered her to go to sleep. That was all she'd done for the past two days, but she didn't have the energy to argue with him. She rolled over, turning her back to him. He was in a foul mood, and she wondered where he'd been and what had happened.

"Oh, no," she said when he crawled in bed with her. "I'm not sleeping with you."

"Shut up, Quinn."

You shut up. He didn't touch her, and after a few minutes his breathing evened out. An hour later, she realized there was no way she could fall asleep in the same bed with him. That, and she was thirsty. He hadn't given her anything to drink with the burger.

When Jasper started snoring, she eased out of the bed inch by slow inch. Fortunately, she was on the side closest to the bathroom, so she didn't have to work her way around the bed. Careful to keep the chains tight so they didn't scrape on the floor, she made her way to the bathroom.

She cringed when the pump squeaked, but she needed water. After satisfying her thirst, she braced her hands on the sink, cringing again when the chains scraped across the porcelain. Exhausted, she lowered her body to the floor. It was probably dirty, but she didn't have the energy to care. She couldn't get back in that bed with Jasper, she just couldn't. She was so hungry, her stomach felt like it was eating itself, and she was feeling sorry for herself. For the first time, she cried. And as she quietly cried, her eyes grew heavy, and she closed them.

She shot up from the bathroom floor gasping for air. The nightmare was horrible. Jasper had wrapped the chain holding her prisoner around her neck and was demanding that she give him the thumb drive. When she refused, he twisted the chain so tight that she knew she was going to die.

She breathed in and out until she wasn't gasping. How long had she been asleep? How had she even fallen asleep on the hard floor? She lifted her hands, feeling the weight of the heavy chain. How was she supposed to escape?

The chains moved as the bathroom door opened. Okay. Okay. This was it. Jasper was coming in, and he was going to demand answers. Time to…what? If not for being chained to the wall, she would fight him. Even if she could somehow wrap the chains around his neck, see how he liked it, then what? She'd still be a prisoner.

Except the man dressed all in black wasn't Jasper. Her heart shot up, landing in her throat, and she opened her mouth to scream. The man was unhumanly fast as he reached her and clamped his hand over her mouth.

This was the day she was going to die.

"Shhhh," the man whispered. "Don't scream. Your father sent me. I'm here to rescue you."

She was being rescued?

"You'll be quiet?"

When she nodded, he removed his hand from her mouth. She'd be quieter than a mouse if it meant she was getting out of here. He held a penlight, and he shined it on his face, letting her see him. Jet-black hair, a face sculptured by the gods, and eyes the color of a deep blue ocean stared back at her. Mother Mary, he was beautiful.

"I'm Liam O'Rourke," he whispered after he closed the door behind him. "Nice to meet you, Quinn Sullivan."

A fellow Irishman. Did he believe in love at first sight? Because she suddenly did. "Ah, you, too." But Jasper had taught her to be wary. "What's my father's name?"

"Robert Sullivan. He knew something was wrong when you missed your Wednesday check-in, so he asked me to come find you."

He wouldn't know any of that if he hadn't been sent by her father, and the relief would have brought her down to the floor if she wasn't already on it.

"Are you hurt anywhere?"

"I'm okay. Just hungry. You got a steak on you?"

He chuckled. "Sadly, no."

"Drat. Can we go now?" She wanted to be as far away from Jasper as she could possibly get.

"That's the plan, but first, we have to get you out of these cuffs." He reached into a pocket of his cargo pants and pulled out a small pouch.

"What's that?"

"My breaking-and-entering kit."

They were still whispering, which made this strange encounter feel intimate, like they were the only two people in the world. "Are you a criminal?" Figured her father would find a man talented in getting in and out of places without getting caught. And even if he was a thief, her instincts, honed over her years in war-torn countries, said she could trust this man she'd just met.

"No, ma'am. Just a man helping a lady in distress." He put the penlight between his teeth, aiming it to light up her hands. "Hold still."

"You need to know that Jasper has a gun. He'll use it on you if he wakes up."

"Then let's be gone before he does. Do you know him?"

"Unfortunately." She was too embarrassed to admit she'd had a fling with the bastard.

"Not a stranger then. There, one down."

She blinked at seeing him remove the handcuff from her left wrist. Her arm felt almost weightless without the heavy chain.

He wrapped his fingers around her wrists and lifted her hands so she could see them. "Voilà! All gone."

"Thank you."

"You're welcome. Now let's blow this joint."

She was all for that.

"We need to be very quiet. Walk right behind me."

"Consider me your shadow." He eased the door open, and she slipped her fingers around the back of his belt. No way was he going to leave without her. They were halfway across the room when she tugged him to a stop.

He turned and put his mouth to her ear. "What?"

"My camera bag," she whispered. "I need it." She had

thousands of dollars of cameras and equipment that she wasn't going to leave behind.

She expected him to argue that they needed to get out of the cabin, and they did, but not without the only things that mattered to her. Instead, he surprised her by putting his finger to her lips to hush her, and then he shined the penlight around the room. When he paused the light on the bag that held her cameras, she nodded. Without making a sound, he went to the bag, eased the strap over his shoulder, and returned to her. She slipped her fingers back around his belt, and they started off again.

Where was he going? The door was the other way. She followed him into what she'd assumed was a pantry, but since her chain wouldn't reach that far, she hadn't checked it out. It wasn't a pantry, but a small cellar. He went down first, then shined the light on the steps for her. After she reached the bottom, he went back up and eased the door shut. He led her to another set of stairs, and through the opening, she saw the sky. She saw freedom.

"Stand by a sec," he said after they exited the cellar.

"Okay." Although, it was almost impossible to stand by when she wanted to run away as fast as her legs could carry her.

He closed the outside doors to the cellar, then he took her hand. "Let's go."

They fast walked around the cabin and passed Jasper's car. "Ouch."

He stopped, and she bumped into him. "What's wrong?"

She lifted her foot and brushed away the pebbles sticking to it. "Sorry. I stepped on a rock. I'm okay." Fortunately, she had refused to undress in front of Jasper, so she had on the jeans and T-shirt she was wearing when he'd taken her. Unfortunately, she had taken her shoes off, not wanting to wear them in bed.

He took his penlight out and shined it on her feet. "I should have gotten your shoes."

"I'm fine. Really."

"We have a ways to go." He turned his back to her and crouched. "Get on."

"Your back?" At five-seven, she wasn't a small girl.

He glanced over his shoulder. "Yes. You can't walk to my car without shoes. Get on my back, Quinn."

At the commanding tone in his voice, she almost saluted him. She settled for, "Yes, sir." She climbed onto his back, and he slipped his arms under her legs. When he took off at a jog, she expected him to struggle with the awkwardness of her camera bag bumping against his side and her bouncing against his back, not to mention the strain of her weight. There was no struggle. He wasn't even breathing heavily.

"Are you Superman?"

"Yeah, that's me," he said, still breathing normally.

She almost wouldn't be surprised if he jogged them to a phone booth where he could change into his Superman costume. The driveway was long, and she guessed he'd been running for three or four minutes when they came to a car. She was happy to see it, because it was going to get her far, far away from Jasper.

Liam stopped next to the passenger door and dropped his arms from under her legs. She slid down his body, and boy oh boy, what a body. She doubted he had an ounce of fat on him. She sure hadn't felt any while wrapped around him like a spider monkey.

"Thanks for the ride," she said.

"My pleasure." He opened the door.

No, it was very much her pleasure. She got into the car,

and he closed the door. After putting her camera bag into the back seat, he jogged around the hood. When he was seated behind the wheel, he shifted to face her.

"I have to make a decision, and for that, I need intel."

"What decision? Can't we just go?"

"Do we just go, or do I need to take care of the man in the cabin?"

Her jaw dropped. "You mean like, kill him?"

"I guess that's an option, but I'd prefer to hand him over to the police. He did kidnap you. Why, and who is he?"

"His name's Jasper Garrison. And I honestly don't know exactly what's going on. He seems to think I have something of his."

"What's that, and do you?"

"A thumb drive. I might or might not have it. I don't know."

"What's on it?"

"Don't know that either, but whatever's on it, Jasper's planning to trade it to someone for a million dollars."

He whistled. "Okay. I think I need to have a little chat with your friend in there."

"I don't think that's a good idea. I told you, he has a gun. Let's just go."

"And then what? If what you have—"

"Might have."

"He seems to think you do, and for that kind of money, he'll come after you."

She knew that. Of course she did. But she didn't want to be here a minute longer. When she got home, she'd look for the thumb drive, see what was on it if she did have it, then decide what to do with it.

"I just want to go," she said. "Please."

Chapter Seven

Liam tapped his fingers on the steering wheel as he glanced up the dirt lane. It went against all his years of military training to turn his back on the enemy and leave him to fight another day, but her father had only hired him to find her and bring her home.

"If we leave now, we're going to the police. You need to file kidnapping charges against him."

"You're right, I do, but I want to go home first and find that thumb drive…if I have it, that is. I need to know what's on it and just what Jasper's gotten himself into. What if he's told someone else I have it? Will that person come looking for me, too?"

She was right. If Garrison thought whatever he had was worth a million dollars to someone, it had to be something big. No offense to the local police, but Hope Corner probably didn't have much of a police department, certainly not anyone with the experience and knowledge this situation might require.

"Okay," he said. "Here's the deal. I'll take you home, we see if you do have what he's looking for, and if you do, decide where to go from there." He wasn't going to just drop her off at her home, not knowing what kind of danger she was in. If it was something she needed to turn over to law enforcement, he'd call his friend in the FBI. And he'd convince her to report the kidnapping.

"Okay."

"Good, but first." He'd noticed the red marks on her wrists when he'd freed her. "We need to get pictures of your wrists. Visible proof that he chained you up. Should've done that before I took the manacles off." He clicked on the car's interior light, then got his phone. "Hold out your hands." He seriously wanted to go back inside that cabin and teach the man a lesson.

The most beautiful green eyes he'd ever seen peered up at him as he snapped the pictures. A need to protect her rose in him, a determination to keep her safe so fierce that it surprised even him. When he finished, he dropped his phone in the cup holder. Unable to stop himself, he wrapped his fingers around her wrists and gently massaged the bruises.

She closed her eyes, and her sigh went straight to his groin. Her long hair was a mess, her T-shirt was wrinkled, and exhaustion lined her face, but she was stunning. He glanced down at her feet, dirty now from walking down the driveway without shoes, and he made a split-second decision. He was going to take her home with him, where he could keep her safe until the threat to her was over.

He eased her hands down to her lap and forced himself to let go of her. "Let's get out of here."

"I'm all for that." She leaned her head back on the seat. "Oh, I have a rental car at the motel. You don't have to take me all the way to Savannah. That's where I live."

"Yeah, your father told me. He said you stay at his house between assignments."

"No reason to pay rent when I'm rarely home. He has a big house, so when he is there, we don't get in each other's way. He also has a log home in Maggie Valley. That's a little west of Asheville. He spends a lot of his time there in the summer because it's cooler. That's where he is now."

Her father hadn't told him that. He picked up his phone and put his finger on it, bringing it to life. He handed it to her. "Call him so he can stop worrying about you."

She took it from him. "Saying thank you isn't close to adequate for getting me out of there."

"It's enough for me." He glanced at her and smiled. As he drove away from the cabin, he listened to Quinn's end of the conversation with her father. It was obvious they were close, and a pang of regret bubbled up from the deep hole where he'd buried his hurt at being disowned. After ten years, he should be over it. Maybe one never got over losing their family.

A few years ago, he'd called his father's office, hoping his dad was ready to put the past behind them.

"May I tell him who's calling?" his father's assistant had said.

"His son."

She'd put him on hold and less than a minute later come back on the line. "I'm really sorry, but he said he doesn't have a son."

And that was that. He'd crushed the ache from missing his family and went on with his life.

"My dad said to tell you thank you, and that he owes you big-time," Quinn said, handing his phone back.

"I'll take a dinner with you and your dad as thanks." He'd very much like to see her again after this was over. At least she didn't live on the other side of the country. Savannah was only about a four-hour drive from Myrtle Beach. Not that she was there much, but maybe they could see each other when she was between assignments.

"Deal."

He almost asked if she could tell him how their fathers knew each other, but he held the question in. That might open the door to her asking questions about his family, and he didn't want to have to explain why he was dead to his father.

The sun was starting its rise over the mountains, and when he glanced at her and saw she was nodding off, something tender settled in his chest. He wanted to protect her from all the bad in the world, wanted to get to know her, to learn what made her laugh.

He didn't know what it was about her that called to him, but from the moment he'd seen her photo, he'd been intrigued. She'd had a rough few days and probably hadn't slept much. It had been near dawn when he'd heard her crying, so she likely hadn't slept last night. He wished he'd brought a pillow for her to rest her head against. He—

He narrowed his eyes as the headlights of a car racing up behind them appeared in his rearview mirror. If the car hadn't been driving that fast, he wouldn't have thought much of it, but the speed the driver was going was dangerous on these mountain roads. As it closed in on them, the sun was up enough to see that it was a green Toyota Corolla, the same model and color car that was at the cabin. Damn.

Liam wasn't worried about outrunning the Toyota. His BMW could leave the Toyota in the dust, but there was nothing but sharp curves and narrow lanes. Too much could go wrong taking these roads at high speed. If the man only followed them, Liam would keep to the speed limit until they came to Hope Corner. The small police department was on the main drag, and he'd go straight there.

He debated letting Quinn continue to sleep but decided

to wake her. Better she be aware and ready if the man decided to get foolish and do something reckless.

"Quinn, wake up." When she didn't stir, he put his hand over hers and squeezed. "Quinn, I need you to wake up."

"Hmm?" She stretched her neck.

"Pretty sure Garrison's behind us."

"What?" She shot up and looked back. "Oh, God. What are we going to do?"

"Nothing as long as he doesn't get stupid."

"You can count on him doing something stupid."

As if to prove her point, the bonehead rammed them. How did he know Quinn was even in the car? Was he so desperate that he'd take that kind of chance that she might be? Granted, his was the only car on the road coming from the direction of the cabin and not that far from it, but to risk possibly hurting innocents?

"He's going to kill us," Quinn said, fear in her voice.

"Not under my watch." They were approaching a sharp curve, and Liam slammed his foot down on the gas pedal, trusting the BMW to keep them on the road. And it would have if Garrison hadn't rammed them again before the BMW could outrun him.

The Toyota caught the end of his car's left bumper, spinning it out of control. Tires screeched on the asphalt, the sound of metal against metal filled the car, and the world outside became a blur of trees and pavement. They passed the last of the guardrail going off the road sideways, and at seeing it was her side that would collide with a massive tree, Liam jerked the steering wheel to the right, barely missing the tree that would have killed her. Instead, the front wheels sank into the muddy ditch, and the car came to a shuddering stop. They hadn't impacted with the tree, so the airbags didn't deploy.

The sudden silence seemed out of place after the noise of the crash. Liam took a second to berate himself for not expecting and preparing for Garrison to come after them. The Toyota passed them, and at the squeal of brakes pressed hard as the car came to a grinding halt above them, Liam threw the BMW in Reverse. All he got for the effort was spinning tires.

"He's coming back," Liam said. "We have to get out of the car." He released his seat belt, and Quinn did the same.

Garrison was backing up his car. Quinn had said he had a gun, and they didn't need to sit here and be targets. They only had a few minutes to disappear into the woods. Quinn appeared to be unhurt. He hoped that was the case because he didn't have time to ask.

"Get out and head for the woods."

"What about you?"

"No time to talk. Just go. I'll catch up." She did as he'd asked, and after picking up his phone, he exited the car. He ran to the other side and yanked open the back door. His weapons bag was on the floor, and he grabbed it, his duffel bag, and was backing away when he noticed her camera case. He should leave it, but it was her life, so he grabbed it, too.

He disappeared into the tree line just as the Toyota came to a stop. Quinn poked her head around the tree she was hiding behind, relief on her face at seeing him. He jogged to her.

"Give me something to carry," she said.

"I'm good." He was impressed by how calm she was, but maybe that was because of her experiences and the time she'd spent in war-torn countries as a photojournalist. "Are you hurt anywhere?"

"Just my feet, but that's not from the wreck. I'm good."

That was the reason he'd grabbed his duffel. A car door slammed, and he took his bearings. If he didn't have her to protect, he'd stay and fight, but he wouldn't risk her getting caught in the cross fire. "He's coming this way, so we need to go." As soon as it was safe to stop, he'd take care of her feet. "Stay close to me."

"I'm your shadow."

He chuckled. "You'd make a great Marine."

"Oorah!"

She knew the Marine battle cry? He could only grin at this woman who kept surprising him at every turn. She intrigued him, and he wanted to get to know her better, but first, he had to keep her safe.

This was one mission he wasn't going to accept anything less than success.

Chapter Eight

"Whoever you are with Quinn," Jasper called. "It would be better for your health if you sent her back to me." As if to back up his threat, the bark exploded from a nearby tree.

"He shot at us!" Quinn shuddered. That was close. Liam didn't respond to Jasper, just reached back with his hand, found hers, and squeezed. Her feet were screaming in pain, and she wanted to yell at herself for not getting her shoes. At the time, all she'd cared about was her cameras and getting out of the cabin.

If they got lost in this forest, at least she'd be with a man she already liked a lot and who was real easy on the eyes. They could build a cozy cabin, he could hunt for their food, she could grow potatoes, and they could have endless babies with his startling blue eyes.

"Damn it, Quinn, you can't hide from me forever. Just give me my thumb drive, and I'll leave you alone."

Yeah, right. His voice was farther away, now to the left instead of behind them. They were losing him. It amazed her how quiet Liam was compared to Jasper. She could hear leaves and sticks crunching under Jasper's shoes and his grunts as he tried to find them. Liam was a ghost, not a sound coming from him as he took them deeper into the woods on silent feet. He'd told her she'd make a good Marine, and she meant to make that true. She made sure to step exactly where he had, determined to be a ghost, too.

Eventually, any sounds from Jasper were gone. They'd lost him, and knowing that, she could breathe again. She wasn't sure how long they walked before Liam stopped, his head cocked as if he heard something, but what, she didn't know. And although the sun was peeking over the mountain, giving them light, she didn't see anything that might have captured his attention.

"There's a good place just ahead," he said.

"Hope it's a spa." That got her a chuckle. It was a nice chuckle. Strike nice, it was sexy, that low, throaty sound. Even with hurting feet, scared out of her mind, and thirsty, she liked one thing about the mess she found herself in. Liam. The man fascinated her, but even more than mere fascination, there was attraction. And, boy, was she ever attracted to him. Maybe once they were safe and back home—

"No spa here, but I promise you something even better," he said with a wink.

—maybe they could have a little fling. Flings were all she would allow herself because of her job. She never knew where she'd be or for how long, and she'd learned early on even though men claimed they were okay with how much she traveled, they never were.

She liked men, liked their minds, their bodies, the sex. She did not like the jealousy, the demands for more time that she didn't have to give, or even as Aiden—the man she'd been engaged to—had demanded, that she give up the job she loved and her soul needed so she could be there for him every day.

Funny that when she told him he could give up his job

and travel with her, he hadn't understood how she could even ask that of him. "Back atcha, pal," she'd said after their worst fight as she handed him back his ring. How could she marry a man who didn't think her career mattered? The love she had for him would have died a miserable death if she'd stayed, giving up her dream. Better that she leave before they ended up hating each other.

After Aiden, she'd adopted a new policy. Flings only with men who were following their own dreams and didn't have the time or the inclination to poke their noses into hers. Pretty much a wham, bam, thank you, sir. Now be off with you. Worked for her.

That was one reason she'd left Jasper. Even though he'd agreed theirs was a temporary thing while they were in California, he'd started to make noises that she should be all about him. The closer she got to finishing up her assignment, the more Jasper pushed her to stay. She refused to even consider it, because she knew exactly how it would go. His career would matter. Hers? Not even.

Then there was his jealousy and possessiveness. It never entered her mind that he'd stalk her, kidnap her, shoot at her. Yeah, that was mind-blowing. Maybe she should consider ditching the flings if her judgment was that whacked. The thought of no more intimate moments with a man, though?

"Do you get possessive and make unreasonable demands of a woman you're dating?" she asked as she followed Liam around a boulder.

He stopped and faced her. "The answer is no. I don't have the right to tell another person how to live their life, man or woman." His brows scrunched together as if he was confused. "What brought that question on?"

Okay, the man was perfect. She shrugged. "Just curious." Obviously, the trick was to be more discerning than she had been. Before allowing any kind of intimacy from here on, maybe she should write up a questionnaire to give to a man she was interested in.

He gave her a quizzical glance before continuing, but she didn't miss the interest in his eyes. She smiled at his back, liking that she had him wondering. A few steps more and then he stopped, stepped to the side, and swung his arm out. "Your 'something even better.'"

"Oh," she murmured at seeing the crystal-clear creek. "Can I put my feet in it?"

"That's the plan."

A few minutes later, she sat on a rock and sighed as she lowered her feet into the cold, foot-numbing water. "Ahh-hhh. Heaven."

Liam squatted, zipped open one of his duffels, and rummaged around in it. He brought out a bottle of water, and seeing it, she wanted to kiss him. Next came a box of power bars, then a small first aid kit.

"Good Lord, what all else do you have in there?" She leaned over and peered inside.

"Just a change of clothes and one more bottle of water." He twisted the cap off and handed her the bottle he held. "We have to ration the water, so only drink a little."

Although she wanted to chug the entire bottle, she limited herself to three swallows before handing it back to him. "You're handy to have around when one is lost in the woods."

"I'm not lost."

She laughed at his affronted expression. "Silly me. Of course you aren't."

"Lift your feet out of the water."

"But it feels so good."

"Your superior officer has given you an order, Little Marine. Feet up."

"Aye, aye, sir." She lifted her feet, and he put his hands under her ankles and brought them to his lap.

"That's sailor talk. You would say, 'Sir, yes, sir.'"

"Would I now?" Their eyes met, and she would swear that the air sizzled between them. Would he be bossy in bed? That gleam in his eyes said yes. She imagined him naked beside her, him giving her orders in that commanding voice, and she, being a brat, would resist obeying until he—

"What's going on in that mind of yours right now, Quinn?"

Drat. He interrupted her daydream. It was a good one. "Um, so, what do we do now?"

Amusement danced in his eyes. "A bit of deflection there, but the answer is, we take care of your feet." He lifted the sole of her right foot, frowning as he studied it. "How were you even walking on these?"

"One does what one must." Especially when worried about getting shot. She watched, fascinated, as he tenderly doctored her feet. He used a cotton ball to clean them with antiseptic, then he covered the cuts with a cream that soothed them, and lastly, he wrapped them in gauze. She thought he was done, but no. He took two pairs of socks from his duffel and put them on her.

"Maybe doubling them up will give you more cushion and help you walk."

"Thank you," she whispered, tears burning her eyes at the care he'd given her. Other than her father, no one cared about her. Not really. She didn't do boyfriends, and she wasn't in one place long enough to make girlfriends, so it had always been up to her to take care of herself.

Sometimes, she missed having people in her life, but it was her choice. She couldn't imagine not doing what she loved, even if it meant sacrificing having relationships of any kind. Her work was her passion, but she sometimes got lonely. Thus, the occasional fling. It was a way to touch and be touched by another person, if only for a short time.

He took out his phone, eyed the screen, and frowned. "No signal."

"That's not good."

"Ah, but have faith, my friend." He rummaged around in the other duffel.

"What's in that one?"

He held it open so she could see inside.

She blinked. "Whoa. Are you planning to go to war?"

"I hoped not, but I didn't know what I'd be walking into, so it's always best to be prepared."

"Says the Marine. With all these weapons you have on you, why didn't you shoot back at Jasper? Do you not have a gun on you?" She would've expected him to be armed.

His eyes locked on hers as he lifted his shirt to show her the gun at his waist. "Because you might have been caught in the cross fire, and that was unacceptable. The mission is to keep you safe, not put you at risk. The best way to do that was to lose him. I also have no desire to kill a man if I don't have to."

"Oh." Who was this man who kept surprising her with the things he said? "What's that?" she asked when he removed what looked like a strange phone.

"It's a satellite phone." He punched in some numbers. "It's me. I need an exfil."

Who was he talking to, and what was an exfil?

"I'm in the middle of the woods and can't see where a good LZ is. Get my coordinates and call me back. My rescue's feet are shredded, so find a place not too far. Also, I crashed my car in a ditch and need you to arrange for it to be towed to a repair shop." He gave whoever he was talking to some coordinates, which she assumed was for the car.

"Who was that, what's an exfil, and LZ is a landing zone, right?" she asked when he set the phone next to his side. "How would they know where we are?"

"That was Grayson, one of my teammates, an exfil is an extraction of personnel, and yes, an LZ is a landing zone, and we can all track each other."

"He's sending a helicopter?" When he nodded, she said, "Wow. Who are you guys?"

"The Phoenix Three is me, Grayson Montana, and Cooper Devlin. Our mission is rescuing children from dangerous situations."

Oh, man, he had no idea what hearing that did to her heart. But wait. "I'm not a child, so why did you come to rescue me?"

He chuckled. "To quote your father, 'She is a child, my damn child,' so here I am."

"Sounds like him. Your friend…teammate didn't want to know what happened and why you need extracting?"

"No, if I say I need a ride, a ride I'll get, no questions asked. He'll want to be debriefed when we're back."

"I need to turn my rental car in."

"When we get back, I'll call the rental company and arrange to get it picked up."

She poked his arm.

"What was that for?"

"Just wanted to know if you're real."

He poked her back. "Maybe you're the one who isn't real."

Gah, she liked this man. More than she could remember

liking any man, and maybe that was a problem. She could fall for him so easily, but she didn't fall for any man. She had things to do and places to go.

Chapter Nine

"You've been surprisingly calm about all this," Liam said as they sat by the creek. She really had been. Most people not trained for dangerous situations would be scared, even falling apart. She'd been calm, had followed his orders without question, and had even teased him.

She stared at the water tumbling over the rocks in the creek. "I don't know. I guess when you've hidden in a basement with families praying the so-called soldiers raiding their village who'll shoot anyone without question don't find you… When you've watched a child die, his belly bloated with hunger, or carried a little girl who had her leg blown off a mile to where you knew Doctors Without Borders were so they could save her life…" She lifted her eyes to his. "I guess in the grand scheme of things it's all relative, you know? Like this crap with Jasper is more like an annoying mosquito buzzing around your face."

"I do know." And right then, that very second, this woman claimed a piece of his heart.

She smiled. "I guess as a former Marine, you do."

He smiled back, then to lighten up the mood again, said, "So, the good news is we won't have to spend the night in the woods. Grayson will have that chopper to us in a few hours. Until we get the coordinates to an LZ, we'll stay put." He was good with that. It would give him time to get to know her a little. From the first, seeing her photo, her work on behalf of children the world over, reading about her accomplishments and awards, and hearing the love for her in her father's voice—he'd been a little envious of that— he'd been fascinated.

"What got you interested in photography?" he asked as he opened the box of power bars and handed her one.

"Oh, fun, a picnic." She grinned, taking it from him. "With the excitement of being chased, I forgot I was starving."

Even with a dangerous man after her, stranded in the middle of nowhere, and with ruined feet, she remained upbeat. She impressed the hell out of him.

"To answer your question, my mom loved taking pictures, and I wanted a camera like hers so I could take pictures, too. I was nine when she gave me one. It wasn't as fancy as hers, but I loved it. She was killed a few months after giving it to me. An elderly man got confused and went the wrong way on the highway and hit her head-on. After she was…um, gone, the camera made me feel close to her. I still have it."

Her voice caught when speaking of her mom, and instead of hugging her like he wanted to, he put his hand over hers and squeezed. "I'm sorry you lost her." He could relate a little because, although in a different way, he'd lost his family. "What made you want to be a photojournalist and specialize in children?"

"One of my college professors had a sister who was a photojournalist, and he had her come speak to the class. By the time she finished talking about the places she'd been and after watching her incredible slideshow, I wanted to be her. She didn't really focus on any one thing, but she had a section of photographs of children caught in a tribal war, and…" Her eyes watered with unshed tears. "Those children were starving, many of them orphans, yet their too-big eyes for their little faces looked into the camera and they smiled for her. That was the moment I knew what I'd do with my life. Bring the plight of these children and others who are suffering to the attention of the world." She shrugged. "Do my small part in helping them."

Be still my heart. She was perfect, and he fell a little in love with her right then and there. How could he not when she was everything and more that he could want in a woman?

His sat phone chimed with an incoming call. "Liam here." After getting the information from Grayson, he set the phone next to him. "The good news, we only have a mile to get to the LZ, but the helo won't be here for three more hours. We're safe here, so we'll stay put for a while longer. Let your feet rest a little."

"My feet thank you. Your turn."

"For?"

"Your story. You said you rescue children. Why?"

He never talked about his kidnapping, but with her, he wanted to. "Grayson, Cooper, and I were kidnapped when we were in high school. We—"

"Wait." She grabbed his arm. "Did that happen during spring break?"

"Yes."

"I remember that being all over the news when I was in high school, that three boys had been kidnapped. Some SEALs found you and rescued you, right?"

"Former SEALs, and yes. We were very lucky. Grayson's father had been a SEAL, and he called in some favors."

"And that's the reason you all created The Phoenix Three?"

"Pretty much." He told her about those dark days of being held for ransom, their rescue, and how he and his Phoenix Three brothers had come up with the idea of rescuing children. When he finished, he smiled. "We have a lot in common, you know?"

She stared at him without saying anything, her gaze dropping from his eyes to his mouth.

"What?" he said.

"I think you should kiss me."

Well, he wasn't expecting that, but he sure as hell wasn't going to refuse. He decided to turn the tables and challenge her. Why? Because he was learning her, and he thought it was a sure bet that she liked a challenge. "I think you should be the one to kiss me."

"Hmm." She tilted her head and studied him as a smirk appeared on her face. "You think I won't?"

"I'm very much hoping you do."

She leaned toward him, her eyes never leaving his as she closed the distance between them. Her soft, warm lips touched his, and as their mouths pressed together, he committed to memory their first kiss. He never wanted to forget this moment. She was someone special, and he had the feeling that she was going to change his life.

She wrapped her hands around the back of his neck and sighed when their tongues tangled. That sigh went straight to his groin as they kissed.

She lowered her arms and leaned away. "Wow. That was—"

"Earth-shattering?" He was pretty sure the ground shifted under his feet.

"I was going to say *amazing*, but *earth-shattering* works."

He hesitated a moment before saying what he wanted to. He didn't want to come on too strong too soon, but something special was happening here. For him, anyway. He needed to know if she felt it, too. "This thing happening—" he gestured between them "—between us, tell me it's not just me feeling it."

"It's called chemistry."

Yes, there was chemistry, but it was more than that. He didn't believe in love at first sight. How could you love someone you didn't know? But for the first time in his life, he believed he could fall in love with someone, with her. He couldn't know that for sure yet, but he wanted time with her to explore the possibility.

First order of business was to get her safely home, then he'd ask her out on a date. Savannah was a doable drive if she was interested in seeing him. He sure hoped she was.

"Now that we kissed, I want to know more about you," she said. "Did you grow up in Myrtle Beach?"

"No, Kansas City."

"I've never been there. Is that where your family lives?"

"Yes."

"Hmm, I hear tension in your voice. Are you not close to them?"

As much as he didn't want to talk about his father, he wanted her to know him, and the only way for her to do that was to answer her question. And, maybe, sitting here in the woods in the middle of nowhere was the best place for confessions.

"When I was eighteen, right after I graduated high school, I told my father I was joining the Marines. He disowned me. I haven't seen him since."

She stared at him for a moment. "I don't know what to say. I can't imagine a parent disowning their child for any reason. That's really sad, because you're an amazing man, Liam, and he's not around to see that."

"I secretly talk to my mom once a month."

"So, she didn't disown you but isn't allowed to talk to you?"

"Correct." Since he'd told her that much, he told her the rest of his story.

"That's sad for you both that she has to sneak to talk to you," she said when he finished. "I'd like to have a few words with your father."

He grinned as he imagined her doing just that. "I'd love to see that." He glanced at his watch. "It's time to head to the LZ."

Her gaze scanned the area around them. "Do you think Jasper's gone?"

"Probably for now, but he's not going to give up. We're going to talk about that." He packed everything up. "Let's go." He stood and held out his hand to help her up. "We have plenty of time, and we're going to take it slow so you don't ruin your feet even more."

"Why don't you let me carry one of those bags?"

"I'm good. I've carried twice this weight when on an op, so I'm used to it. You just worry about where you step and not hurting your feet."

"You really are a knight in shining armor."

"No, ma'am. Just an ordinary man here."

She snorted. "Right."

Fine. Maybe he wasn't quite ordinary, and if his special skills kept her safe, all the better. Whether she was his future remained to be seen, but for now anyway, she was his to protect.

Trooper that she was, she didn't complain once as they traveled to the LZ even though her feet had to be on fire.

When they reached the designated pickup, they had twenty minutes to wait for the bird. The LZ was in a flat meadow surrounded by forest.

After he got her settled inside the tree line where she was hidden from sight, he made a sweep of the area around them. He knew they hadn't been followed, and he didn't expect to find anything of concern, but he wasn't taking any chances where Quinn was concerned. Finding all was quiet, he returned to her.

"Your feet must be in agony," he said as he squatted next to her, dropping the three packs next to him.

"Kind of, but better than they were before you doctored them."

At the sound of a helo in the distance, he said, "I think a kiss would be just the right ending to this little adventure."

She grinned. "Adventures should always end with a kiss."

With permission granted, he covered her mouth with his, and damn, she tasted like the sweetest honey. An addiction he didn't want a cure for. Too soon, the shadow of the bird hovering above and the *whup, whuping* sound of the machine had him breaking the kiss.

When she leaned toward him, eyes dreamy, her mouth seeking his again, he smiled as he brushed her hair away from her face. "I'm going to kiss you again, Quinn. You can count on that, but right now, our transportation is here."

"Why couldn't it be late?"

He laughed. "Not gonna argue with that." He slipped the straps of their bags onto his shoulders, then he scooped her up, laughing again when she yelped.

"Liam! Put me down."

"Nope. I've got you." He ran toward the bird. *I'll always be here for you.*

Chapter Ten

After Liam buckled her into the seat, Quinn glanced around. Two pilots were in the seats in front of her, and the one on the left leaned his head around his seat and grinned.

"VIP transport at your service, ma'am. We can't offer you first-class luxury. No champagne or sweet chocolates, but we'll try to give you a smooth ride." He winked.

He was cute, and when she grinned back at him, Liam growled. Well, that was hot. *Liam.* What was she going to do about him? He was mysterious. He excited her. He was a man she would consider fling material without a second thought if…

It was a very big *if*…if he didn't check every single one of her boxes, even boxes she didn't know she had. That made him dangerous to her heart. She didn't risk her heart for any man. Ever.

Yet she wasn't sure she could walk away from him. It was kind of ridiculous actually. She didn't know this man, not really. They'd spent, what, all of a day together? She should be able to walk away. She'd always been able to in the past without a glance back.

Her feet that he'd taken such gentle care of weren't going to be happy leaving him behind. *It's not just your feet, girl.*

She laugh-snorted, which the noise of the helicopter thankfully covered up. What a freaking few days. She honestly didn't know if she was going or coming, so no surprise she wasn't thinking clearly.

She leaned her head back against the seat, closed her eyes, and relived kissing him. It might have been the best kiss she'd ever had. Who was she kidding? It was the best kiss she'd ever had. She smiled as she let the dream of Liam's mouth on hers take her.

"Quinn, wake up. Hey, we've landed. Time to go."

"Hmm?" She opened her eyes and stretched. She could probably sleep for days. Of course, she'd gotten very little rest from the time Jasper had kidnapped her, then an escape and a trek through the woods, so it was no surprise that she was exhausted. If only she could blink herself home and into her bed.

Liam moved in front of her and unbuckled the shoulder harness. Gosh, his eyes were beautiful. Indigo blue, she decided. She wished she had her camera in her hand.

"Come on, sleepyhead. Let's get you to a bed."

"Yes, please." With him in it. She glanced out the window. "Are we in Savannah?"

"No, Myrtle Beach."

"I don't live in Myrtle Beach."

"True, but I do." He jumped out of the helicopter with the ease of a man who'd done so many times, then held out his hand.

"Why are we stopping here," she said as she put her hand in his and he helped her down. Once she was standing on the pavement, he reached inside and grabbed their bags, strapping them over his shoulders. She wanted a bath, a glass of wine, and her bed. Her bed was not in Myrtle Beach.

He leaned his head back into the helicopter. "Thanks for the ride, guys. We owe you." He then took her hand and started walking toward a black SUV. "You need dinner and a good night's sleep. In the morning, we're going to talk."

"And exactly where am I doing this eating and sleeping?"

"My place."

Before she could respond to that, they reached the car where two men built like Liam leaned back against the SUV with their arms crossed over their chests. Two pairs of eyes fell on her, and both men smiled. Double whoa! Where did they grow these hotties?

It was the man holding her hand, though, who did it for her. He stopped them in front of the other two men. "Quinn, these two jokers are my mates. Grayson, meet the lovely Quinn Sullivan."

Both men's gazes dropped to Liam's hand holding hers before exchanging a glance, and it seemed to her that an unspoken message passed between them. The blond man to her left, Grayson, nodded. "A pleasure, Miss Sullivan."

"Just Quinn. Nice to meet you, too."

"He saved the best for last," the man with the chestnut brown hair said with a mischievous grin. "I'm Cooper. The most fun of our little band of brothers."

She didn't doubt that from the playful gleam in his coffee-brown eyes and his flirty smirk. They were both gorgeous men, but she preferred Liam's looks, his black hair and indigo blue eyes, his...well, his everything.

"Feel free to ignore him," Liam said.

It was said with humor, but underneath that humor was a bite. A warning to his friend. Was Liam jealous? She grinned and, unable to resist testing the water, said, "Now why would I want to do that?" He scowled, answering her question. She very much liked that answer.

Grayson's gaze homed in on Liam, and he chuckled as if something amused him.

"This is gonna be fun," Cooper said.

"Why are both of you here?" Liam opened the rear hatch and set their bags inside the SUV. "Don't you have other things to do?"

"Nope," Cooper said. "I for one am curious where you found the lovely Miss Quinn." He winked at her.

"Behave, Coop," Grayson said.

"Where's the fun in that?"

She laughed. She liked both men, but Cooper had an easy way about him that made her feel comfortable with him. Grayson was harder to read.

"It's been a long, exhausting day for Quinn," Liam said. "We'll debrief in the morning, but for now, how about we get this show on the road so she can get off her feet."

"My feet would thank you for that." They loaded up, Grayson driving and Cooper in the front passenger seat. She and Liam got in back, and she sighed as she sank into the soft, buttery leather. She could sleep right here, which she apparently did as sometime later, Liam was waking her again.

She still wasn't home in Savannah where she wanted to be, but right now she didn't care. She just wanted a bed. Once again, Liam played the pack mule and loaded himself up with their bags. She swayed on her aching feet as he had a brief conversation with his teammates. That done, she followed him into a high-rise, where he nodded at a man behind a desk. "How's it going, Wilson?"

"Good, Mr. O'Rourke. All's quiet here."

Wilson's gaze raked over her, ending on her sock-clad feet. She gave him credit for his expression not changing at seeing Liam drag home a dirty, sock-wearing woman.

They continued through a lobby with a beach theme and colors, and into an elevator, where he pushed the button for the fifth floor.

He smiled when she leaned against the wall and sighed. "After what you've been through, I'm impressed you're still upright. We'll have you off those feet and food in your belly soon."

"Not sure I have the energy to eat." She didn't know what he had planned and what tomorrow morning's meeting was about, but if it involved her sticking around, not happening.

"You need something in your stomach, Quinn, and I'm sure you'll feel better after a shower."

"I'm salivating over the thought of a bubble bath and a glass of wine."

"We can make that happen." The elevator door opened, and he gestured for her to walk out first. Halfway down the hall, he stopped in front of a door, unlocked it, and pushed it open. "After you."

She stepped inside, and she didn't know what she was expecting his home to look like, but it wasn't this. "You need to go furniture shopping." There was the biggest flat-screen TV she'd ever seen mounted to the wall, a leather recliner situated in front of it, and a small table next to the recliner. That was it.

His gaze scanned the room, and he frowned as if his lack of furniture was a surprise. "I guess I do." He set her camera bag and his two on the kitchen counter. "I'm not here much, but let me show you where you can find me when I am, unless I'm watching a game or sleeping."

"Oh, this is where I'd be, too." He'd taken her out to the balcony, and his condo was right on the ocean. She spied a comfy-looking lounge chair and headed for it. "I think I'll just crash right here," she said as she stretched out. The sound of the waves lapping onshore and the gentle warm breeze was heaven after the nightmare of the last few days.

"What about that bubble bath?"

Chapter Eleven

No answer. Liam chuckled. She was out cold already. His gaze traveled over her. Even a mess—clothes dirty, hair tangled, and filthy socks on her feet—she was beautiful. That she needed a bath and a brush but hadn't seemed to care how she looked to him or his teammates was pretty cool. This woman was comfortable in her own skin, even when she wasn't at her best.

He'd let her sleep while he took care of some things. First order of business, a shower and clean clothes. That done, he checked on Quinn. Still sound asleep. There was a grocery store two blocks away. He should be able to make a quick trip there and be back before she woke up. To be safe, he left her a note on the kitchen counter that he'd be back in a few minutes.

The store had a deli where they made subs to go, and not sure what she liked, he got three varieties and added three bags of assorted chips to his order. After picking up a few more items, including bubble bath, he hit the checkout. He was back home twenty minutes after he'd left.

As expected, when he checked on her, she was still asleep. He put the subs in the refrigerator along with the bottle of white wine and the beer. That done, he readied the guest bathroom for her. He'd never had overnight company, never brought women to his condo. It was his sanctuary, his place to retreat to when he needed alone time. It seemed like it should bother him that Quinn was invading his space, but it didn't. Something to think about.

He scanned the guest room with a critical eye. It had never been used. Quinn would be the first to sleep in the bed that he'd bought with the hope that someday, his mother might come for a visit. That was probably never going to happen. Before the hurt of losing his family took him, he walked out.

Back in the kitchen, he noticed the three bags he'd left on the counter, his go bag with extra clothes, his weapons bag, and her camera bag. She didn't have any spare clothes to change into. That needed fixing, and he called Harlow. Arrangements made to fix that problem, he went to his bedroom and found a T-shirt, a hoodie, and a pair of his boxer briefs. Those, he took to the bathroom.

Time to wake Quinn. When he returned to the balcony, she was curled up in a ball. The sight of her vulnerable and at peace stirred something within him. He was a protector, and this woman needed him. She might not like it, but until he was sure she was safe, he wasn't leaving her side.

He leaned over her and shook her shoulder. "Quinn, open your eyes." As if he were a pesky fly, she batted at his hand. Her eyes stayed closed, and she turned over, away from him.

"All right then." He slid his arms under her and lifted her.

She stirred, her eyelids fluttering before slowly opening. Her gaze met his, still hazy with sleep. "Hey."

He smiled down at her. "Hey, yourself."

"Where are you taking me?"

"Bubble bath. Remember that was on your list of must-haves tonight?"

"Are you getting in with me?"

"Not tonight." As much as he wanted to do just that, she was still half-asleep, and he wasn't sure she knew what she was saying. "I'll take a rain check."

"Is it raining?" She closed her eyes and went back to sleep.

This girl had him amused, had him thinking of possibilities, and had him aroused. All those things and wanting to kill anyone who dared to hurt her. He'd been with women he liked a lot, but never had there been one who'd made him feel like a growly, possessive bear ready to swipe deadly claws at anyone with malice on their mind coming near her.

He took her to the guest bedroom, lowered her so that she was sitting on the bed, and had to keep his hands on her shoulders to keep her from falling over. Did she always sleep this deeply, or was it because she was mentally and physically exhausted? Just another thing he wanted to learn about her.

"Quinn, sweetheart, open your eyes."

"Mfff."

He chuckled. "Not sure what that word means."

She blinked her eyes open. "What?"

"There's a bubble bath waiting for you."

"Okay."

"Let's get these socks off you."

She peered down at them. "I ruined your socks." She lifted her feet to show him the holes on the bottom. "I'll buy you new ones."

"I think that's something you don't need to worry about. After your bath, we'll doctor your feet again."

"You're so nice. Are you going to kiss me again?"

Hell yes. "Maybe, if you want me to."

She batted her eyelashes. "Maybe I do."

This girl. "I think you're punch-drunk."

"What does that mean, anyway?"

"It means you're beyond tired and being silly."

"Do you like me silly?"

He lowered her feet to the floor, then let his eyes settle on hers. "I pretty much like you in all the ways I've seen you. Come on." He scooped her up and carried her to the guest bathroom, where a bath was waiting for her. "The bubble bath is a mild formula, so it's not going to sting your feet. There's one of my T-shirts and a pair of boxer briefs you can put on when you're done."

"Oh, goody. I'm getting in your undies."

He laughed as he left her to take her bath and tried not to think about her being naked with only a closed door between them.

After her bath, he doctored her feet, then fed her a sub. She'd only eaten half of it when her head almost fell to the table. She jerked up, giving him a sheepish smile.

"I'm sorry. I don't know why I'm so tired and sleepy."

"Because you're exhausted. You've had a hell of a few days. You want the rest of that sub?"

"No, I don't have the energy to eat it."

"Okay, let's get you to bed." He took her hand and led her to the guest room.

"Will you stay with me until I fall asleep?" she asked softly, her eyes heavy with sleep.

He smiled, brushing a lock of hair away from her face. "Of course, I'll be right here."

"Maybe you could hold me? I feel safe with you."

He toed off his shoes, then slid onto the bed. "Turn your back to me."

She turned, then sighed when he wrapped his arm around her waist. "Thank you for finding me."

"You're welcome." He wanted to thank her for needing him to find her. As she drifted off, he watched over her, his heart full of tenderness. The events of the day replayed in his mind, the way she had trusted him, her vulnerability touching something deep within him.

In the quiet of the room, he realized that his feelings for her had grown beyond simple liking. He would do anything to keep her safe and make her smile.

With a soft sigh, he leaned over and pressed a gentle kiss to the corner of her eye before easing out of bed. "Sleep well, beautiful girl," he whispered.

THE NEXT MORNING, he was up early and gathering ingredients for breakfast when his doorbell rang. He knew who it was, and after opening the door, he smiled as he kissed Harlow's cheek.

"Get your mouth off my woman," Grayson growled from behind her.

Harlow's eyebrows shot up as she scowled at him. *"Your woman?"*

"Yep. Deal with it." He put his hand around her neck, brought her to him, and soundly kissed her.

"When you two finish making out like teenagers, I'll be in the kitchen."

Liam left them to it. His phone buzzed with a text, and he glanced at it. It was from Cooper, telling him he was on the way.

"I have the things you asked for," Harlow said as Grayson set bags from a local department store on the counter.

"Appreciate you shopping for Quinn." He'd given her a list of things he thought Quinn needed until she could get home, and Harlow had gone to the store last night.

"No problem. Is she up yet?"

"I'll go see." At the guest room door, he knocked. "Quinn, you up?"

"Yeah. You can come in."

He opened the door and found her sitting on the edge of the bed wearing his T-shirt with the bottom of his boxer briefs peeking out. "Morning. How are you feeling?" She looked lost, and he wanted to send everyone home, and when they were alone, he'd gather her up and hold her, take care of her.

"Better than yesterday." She frowned down at herself. "I can wash my clothes, but I'm going to need shoes."

"Stand by a sec." He went to the end of the hallway. "Harlow, can you bring the things you got? She seems a little lost today," he quietly told Harlow. "Maybe having something besides my T-shirt to wear will help."

"Can't hurt," Harlow said. "I want to meet the woman who has you sending me to the mall with a list of things most men wouldn't even think of." She grinned. "You like her."

It wasn't a question, so he didn't answer. Harlow followed him into the bedroom.

At seeing her, Quinn's gaze darted between them before stopping on Harlow. "Oh, um… I'm just here until I get some shoes. I slept in here. In his guest room. We're not—" she gestured between her and him "—ah, you know. He didn't tell me he had a girlfriend."

Harlow laughed.

He frowned at Quinn. "What are you talking about?"

"She's afraid I'm going to get mad at my boyfriend because he brought a woman home with him," Harlow said.

Say what now? "I'm not your boyfriend."

"Get lost, Liam. I got this." She smiled at Quinn as she walked into the room with the department store bags, closing the door in his face.

"Right, I'll get lost," he muttered.

He didn't like…well, whatever just happened. He was the one who was supposed to be a hero in Quinn's eyes, bringing her new clothes and shoes. And panties. He was kind of hoping she would need his help putting on the panties. Guess not.

By the time he returned to the kitchen, Cooper had arrived. "Your fiancée's mean," Liam told Grayson. "She kicked me out and slammed the door in my face." His two friends laughed, and he scowled at them. "Not funny."

"Quit pouting and feed me," Cooper said.

"Dude, are you ever not hungry?" The man was a bottomless pit.

Cooper lifted his gaze to the ceiling, pretending to think about it. He snapped his fingers. "Yup. After dinner last Thanksgiving. You gonna do that again this year, right? It was awesome."

Having grown up working in his father's pub, he was the appointed chef in the group. "If I'm in town, sure." He pushed the plate of bread and the toaster across the counter. "Here, start making toast while I bring you up to speed on what happened."

The bacon was cooked, the hash browns were keeping warm in the oven, and he just needed to scramble the eggs. He was keeping this meal a simple one. The purpose of getting everyone together was to make a plan for keeping

Quinn safe and getting his teammates' help in investigating what Jasper Garrison was up to.

"How's Quinn this morning?" Grayson asked.

"Not sure. Didn't really get to talk to her before your woman kicked me out."

Grayson chuckled. "Better not let her hear you call her that."

"Yeah, she's mean." Truthfully, Harlow was one of the nicest people he'd ever known, and Quinn couldn't be in better hands...except for his.

Chapter Twelve

If not Liam's girlfriend—and funny how happy that made her—who was this beautiful woman smiling at her as if they were besties? Quinn wished she had on something besides an oversize T-shirt and Liam's underwear.

"I'm Harlow Pressley, Grayson's fiancée. I understand you've had a lousy few days."

"Quinn Sullivan. Nice to meet you, and you could say that."

"Well, I have a few things here that might help you feel better." She set several bags bearing a popular department store's logo on the bed.

Quinn peeked in one of them. "You brought me clothes? You're an angel."

"Thank Liam. He sent me shopping with a list of things to get you."

"I'll thank him, but still, thank you for going shopping." She dumped out the items in the bag, revealing two pairs of shorts, two jeans, several T-shirts, and two nice tops. In the next bag were panties and two bras, a nude one and a black one. From the third bag came a brush, hair ties, toothbrush, toothpaste, lip gloss, deodorant, a lady's razor, shampoo, conditioner, body wash, and body lotion. In the last one, she found flip-flops, a pair of white canvas tennis shoes, and a package of socklets.

"All this was on his list?"

"Yep."

"The sizes are right. How did you know?"

"When Liam called me last night and said your clothes were a lost cause and asked me to shop for you, I had him look at the sizes in your clothes to give me some sort of direction." She grinned. "He actually measured your feet since you didn't have any shoes."

"He thought of everything." Not that she needed this much, since she was going home today, but she couldn't imagine another man doing this for her. She was going to miss him, that was for sure.

"Why don't I let you get dressed. Liam's making breakfast, so come on out as soon as you're ready."

"Okay. And, Harlow, I truly appreciate you shopping for me."

Harlow smiled. "Who doesn't love shopping? Found a few things for myself while I was at it."

When she was alone, Quinn gathered up the toiletries and took them to the bathroom. Ten minutes later, she had her hair tamed in a ponytail and was wearing a pair of the shorts and a T-shirt. She decided on the flip-flops as they seemed the best choice for her feet. She then followed the aromas of bacon and coffee to the kitchen.

"Oh, everyone's here. Morning, y'all." She waved her fingers at the guys, getting smiles from Grayson and Cooper. Harlow was pouring coffee into cups.

Liam, standing at the stove, glanced over his shoulder and smiled. "Breakfast is almost ready."

A man who sent someone shopping for her and cooked?

Sign her up. Grayson stood from the bar stool where he was sitting next to Cooper. "Have a seat."

"Thanks." She'd only been on her feet for a few minutes, and already they were hurting from walking on them.

"Coffee?" Harlow asked.

"Lord, yes. About a gallon, please." After adding cream and sugar to the cup Harlow set in front of her, she took a sip. "Ah, perfect." She hadn't had any coffee since the morning of the day Jasper kidnapped her. Another reason to wish him to the devil.

"Breakfast is up," Liam said. "Eat here or on the balcony?"

"I'm good with eating here if the ladies are," Cooper said as he stood. "Harlow, you can have my seat."

"I'm fine here," Quinn said.

"Me, too." Harlow brought her cup of coffee around the island and slid onto the stool Cooper had vacated. She handed Grayson her plate. "Load me up, babe."

"I'll load you up all right." Grayson gave her a wicked grin.

"Hey, no talking dirty in my kitchen," Liam said. His gaze fell on Quinn.

When he winked, she glanced down at her plate, hiding her smile…and the heat that she knew was in her eyes. This man was dangerous to her in all the right ways. As much as he fascinated her, she didn't have time to mess around. She had to find that thumb drive and figure out what Jasper was up to.

"I need to rent a car." She'd considered flying home, but it would actually be easier to drive than deal with airports and flights. She could be home just about as fast. "Oh, crap. I just realized my purse is back at the cabin." That was a problem. She didn't have any money or her credit cards. She'd have to borrow money from him until she got her purse back.

"Let's finish breakfast, and then we'll talk," Liam said.

"Okay."

As she ate, she tuned their conversation out while she tried to think of how to get her purse back. The things in her suitcase, also left behind, could be replaced, but her IDs, credit cards, and cash not so easily. She had about a thousand dollars in her wallet, not a small amount for her.

Few people carried that much money around with them, but it was one of her dad's rules. Call home every Wednesday and Sunday, have enough money in her wallet to get out of a foreign country on the spur of the moment if things went south—which she'd actually had to do once and she'd only accomplished it because she had the cash to bribe a man who could get her on the last plane out—and never drink anything that she hadn't poured herself or watched poured. None of those things were too much to ask of her for her father to not have to worry about her...well, not too much.

"Why don't y'all go talk," Harlow said. "I'll clean up the kitchen, then I need to go home. I have a conference call with a baseball player and his PR person this morning."

"That sounds cool. What do you do?" Quinn asked.

"I design websites, handle social media for celebrities, things like that."

"Girl, we need to talk. My website could use some work. I just never seem to have the time to get to it."

"You have a card?" Harlow said. "I'll take a look at it."

"Not on me." They were in her purse. Oh, wait. She had some in her camera bag. "I'll be right back." From now on, she was going to keep her wallet in her camera bag because that was the one thing she'd never leave behind.

When she returned, she and Harlow traded cards, promising to talk soon. After Harlow left, Quinn said, "I like her."

Grayson grinned. "I kind of like her, too."

She laughed. "Yeah, you'd be a fool not to, and I don't take you as a fool."

"He's a fool in love," Cooper sang.

"That I am," Grayson cheerfully said. "Ready to get down to business?"

"I guess. I could use another cup of coffee, though." When she got up to make it, Liam took her cup from her. While he was refilling it, she glanced out the sliding door. "Can we sit outside?" She loved the beach, but rarely had time to go.

"Sure," Liam said.

Once they were settled around the table for four on his balcony, the guys also with coffee refills, she said, "I'm not sure what there is to talk about except how I'm going to get home. I realized I left my purse at the cabin, which I need to figure out how to get back." Would Liam go back to Hope Corner with her? "Maybe—"

"If you're thinking of going back to get your purse, think again." Liam set down his cup, an unhappy expression on his face.

Men! Why couldn't they discuss things without getting bossy? She had no intention of returning to the cabin by herself, but she didn't like being told what she could and couldn't do. "You're not the boss of me."

"Ruh-roh," Cooper muttered. He poked Liam's arm. "Didn't your mama teach you better than to say things like that?"

Grayson snorted.

"Apparently not." Liam sighed. "I'm not trying to boss you around, Quinn. But—"

"If you'd give me a chance to finish, I was going to ask if you could come with me to get my purse."

"I thought you wanted to go home and look for that thumb drive, see if you have it. That's not your priority?"

"Well, yes." Why did he have to make sense? And as much as she wanted her purse back, it was ridiculous to even think of going back to the cabin.

"Liam filled us in before you came down," Grayson said. "You don't have any idea what's on the thumb drive?"

"All I know is that I overheard his end of a phone conversation where he said children were getting sick because of someone dumping something into the lake, and it sounds like he's blackmailing that person. Apparently, there's a thumb drive with photos on it that I might have accidentally taken when I left." Her gaze scanned each of their faces. "I can't turn my back on that if children are getting sick and it's something I can stop."

"I have a question," Cooper said. "Why don't you just turn all this over to the police? Report the kidnapping?"

"Not yet. I need to find that thumb drive if I do have it, see what's on it. If children are getting sick because of illegal dumping, it's bigger than me being kidnapped."

"I agree with Quinn," Liam said. "The police might not be the best people to bring in on this, depending on what is on the thumb drive. If it's something making children sick, then we're probably talking about the EPA or the Feds."

Grayson nodded. "We need to find that thumb drive."

"Then I have a solution," Cooper said. "Why don't you and Liam go look for the thumb drive, and I'll go to the cabin and get your purse."

"Not a bad idea," Liam said. "You'd be able to nose around, see if you can pick up anything of interest. You can also check on my car, see if it can be fixed there, or if I need to have it towed to Grayson's dealership."

"You have a dealership?" Quinn asked.

Cooper was the one to snort this time. "The boy has what? Eleven of them? All luxury car dealerships. Need a new car, he's the man to see."

Grayson shrugged as if it wasn't a big deal, but jeez, if he had eleven of them, he must be loaded. She was impressed that he was so down-to-earth, that he came across as just another one of the guys.

"Good to know if I'm ever car shopping." She was relieved that they weren't fighting her and insisting she go to the police. "Thank you for understanding that I can't turn my back on the children."

"Neither can we," Liam said. "Which means you have a team of skilled investigators on your side."

"What he said." That from Grayson. "While you and Liam are looking for the thumb drive and Coop's nosing around Hope Corner, I'll start looking into Jasper. I'd like you to write down everything you know about him before you head home."

Cooper grinned. "We got a plan, folks."

Honestly, she was a bit overwhelmed by these guys who weren't hesitating to help her find out what Jasper was up to. Jasper had no clue who was gunning for him. If he did, he'd make like a rabbit and haul ass.

Chapter Thirteen

"Awesome house," Liam said as he parked the car Grayson had loaned him until his was repaired.

"It's too big for my dad, but he's lived here since he and my mother married, and all his memories of her are here."

Liam guessed the two-story Victorian house was four or five thousand square feet, and it fit the landscape of giant oak trees dripping with Spanish moss. The wide front porch was perfect for sitting in the swing with a book and a sweet iced tea. The ceiling fans would make hot summer days tolerable.

"You said your father's in Asheville?"

"Maggie Valley actually, but that's in the Asheville area. He'll come back to Savannah in early October when it starts to cool down a little. He does come home if I'm here so he can spend time with me. He wanted to be here now, but I told him to stay at his cabin, that I was only going to be here for a day, two at the most."

She unlocked the door, and he held it open for her to step inside. He followed her in and paused to appreciate the entrance. They were in a large foyer, the feature a wide staircase, and he could imagine her walking down it on prom night, her date standing at the bottom, his gaze focused on the beautiful girl floating toward him. In Liam's vision, the girl wore a green gown that fit her curves and matched her eyes. He was jealous of that faceless boy.

"You look a thousand miles away," she said. "What are you thinking?"

"Did you go to the prom?"

"Yes, why?"

"Did you walk down those stairs while your boyfriend tried his best not to drool at seeing you?"

She laughed. "I don't know about the drooling part, but yes."

"What color was your dress?"

"Emerald green. Why are you asking these questions?"

Because he'd seen her clear as day slowly descending the stairs, a soft smile on her face for the boy waiting for her to reach him. "I just wanted to picture it." If he married her, he'd ask her to walk down those stairs in her wedding dress, so he would experience that soft smile meant just for him. He shook his head. Where had that thought even come from?

"You want something to drink?"

"I'm good for now." They walked past the stairs and into a formal living room. "Your home is beautiful."

"Thank you. I think so, too, although I sometimes forget to appreciate it. It's the only home I've ever known."

"Your father's retired I take it?"

"For five years now. He owned a real estate company specializing in commercial property and decided one day he was working too hard, so he sold it. He dabbles in the stock market now, more as a hobby than a job. He seems to have a knack for it, though."

It was obvious father and daughter were close, and he envied that. Even before he'd been declared dead to his father, they hadn't been close. What Patrick O'Rourke saw when he looked at his son was a means to an end, just someone to carry on the O'Rourke legacy. There had never been affection between them, and as hard as the boy he used to be longed for approval from his father, it never came. Yet he still held on to the hope that someday, his father would… well, undead him. That he'd be welcomed back into the family again.

She headed down a hallway. "Come on. I want to look for that thumb drive."

"Right behind you." He took those unwanted thoughts of his father and crammed them back into the box where they belonged.

"Cool room," he said after following her into what he was expecting to be her bedroom but was not. He turned in a circle, taking in the two large monitors sitting on a glass desk, a small blue leather sofa, the photos on the walls, the shelves of awards, and a long, chest-high table in the middle of the room. Scattered across the table were cameras, two closed laptops, and things he couldn't identify.

"Where's your darkroom?"

She walked straight to the table. "You don't know much about photography, do you? With digital cameras, computers, and hundreds of photography software, darkrooms aren't much of a thing anymore."

"Who knew?"

She glanced up from scattering thumb drives over the table and smirked. "I did."

"I want to kiss that smirk right off your face." When she laughed, he stepped around the table. "You find that funny?" He was close enough now to catch her scent, something that made him think of the sea, summer nights, and satiny sheets.

"Are you smelling me?" she asked when he leaned his nose close to her neck and inhaled.

"I am. What's that scent? Makes me want to lick you."

"Harlow brought me coconut-and-vanilla body wash and shampoo." She tilted her head, giving him access to her neck. "You like?"

"*Like* is such a mundane word for what I think." Keeping his lips close to her skin, but not touching, he moved his mouth until it was an inch from hers. "Stop or go?"

"Go?"

"As in can I go ahead and kiss you?"

"If you want."

"Oh, I want." The first time he'd kissed her, he'd committed the taste of her to memory, but maybe his memory was faulty. When his lips met hers this time, it was…different. Their kiss in the woods had been sweet and tentative with a hint of possibilities. This one, man, this one was electric, sending a shock wave of desire through him.

She tasted like sin and a craving only she could satisfy, a dangerous combination that had his head spinning. When they finally broke apart, he was breathless, his heart hammering in his chest. He leaned his forehead against hers. It was in that moment that he realized this wasn't just a passing attraction; there was something deeper between them, something he wanted to explore.

"Wow," she whispered.

"Yeah, that kiss was definitely a wow." He cupped her cheek, her skin soft against his palm. "There's more where that came from. All you have to do is ask."

"I just might do that, but right now, I want to know if I have Jasper's thumb drive."

He picked up one that looked different. "What's this?"

"It's a SanDisk. Sometimes we store our photos on those,

sometimes on a thumb drive. Jasper wants his thumb drive, and he knows the difference, so that's what we're looking for. Purple's my favorite color, so mine are all purple. Jasper's are black, and it's not here."

"So, you don't have it?"

"Don't get excited yet." She got a bigger camera bag. "This is the one I had with me in California. I didn't really go through it when I got back. You'd think if he has photos stored on a drive that are worth a million dollars to someone, he'd keep it safely locked up somewhere. But that's Jasper for you. Never takes care of his things."

"Most people would." He leaned against the table. "Tell me about him."

"He's also a photojournalist. I met him in California when we were both covering the wildfires. He likes to think he's a macho man, gets embedded with teams on the front lines of wars or in California with the hotshots." She stared down at her hands where she rested them on the camera bag. "It embarrasses me to admit that I had a short fling with him."

"Why? You're single, and if you were attracted to him and it was consensual, you have nothing to be embarrassed about." Thinking of her being intimate with another man, though? Not a picture he wanted in his mind. "Did he treat you right?"

"He did in the beginning. Around the time for me to head home, he started getting possessive and talked about me staying even though my assignment was coming to an end. When I reminded him that I didn't do relationships, something I'd been up-front about from the beginning, he just talked over me. By then, I knew I'd made a mistake getting involved with him."

"You don't do relationships at all?" That was not something he wanted to hear.

She lifted her gaze to his. "No."

"How come?" If she wasn't interested in him, he'd walk away, but she was. He could see it in her eyes and in the way she kissed him back. He wasn't a man who let obstacles get in his way. There were always a way around them. To do that, he needed to know what her obstacles were and why they were there.

"Why not, Quinn?"

Chapter Fourteen

Quinn considered her answer. If he were any other man, she'd tell him because that was the way it was, because it was her choice, and she didn't owe anyone an explanation. To explain, she'd have to share her past, talk about Aiden. But Liam wasn't any other man, and she wanted him to understand.

She glanced at her watch. They had all night to look for the thumb drive, and she sensed this was an important conversation to have. "You know what, it's wine time." She didn't want to talk about this while they stood in her photography room at her worktable, looking for Jasper's thumb drive…thinking of Jasper. "Let's go sit out on the patio."

"Is this a diversion tactic?"

"No." She held out her hand, and he took it. "I'm going to bare my soul. I just need a peaceful setting and a glass of wine while I do it."

"All right, then. Lead on."

He was so easy to get along with…now anyway. She knew how that could change if feelings became involved. It was always the woman who was expected to change her life for her man. Even her mother had.

"White or red?" she asked when they reached the kitchen.

"Or maybe you'd like something stronger? Dad's bar is in the butler's pantry if you want to check out what he has."

"I'll have what you're having, but I've never seen a butler's pantry, so I need to check it out."

She gestured to the door past the refrigerator. "It's right over there." After he walked by her, she took a moment to appreciate the rear view. His T-shirt wasn't so tight that his muscles stretched the fabric, but they were there. Broad shoulders, a tapered waist, a mouthwatering butt, and long legs made for a very sexy man. That wasn't even taking into account his face, those blue eyes, and that black hair.

"Yummy, yummy, yummy," she murmured after he disappeared into the pantry. Hopefully, he would be agreeable to a brief fling with the condition that there would be absolutely no feelings involved and they would go their separate ways when their time was up. She ignored the little pang in her chest at the thought of walking away from Liam.

She took a bottle of Pinot Grigio, her favorite wine, from the wine cooler and poured each of them a glass. Was she really going to dredge up memories that still had the power to hurt? After everything went down with Aiden, she'd promised herself never again would she let a man hurt her the way he had. Walls had been erected, and she'd been perfectly happy with life after Aiden.

Aiden had been her first and only love. Although she saw nothing wrong with consensual sex, she was selective and cautious, but she wished she could have a do-over on the last one. She'd like to bleach her brain of any memory of Jasper.

Liam stepped out of the butler's pantry. "If I ever build a house, it's going to have one of these."

She grinned. "Most people want a big walk-in closet or a pool. You just want a pantry."

"Not just any pantry." He took the glass of wine she offered. "One like that."

"Let's take our drinks outside." She started walking toward the sliding door to the patio.

"Can we sit on the front porch instead? I think that swing has my name on it."

"Sure. It's Dad's favorite place to sit in the morning with his cup of coffee." She flipped the switch to turn on the ceiling fans as they walked out.

"Ah, this is nice," he said after they were seated.

She tucked her feet under her so he could push the swing with his long legs. The breeze from the ceiling fans kept it from being too hot, and as he rocked them, she closed her eyes, inhaling the sweet scent of her dad's roses. It was good to be home.

"You're beautiful," he softly said.

She opened her eyes to see his gaze on her, and she smiled. "Thank you."

"Talk to me, Quinn. Why don't you do relationships?"

"Why do you want to know?" She'd kind of hoped he would forget that was why they'd taken a break from looking for Jasper's thumb drive. The weight of his question settled between them, and she wished she hadn't said she'd give him an answer.

"Because I…" He glanced away for a moment before his gaze returned to hers. "I like you, and I think maybe we could have something good between us. Suppose we don't give it a name? We just spend some time together, see how it goes. Would you say yes to that?"

"I'd be more likely to agree to a short fling." If she was ever tempted to be in a relationship again, it would be with him. "Relationships don't work for me because—"

Liam's phone chimed. He pulled it from his pocket and

turned the screen toward her, showing her it was Cooper calling. "Whatcha got for me?" As he listened, his eyes locked on her. "I'm with Quinn now. I'm going to put you on speaker."

"Hi, Quinn," Cooper said.

"Do you have my purse? Oh, and hi."

"I'm sorry to say that I don't have it. We've got a problem. Garrison's dead. Murdered, and—"

"What?" Jasper was dead? Murdered?

"Do you have any details?" Liam asked.

"When I got to the cabin, I found him on the floor, shot in the back of his head, execution style."

Quinn gasped. "Oh, my God." She was furious with Jasper, regretted every moment she spent with him, but she'd never wish that for him. What in the world had he gotten into? What had caused him to kidnap her, chain her up, and in the end get himself killed?

"It gets worse. I have your suitcase, Quinn, but your purse was nowhere to be found."

Her heart fell to her stomach. "What does that mean?"

Liam took her hand and squeezed. "It's not good. Whoever shot Garrison has your purse, knows who you are."

"I think I'm going to be sick." Liam tugged on her hand, pulling her against him. She tucked into him, wishing she could stay wrapped in his arms where she knew she'd be safe.

"Are the police aware?" Liam asked.

"Not yet. I'll make an anonymous call to the local police telling them where to find Garrison as soon as I get back to town. His phone and wallet aren't on him, so I assume whoever took your purse took them, too. I'm going to wipe down anywhere I think your prints might be, Quinn."

"Why not just tell the police I was there?" She didn't kill him. "I could tell them what happened."

"For one, the Hope Corner police department won't have the experience to deal with something like this," Liam said. "They'll want you to go there, and that's not going to happen. We don't know who killed Garrison. Was it someone local? Someone who might have an in with the police? We won't risk it." A fierce light entered his eyes. "I won't risk you."

"He's right," Cooper said.

"So, what do we do?" How in God's name did she end up in the middle of a murder? She never bothered anyone. She just wanted to take pictures of children who needed a helping hand.

"We find that thumb drive, see who Garrison was trying to blackmail and what he had on them. We find out who killed him and how they're involved. Then we fix it and make you safe. Bring in the proper authorities when we know what we're dealing with. Probably the FBI. Until then, I'm not leaving your side."

Her stomach settled a little, knowing he would keep her safe, but still… She was scared, really scared. She didn't want to ask the question in her mind, but she had to. "Does whoever has my purse think I have the thumb drive?"

Liam nodded. "We have to assume that's what they think."

And they knew where she lived. "We have to find it. Right now."

"I'm going to nose around here a little," Cooper said. "See what kind of vibes I can pick up. Keep in touch."

"Will do, and be careful." Liam slipped his phone back into his pocket. "We're not staying here tonight after all. I'm going to get my weapons bag from the car, then let's go see if we can find that thumb drive so we can get out of here."

She waited on the porch for him, and once they were inside, he locked the door while she went to the alarm and set it. Once that was done, she leaned against the wall. "What if you weren't here? I'd be by myself, not knowing what happened after I left the cabin. I wouldn't know someone was looking for me." What she really wanted to do was crawl into the bed and pull the covers over her head.

He dropped the bag to the floor, then wrapped his arms around her. "I am here, so don't even go down that road. You couldn't find anyone better to have your back than the three of us. And I meant it when I said I'm not leaving your side until this is over."

"Thank you," she whispered. She buried her face against his chest. "How did I end up in the middle of a murder?" She stepped away from him. "Come on. Let's find that damn thumb drive." She still wasn't sure she had it.

Back in her office, he set his bag on the sofa. He opened it, took out a holster that he clipped to his belt, then he brought out a gun, slipping it into the holster. At her raised brows, he said, "Best we be prepared for trouble."

"I hate this, but you're right. I'll get mine out of the gun safe and keep it near me."

"Probably not a bad idea."

It gave her the warm fuzzies that he didn't balk at her also arming herself. She'd told him she knew how to use a gun, and he didn't question her, just trusted that she wasn't blowing smoke. He came and stood next to her as she took everything out of her large camera bag, and at the bottom, where she'd hurriedly tossed her own accessories, was one black thumb drive.

"That's it?" Liam asked.

"I think so. I don't have any black ones." She didn't know how she felt about actually having it. A part of her wished she'd never touched it, but if whatever was on it showed why children were getting sick? She would be able to do something about it. At the very least, she could make sure the right someone or agency was made aware.

"Let's see what's on it," Liam said.

"In a way, I don't want to even know, but I guess we need to." She took the thumb drive to her desk computer, logged in, and then slipped the drive into the port.

"It's the only way we'll find out what Garrison got involved in."

She frowned at what they were seeing. "What in the world?"

Chapter Fifteen

"He's dumping something into the lake," Liam said. "That's never good." The video was of a man who had a steel drum turned over on its side, and a colorless liquid was flowing into the lake. The camera panned to where more drums behind the man had either been already dumped or were going to be. "We need to find out what that stuff is."

"Whatever it is, it's making children sick." After the video, there were photos. Still shots of the drums, then one of the lake.

It wasn't a big lake, which also wasn't good, since the liquid didn't have much space to disperse. The next picture was of a section of the lake that had a sandy shore and children playing in the water. There was a playground in the background and picnic pavilions, so the area had been created for people to enjoy the lake.

"That's Black Bear Lake," Quinn said. "I took some photos of it."

He leaned closer to the monitor when she moved on to the next photo. "What's that building?" The picture of a large structure was taken from a distance. "Can you zoom in on the name?"

"Sure."

"Hanson Textiles," he read when the name was enlarged. "We need intel on that business."

"It's a textile mill. I saw it when I was snooping around. It's about a half mile from the lake."

He called Grayson, and when he had his teammate on the phone, he said, "Get Cooper on here with us. I have an update." A minute later, Cooper was on the call with them. Liam told them what they'd found on the thumb drive. "I need you to look into Hanson Textiles," he told Grayson. "We need to know who owns it."

"I'm on it," Grayson said.

"As long as I'm in Hope Corner, I'll see what I can learn on this end," Cooper said. "The big question, if those drums belonged to this textile mill, are they still dumping whatever's in them?"

That was a question Liam wanted an answer to. "And exactly what was in them. Once we find that out, we'll be able to notify the authorities. We know that Garrison was planning to blackmail someone. The question is who. And was this person the one who killed him? Or maybe he sent someone to do his dirty work?"

"I'll do a deep dive on the mill as soon as we hang up," Grayson said. "What's your plan? If our bad guys know about Quinn and think she has the thumb drive, you're not safe there."

"Agreed. Quinn's going to email you a copy of what's on the drive, and then we're going to pack up and come back to Myrtle Beach. It's where she'll be the safest."

Quinn scowled. "Maybe you should ask me what I want to do."

"So, you're good with staying here knowing it's not safe?"

Grayson chuckled. "Sounds like it's time for Coop and me to sign off."

"See you tomorrow." After disconnecting, he crossed his arms and raised a brow. "Back to my question. You want to stay here even knowing someone who's already murdered knows where you live?"

"No, of course not. I just don't like being told what to do. I would appreciate being a part of the decision."

"My bad." He wanted to grin at her disgruntled expression, but he doubted she would appreciate that. He very much liked that she stood up for herself. "Allow me to remedy my blunder. I'm of the opinion that we need to skedaddle ASAP. What would you advise on this situation, Miss Sullivan?"

She scowled at him. "Stop being so entertaining." One corner of her mouth twitched before she caught it.

"Why?"

"Because I don't need to be liking you any more than I already do."

"Sorry, but I can't help myself, sugar pie." He almost laughed when she wrinkled her nose at the endearment. Somehow, he'd known that would rile her up.

"No, no, no. Don't start with the pet names. My name is Quinn. Period."

"Got it. I'll try to refrain from affectionate cute little names. Now that we've got that cleared up, we really need to leave before unwanted visitors show up."

"Give me Grayson's email, so I can send this to him, and then we can do as you advise and skedaddle." After he told her Grayson's email address and she'd sent him copies of the files, she handed him the thumb drive. "You're in charge of keeping this safe."

He put the drive in the front pocket of his jeans. While

she was packing her cameras and accessories, he retrieved his weapons bag. After putting on his shoulder holster, he moved his gun from at his waist to the holster, then slipped a shirt over his T-shirt, leaving it unbuttoned, hiding the gun. With another gun secured in his ankle holster, and a knife in a sheath at his belt, he zipped the bag up.

She'd disappeared into what he assumed was her bedroom, and as he waited for her, he went to a front window and looked out. All seemed quiet outside, but his skin prickled with unease. It was a warning he'd learned to pay heed to.

"We need to go, Quinn," he called.

"Do you see anything?" she asked, coming next to him, carrying her camera bag and a small tote.

"No, but the hair on my neck is standing on end, so I'm uneasy about us walking out to the car. I should've parked it in your garage."

"Would Grayson be unhappy if we left it here?"

"If he has to choose between our safety and the car, he'll pick us. Why? What are you thinking?"

"Get your stuff and come with me."

He followed her through the kitchen and after she set the alarm, they went out to the garage. "Well, well, what do we have here? Is that yours?"

"Yep. And she's fast."

"I just bet she is." He whistled as he eyed the black beauty, a Porsche Cayenne Turbo.

"My dad said I could have any car I wanted for my graduation present from college, and this was what I wanted. It's almost a crime that she sits when I'm gone so much, but Dad does enjoy driving it, too." She tossed him the keys. "You drive."

"Be happy to." They loaded their bags in the back, and once they were seated in the car, he said, "Do you have your gun on you?" She'd told him she knew how to shoot, and he was going to trust her on that.

"Oh, I was in a hurry and forgot to get it. I'll be right back."

He put his hand on her arm. "No, I don't think we have the time." That sixth sense he was known for was screaming that danger was near. "I can loan you one when we get to Myrtle Beach if need be."

"Okay. Let's get out of here."

"All right, time to see if anyone's waiting for us." He leaned over and caught her eyes. "Listen carefully. If we do have company, or pick up any on our way, you do everything I say when I say, no exceptions."

"Sir, yes, sir." She saluted him. When he narrowed his eyes, she shrugged. "Sorry, couldn't resist. I will obey you without question when it comes to our safety." Her lips ticked up in a grin. "Can't promise that at other times. Just so you know."

"I wouldn't expect otherwise." He glanced up at the visor. "That the garage door opener?"

"Yes."

"I'm going to start the car, then hit the opener. Be ready for anything." He prayed he was wrong and bad guys with guns weren't waiting for them.

"Just try not to let them shoot up my car."

"I'll do my best." Before he started the car, he leaned over and gave her a quick kiss. "That was for good luck. Ready?" She nodded, and after the car was running, he pushed the opener. The door rumbled open. As he was backing the Porsche out, the sound of breaking glass pierced the air, and the house's alarm blared.

"They're breaking in." Fear tinged her voice.

He wished he could take the time to reassure her that he'd

keep her safe, but his one goal at the moment was to get her away from danger. He pressed down on the gas pedal, the tires screeching against the garage floor. Clear of the garage, he stopped long enough to throw the gear from Reverse to Drive. Rubber burned as he gave the Porsche gas and spun it around.

"Oh, God," she screamed as a man wearing a black face mask stood in front of them, a gun pointed at their windshield.

"Get down," he ordered, and as she'd promised, she instantly obeyed, lowering her head to her knees.

"Stop or I'll shoot," the man yelled.

It was time to play chicken, as there was no way he was stopping. If he did, they'd both end up dead. He gunned it and headed straight for the man. The man dived out of the way. Shots were fired at them from behind, but he didn't slow down.

Two white SUVs were parked at the end of Quinn's driveway. One was empty, and one had two men in it. Liam managed to get the plate number on one of the cars as he blew by them over the grass. "Sorry about your dad's lawn."

Fortunately, there wasn't anything blocking his view of the road, and not seeing any cars coming, he took the turn onto the street at a speed that if he'd been driving another car, they probably would've fishtailed. The Porsche, though, handled the maneuver as if it had been only waiting to show off what it was capable of.

The occupied SUV tore off after them. He grinned. "Catch me if you can."

"Can I get up now?"

"Yeah."

"Who are they?" she said as she leaned around the headrest and watched the car chasing them.

There was fear in her voice, and he wanted to knock some heads for scaring her. "I don't know, but we'll find out. Sit back and make sure your seat belt is tightened. We're going to see what this baby can do."

"She can do whatever you ask of her."

"Counting on it." The SUV was coming up fast on their bumper, and Liam was sure the intention was to hit them and run them off the road. The Sullivans' house was outside Savannah city limits, in a somewhat rural area. The road they were on was a two-lane and not heavily traveled. He needed to lose the SUV before they got to heavier traffic. The last thing he wanted was to put any innocents in danger.

"Hold on. We're going turbo." He pushed the gas pedal to the floor, and the powerful engine roared to life. As they raced down the narrow road, trees blurred past them in a green-and-brown whirl. The SUV behind them struggled to keep up, and its headlights grew smaller in the rear-view mirror with each passing second. The Porsche's tires gripped the road as he took a sharp curve faster than was safe.

An intersection with a four-way stop loomed ahead. "Which way will take us to an area we can get lost in?"

"Left. There's a mall and a bunch of restaurants."

"Perfect." Now the trick was to get lost in traffic.

Chapter Sixteen

Adrenaline rushed through Quinn's veins as Liam wound their way up and down streets, sometimes taking left turns, sometimes right ones. She'd been watching in her side-view mirror and hadn't seen the SUV since they'd taken that first left at the intersection.

"You okay?" Liam asked.

"I'm good." Mostly. That had been scary, though.

"How do we get to I-95 from here?"

"Keep going straight for a few miles. I'll tell you when to turn." As they traveled, she kept her gaze on the mirror. "I think we lost them."

"For now. We just need to hope they don't connect you to me or The Phoenix Three. I'd rather not see them show up in Myrtle Beach."

She definitely didn't want to bring trouble to her new friends. Since they'd lost the men chasing them, she relaxed…somewhat. "Do you think those men are from whoever was dumping that stuff from those barrels?"

"That would be my guess."

Hopefully, Cooper and Grayson would know more by the time they got to Myrtle Beach, but she needed a break from thinking about men out to kill her. His phone chimed, and he pulled it out of his pocket and glanced at the screen.

"It's your dad." He handed the phone to her. "Just hit Accept."

"Hey, Dad."

"Where are you? The alarm company called. Are you okay?"

She told him what had happened, including why they weren't involving the police.

"I'm coming home."

"No, don't. I'm with Liam, and we're going back to Myrtle Beach. It's not safe to be at the house right now. Hold on. I'm putting you on speaker." She turned the phone toward Liam. "Tell him he needs to stay in Maggie Valley."

"Sir, she's right. It's not safe right now, and there's nothing you can do here."

"I don't like it, but I'll stand by for now. All I care about is that you keep my daughter safe."

"That's all I care about, too. Call the alarm company back and tell them it's a false alarm."

Her father loudly sighed. "I'm not liking this. Quinn, get a damn phone so I can call you."

She'd called when they'd returned to Myrtle Beach from Hope Corner to tell him she'd lost her phone and he could reach her through Liam.

"We'll get her a phone as soon as we get back to Myrtle Beach," Liam said.

"Love you, Dad."

"I love you, too, but I need you to stop turning my hair white."

She laughed. "Your hair was already white. Nothing to do with me."

"Humph." Then he disconnected.

She handed Liam his phone. "Can we talk about something besides men with guns and whatever all this is?"

"Sure." He tapped his finger on the steering wheel, then glanced at her. "Cooper's phone call interrupted our conversation, and I want to finish it. You were about to tell me why you don't do relationships."

"Was I?" She was kind of hoping he'd forgotten about that, yet, because he'd said he wanted to explore what this thing between them was, she wanted him to understand.

"You know you were, but if you don't want to talk about it…" He shrugged.

"Okay, here's the thing. Men can't handle my career, and I'm not giving it up to make a man happy."

"You shouldn't have to."

She huffed. "Tell that to Aiden, or even Jasper."

"Who's Aiden?"

His voice had turned growly, and it wasn't the sexy kind of growl. "A man I was in love with. We met right after I graduated college, and I told him right up front that I was going to be a photojournalist and I'd be traveling a lot. He assured me he was fine with that."

"I'm guessing he wasn't?"

"He seemed fine with it until he asked me to marry him. As soon as I said yes, everything changed. At first, it was small things, like couldn't I shorten my assignment to a week instead of the two I'd planned. Then it grew to be all about him. Aiden was a trauma doctor, and his job was stressful to say the least. That was his reason for asking me to give up traveling, that he needed me at home. He said he was saving lives while I was just taking pictures."

"He was wrong. Your work is important. You bring attention to children who need it the most."

"I like to think I make a difference."

He reached over the console, found her hand, and squeezed it. "You do. Never doubt that."

"My mother gave up her career for my father. I didn't know she was unhappy until a few years ago. I don't think my father even knew that. She was never happier than when she had her camera in her hand. A few years ago, I found her diary in a box in the attic. It was an eye-opener. She wrote about how much she loved me and my dad, but she also talked about how something was missing. That if she had it to do over again, she wouldn't have given up her career for my father, but that she hadn't understood back then that she could have both."

"I'd say it was probably a generational thing. That she did what was expected of her and put her marriage first."

"Maybe. In her diary, on my first birthday, she wrote about how much she loved me and how she was going to teach me to go after my dreams, whatever they were. She was going to teach me that my dreams were important, and I should never let anyone come between me and what fed my soul. I found her diary after Aiden, and reading it, I vowed I'd honor her wishes for me. In my experience, it seems that men feel they're the important ones. So, I decided short flings are safe. Relationships for a woman means what you do, what feeds your soul isn't so important."

"I don't think anyone, man or woman, should have to give up something they love for another person," he said. "If you love someone, why would you want them to be less than they are? I can't judge why she gave up a part of herself to make your father happy. Maybe it was because they lived in a different generation, and she didn't know how to speak up for herself. Maybe she loved him so much that she felt like she needed to make him happy, and she wanted to make the sacrifice."

"Didn't sound like it in her diary."

"Maybe not, but I'm not Aiden, Quinn."

"I know." But did she?

After their conversation, they each grew quiet, and she hoped he understood why the only thing between them could be a fling. He might say he wasn't like Aiden or her father, but she wasn't willing to risk it. It was different with her because she was gone so much, so her job wasn't one where she had a career but was home every night.

If she took a chance and, in the end, she fell in love with him and he demanded she give up the one thing that fed her soul, it just might destroy her, because she just knew that given half a chance, she could love Liam so hard.

Sometime later, he shook her. "Wake up, Sleeping Beauty. We're here."

"Hmm?" She stretched. "Sorry. Didn't mean to fall asleep on you."

"That's okay. You needed the rest. Let's unload our stuff, then I want to hide your car. It's too recognizable. We'll get one of Grayson's loaners until I get my car back."

"That's a good idea."

As soon as they dropped their bags inside his condo, they were back on the road. "What about the car we left at my house?"

"I called Gray while you were sleeping, brought him up-to-date. He has a dealership in Savannah. Two of our friends are going to your house to check things out, and then they'll take the car to the dealership."

"Isn't that dangerous for them? What if those men are still there?"

"Doubtful they'll be hanging around. They probably

searched your house, and when they didn't find the thumb drive, they would've left. Hopefully, without doing much damage. If they are still around, our friends aren't the kind of men you want to mess with."

"What's this place?" she asked when Liam parked in front of a commercial building.

"Ours. The Phoenix Three's on the top floor. We rent out the other floors."

"Cool." She was curious about their offices.

The lobby was disappointingly plain. Nothing but an elevator straight ahead and two doors, one to the left with a sign for a group of attorneys and the other an insurance agency. She followed Liam into the elevator. As soon as the door closed, he pulled her in front of him, her back to his chest, and he slid his arms around her waist. It was a position she very much liked.

"Hey," he said, his voice next to her ear, his breath warm and tickling. How was one word that sexy?

She leaned against him. "Hey." She glanced up at him and smiled.

His eyes locked on hers. "If I didn't know for a fact that Gray was watching us right now, I'd kiss you senseless, maybe let my fingers go exploring."

"He's watching us?" she squeaked. She'd never kissed a man in an elevator, and the thought of Liam backing her up against the wall did funny things to her stomach and other places. But it was a big no on being watched. She moved to the opposite wall, and the dang man laughed.

The elevator door opened, and she couldn't resist messing with Liam after stepping out. She bent over to retie the laces of her sneaker and threw in a little butt wiggle.

"You're a very naughty girl, Quinn."

"Me? Never." She walked out, exaggerating the sway

of her hips and hiding her smile when the man behind her growled. There wasn't anyone in the reception area, and although she didn't know where she was supposed to go, she headed down the hallway. Footsteps on the wood floor sounded behind her, those of a predator stalking his prey, and she, being the prey, felt a rush of excitement.

Suddenly, an arm wrapped around her waist, and she was pulled into an office. He closed the door, and then turned them so that her back was against the wall. A thrill shot through her at his dominance.

He put his hands on the wall, caging her in. "You like playing games, Little Marine?"

The heat in his eyes matched what she knew was in hers. She wanted him in a way that she'd never experienced with another man. And funny in that she hated pet names, but she liked him calling her Little Marine. It was cute.

"Only when I know I'm going to win," she snarked.

A wicked grin appeared on his face, one that made her heart flutter in anticipation. "This is a game where we both win."

His lips crashed down on hers in a fierce kiss that stole the breath from her lungs. The world around them faded away, leaving only the electrifying connection between them. In that moment, there was no one else but the two of them, caught in a whirlwind of desire and unspoken promises. She put her hands on his chest and felt the rapid beat of his heart. He wanted her as much as she wanted him.

He rested his forehead against hers. "You drive me crazy, woman."

"Just so you know, I'm not sorry." She ducked under his arm and walked out.

Chapter Seventeen

Not sorry, eh? Grinning, Liam put his hand on her lower back as he followed her out. "Last door on the left."

"That's your office?"

"No, it's the war room."

She stopped so fast that he almost bowled her over. "War room?"

"Yeah, where all our equipment is. Where we plan our missions."

"Cool. Let's go play with your toys."

He chuckled. "A woman after my own heart."

"Let's keep our hearts out of it. Our mission is to learn who's making children sick and how." She glanced over her shoulder at him and grinned. "But no reason not to have a little fun along the way."

The last thing he wanted was to clue her in that his heart was already in it. That would only scare her away. So, he winked and said, "No reason at all." He'd just have to show her he wasn't like Aiden or any other man of her experience, his own secret mission to win that heart she so closely guarded. He wasn't in love with her...not yet. But he thought he could be if only she'd open her mind to the possibility of a future with him.

At the door to the war room, he put his palm to the security reader, then opened the door.

"That's neat," she said.

"We have some top-grade, expensive equipment in here. Don't want to make it easy for anyone to break in. The door's steel and bulletproof. Gray will be here in a minute."

"Oh, wow. You weren't kidding about having expensive equipment."

He stood back while she explored the room. In the middle was a conference table that would seat ten. In front of each leather chair was a monitor. They'd come in handy when they'd had occasion to have meetings with the police, and twice with the FBI. Everyone in attendance was able to follow along on their own monitor.

The top half of one wall was a flat screen that was connected to the three high-tech computers placed on the three desks along another wall. They could project any location in the world onto the screen as long as their computers could find it on Google Earth or other satellite imagery options such as NASA Worldview.

She stopped at a whiteboard, and her gaze roamed over the photos of the children they'd rescued. There weren't any names identifying the children, but he and his brothers knew every child's name.

"Most of those children were reunited with their families," he told her. "We had to find foster families for the few unfortunate ones who didn't have a family to claim them or that wanted them back." They kept tabs on their rescues, making sure those children were being taken care of and treated right.

"That's awesome, Liam. What all does The Phoenix Three do?"

"Anything that involves the safety and well-being of a child."

She turned to him, looking at him with soft eyes. "You guys are heroes. I'm in awe of you."

"Don't be painting us with something we're not. We're just three guys doing our small part to hopefully make the world a better place."

"Heroes."

Okay, if that was how she wanted to see him, he wouldn't argue. He kind of liked that admiration shining in her eyes. In reality, though, he was just a man sometimes haunted by his past and the resulting invisible scars of his kidnapping. He was a man without a family, and even now, years later, he was still trying to heal from that.

"All this must have cost a fortune."

Beyond what he and Cooper could have come up with. "Gray funded it all." And had refused to accept his and Cooper's offer to repay him over time. Liam headed to the corner where they had a kitchenette with a mini fridge, microwave, and sink. "Do you want something to drink? We've got water, sodas, beer, or I could brew a pot of coffee."

"Water's fine."

"Sorry," Grayson said, walking into the room with his laptop in one hand. "I got held up on the phone. Good to see you again, Quinn."

"Thanks. It's been a bit exciting recently."

Liam snorted. "Only you would think getting shot at by bad guys is exciting." He handed her a bottle of water.

"I didn't say it was fun exciting. I can definitely do without people shooting at me."

"You got shot at?" Grayson said.

"We sure did," she said.

While she told Grayson about the men who'd shown up at her house, Liam pulled out a chair and motioned for her to sit. He took the seat next to her, and Grayson settled across from them. Grayson already knew the men had guns and had used them. Liam had told him that when he'd called in, but his teammate grasped that this was a new experience for Quinn and that she was eager to tell him the story.

"And they didn't even hurt my car, so that was good."

"Sorry about having to leave your car behind," Liam said.

"Not a problem. Vic's already brought it to my Savannah dealership." Regret filled his eyes as he focused on Quinn. "I am sorry to have to tell you that they tore your house apart."

She sighed. "I figured they would. We have a woman who takes care of the house when my dad's away. I'll call her today and get her to go over and clean up as best she can."

"Let us know when she'll be there," Liam said. "We'll have Vic and Mason be there when she is, just in case."

"You think those men might come back? I don't want to put her in danger."

"They probably won't, but we'd rather err on the safe side."

"Y'all are pretty awesome, you know? Thank you."

"We aim to please." He got a little lost in those green eyes shining up at him, and they stared at each other until Grayson cleared his throat. Right, they were here to go over what they had so far. When he glanced across the table at his teammate, Grayson smirked, his amusement obvious. Liam shrugged. What could he say? He wasn't going to deny his interest in Quinn.

It wasn't that long ago that Grayson was falling in love

with Harlow while protecting her and her son from her ex-husband, a man about as evil as they came. Maybe Grayson could give him some advice when he got a chance to talk to his friend alone.

Until then, back to business. Liam took the thumb drive from his pocket and slid it across the table to Grayson. "Your turn to keep this safe. What were you able to find out about Garrison?"

"Nothing particularly remarkable about the man. Thirty-two years old, a photojournalist who likes to put himself in his stories. If you look at his published photos, he's in many of them."

"That's true," Quinn said. "He loves the attention."

Liam twirled his chair to the side, facing her. "Unlike you. You're not in any of yours." He knew because he'd deep dived into her published photos, his amazement of her talent growing with each one he viewed.

"Because I'm not the story. The children are."

"You are very good at what you do," Grayson said. "Your photos have a way of tugging at the heart of the viewer."

Liam nodded. "Makes one ask what they can do to help those children."

"That's my goal. Back to Jasper, what else did you learn?"

Grayson's gaze shifted over his laptop screen. "Nothing spectacular about him or his work. He has gotten some good up-close photos of fires, some war zones, and natural disasters, just not anything that's won him any awards."

Quinn frowned. "Really? He told me he's won awards."

"Not any that I could find. He has one DUI arrest from when he was twenty-one. That happened the night of his birthday. Guess he was out celebrating. Other than that, no record. There really isn't anything interesting on him."

"I could've told you that," Quinn said.

Liam didn't like thinking of her with Garrison, but the questions that needed to be asked couldn't be avoided. "How long were you…ah, with him?"

"Almost three weeks. He was fun at first, but then he started getting weird."

"How so?" Grayson asked.

"Demanding. Possessive. Jealous. He thought his work was important, mine not so much. After all, he was getting up-close shots of a massive wildfire while I was just taking pictures of children."

Another man in her life who'd proved her point. "Not all men are like that, Quinn." He wasn't.

"So you say."

They'd veered off onto a road he didn't want to travel, especially not in front of Grayson, who was watching them with curiosity. How hard was she dug in on that belief that all men were alike? Would he ever be able to prove to her that he was different? Was he willing to put in the time and effort if there wasn't hope for mission success? All questions he didn't know the answer to.

"Moving on," Grayson said as he inserted the drive into the computer. "Let's watch what's on here one more time while we're together, then I'll tell you what I learned about the textile mill."

The video appeared on all the monitors around the table. Liam focused on the screen, looking for anything he'd missed the first time around. He hadn't counted the drums, and he did so now. There were sixteen of them. How often did whatever was in the barrels get dumped into the lake?

"We need to find out if this is a onetime thing or something they do on the regular," he said. "Although, with Garrison attempting to blackmail someone with what's on this thumb drive, I'd say it's something they do on the regular."

"Agreed," Grayson said. "Cooper's bringing us samples from the lake we can send to a lab. Find out if the lake is contaminated and if so, by what."

"These drums are from that textile mill?" Quinn asked.

"Probably. We'll find out for sure." Liam watched the man on the video roll the empty drum aside, then he pushed over another one. "Who do you think Garrison was talking to on that conversation you overheard?"

She lifted her shoulders in a shrug. "I don't know who he expected to get money from or who he was talking to. It did sound like he was talking to a friend."

"The question is, is that who killed Garrison, maybe didn't want to share a million dollars?" Grayson said.

Liam shook his head. "That doesn't feel right. The men who showed up at Quinn's were professionals, and there were four of them in two Chevy Suburbans. Bodyguard cars. Going on the assumption that only Garrison and a friend, or maybe a family member, were working together—"

"Professionals? Like hit men?" Quinn said. "Unbelievable. This is like a bad movie."

Liam smiled. "Just keep in mind that the bad guys always lose, and the good guys live to see another day."

"I think Garrison and whoever was in this with him got in over their heads," Grayson said. "Messed with someone more powerful and dangerous than they could imagine."

Liam nodded. "That's my thinking. Anything on that license plate number I gave you?"

"Not yet. It belongs to what appears to be a shell company. It might take a little time to follow the trail back to whoever's behind it."

"I kind of know the concept of a shell company, but what is it exactly?" Quinn asked.

"Easy answer," Liam said, "it's a company or companies within companies set up to mask the true identity of the individual or individuals behind it."

"Is that legal?"

"Sometimes they're legit, sometimes not. I wouldn't be surprised to find this one isn't." He glanced at Grayson. "What did you find out about Hanson Textiles?"

"Something interesting. Hanson Textiles is owned by Senator Charles Hanson's family. The mill is the biggest employer in the county. The senator sits on numerous committees, is serving his fourth term, and is on the short list of vice presidential candidates in the upcoming election."

Liam whistled. "In other words, powerful and has much to protect. He'd also have the connections and money to hire the kind of men who showed up at Quinn's house."

"Exactly," Grayson said.

Quinn groaned. "This just gets worse and worse."

No, it just got more interesting. From the expression on Grayson's face, his teammate agreed. They'd never gone after anyone as powerful as Hanson, not in civilian life, but they were trained to beat the odds. With careful planning and execution, they could win this battle…if it was indeed the senator at the wheel of a murder. More than that to Liam was they'd scared Quinn. The senator would go down for that alone if those men were his hired guns.

Chapter Eighteen

Like Cher, Quinn wished she could turn back time. But would she do anything differently, knowing whatever was being dumped in that lake was making children sick? What if children started dying? No, she'd do the same thing all over again.

If she hadn't accidentally taken the thumb drive and hadn't heard Jasper's phone conversation, there would be no one to stop the illegal dumping. Because both those things had happened, she'd ended up with three formidable men at her back, one of whom had probably saved her life.

Whoever was hurting those children had to be stopped, even if it was a powerful senator. "So, what do we do now?" She didn't miss the glance exchanged between Liam and Grayson, and if they thought they were going to keep her out of this, they could think again.

"I understand your father's in Asheville, where he has a vacation home?" Grayson said.

"Maggie Valley, actually, but close enough." She knew where he was going with this, but she'd let him say it before she told him what he could do with his suggestion.

Grayson tapped a finger against his lips, then said, "I don't suppose you'd consider staying with him for a while?"

When Liam snorted, she almost smiled. That he got her gave her the warm fuzzies. "I don't suppose I will. So, again I ask, what do we do now?"

"Now we take your car to Grayson's dealership, where they'll keep it until this is over, pick up another car, and then go get some dinner," Liam said.

Grayson scowled. "You need to stop losing my cars, brother."

"He loves me," Liam whispered loudly enough for Grayson to hear.

"So you say." Grayson removed the thumb drive from his laptop. "I'll put this in the safe." He stood. "Cooper's coming back tonight. Let's plan to meet at my house for breakfast in the morning. Nine o'clock good?"

Liam glanced at her, his brows raised.

"Sounds good." She eased out of her chair. "Thanks for hiding my car. She's my baby."

Grayson walked to the window and peered down at the parking lot. "Is it that Porsche?"

"Yes, a present from my dad."

"Nice. I'll call the dealership and tell them to have a car ready for you." He lifted a hand as he walked out. "See you kids in the morning."

"He's really nice," she said when they were alone.

"Yep." Liam stepped in front of her. "But I'm even nicer."

"And sexier." She trailed her finger down the front of his shirt. "Maybe."

"Maybe?"

"Well, that's my impression, but I could be wrong." She shrugged as if she wasn't sure, then walked out of the war room.

"Where're you going?" he said from close behind her.

"To hide my car so you can get busy proving I'm not wrong." She inwardly smiled when he grabbed her hand and urged her to walk faster.

THEY TRADED HER car for a used white Mercedes SUV that would blend in with other cars on the road. The sales manager assured them that the Porsche would be hidden in a warehouse they had on the property.

Since they didn't feel like eating out, they stopped at a small, hole-in-the-wall Italian place that Liam promised had the best pizzas in town and ordered a large one to go. When she asked for a meat lover's with extra cheese, Liam declared her the best date in the world.

After quick showers—him in his bathroom and her in the guest bath—because they both felt grimy, they were now sitting on his balcony. Each with a craft beer and the large pizza on the table in front of them, they were eating as if they hadn't had a meal in a week. In all the excitement of getting shot at, they had missed lunch and were starving.

"You're right. This pizza is soooo good. I can't believe I ate four pieces." She licked her fingers.

"I'm done, too." He closed the lid on the pizza box. "Another beer?"

"No, thanks." She held up her bottle. "Mine's still half-full."

"Hold on to your beer."

"Eeep," she squeaked when he scooped her up from the balcony table where they'd sat to eat their dinner. He carried her over to a chaise longue with no more effort than it took her to carry a sack of groceries. Who knew a man carrying her would be such a turn-on? "You Tarzan, me Jane," she said with a giggle when he let her feet fall to the floor.

His eyes gleamed with amusement as he stared down at her. "Should I be wearing a loincloth?"

"Yes, please."

He laughed as he settled onto the chaise, then he pulled her down so that she was sitting in front of him, her back to his chest. "I'd wear one for you." He kissed the side of her neck.

Shivers traveled across her skin at the touch of his lips, and she arched her neck, giving him access. She'd wanted him from the day they'd sat by the stream and he'd gently doctored her feet. With all that had happened since then, it felt like that was ages ago. But finally, he was going to be hers for as long as this thing between them lasted.

He sat back, taking his mouth away. She wanted to protest, to beg him to go on with what he was doing. "Don't stop," she said.

"Watch the sunset." He slid his arms around her waist and rested his chin on her head.

She'd rather have his mouth back on her, but she lifted her gaze to the sky. "Oh, wow."

"Hmm," he hummed next to her ear. "Beautiful."

Without even looking at him, she knew that his eyes were on her and he didn't mean the sunset. She smiled, loving this moment with his arms around her, the gentle sound of the waves lapping onshore, and the soft breeze caressing her face. It struck her that Liam was romancing her, and it was a new experience. She'd never been romanced before, not even by Aiden. He'd been too busy with his medical career to think about romancing her.

As they watched the sun set to the west, the sky a brilliant painting of pinks, blues, and yellows, she changed her mind about living in the woods with Liam and growing potatoes. Instead, they'd live on a deserted island. He'd build them a hut house and fish for their dinner while she gathered coconuts and made coconut pies. After watching the sunset, they'd make love each night under a sky filled with glittering stars that looked like diamonds on black velvet.

Liam slipped his hands under her T-shirt, and as the sky grew dark and the scent of salt was heavy in the air, he danced his fingers over her stomach and up to the curve of her breasts. She softly sighed as she closed her eyes.

"You like that?" His mouth was next to her ear, his breath a warm tickle that gave her goose bumps.

"Yes." A thousand yeses.

"Give me your mouth."

She lifted her face.

"Such an obedient Little Marine," he said.

"Only for you."

"Good answer."

He kissed her then, softly, his lips brushing over hers, teasing, a little playful. Then the kiss grew demanding, possessive, and when his tongue sought entrance, she welcomed him in. He tasted delicious, and she lost herself in the desire for him building inside her. His hands covered her breasts, toying with them, igniting a fire that burned hotter with each touch of his fingers on her skin.

Suddenly, without Quinn quite knowing how he did it, he lifted her and turned her to face him. "Much better," he said as he positioned her legs so that she was straddling him. He took the bottle from her hand and set it on the table next to them. "Now kiss me."

"You're a bossy one. I like it." He'd told her to kiss him, so she did. He kept his hands on her hips but made no other move to try and control her. When she sucked his lower lip into her mouth, he groaned, and the sound of that low groan rippled through her.

His fingers tightened on her hips, and something about that possessive hold thrilled her. Heat coursed through her veins, fueled by the raw passion radiating from him.

"You're driving me crazy," he whispered, his voice low and husky, before capturing her mouth in another searing kiss.

"Good."

He chuckled, then surged up, bringing her with him. "Need a bed."

"A bed sounds lovely." She wrapped her arms around his neck as he carried her to his bedroom. When he began to lower her, she said, "Throw me."

He stilled, his eyes locking on hers. "Throw you?"

She nodded. "Like you're a barbarian about to take his spoils of battle...that would be me. The barbarian, that would be you, finds me hiding in a corner of my thatched-roof house, and your eyes light up at seeing such a pretty girl that is yours for the taking. So, take me you do. You bring me back to your home, throw me on the bed, and ravage me."

His mouth slowly curved up in a grin. "Your mind is..."

"Weird?" Sure, her imagination often ran wild, but she didn't like him thinking she was strange. Even if she was.

"I was going to say *fascinating*."

Okay. *Fascinating* was so much better than *weird*. She'd take it. She really hadn't meant to give voice to the movie playing in her mind. She'd never before given a man even a hint that she created these little scenarios in her head. They just appeared through no effort on her part. She did think she was a little weird.

His grin grew sly, and... He threw her!

She bounced on the bed, laughing and ridiculously happy. He came down on top of her, catching his weight on his elbows. "Hi," she whispered as she stared up into his beautiful blue eyes.

"Hi," he whispered back. "Did I pass the barbarian test?"

"You get a five-star review on Yelp."

"So, what does a barbarian do next?"

"Well, ravish me, of course."

"I can so do that."

And he did. Magnificently, in fact.

Chapter Nineteen

Liam awoke to the feel of Quinn's body wrapped around his with her head on his chest. She was mumbling in her sleep, something about coconut pies. Smiling, he pressed his lips against the top of her head. Lord only knew what she was dreaming.

He tried to think of something he didn't like about her or that annoyed him, but he couldn't think of a thing. She was brave, funny, incredibly talented, and sexy as hell. They'd made love, and it had been amazing. She was comfortable in her body and her sexuality. She preferred to sleep in the nude. She loved pizza and beer. Pretty much the perfect woman, and he didn't want to give her up when what she insisted was only a *fling* came to an end. He didn't want to think of her not being in his life.

What he did want to think about...losing himself in her body again. He slid his hand down her bare back to one round butt cheek. "Sweet," he murmured. He shifted his body toward her and brought his other hand to her breast. They were on the small side, but they fit perfectly in his hands. He flicked his thumb over a nipple and got a soft moan.

The gray light of dawn chased away the night. He turned

his head and eyed the clock. It was only six in the morning. He should let her sleep another hour, but he wanted... no, needed to bury himself inside her.

She stirred, her eyelids fluttering a little, then her eyes opened and met his. She smiled. "Good morning."

"Yes, it is, and it's about to get even better." He trailed kisses down her neck to her shoulders. "Do you want this? Me?"

She rubbed against him. "Morning sex is the best."

The perfect woman. He dipped his fingers between her legs. "I love how wet you are, and it's just for me."

She lowered her hand to his erection and wrapped her fingers around him. "I love how hard you are, and it's just for me."

"You got that right." He nuzzled her neck. "I want to be inside you right now, but if you need a little foreplay, we can start with that."

"You foreplayed me enough last night to carry some over to this morning. Just slide right on in, hot stuff."

How could he not laugh? This woman was something else. She checked all his boxes and some boxes he didn't even know to wish for. He reached over to the night table where there were still a few condom packages left from the night before.

"Let me." She took the condom from him and scooted to her knees between his legs.

He put his hands behind his head and watched her. Her tongue stuck out to the side as she concentrated on rolling the condom on him, and when she finished, she looked up at him and grinned.

"All covered up and ready for me."

Was he ever. "Ride me, Quinn."

Her eyes lit with pleasure, and she lifted and moved up

until she was positioned over him. "Giddyap," she cried out as she slid down on him.

When they'd made love earlier, it had been deep and emotional, both of them stunned by the hot and heavy chemistry between them. Well, he had been anyway, and he was pretty sure she'd felt it, too.

This morning, she was full of fun with mischief shining in her eyes. He let her play until he was on the verge of climaxing. When he was close, he flipped them so that his body covered hers. "Playtime's over." He rested on his elbows and put his hands along the sides of her face. "Beautiful girl." And for now, his.

Her eyes softened, and she ran her fingers through his hair. "Beautiful boy."

"Let's make some magic." He kissed one corner of her mouth, and then the other. When she parted her lips, he slid his tongue inside, and with their bodies joined, he began to move. Their rhythm built, and their movements became more frenzied, their hearts beating in sync, their lovemaking raw and untamed.

Her fingers dug into his back as she gasped his name, and he let go, joining her as she arched up, her body trembling with the aftershocks of her climax. He buried his face against her neck, put his mouth on her throbbing pulse, and felt his heart pounding as hard as hers.

"Wow," she said. She gave him a soft smile as she nestled her head against his chest. "Did you see stars?"

"Still seeing them." He wrapped his arms around her and rolled them over so they were on their sides. As his heart slowed back to its normal rhythm, contentment washed over him. Surely she felt this connection between them, but he didn't ask, too afraid she'd dig in on her insistence that this was nothing more than a fling, soon to be over.

The trick was to consider this a mission, the end result being to win her heart. He would not fail.

THEY ARRIVED AT Grayson's ten minutes late. He blamed their lateness on the shower they'd taken together. Not that he was going to share that with Grayson.

"Good to see you again, Quinn," Grayson said after opening the door to them. "Harlow's dropping Tyler off at school and should return any minute. Come on back."

"What about me?" Liam asked.

Grayson raised his brows. "What about you what?"

"Isn't it good to see me again?"

"You're a needy one this morning, but if it makes you happy, sure, it's good to see you again." Grayson smirked. "Happy now?"

"Ecstatically so," Liam answered with a silly grin. "Love you, too, bro."

Grayson leaned close to Quinn. "The boy's a cute one, isn't he?" he stage-whispered.

"He is, but don't tell him I said so," she said, also stage-whispering. "It might go to his head."

"You two are hilarious." He slung his arm around Quinn's shoulders. "Come here, you." She tucked herself into his side, right where he liked her. If she didn't have a dangerous threat hanging over her that they needed to discuss and make a plan for keeping her safe, he'd turn her right around and take her back home, where he'd spend the day loving on her. But keeping her safe was the only thing that mattered, so he didn't throw her over his shoulder like a caveman and carry her off to his lair.

Grayson's phone dinged, and after reading what was on the screen, he said, "Cooper's on the way. You two go on out to the deck while I finish up breakfast."

"Can I help?" Quinn asked.

"Thanks, but it's pretty much done. Go enjoy a morning on the beach."

"Well, hello. Who are you?" She bent over to pet the cat winding around her feet and talking up a storm.

"That's Einstein," Liam said. "He always has a lot to say."

"Nice to meet you, Einstein. You're a fine-looking boy."

"And he knows it," Grayson said. "He'll talk to you all day if you let him. Go on out to the deck and enjoy the beautiful morning."

Quinn gave him one last pet. "I'll come talk to you later."

"This is awesome," she said when they stepped out on the large deck. "I want to live on the beach."

His place was on the beach. She could come live with him. A few minutes after he and Quinn were seated, Cooper came around to the back of the house. "What's that?" Liam asked as Cooper walked up the stairs to the deck.

Cooper glanced down at the creature that was glued to his leg. "Have you never seen a dog before?"

"Yes, but not one that looks like it was patched together like a quilt of many colors." The dog was seriously weird. Long-haired with a patch of black, another of brown, one golden, with some red and white thrown in. He'd never seen anything like it.

"Aww, he's strangely cute," Quinn said.

"She." Cooper put his hand on the top of the large dog's head. "She's on the lam and a bit afraid of everything."

"Who's on the lam?" Grayson said, joining them on the deck.

"Ruby."

"Who?" His gaze fell to the dog trying to hide behind Cooper's legs. "What the hell is that?"

Cooper rolled his eyes. "Has no one ever seen a dog before?"

"Are you sure that's a dog?" Grayson said. "And why is it on the lam?"

"Yes, it's a dog, and if you'll give me a minute to get a cup of coffee, I'll tell you Ruby's story. It's a good one."

"Harlow's here now and bringing out the coffeepot in a minute, as soon as she takes the breakfast casserole out of the oven."

"I'll go help her," Quinn said.

"That's why I came out, to tell everyone to come help." He pointed a finger at Cooper. "You, though, can stay out here with whatever that is, because that is not a dog."

"You're hurting Ruby's feelings. Tell her you're sorry."

Liam laughed when Grayson rolled his eyes before walking inside.

With everyone helping, it only took a few minutes to have the table on the deck set and the food and coffee brought out. Once they all had their coffee cups filled and food on their plates, Liam said, "Story time." He leaned back and glanced under the table, where Ruby was curled up in a tight ball next to Cooper's feet. "Why is Ruby on the lam?"

"Not sure, but I suspect she was being terribly mistreated. She's not in bad shape physically, no ribs showing or anything like that. I'm taking her to the vet this afternoon and getting her checked out to be sure. But I think she's been mentally abused, maybe even used to being hit. She shies away if you make a sudden move."

"Poor girl," Quinn said.

Grayson pointed his fork at Cooper. "How'd you come to have her?"

"Funny story. I was gassing the car up, getting ready to

leave Hope Corner. I'd left my door open, and here comes this animal…" He grinned. "At first glance, I honestly thought it was a wild boar or something. Then I saw the chain she was dragging and realized it was a dog. She jumped into the car and parked herself right on the passenger seat."

Harlow put her hand on her chest. "A chain? Like she'd been chained up?"

Cooper nodded. "Yeah. It was around her neck, and she was dragging about three feet of the chain. It wasn't a heavy one, and it looked like she'd pulled on it hard enough to break one of the links."

"Thinking of her chained up like that makes me want to cry," Quinn said.

Liam reached over and clasped her hand. She had to be thinking of being chained up herself and the fear and help-lessness she'd experienced.

"I was trying to urge her to get out of the car when her ears suddenly perked up," Cooper said. "I looked up and saw a piece-of-junk pickup truck in dire need of a new muffler coming down the street. She whimpered, and let me tell you, it was about the saddest sound I've ever heard. She scrambled to the floor and tried to crawl under the seat. She could only fit her face just past her eyes under there, but I guess she thought she was hidden."

Liam glanced around the table and guessed that, like him, everyone was on the edge of their seat, waiting for the rest of the story.

"I got in the car and closed the door. As I was leaving, the pickup stopped next to me, and this dude with the mean-est eyes I've ever seen wanted to know if I'd seen an ugly-assed dog. At the sound of his voice, Ruby whimpered, and afraid he was going to hear her, I told him I hadn't seen any dog, then took off."

"You saved her," Quinn said.

Cooper shrugged. "I guess I did. About a mile down the road, I pulled over. She was violently shaking, and I started softly talking to her. The Stones' 'Ruby Tuesday' came on the radio, and I just started calling her Ruby. She seemed to like it, so I guess that's her name now."

"I think it fits her," Quinn said.

Cooper nodded. "I looked up the lyrics to 'Ruby Tuesday' last night. There's a line in it, 'She just can't be chained,' and Ruby felt like the right name for her."

"What are you going to do with her?" Liam asked as he set his silverware on his empty plate.

"The only thing I can do. Keep her."

Quinn smiled at him. "You're a softy, Cooper."

"Only for pretty girls in dire need of a bath. She's getting the works at the vet, an exam, a bath, and toenails clipped. It's going to be traumatic for her, so I'm going to hang there with her." He looked at Quinn. "I need to leave for her appointment in about an hour, which leads to let's talk about your situation."

Harlow stood. "I'll clear the table while you guys talk."

"I can help," Quinn said.

Grayson pushed his chair back. "We all can."

"No," Harlow said. "Cooper needs to leave soon, and this is important. Sit. It won't take me long."

Quinn picked up her plate, handing it to Harlow. "Thank you. Breakfast was delicious."

"Yes, it was," Liam said, handing Harlow his plate. He sat back, thinking about how easily Quinn fit in with his friends. They all liked her, but then, she was easy to like. He was pretty sure she'd be easy to love, too.

Chapter Twenty

Quinn wished she didn't have to ruin a perfect morning with her new friends by talking about anything to do with Jasper. Temporary friends that was. When this was over, they'd go their way, and she'd go hers. She would miss them when that time came, especially Liam. If she was a different person, one who could be happy staying put and taking wedding photos or whatever, she'd open her mind to a possible future with him. But that wasn't who she was.

"I stopped by the office and left the water samples on your desk," Cooper said.

She pushed her musings aside and glanced up to see that Cooper was talking to Grayson. Getting the water samples was a big step forward. "How soon do you think it will take to find out if the water is contaminated, and if so, what's in those barrels?"

"Normally one to two weeks," Grayson said. "But I pulled in a favor, and we'll get the results back in a few days."

"I hate the waiting part," she said. "I really want to know what they're dumping in that lake. If it's something that's making children in that area sick, we need to notify the Environmental Protection Agency as soon as possible. They'll be able to find any sick kids."

"While we wait, we need to find out if there's a connection between the men who showed up at Quinn's and Senator Hanson," Liam said.

"I want to go back to Hope Corner and get some more pictures. We have the photos from Jasper, but what if we can get photos with those kinds of drums located at the mill? It would be another link to who the drums belonged to."

"That's not a bad idea," Liam said.

She beamed at him. She'd expected him and the others to tell her that it was in fact a bad idea. He kept surprising her in the best kind of way.

"You do plan to go with her?" Grayson said, his gaze on Liam.

Liam scowled as if the question was ridiculous. "Do you really have to ask?"

Wow, no pushback from any of them on her returning to Hope Corner. Who were these guys?

"I really did," Grayson said with a smile as he looked at her. "I was just checking that I was reading the room right."

"Huh?" What did he mean?

"You're reading the room perfectly," Liam said.

Both men exchanged a smile she didn't understand, but they weren't fighting her on going back, and that was all she cared about.

Harlow returned, taking her seat next to Grayson. "What'd I miss?"

"An interesting development." Grayson leaned over and gave her a quick kiss. "I'll fill you in later."

She still didn't know what they were talking about, but her mind was on the things she wanted to do when she returned to Hope Corner. Along with the photos she wanted of the drums and their locations, she'd like to get pictures of children playing in the lake.

"Ruby and I are off to the vet," Cooper said as he stood. Ruby moved with him as he stepped away from the table.

"Oh, Einstein got out," Harlow said, jumping up. "No, Einstein, no!"

The cat swerved to stay out of Harlow's reach as she tried to grab him. He ran straight to Ruby. Quinn held her breath, fearing they were about to witness a fight in which poor Ruby had no chance of winning.

Seeing the cat coming at her, Ruby dropped her belly and chin to the deck, closed her eyes, and made a sound of distress. Before anyone could get to Einstein, he stopped right in front of Ruby and sat. Then he started chattering to the dog. As he talked, he gently lowered a paw to the top of Ruby's nose and patted it.

Ruby opened one eye, then the other, and Quinn could swear she saw relief on Ruby's face that she wasn't being clawed to death.

"I'll be damned," Cooper said when Ruby lifted her head and stretched her leg out until she was touching Einstein's fur. She tentatively sniffed Einstein's outstretched paw as her tail made a slow sweep over the deck.

"Someone has a new friend." Quinn wished she'd brought her camera. Einstein was still talking to Ruby, and Ruby appeared to be raptly listening as her tail continued to swish across the deck. Didn't dogs wag their tails when they were happy? She'd never had a pet, so she didn't really know anything about them.

"Why don't you bring her back here after you finish at the vet's," Harlow said. "I think time with Einstein might be just what she needs."

"I'll do that." Cooper took a few steps back. "The question right now is, who will she choose? Me or Einstein?"

"I'd pick the cat," Liam said, making everyone laugh.

Cooper slapped his hand over his heart. "Harsh, brother."

Ruby's gaze swiveled from Einstein to Cooper, and then after one last look at the cat, she rose and hurried to Cooper's side.

"That's my girl," Cooper said. "Although, she might regret her choice when she finds out where she's going."

Einstein tried to follow them as they walked down the steps, and Harlow grabbed him. "You really don't want to go to the vet."

Two hours later, after a stop at The Phoenix Three for Liam to get some weapons and equipment he wanted and then back to his condo to pack, they were on the road to Hope Corner.

"THIS IS NICE," Quinn said when they arrived at the cabin Liam had rented. They hadn't wanted to stay at the same motel she had when she'd been here before or any motel, preferring to keep a low profile while in Hope Corner.

"I would never bring you to a not nice place." Liam set their bags down. "I'll get the groceries if you'll put everything away."

"Deal." They'd made a stop at the grocery store one town over so they wouldn't have to go out to eat. He brought in the cold food first, and she put everything in the refrigerator.

"That's the last of it," he said as he set three bags on the counter.

He unloaded the bags, and she put everything away in the pantry. For a cabin in the middle of nowhere, the kitchen was really nice with new stainless steel appliances and granite countertops. The first floor was an open concept with a view of the mountains out the floor-to-ceiling windows. The stone fireplace that went all the way up to the vaulted ceilings was stunning.

"Is that a creek?" She walked to the French doors. "It is. And a small waterfall."

Liam came up behind her and slipped his arms around her waist. "There's a grill and a table on the deck. Let's have our dinner out there."

"I'd love that."

He nuzzled her neck. "Are you in a hurry for dinner?"

"Depends on what you have in mind." She tilted her head, loving the feel of his mouth on her.

"I have in mind having you for a predinner treat."

"Hmm, I could be on board with that."

"Good answer." He scooped her up in his arms and carried her up the stairs without a single gasp for air. "Do you want me to throw you?" he said when he stopped at the bed.

"Yes, please." They'd need an air mattress on their deserted island so that after she finished making their coconut pies, he could toss her on it like a barbarian setting about the business of claiming his spoils, her being the spoils, of course.

"Commence throwing." He tossed her into the air.

She laughed as she bounced on the mattress. Liam O'Rourke might be the coolest guy on the planet to humor her in her secret fantasy of being dominated by a really hot guy. Maybe she'd eventually get up the nerve to tell him the rest of her fantasy.

Also, dinner was very late, but she wasn't complaining.

Chapter Twenty-One

The sun was peeking over the top of the mountain when Liam woke up. He then spent the next twenty minutes watching Quinn sleep. She was on her side facing him, both hands tucked up under her chin. Her hair was a wild mess covering her pillow, and he took satisfaction knowing that he was the cause of that wild mess.

She had a smattering of freckles across her nose she said she hated. Why, he didn't understand because he thought they were adorable. A slight smile was on her face, and her lips were moving as she murmured something unintelligible. Maybe she was dreaming about him.

He thought about waking her up for a little morning sex, but they'd been up half the night making love. She needed her sleep. He placed a soft kiss on her cheek, then eased out of bed. By the time she came downstairs an hour later, he had coffee brewed, scrambled eggs ready to cook, and bread in the toaster.

"Do I smell coffee?"

"You sure do." He poured a cup and doctored it just the way she liked it, one sugar and enough cream to turn the coffee milky white.

She took the cup from him and brought it to her nose, inhaling the aroma. "You're awesome."

He was trying to be. "What's the agenda for the day?" This was her trip, and he wanted to show her that he was cool with her being the boss.

"Since it's summer and the kids are out of school, I'm hoping we can get some photos of kids playing in the lake. This afternoon is probably better for that. Let's start with checking out the mill, get some pictures there, and if we're lucky, of some of those drums."

"Sounds like a plan."

After breakfast, he googled the mill's address, and when they got in the car, entered the address in the GPS. "Twelve miles from here. We'll do a drive-by, get the lay of the land."

The drive to the mill took them through Hope Corner. Because they'd both been here, to help disguise their appearances, they wore ball caps—her hair tucked up under hers—and sunglasses. Just tourists out to see the sights. Not that there was a lot to see. But there were a dozen or so cabins for rent on the town's only Realtor's website, so they did get tourists.

"If we're questioned, our cover story is that we're on our honeymoon," he said.

"Well, hello, husband." She grinned at him.

"Hello, wifey." He winked at her.

"Don't you dare call me wifey in front of anyone."

He laughed. "But I can in private?"

"No, you cannot. I have a name. Use it."

"Yes, ma'am. Just curious, but what's your aversion to pet names."

"They're silly. Like you'd want to be called a silly name."

"I wouldn't mind it so much if it was you doing it."

"So you'd be okay with love nugget or pookie?"

He laugh-snorted. "I'd hope you'd come up with ones better than that."

"What was your Marine nickname?"

"Irish, not very original."

"Maybe that's what I'll call you."

She could call him anything she wanted as long as she called him. "I guess I should stop calling you Little Marine."

"For some reason I can't comprehend since I have such strong feelings about pet names, I kind of like that one."

"Good to know. Target coming up on the left."

"It's bigger than I expected," she whispered.

"You do know you don't have to whisper right now?" He grinned when she punched his arm. "Little Marine's got muscles."

"Damn straight." She flexed her arm, showing off her muscles.

"We'll drive by it. Maybe there's a place to park nearby where the car won't stand out." A few blocks past the mill, they came to a strip shopping center, and he pulled in. "There's a diner. Let's get coffees to go and walk around." He parked between two other cars at the end of the lot, closest to the mill.

They walked past an insurance agency and a Laundromat before reaching the diner. When they entered, the five people scattered around stared at them. He tagged them as breakfast regulars not used to seeing strangers in their restaurant. They would be remembered, but that was okay. No one would be asking about them.

"Good morning," he said to the woman behind the counter. She looked to be in her sixties with gray hair held back in a tight bun and kind but tired eyes.

She smiled. "Good morning. Do you want a table?"

"No, ma'am. We'd like two coffees to go, and maybe a couple of those breakfast pastries. They look delicious."

"I can rightly say they are, since I baked them fresh only a few hours ago."

He put his arm around Quinn's shoulders. "What would you like, sugar?" She ground her heel on his toe, and he bit back a laugh.

"Well, that cheese Danish looks amazing, but so does the apple muffin."

"Then let's just get you both, sweetie." She elbowed his side, and he snorted, then coughed to cover the snort. "My wife will have those two, and is that a cinnamon coffee cake?"

"Cinnamon and walnuts, and it's a favorite."

"Awesome. I'll have one of those and a dozen assorted doughnut holes." He glanced out the window. "It's a beautiful morning. Is there a park nearby where we can enjoy our breakfast?"

"There's one at the lake," the woman said as she poured their coffee. "You just go about a half mile past the mill, and you'll see a sign on your left directing you to the park. You folks on vacation?"

He smiled at his lovely wife. "My honey bear and I are on our honeymoon." He smirked, and she glared back at him. He was going to pay for this, but he did love that riled-up fire in her eyes.

"Isn't my pookie the cutest thing ever?" She beamed at the woman as she stomped on his foot again.

The woman handed over their coffee and pastries. "The cutest thing ever is a puppy." She studied him for a moment. "Now, if you said he was a handful, I'd have to agree with you. Good luck with him."

Quinn laughed, and after they exited the diner, said, "You got that right, lady."

"Hey now. Don't be talking about your husband like that. Besides, you can't be mad I called you honey bear. That wasn't you I was talking to. It was my imaginary wife who happens to love my little pet names for her."

"You're ridiculous."

"What I am is the best pretend husband you'll ever have, who just happens to be hot in bed. Go ahead. Try to deny that."

She rolled her eyes but couldn't stop a grin. "You have me there."

"Here's a secret." He leaned his mouth close to her ear. "I'd like to have you here, there, and everywhere."

"You're starting to sound like Dr. Seuss."

"Dr. Seuss wishes he could come up with lines like mine. But hey, if you're not into cheesy rhymes, I can always switch to Shakespearean sonnets. 'Shall I compare thee to a summer's day?'"

She was trying to pretend he wasn't amusing her, but he could see the laughter in her eyes. He'd read somewhere that women loved a man who could make them laugh, and he'd take all the help he could get.

Chapter Twenty-Two

It wasn't the first time that Quinn thought the man needed to stop being so amusing. It hadn't been easy, but she'd managed not to give him the satisfaction of laughing. She liked him so much it wasn't funny.

The day really was beautiful. Much cooler in the mountains than at home in Savannah or even in Myrtle Beach. "Are we going to walk awhile or drive to the park?"

He shrugged. "It's your operation. Just waiting for my orders."

This man just kept surprising her. "Let's walk awhile. See how close we can get to the mill without being noticed."

A high school was between the strip center and the mill, and a group of teens were playing a game of volleyball. She'd finished eating the cheese pastry and only had her coffee in her hand.

Liam held out the white bag. "Want the muffin now or some doughnut holes?"

"Maybe later. Hold this a sec." She handed him her coffee so she could get her Nikon out of her purse. She took back the cup, drank the last of her coffee, and then crushed the cup.

"Here, I'll hold that while you do your thing."

She gave it to him. "You're a great photographer's assistant."

"Totally indispensable, eh?"

"For now."

"Tough crowd," he muttered, making her laugh.

She glanced around and, seeing no one was paying attention to them, she snapped some photos of the school, the kids, and in the far background, the mill.

His phone chimed, and after taking it out of his pocket, he showed her the screen before answering Grayson's call. "You got me." As he listened, his expression hardened, and his eyes turned cold.

That was his warrior face, and fascinated by the sudden change in him from a goofy pretend husband to a battle-ready Marine, she lifted her camera to her eye and snapped pictures of him.

After a lengthy call where he mostly listened, he put his phone back in his pocket. His gaze was distant, as if he was mulling things over.

"What was that about?"

"That was Gray. His car that we left at your house when we ran, his service manager found a tracking device on it."

"How did that happen?"

"We assume they put it on before they broke in, before we left."

"So, what does that mean?"

"Right now, only that they know the car was taken to Gray's Savannah dealership, but we can't discount that they made a note of the license plate number. That means they'll learn the car is a dealer's loaner out of his Myrtle Beach dealership."

"That's not good. That's all they can find out, though, right? That it belongs to the dealership."

"Depends on how smart they are. It won't take much to connect the dealership to Gray and Gray to The Phoenix Three.

"He also said he did a deep dive on Garrison. Turns out Garrison has a cousin who lives in Hope Corner. Name's Joey Garrison. Their fathers were brothers. My guess is that Garrison was visiting his cousin and stumbled on the illegal dumping."

"Oh. And you think the conversation I overheard was Jasper talking to Joey?"

"Exactly." He put his hand on her lower back. "Let's start walking before we draw attention just standing here."

Were people already watching them? The mill was just ahead, and she slowed. The sidewalk they were walking on ended on this side of the street. "Will we look suspicious walking past it?"

"Not if we play it right."

"What do you mean?"

He handed her the muffin. "Who's going to suspect an infatuated couple out for a stroll while eating their goodies?"

"I'd like to get a picture of the mill."

"Wait until we're across from the entrance."

"Okay." She bit into the muffin. "This is delicious. Want a bite?"

"I'd rather have a bite of you, but I'll settle for your muffin."

She giggled as she held it out to him. "That almost sounds dirty."

"You want dirty? All you have to do is ask."

"I just might do that."

After taking a bite, he put his arm around her shoulders. "That is good. Let's stop and get a selfie. Is your camera set where I can just push a button?"

She changed the setting to auto mode, then pointed to the button he needed to press. "It's that one."

"Okay, turn your back to the mill."

He held the Nikon up. "Smile." The camera wasn't aiming at them, but just over their shoulders. After taking several pictures, each time slightly moving the camera angle to get different parts of the mill, he said, "There's a man standing at the entrance watching us." Before she could answer and still clicking the button, he kissed her.

Chapter Twenty-Three

Liam angled the camera to get a picture of the man watching them, and then he took one of him kissing Quinn. That one he took for himself. It was time to move on, though, before they drew any more attention. "Don't look at the man or the mill," he murmured against her lips. He lifted his head and smiled at her. "We need to go."

"Is he still watching us?"

"Yep." It could be nothing, but his gut said the man had more interest in them than normal. From the corner of his eye, he could see that the man watched them until they disappeared. Just curiosity or suspicion? He risked a glance at the windows on the side of the mill. Good, no one inside the building seemed to be paying them any attention.

"Liam," she said.

The urgency in her voice had him looking around them for the threat. "What?"

"Look over there. Are those the same two cars that showed up at my house?"

There was a parking lot behind the mill, probably for employees, and parked side by side in front of an entrance door were two white Suburbans. "I'm guessing so, but we need to get pictures of the tags to be sure."

"If I can get a clear shot from behind them, I can zoom in."

The lot was fenced in, so they couldn't just mosey over. He scanned the area around them. "Let's go over there." He pointed to a tree that was just outside the corner of the fence.

"I can't see the license plates from here," she said.

"Show me how to zoom in." After she did, he said, "Keep an eye out." The tree had a low branch, and he pulled himself up to it. "Hand me the camera." From his vantage point, he was able to zoom in over the top of the other cars and get a clear shot of both plates. He jumped down and gave her back the camera. "The car on the left has the plate number I memorized when we were being chased."

"Wow," she said. "We did it. We connected what's going on to the mill."

"And maybe a powerful senator."

"Yeah, that part makes me nervous. Like what have I gotten myself into?"

"Whatever it all turns out to be, you're not alone in this, Quinn. Let's head down to the lake before someone notices us hanging around here." At the entrance to the park, he tossed their empty coffee cups into a trash can.

"Do you think it would be safe to look for those drums?"

"The mill probably operates overnight shifts, but it should be safe enough to nose around after it gets dark." He slipped his hand around hers and walked them to a picnic table. They sat, facing the lake.

"It's pretty here." She lifted her camera and started snapping pictures of the lake and the surrounding area.

"Very pretty," he agreed, his eyes on her. He thought about standing on Grayson's deck and feeling envious of his relationship with Harlow. That he wanted someone special in his life, and that he just needed to find *her*. Had he? Was Quinn the one?

What was it about her that called so strongly to him? He thought about that for a minute and what he liked about her. It was nice that she really was pretty but *needs to be pretty* wasn't at the top of his list. She was feisty and would challenge him, keep him on his toes. He very much liked that about her. He admired her and what she stood for and who she was. When they made love, he had the sense that he'd found his home, something he'd never felt with another woman. He loved her smile and how her eyes would light up like glittering emeralds when she was happy or when she teased him. She was fearless but not reckless. She always smelled so damn good.

Things he didn't like about her... He drew a blank.

"No one's at the lake this morning," she said. "We need to come back this afternoon, see if there are any kids playing in the water I can get pictures of."

"Okay. Why don't we drive around a little, then go back to the cabin and have lunch. Come back here—" A white Suburban came into view, driving slowly. He put his hand on Quinn's cheek, turned her to face him, and kissed her. "We've got company," he said against her lips. Without trying to see for herself, she put her arms around his neck and kissed him back.

He had on sunglasses, so his eyes were hidden, and he was able to watch the car. Two men were in it, and both were looking their way. *Keep going. Nothing to see here.* The driver said something and both men laughed, then the car picked up speed and disappeared down the street.

He lingered for a moment with his mouth on hers, then reluctantly pulled away. "Let's go before they decide to come back."

It was a ten-minute walk back to the car, and they reached the Mercedes without incident. He needed to call Grayson and let him know they'd confirmed the Suburbans were connected to the mill. He'd do that when they got back to the cabin.

Speaking of phone calls... "Did you have time to call and cancel your credit cards?"

"My dad's canceling my credit cards. I did call the DMV and reported my driver's license stolen. They're sending me another one."

"Should've known you'd be on top of things." He reached over and put his hand on her leg. "Want to be on top of me?" That got him an eye roll and a grin.

"You have a one-track mind, sir."

"Appears so where you're concerned. All your fault, Miss Sullivan."

"Well, maybe a little playtime after lunch before we go back to the lake would interest you?"

"The answer is yes, yes it would." He might've exceeded the speed limit to get back to the cabin.

KIDS WERE PLAYING in the water when they returned later that afternoon. To look like they were here to enjoy the lake, they'd changed into shorts and had brought towels to set on the sand.

"It's hard to sit here and stay quiet," Quinn said. "I want to tell them to get out of that water."

"Since we can't do that and risk the mission, we just have to prove the lake is contaminated so we can warn the town." There were five families enjoying a summer afternoon at the lake. He guessed the kids ranged in age from two or three years to sixteen or so. It was hard to stand by and not say anything. It was also possible there wasn't anything wrong with the water.

Quinn lifted her camera and started taking pictures. He couldn't take his eyes off her. When her camera came up, she was in her element, and he didn't doubt that anything not in that viewfinder ceased to exist for her. He could take pictures that were just that, a picture, nothing special. He'd studied her work, and she had a keen eye for detail and composition that set her photos apart from those of an amateur. She impressed the hell out of him.

Since he'd forgotten to call Grayson when they returned to the cabin because a certain woman had wanted to play, he called his teammate while she took her pictures. Liam updated him on finding the Suburbans at the mill, then got an update from Grayson.

"Anything new?" she asked after he finished his call.

"Gray's still trying to trace the shell company back to the owner or owners. He said it's sophisticated and that there are layers and layers, which tells us it isn't a run-of-the-mill operation. There are powerful people behind it."

"Like a certain senator?"

"Quite possibly. He has made progress on developing a profile on Joey Garrison. He was a mechanic in the Army for three years until he was dishonorably discharged for stealing Humvee parts."

"Doesn't surprise me then that he and Jasper are cousins. Do you think he's the one who killed Jasper?"

"Hard to say at this point, but I don't feel like he's the one. From what Gray said, Joey doesn't have the smarts to pull their scheme off by himself. I think he needed his cousin for their plan to be successful, so he wouldn't have killed him. Or he wanted all the money for himself and did kill his cousin. Did you get all the pictures you wanted?"

"For now. Until we can come back tonight and see if we can find those drums."

"Good. Gray texted me Joey's address, so I thought we might do a drive-by."

They gathered their things and headed to the parking lot. Once in the car, he put in the address Grayson had sent him. "It's not far from here."

"How do you guys find these things out?"

"If I told you, I'd have to kill you." He gave her a sad face. "I'd miss you."

"I'd come back and haunt you."

"Now I'm afraid." Following the GPS's instructions, he turned onto Cow Creek Road.

"Fun name for a road."

"Small rural towns have some great road names." The GPS announced that they'd reached their destination, and he slowed as they drove by. The neighborhood was run-down, the small houses close together.

"Doesn't even look like anyone lives there," she said.

The yard was overgrown, and an old car missing its tires and back bumper was up on blocks in the driveway. "The windows are open, so someone must be around."

A man talking on a phone came around from the back of the house. The man had a full beard that could use a good trim, and he could also use a haircut and some clean clothes.

"Looks like he's been mud wrestling," Quinn said. "Do you think that's Joey?"

"Joey's twenty-seven. This guy looks like he's in his forties, so I'm thinking maybe not. Still want to go drum searching tonight?"

"Definitely. I wonder if there's a box store close by. I need to go shopping."

"What for?"

"You'll see." She got out her phone and after a few minutes of searching said, "There's one about thirty minutes from here. We've got time to go there."

What was she up to? At the store, she told him she'd meet him back at the front of the store in twenty minutes. Guess whatever she was up to would remain a mystery for now. When they returned to the cabin, she spent the evening getting her cameras and what she called her spy outfit ready. He spent it getting his weapons ready and worrying about keeping Quinn safe.

Chapter Twenty-Four

"You look like a cat burglar." Liam's gaze traveled over her. "A very sexy one."

Quinn bowed. "Thank you, kind sir." She'd found everything she wanted on her shopping trip: a black, long-sleeved T-shirt, black leggings, black socks and running shoes (she sure hoped she didn't have to do any running, though), and a black knit beanie to hide her hair under. That had been her most important purchase since her red hair was memorable. Overkill maybe, but this was her first spy operation, and she wanted to be an invisible spy.

"Did you shop for black clothes, too?" He wore a black T-shirt and black jeans.

"No, brought them with me. Never know when you might need to blend into the shadows. Open your phone and give it to me."

She handed it to him. "What are you doing?"

"Adding a tracking app. I'm not going to let it happen, but I'm trained to prepare for the unexpected. If we should get separated, I want to be able to find you."

"Oh, good idea."

He handed her back the new phone he'd gotten her before they'd left Myrtle Beach. "You ready for this?"

"As ready as I can be. Do you have your gun?"

"Let's hope we don't need it, but…" He lifted his T-shirt to show her the gun holster on the right side of his belt and a knife holster on the left side. Then he lifted a pant leg to show her his ankle holster.

"You forgot to give me a gun when we were in Myrtle Beach."

"You just worry about taking pictures, and I'll worry about keeping you safe. Deal?"

"Deal." She held her hand up for a high five. Instead of high-fiving back, he wrapped his hand around hers and pulled her to him.

"I think a kiss for good luck is necessary."

"Is that so?"

"Yes, ma'am."

He lifted his hand to the back of her neck and lowered his mouth to hers. No one had ever kissed her the way Liam did. He had a way of kissing her that was soft yet demanding and possessive. It wasn't just that he was a great kisser, which he was, it was that he made her feel as if nothing and no one in this world mattered to him but her.

He pulled away and pressed his forehead to hers. "Want to blow off this op, get naked with me, and let me kiss my way from your toes to your nose?"

"Hmm." She gave him a quick peck on his lips. "Save that thought for later."

"You're no fun," he grumbled as he followed her to the car.

She only smiled because she had her back to him and he couldn't see.

LIAM FOUND A secluded stretch of land a mile from the mill where he was able to park the car so that it was hidden from the road. It took them fifteen minutes to fast walk to the mill, and Liam was right, they did operate a night shift. She stood next to him at the tree line, scanning the area around them.

All the windows were lit up, and there were cars in the parking lot. A small group of men and women were standing outside the entrance smoking cigarettes. "It must be break time."

"Yeah." He put his hand on her back. "Let's circle around the building."

It was dark, they were dressed in black, and were far enough away that no one noticed them. Even knowing that, Quinn's heart raced. If someone did see them, what would they do? Chase them? Call the police? "How do you stay so calm?"

"Training. It also helps knowing there's not an enemy sniper or two out there with me in their sights."

"Well, when you put it that way." There weren't any drums in the back that they could see, which was a disappointment. "Maybe they keep them inside." If so, it would be impossible to get photos of them.

"Maybe, but it appears like they have a good bit of property back here. Let's look around."

It took about ten minutes, but behind a shed set back in the trees, they found the drums. She counted sixteen of them. "Yes!" She pumped her fist in the air. "It feels like we found gold."

He chuckled. "Most women want flowers and candy. My girl just wants rusty barrels."

She should take umbrage at being called his girl, but she kind of liked it. She got her camera out of the fanny pack she'd bought with her spying outfit.

"You don't need light to take your pictures?"

"It would be nice to have light, but I don't need it, thanks to the light posts in the parking lot. I can work with that." She adjusted her camera settings, and when they were to her liking, she took her pictures. She got shots of all of the drums together, then up-close ones of several of them. For the last few, she backed up, wanting to get the drums with the mill in the background.

"All done," she said after she finished. "What are you doing?" He was prying open the lid on the top of a drum.

"This one's full. We can get a sample of what's in it to send to the lab. If the lake is contaminated, and the chemicals in here match, that's pretty good proof, don't you think?"

"You're so smart. You even thought to bring a vial. Where'd you get that?"

"At the store today while you were getting your spy clothes. Thought if we did find the drums, we might get lucky and find one that was full." After filling the vial, he stoppered it then handed it to her. "Put that in your pack."

As soon as her camera and the sample were put away, she said, "Let's get out of here before our luck runs out."

"Roger that."

They hadn't taken ten steps when their luck ran out.

"Stop unless you want to be shot," a man said, stepping around the shed, his gun aimed at them.

Oh, God. It was the man who'd shot at them when they were fleeing her home.

Liam shoved her behind him. "We don't want any trouble. We were down at the lake and got a little turned around trying to find our car."

"You think I fell off a turnip truck? I know who you are, and the little lady has something that doesn't belong to her. We want it back. There's no getting out of this."

She peeked around Liam's shoulder. "How would I have something of yours? I don't even know you."

"I'm not playing games here. Jasper said you have the thumb drive. I want it and the camera you had in your hands a few minutes ago."

What he didn't know was that she had her Nikon set to automatically store any photos she took in the cloud, so they'd still have the proof that the drums were here. He also didn't seem to know that they had a sample of what was in the drums.

Since she wasn't going to argue with a man pointing a gun at her, she unzipped her fanny pack, removed her camera, and tossed her very expensive Nikon to him. "It's all yours, but I can't give you what I don't have, and I don't have your thumb drive."

As the man reached his hand out, his attention on catching the camera with his free hand, Liam did some kind of body twist in midair and slammed his foot against the hand holding the gun. The weapon went flying, landing ten feet away. She rushed to it and grabbed it.

The two men were circling each other, but then Liam stopped and dropped his hands to his sides. He smirked at the man. "I'll give you a chance to walk away without a broken nose or worse. You should take it."

What was Liam doing? That man wasn't going to just walk away.

The man laughed. "You're a dead man. You just don't know it." He glanced at her. "And you and me, pretty lady, we're gonna have a little fun before I send you to hell with him."

Should she shoot him? She'd never wanted to shoot a person before, but she sure wasn't up for the kind of fun the man insinuated, and also, she'd do it to protect Liam.

As if he knew what she was thinking, he positioned himself between her and the man, taking away her chance to pull the trigger.

"You touch her, you die," Liam said in the coldest, deadliest voice she'd ever heard in her life.

The man growled and launched himself at Liam, aiming her Nikon at Liam's face.

"Liam," she gasped. He was going to let the man hit him with her camera, and that was going to hurt. Just as the Nikon was inches away from connecting with Liam's jaw, he ducked, and at the same time, he brought his fist up, landing an uppercut right into the man's gut. The man doubled over, wheezing as he tried to get air into his lungs. He dropped her camera, and Liam picked it up, tossing it to her. One hard hit to the man's jaw and he crumpled to the ground, out cold.

"Let's go," Liam said.

She was all for that. She handed Liam the man's gun, then dropped her camera into her fanny pack. He grabbed her hand, and they ran through the woods.

At the car, she put her hands on the hood and tried to catch her breath. "Not fair. You're not even breathing hard," she said.

He grinned. "I could give you mouth-to-mouth."

Did nothing faze this man? "We almost got killed and all you can think about is kissing me?" He'd been magnificent and seeing him in his element had been hot. She could have done without having a gun pointed at her, though.

"I think about kissing you all the time, and trust me, you didn't come close to getting killed. I wouldn't have allowed that to happen on my watch. Now, get in the car and let's get out of here before they come looking for us."

As they drove back to the cabin, he took her hand and put

it on his leg. "I'm proud of you. You did good back there. You need a reward."

"I think so, too, and I know just what I want."

"And what's that?"

"You. You're my reward."

"Oh, the sacrifices I make." He grinned at her. "But if you insist…"

Chapter Twenty-Five

Liam recognized that Quinn was high on adrenaline, a common feeling after a tense or dangerous event, like having a gun pointed at her by a man who'd threatened to kill them. When the bastard said he would play with her first before killing her, he'd had to use every bit of his discipline not to tear the man's tongue out of his mouth.

He wasn't complaining, though. That adrenaline had turned her into a wildcat. Within seconds of entering the cabin, she turned to him, put her hands on his chest, and pushed him against the wall. He raised his brows. "Want something?"

She tugged on the hem of his T-shirt. "My reward and this off."

"Yes, ma'am." He pulled his shirt over his head and dropped it on the floor. "Now what?" Indecision was in her eyes, but he wasn't going to help her. He liked this game and wanted to see how far she'd take it.

"Now you ravish me."

"There's a word I can get behind. Tell me a fantasy you've had but never experienced."

"I have lots of fantasies I've never experienced."

"You stick with me long enough, and I'll give them all

to you. For right now, tell me just one of them." He brushed his thumb over her bottom lip. "Make it one that really excites you."

"I've always wanted to be taken against the wall. The idea of it sounds hot, but I just don't see how it could really work. I think all those romance novels exaggerate how sexy it really is. I want to know if it's even possible."

"Stop talking." He crashed his mouth down on hers. He'd never had sex against the wall either, but he was determined to live up to those scenes in romance books. And yes, he'd read quite a few. When on deployment, during downtimes, when he was bored, he'd read anything he could get his hands on. Many of the guys would, and the women on base thought that was cool and would pass their romance books around.

He put his hands on the wall above her head and pressed his body against hers, trapping her between him and the wall. Her throaty moan went straight to his groin, and when she scraped her nails down his back, he growled and deepened the kiss. She arched against him, and damn, he'd never been this hot for a woman in his life.

"I need to feel your skin against mine," he said.

"Yes. Naked is good."

They shed their clothes with frantic haste, and thankfully, he was still coherent enough to remember to get a condom out of his wallet before dropping it and his pants to the floor. She watched him put the condom on, and seeing her eyes on him as she swiped her tongue over her lips almost sent him over the edge.

"You're the sexiest, most beautiful woman on the planet, Quinn. Are you ready for me?"

"I've been ready."

"Good, because I'm going to bury myself so deep inside

you, you're going to think we're one person. Wrap your legs around my hips."

She did, and he slid his arms under her bottom and held her close to him as he pressed her against the wall again. In this position, it was on him to do all the work since she didn't have room to move, and he was good with that. He thrust into her, pulled back, and did it again. Nothing in his life had felt this good. *Good* wasn't even the right word. Amazing. Incredible. Mind-blowing. Those were so much better words for how being inside her felt, and underneath those words was a feeling he never wanted to lose. He'd found his home, and it was with her.

She scraped her teeth along his shoulder. "I want to bite you."

"Do it." When her teeth clamped down on his skin, he almost lost it then and there. Only by sheer will did he hold off. "Can't wait much longer. Come for me, little vampire."

"Liam."

That was all she said, but it was how she whispered his name, as if he meant more to her than just the fling she kept insisting this thing between them was. He was done for. "Now, Quinn." He found her mouth and stroked his tongue over hers. Her body tensed, then shook as her climax crashed through her, driving his own release.

He let go of her mouth and buried his face against her neck as he struggled to get air back into his lungs. What just happened? He'd never come that hard, and before his legs— the same ones that could walk miles across the desert with eighty pounds of gear on his back without a quiver—threatened to quiver him right down to the floor in a heap with her on top of him… Before that could happen, he managed to get them to the couch, where he fell back, still holding her. He might never let her go. Never wanted to.

"You okay?" he said. She'd snuggled against his chest with her head resting in the crook of his neck.

"Better than." She gave a sigh of contentment. "You zapped all my energy. I think I'll sleep right here."

He refused to sound needy, so he didn't ask if what just happened was as good for her as it had been for him. But he wanted to because, eff him, he was feeling pretty damn needy right now.

When her breaths slowed and he realized she was asleep, he rose with her still wrapped around him and carried her to the bedroom. Lowering her to the bed, he pulled the cover over her, then kissed her cheek. "We have some talking to do," he quietly said. After what just happened between them, there was no way she could deny there was something between them. They were not going their separate ways when this was over because it would never be over.

He let her sleep for two hours while he gathered their things and had all but her bag set at the front door, waiting to be put in the car. That done, he made some sandwiches and packed them along with apples, chips, and bottles of water. He didn't want to make any stops on the road where their route home could be tracked. The remaining groceries they'd bought went into a trash bag. There was a bear-proof can at the end of the driveway, and he took the bag out to it.

They hadn't planned to leave for another day, but the men after her would be out looking for them even now. He had no intention of sticking around long enough for them to find her. It was time to wake her up, and he went into the bedroom. She was still asleep, all that magnificent red hair that he'd had wrapped around his fist spread over her pillow. One leg was out from under the covers, something he'd noticed before that she did when sleeping.

His girl did love her sleep. Affection for this woman swelled in his chest, and he wanted nothing more than to crawl back into that bed and spend the day loving on her. The risk of being found was too high to stay any longer, though.

He sat on the edge of the mattress near her waist. "Quinn, wake up." He shook her shoulder. She mumbled something and burrowed deeper into the covers. He shook her again. "Up and at 'em."

She squinted her eyes open. "Still dark."

"I know, but it's not safe to stay here any longer. We need to go."

"'Kay." She closed her eyes and went back to sleep.

"Sorry about this." He pulled the covers off her, then the pillow out from under her head. "Up, Quinn." And…he'd forgotten she was naked. He briefly considered risking a few more hours at the cabin, but she was too important to take that kind of chance.

"I don't like you." She stuck her tongue out at him.

He grinned at that. "That's not what you were saying a few hours ago. In fact, I seem to recall these exact words. 'Oh, Liam, you're amazing. You're the best thing that's ever happened to me, Liam.' Admit it, you really like me."

"I never said any of that."

"Maybe not, but I know you thought it." He stood. "Up. We really do need to go."

"You're no fun," she grumbled as she rolled out of the bed.

"Not true. I'm the funnest guy you know. The bag with

your clothes and girlie stuff is on the counter in the bathroom. I'll make us coffees to go while you get dressed."

He had their coffees made and in travel mugs he'd found in a cabinet by the time she walked into the kitchen. "Ready to go?"

"If we have to. I wish we could stay a few more days."

"Too risky. We got what we came for, pictures of the drums and the lake with children playing in it. Even got a sample of what's in the drums, which is a great bonus." He handed her the coffee mugs. "Carry these. I'll load our bags in the car."

It was a little after midnight when they drove away from the cabin, and there were only a few cars on the road. Liam tensed each time a car passed them, but no one paid any attention to them. He only relaxed when they made it to I-95 without incident.

"What if they move the drums before we can get the proper authorities involved?"

He pulled over to the left lane to pass a slower moving car. "Won't matter. We have plenty of proof with the thumb drive, your photos, and the samples from the drum and the lake."

"I'm ready for this to be over. I want my life back."

Did she include him in that picture? He wanted to talk to her about where they went from here, and the long trip home would give them plenty of time. Before he could bring up the subject of a future, she yawned. "Why don't you sleep for a little while," he said instead. "We've got about four hours before we get home."

"You don't mind?"

"Not at all."

"Thanks. I can barely keep my eyes open."

She reclined her seat, and within minutes, she was sound

asleep. Although disappointed that he wasn't going to learn where they stood, maybe it was for the best. A better idea would be to bring it up at his condo. Tomorrow night, he'd romance her, make her a nice dinner, and then after, they could sit on his deck, drink a little wine, and talk. It was a much better plan.

Chapter Twenty-Six

It was the morning after they'd arrived back in Myrtle Beach, and they were in The Phoenix Three's war room again. "The lab results came back on the lake water," Grayson said as he held up the vial containing the sample they'd taken from the drum. He eyed the colorless liquid. "The lab found concerning levels of PERC in the water."

"What's that?" Quinn asked.

Grayson set the vial on the table. "Tetrachloroethylene, a chemical commonly used by textile mills and dry cleaners. The chemical has been linked to several kinds of cancer both in adults and children. The EPA has proposed a ten-year phaseout of the chemical. It's definitely not anything a town wants to find in their lake water, and with the thumb drive, we can prove the mill dumped those barrels into the lake. That means serious trouble for them. Another concern is whether it's gotten into Hope Corner's drinking water."

"Wow, that's unconscionable that they would risk the lives of people like that, especially the children." No wonder whoever was after that thumb drive was desperate to get it back. She knew there were evil people in this world, but the thought of what the mill was doing made her sick to her stomach.

As if sensing her thoughts, Liam reached for her hand. "With the lake water results and the sample we got from the drum—assuming the chemicals will be a match, which we do—along with your photos and the thumb drive, we have the proof we need to bring in the authorities."

"We can do that today?" She didn't want to wait another minute.

Grayson tapped the vial. "Let's get a report back from the lab on what's in the drums first. But we have another problem. You're wanted for questioning by the Hope Corner sheriff."

"Me? Why? Cooper got my suitcase, and he said my purse wasn't there for the police to find. He was going to wipe the cabin down so my fingerprints wouldn't be there. And how would they know to call you?"

"They didn't, the county sheriff put out an APB on you as a person of interest in a murder. I've been expecting something like that, so I have a friend in our police department who's been keeping an eye out for me should something like this happen."

"I still don't understand why they're looking for me if they don't know I was in the cabin."

"Since I wondered the same thing, I had your lawyer call the sheriff."

"My lawyer?"

"John Fowler, your attorney for dealing with the sheriff. He's one of the best criminal attorneys in the state."

"I'm not a criminal." She wasn't liking this at all.

"We know that, the sheriff doesn't. According to the sheriff, he received an anonymous phone call that you were in the cabin with Jasper. We have to assume the call was made by whoever killed Jasper."

"Do I have to talk to him?"

"It would be best to before they issue a warrant for your arrest, which the sheriff threatened to do if you don't go in for questioning," Grayson said. "John told him you'll talk to him here, and he'll be with you for the interview."

"They'll want to talk to me, too, since I was there," Liam said.

She frowned. "They don't need to know that. What if they think you killed him?"

"We'll have to explain how you got away, so there's no way around involving me. Besides, you're my witness that I didn't kill him." Liam squeezed her hand. He glanced at Grayson. "I'm thinking we don't mention the contaminated water and drums. I hope not, but it's always possible someone in the sheriff's department there is...let's just say favorable to the mill and its owners. We say that Quinn had a short relationship with Garrison and after she broke it off, he stalked her and then kidnapped her."

"I agree," Grayson said. "I'll tell John to contact the sheriff today and make the arrangements."

"What if they insist I go there?"

"The answer will be no, and if they have a problem with that, I'll involve a friend of ours from the FBI."

"I don't like putting you guys in the middle of this. Maybe it would be better to meet somewhere besides here."

Grayson shook his head. "No, we want him to see that you're not alone and without protection. We want him to see us and The Phoenix Three. We're not a fly-by-night operation, and that's obvious to anyone who sees this place."

"A little intimidation isn't a bad thing," Liam said.

"I guess. So, why was I in Hope Corner if I'm not going to tell them the real reason?" Surely, they would ask her that.

"Easy," Liam said. "Your job is taking photos of children in need of help. You were there documenting the poverty the children of coal miners who've lost their jobs were living under. There is a coal mine that has been shut down not far from Hope Corner, so that story holds weight."

"Okay." Honestly, she didn't care about any of this. She just wanted the people making children sick brought to justice. And she wanted her life back. She was scheduled to leave for Ukraine in two weeks, and with everything going on, she'd almost forgotten about it and hadn't thought to tell Liam. It was a trip she had no intention of canceling.

The warmth of his hand still holding hers felt good, too good. As much as she wished otherwise, she wouldn't change her mind on no relationships. Her life wasn't one any man would put up with for long, even Liam, no matter how much he said otherwise.

There was regret, though, that it had to be this way. Men went off to war, some spent weeks working on oil rigs, smoke jumpers were gone during fire season, et cetera, et cetera. They all expected their women to be waiting for them back home. It wasn't fair, but it was the way it was.

"Where's Cooper?" Liam asked.

Grayson chuckled as he glanced at his watch. "Right about now, he's pacing the floor at the vet's office. Ruby's getting spayed today, and Coop's freaking out, afraid it's going to traumatize her."

Liam grimaced. "It would sure as hell traumatize me."

She laughed. Men were such wimps with anything that had to do with the family jewels. If they had to be the ones to push babies out of a tiny hole, there would be no babies.

"I've got some other news," Grayson said. "Harlow and I have set a date for our wedding. The first week of November. You all will, of course, be there. She wants a small beach wedding, just us and our friends. I'm taking her and Tyler to Hawaii for our honeymoon."

"Because surfing," Liam said.

Grayson shrugged. "It would just be wrong not to surf while we're there, but she's always wanted to go to Hawaii, and I live to make her happy."

That soft look in his eyes when he talked about his fiancée almost had Quinn envious. She'd never have a man live to make her happy, but then that was her choice, so no feeling sorry for herself.

"Congratulations," Liam said. "You're a lucky man."

"And well I know it." He pushed his chair back. "Anything else we need to discuss this morning?"

"Not from me," Liam said, and she shook her head when he glanced at her. "It's been an exhausting few days, so Quinn and I are just going to hang out at my place for the rest of the day. If anything new pops up, give me a call."

"Will do." Grayson nodded at her, then left.

"Want to go have a beach day with a little hanky-panky thrown in?"

She grinned. "Where do I sign up?"

AFTER THEY ATE LUNCH, Liam talked her into playing in the ocean for a bit, and when they came back inside, they showered together. There was hanky-panky involved. "You really know how to treat a lady," she said after they got out and he took the towel from her and dried her off.

"There's only one lady I'm interested in impressing."

"Oh? Who would that be?"

He wrapped the towel around her and tucked in the end, and then he tapped her on the nose. "Such a silly question. After you get dressed, let's sit out on the deck and watch the sunset."

"I'd like that. Give me a few minutes to get the tangles out of my hair."

"While you're doing that, I'm going to pour us some wine and make us a snack. Meet you on the deck."

He'd wrapped a towel around his waist, and as he walked out of the bathroom, she sighed at the view. She'd had her hands all over that amazing body, had pressed her fingers into those muscles, finding them as rock-hard as they looked. He was funny and kind, and an amazing lover. He was setting the bar high for any man who came after him. She looked into the foggy mirror and frowned at herself. After him, would she even want another man?

Chapter Twenty-Seven

Liam chickened out. It was the perfect time and place to bring up wanting to see where this thing between them could go. The sky was an artist's abstract painting of yellows and pinks. The soft slap of the ocean against the sand was music floating in the air, and his gaze was drawn to Quinn as she closed her eyes and lifted her face to the gentle breeze.

It was the perfect evening for having that talk, but what if she wasn't ready to admit, to accept that they were past having a simple fling? If he tried and she shut him down, dug her heels in and closed her mind to the possibility of them, he would lose any chance he had with her.

So, instead of that talk he wanted to have, he decided they would have a quiet, romantic night. The situation she'd found herself in was close to breaking open, and this might be their last chance to spend time alone. At the moment, she was staring out at the ocean and seemed miles away.

"Penny for your thoughts." She didn't respond. Had she even heard him? "Quinn?"

She startled. "Sorry, what?"

"Where'd you go? In your mind?" Why was she blushing?

"Oh, just…um, you'll think I'm weird."

"I already think you're weird, so no problem there." He

winked to let her know he was teasing her. She had his curiosity going, though. When she just stared at him, he said, "You can tell me anything."

"You know, you're the first person I've felt I could tell about this little quirk I have."

"Now you have my attention." It had to be a good thing that she trusted him with something she'd never told anyone else.

She picked up her wineglass and took a healthy swallow. After setting it back down, she cleared her throat. "Okay, here goes. Just now, I was imagining us living on an island in the South Pacific. No one else lives on that island but us. Well, along with these cute little monkeys that swam ashore after a shipwreck a hundred years ago. They showed us where there was fresh, pure water. There were mango trees and banana trees and coconuts, and all the fish we could eat. So we had plenty of food, but I was getting kind of tired of eating nothing but fish. We…ah, we didn't wear clothes." She was blushing again. "See, I'm weird."

"That's very detailed." He ignored the weird part for a moment.

She shrugged. "All my fantasies are."

"Do you have these fantasies often?" Quinn Sullivan was more fascinating by the minute.

"I don't know. Just sometimes my mind creates these pictures. Mostly when I'm stressed and want to escape. It started after my mom died. I missed her so much and cried a lot. One day, my dad took me out to her favorite spot in the garden. He had a picnic spread out on a blanket the same way she used to. He told me to imagine she was with us, and we talked about her. It made me feel better.

"After that, when I would cry, he'd tell me to create a story in my mind with her in it. Like someplace special we might be, and he'd ask where we were, what we were doing, what we were eating. I was ten years old, and those stories I'd make up with Mom in them were a comfort. As time went on, the stories would get more creative, more detailed. At some point, I started creating fantasies that didn't have her in it. I've had a few with you in them."

"Yeah? More than this one?" She nodded. "Tell me another one about us."

"The first one I had with you in it was when we were in the woods and Jasper was shooting at us. I was a bit stressed out, so my mind made up a story that took me away from the danger we were in."

"I want to hear it."

"Well, we built a cabin in the woods. You hunted for our food, and I grew potatoes. We…ah, we had babies with your blue eyes."

"Maybe we could have one or two with your green eyes." He was suddenly imagining her pregnant with their baby and his male brain liked that picture.

She laughed. "I guess that would only be fair."

"Right now, I'm having my own fantasy. Want to hear it?" He loved how her eyes lit up when she was happy.

"Tell me."

"I'd rather show you." He stood and held out his hand, pleased when she didn't hesitate to take it.

"Where are we going?"

"Someplace we don't need clothes." He took her to his bedroom, where he tried to show her without words how much she meant to him. He wanted to tell her he was falling for her, but he was afraid that would scare her off. She hadn't given him any indication that he meant more to her than that fling she insisted they were having.

Fling. He hated that word.

THE NEXT MORNING, Liam was enjoying a cup of coffee on his balcony while he waited for Quinn to wake up. He thought about how he should proceed with her. She hadn't said anything about her next assignment. He didn't doubt she had one scheduled, probably had her next year booked out. He frowned. Did she intend to tell him her plans or just leave when the time came?

Should he push for some kind of commitment from her or let things play out? He couldn't decide, and he hated being hesitant to do so. His military training had programmed him to be decisive. She'd told him the reason for her no-relationship rule, and he got why she felt that way after her experiences with other men. He wasn't other men, but how could he prove to her that he would never come between her and the career that she loved?

His phone chirped, Grayson's name on the screen. "What's up?"

"The West Virginia sheriff and one of his deputies are on the way here to interview Quinn. They expect to arrive around one."

"Did they give any pushback on coming here?"

"Big-time. Threatened to issue an arrest warrant if she didn't appear at the sheriff's office by noon tomorrow. John told them she wasn't returning to Hope Corner, so if they wanted to talk to her, it was here or nowhere. Then he dropped the big bomb. Said since she was kidnapped, she wanted to call the FBI to report what Garrison had done. He told the sheriff that he was advising her to do just that."

Liam chuckled. "That must have gone over big."

"It went over like a lead balloon. John said he got about a full minute of sputtering before the sheriff grumbled his agreement to talk to her here."

"Interesting that they don't want the FBI involved."

"John's vibe from the sheriff is that he doesn't want another agency encroaching on his territory, especially the Feds. John wants to meet with Quinn before they get here, so why don't you bring her over to my place for an early lunch. John will be here, and she can talk to him then."

"Sounds like a plan." Their lawyer was soft-spoken and kind to those he liked, and he would like Quinn and she him. Underneath that gentle nature was a man as sharp as a whip and a formidable opponent to any who came up against him. She would be in good hands. "What was his impression of the sheriff?"

"That he doesn't have any other suspects, so he's going to try to pin Garrison's murder on Quinn. This isn't going to be fun for her, so let's make sure she's well prepped before the interview. Since you're going to surprise him with the story that you rescued her, John's also meeting with you. I don't think the sheriff's going to be happy when he finds out you're involved in all this."

"Because he'll realize he can't bully me. Not to mention that I'm a decorated Marine, giving his suspect an alibi."

"Exactly. See you in a few hours."

Liam hadn't even met the sheriff yet, but his hackles were already up. He was going to have to work hard to keep his temper in check if the man tried to terrorize Quinn into making a false confession. Under no condition were they taking Quinn back to Hope Corner with them. If he had to spirit her away and hide her, he would.

Chapter Twenty-Eight

Quinn chewed on her thumbnail—a nervous habit she'd broken years ago—as she waited with John in a small conference room at The Phoenix Three, a room she'd never been in. Grayson had told her it was where they met prospective clients.

It was an impressive room. She wasn't sure what the small table that sat six was made from, but the finish was a glossy black lacquer. The walls were painted a soft gray, and the six cushiony leather chairs around the table were slate gray. Abstract paintings in subdued colors hung on the walls, and a mini fridge was tucked under a counter that matched the table. A fancy coffee maker sat on the counter, and cups and glasses filled two open shelves about the counter.

Grayson was right. The sheriff would see that The Phoenix Three wasn't a fly-by-night operation, but would that matter? She'd be the first to admit she was terrified. What if the sheriff manufactured evidence against her? She so did not want to go to prison.

John reached over and pulled her arm, taking her finger away from her mouth. "It's going to be all right, Quinn. You've got three of the most formidable men I've ever met circling the wagons around you, protecting you, especially Liam." He smiled, and it was such a sweet smile. "Then you have me. They might be the muscle you need right now, but I'm the brains, and I take no prisoners. We got you, okay?"

Something about his quiet assurance calmed her. "Okay." When she and Liam had met with him earlier, they'd told him everything. He knew about Jasper's conversation she'd overheard, the thumb drive, the contaminated water, Jasper kidnapping her…all of it. He'd agreed that the sheriff didn't need to know about all of it at this point, only that Jasper had fixated on her and had kidnapped her after she'd ended things with him. She didn't like having to lie, even if it was only by omission, but agreed it was necessary for now.

Liam came into the room and put his hands on her shoulders. "The sheriff's coming up in the elevator now. I'm going to insist that he interview me first so that you have an established alibi before he meets with you." He leaned down and kissed her cheek. "You got this, but if you feel threatened at any time, walk out. I'll be right outside, and I'll get you out of here."

"Liam," John said, a warning in his voice.

"I don't care," Liam said, staring John down. "She needs to leave, she's leaving. End of discussion."

John let out an exasperated sigh before he smiled at her. "Didn't I tell you they'd protect you, especially this one?"

"You stay in here." Liam squeezed her shoulders. "I'll come to you as soon as I'm done."

"Okay. Where are you meeting him?"

"In the war room. We're giving him a kind of tour by me meeting him in there, and then bringing him here to talk to you." He winked at her, then left.

"I have to go with Liam," John said. He touched her arm. "It really is going to be okay."

Alone now, she dropped her head down on the conference table. How could they know it was going to be okay? What if the sheriff didn't believe Liam? Even worse, what if both she and Liam were arrested for Jasper's murder?

"You hanging in there?"

She lifted her head and forced herself to smile at Grayson. "Yeah. Everyone keeps telling me it's going to be okay, so I'm going to believe it. Do you think Liam's going to get in trouble?" All he'd done was rescue her, and she couldn't bear the thought that he'd be in trouble because of her.

"He's going to be fine."

"I hope so. Did you meet the sheriff?" When he nodded, she said, "What was your impression?"

He slid into a chair across from her. "I don't want to scare you, but I've always believed it's better to be prepared than not."

"Oh, God, that bad?"

"'Fraid so. He's got an attitude, so be ready for that. John will be with you and will put a stop to any questions you don't want to answer. Just keep to the script we've already gone over."

"What if they arrest me?"

"They won't. They can't, not today anyway. First, they don't have any evidence that you killed Garrison other than an anonymous phone call that you were in that cabin. Second, they personally can't arrest you. They'd have to go through our local police with a warrant for your extradition to West Virginia. If they had that, they'd have gone straight to the Myrtle Beach police. Should that happen at some point, we'll fight it with every tool available."

"I can't thank you guys enough for what you're doing for me."

He tsked at her. "Not necessary. You mean something to

Liam, and we protect those we care about. Would you like a cup of coffee while you wait?"

"No thanks. I'm jittery enough as it is. I wouldn't mind some water."

"Coming your way." He stood and went to the mini fridge, grabbed a bottle and brought it to her. "Help yourself if you want more. There are also sodas if you'd prefer one of those."

"Thanks. You don't have to babysit me," she said when he sat back down.

"How about we just sit here and talk until it's your turn. Maybe take your mind off things for a while?"

"If you don't have other things you need to be doing, I'd like that."

"Nothing pressing. Anything you'd like to know about The Phoenix Three?"

"Lots of things. Liam told me about you guys being kidnapped when you were teens, and that was why y'all joined the military. Were the three of you all Marines, serving together?"

"No, we each joined a different branch of the military. Liam the Marines, Coop the Army, and I was in the Navy."

"Liam said he was a Marine Raider. Were you and Cooper also in special ops?"

"Yes. Coop was an Army Ranger, and I was a Navy SEAL."

"I would've thought you'd want to serve together after what you went through."

"That was the plan at first, but then we decided we could learn different things if we each joined a different branch, then come back together and start The Phoenix Three."

"Liam told me what Phoenix Three does, and I have to say that I'm in awe of you guys."

"Pretty sure Liam is in awe of you." He grinned. "He showed me some of your photos that are out there, and I see why he's impressed. The attention you bring to children in need is something the three of us can fully support."

"Thank you. It's—"

Liam came in, followed by John. She jumped up. "Are you okay?"

He held up his hands. "No handcuffs, so I'd say yes. Are you?"

"I was freaking out, but then Grayson came in and talked to me. He took my mind away from what might be happening to you. I guess that was on purpose." She gave Grayson a grateful smile, and he winked, confirming that was why he'd stayed with her.

"The sheriff made a pit stop, but will be here in a minute," John said. "Liam's laid the groundwork, and all you have to do is tell the story we talked about."

"Did he believe you?" she asked Liam.

"He doesn't want to, but he doesn't really have a choice. We're each other's alibi, and unless he can prove we're lying, which we aren't, he's got no case against you." He wrapped his arms around her, hugging her. "I'll be in my office waiting for you."

"I wish you could stay in here with me."

"Me, too, but I won't be far away." Liam kissed her forehead, then left.

"Please excuse me, as well. I need to check for our visitors," Grayson said, exiting the conference room.

She dropped back into her chair. She should've asked Liam to run away with her, go to the Highlands in Scotland, where a county sheriff couldn't find her. They could raise those adorable Highland cows with the long bangs.

John slid into the seat next to her. "Don't let the sheriff

rattle you. If he tries to intimidate you, I'll step in. Anytime you're not sure what to answer, you can say 'I don't know,' or 'I don't remember.' Don't let him make you feel guilty for anything. You didn't do anything wrong. He has one of his deputies with him, and he'll try to make you uncomfortable by staring you down. Ignore him."

"I'll be happy to."

The door opened, and Grayson stepped inside. "Miss Sullivan is waiting for you in here," he said as a uniformed man walked in, followed by a younger man, also in uniform.

The sheriff wasn't what she'd expected. She'd formed a picture of a good old boy, maybe a little overweight, average height, and going bald. He wasn't any of that; instead, he was tall and lean, with a full head of salt-and-pepper hair cut short and icy blue eyes. Although there wasn't any warmth in those eyes, they were sharp with intelligence as they raked over her in a calculating way. She needed to be careful with this man.

"I'm Sheriff Lamott, Miss Sullivan. Before we start, I'm going to read you your rights."

"Why? Is Miss Sullivan a suspect?" John said.

"At this time, she is a person of interest."

"Then you're just here to interview her, not interrogate her, correct?"

"For now."

"Then no need to Mirandize Miss Sullivan if this is only an interview and she isn't a suspect."

John had told her that he'd do little things to throw the sheriff off his game, and he was doing just that if the sheriff's obvious annoyance was any indication.

"Fine." The sheriff glared at John, then turned his attention to her. "Miss Sullivan…may I call you Quinn?"

"No. I only let my friends call me Quinn, and I don't think you're my friend, sir."

"Very well. Do you know why we're here to talk to you?"

The deputy standing against the wall crossed his arms, drawing her attention. She pointed her finger at him. "Who's that?"

Sheriff Lamott narrowed his eyes, apparently not appreciating her question. "That's Deputy Dough. Don't concern yourself with him."

"Deputy Dog?" She grinned at the deputy, who was scowling at her. "Sorry." Out of the corner of her eye, she saw John smile, while the sheriff joined his deputy in scowling at her. Good, they weren't liking that she wasn't cowering in fear as she should be doing if she had in fact killed Jasper.

"It's D-o-u-g-h," Deputy Dog said, emphasizing each letter as he spelled it for her.

"Gotcha." Sorry, he would always be Deputy Dog to her.

The sheriff tapped his finger on the table. "I asked you a question, Miss Sullivan."

"Yes, I know why you're here. Someone killed Jasper, and you think I know something about that. I don't, but ask your questions."

"Do you have any idea who that someone is? You were the last to see him."

"Not true. Whoever killed him was the last to see him. That wasn't me."

"Mr. O'Rourke stated that Garrison kidnapped you. Tell me about that."

After she related the story, she sat back in her chair. "And that's it. After Liam and I escaped into the woods *because Jasper was shooting at us*, I never saw him again. You can verify with the garage that picked up Liam's car that it had been wrecked. That was also because of Jasper crashing into us."

"Why didn't you report him to the police?"

Thankfully, John had prepared her and Liam for this question. "Liam wanted me to, but I was afraid Jasper would find us if we stuck around Hope Corner, and I just wanted to go home. Plus, I felt sorry for Jasper. I mean, I know he chained me up, but it was a case of misguided love... No, *love* isn't the right word. *Obsession*'s a better one. Liam wasn't happy about not telling the police what had happened, so I promised that I'd consider reporting him after I was home where I felt safe. Sadly, Jasper was killed before I could do that."

Liam hadn't been happy about letting her take the blame, but John had convinced him that it was the best answer. She was good with her being the reason Jasper wasn't re-ported to the police. She'd do whatever she could to keep Liam out of trouble.

The sheriff stared at her for a long minute before speak-ing. "What aren't you telling me, Miss Sullivan?"

"I have no idea what you're referring to. Jasper stalked me, kidnapped me, chained me up, all because I broke up with him and his tiny ego couldn't handle the rejection." She sighed. "Men. Such babies, yeah?"

"Miss Sullivan, this is your chance to help yourself by telling the truth. If... No, *when* I find out what you're hid-ing, it will be worse for you. See, there are reports of a man and woman fitting your and Mr. O'Rourke's descriptions seen in Hope Corner after Mr. Garrison was killed, yet both of you claim you left prior to his death."

Oh, boy. That wasn't good. Too late to change their story now. Had this question come up with Liam? If so, why hadn't he warned her? She had no choice but to stick to her guns, so she met the sheriff's gaze. "Listen, my father hired Liam to find me. He did, and he rescued me. Neither one of us saw Jasper again. End of story."

"Sheriff Lamott, unless you have an arrest warrant for Miss Sullivan's extradition to West Virginia that you've presented to the Myrtle Beach police department, Miss Sullivan is done here," John said. "Do you?"

"Not yet."

"Great. Nice talking to you, Sheriff Lamott." *Not.* She stood. "I hope you find who killed Jasper. He turned out not to be a nice man, but he didn't deserve to die." She felt Deputy Dog's eyes on her as she walked out of the room. The man made her uneasy.

"I'm not in handcuffs either," she exclaimed as soon as she saw Liam.

He grabbed her hand and pulled her into his office, closing the door behind them. He put his hands on her cheeks and roamed his eyes over her. "You're okay?"

"Yeah. Just happy it's over. Well, over for now. I'm sure we haven't heard the last from Sheriff Lamott. He asked—"

Someone knocked on the door, and Liam stepped away to open it. Grayson walked in, followed by John.

"John said you did great," Grayson said.

"I was fine until the sheriff told me a couple matching my and Liam's description was seen in Hope Corner after Jasper was killed. It took everything in me not to react to that."

"He didn't ask me that," Liam said. "I wonder why."

"It was an ambush," John said. "He didn't ask Liam that question on purpose. He didn't want you warned that he knew you were back in Hope Corner. You did good not to react, because he was hoping it would rattle you."

"Well, it did. I'm amazed my voice didn't quiver. It was

a mistake to go back. I just really wanted those pictures to prove the barrels belonged to the mill."

"What's done is done," Liam said. "He can't prove it was us, so he still has nothing."

"And if he does prove it was us?"

"Just because you returned to Hope Corner isn't evidence that you were involved in Jasper Garrison's murder," John said. "According to Liam and Grayson, this situation will be resolved soon, and the sheriff can turn his focus from you to the actual murderer."

"I'm supposed to leave for Ukraine in two weeks. Will that be a problem if whoever killed Jasper hasn't been arrested?"

Liam frowned. "You're leaving?"

Chapter Twenty-Nine

"I didn't mean to tell you like that."

"How did you mean to tell me?" Grayson and John had quickly excused themselves. Liam figured it was his scowl at hearing Quinn's news that sent them running.

"When we were alone. I've had this trip scheduled for months, Liam, before I met you. It has nothing to do with you."

"Nothing to do with me? I thought…" He swiped his hand through his hair.

"You thought what?"

"Maybe that I meant something to you. Enough of a something that you would tell me you had plans to leave the country. Guess I was wrong." He was being an ass. He knew it, but he plowed on anyway. "Did you plan to wait until the last minute to tell me, like when you were packing to leave? Or were you just going to walk away without looking back?"

"This is why I don't do relationships." She turned her back on him, walked to the window, and looked out. Her shoulders were stiff, her frustration visible. "Why do men think they have a right to dictate how a woman lives her life?"

"I'm not trying to—"

She faced him. "I thought maybe you were different. My career is my life, Liam. It's what I live for. I've been up front with you about that."

"Meaning you don't have room for me." It wasn't a question because he got it. He was, after all, exactly what she'd said. A brief fling. He should have listened to her from the start.

"I wish…" She shook her head. "Never mind."

"You wish what?" He was close to begging her to make room for him in that life of hers that she guarded so fiercely, but stubborn pride kept his mouth shut.

"That I'd never met Jasper. Then I wouldn't be standing in this room worrying about men after me, children getting sick, and doing my best not to cry because I feel like I just lost a friend."

She wished she'd never met him. That hurt. It also made him feel mean. He held up his thumb and index finger an inch apart. "I was this close to falling in love with you, but I guess I should thank you for showing me the error of my ways."

Tears filled her eyes. "You're welcome." Without another word, she walked out of his office.

Eff him, he was an ass. A pissed-off ass, but an ass all the same. How had it come to this? He scrubbed his hand over his face. If she never intended to include him in her life, it was better this way. Yes, he was hurt. And yes, he was falling in love with her, but he should thank her for saving him from being all in.

His office suddenly felt empty without her in it. If only she had given him a chance, he would have shown her that he wasn't like her ex…whatever the hell his name was, or any other man in her life who didn't encourage her to fly free. He would have been there for her, been her number one cheerleader. He would have never stopped her from doing what, as she'd said, "fed her soul" no matter where in the world it took her. He would have been her safe haven whenever she came home to him.

"Guess that's that," he muttered. He walked to the window, stood where she had, and looked out at the view she'd seen. The Phoenix Three was on the top floor of a three-story building that Grayson's father had bought and rented back to them when they'd started their company. It was two blocks from the beach, and over the tops of the buildings, he could see the Atlantic Ocean.

Was it only last night that he'd sat out on his balcony with her, enjoying that same ocean and feeling so much hope for the future? Her coconut vanilla scent was still in the air, and he breathed deep. He'd almost handed over his heart, not knowing she'd be taking it to Ukraine with her but not bringing it back to him. Good thing he hadn't.

He'd lost his family, and now he'd lost the woman he could love, make a life with. Even years later, he still missed his family, and since losing them, he'd longed to make a new family of his own. A woman who loved him and a home filled with the laughter of children. Maybe the universe was sending him a message that he was meant to be alone. Yeah, he was feeling sorry for himself. He was entitled to a little self-pity, wasn't he? If only for tonight? Tomorrow, he would pick up the pieces and move on.

Too bad he wasn't much of a drinker. If he was, he could go home and drink his misery away. Sadly, a beer in the evenings while sitting on his balcony and decompressing from the day or wine with dinner occasionally when on a date was about the extent of his alcohol consumption.

Where was she? He walked out to the hallway. The small

conference room had an all-glass wall, and seeing that she was sitting at the table where she was safe, he returned to his office.

He went to his desk, hesitated for a moment, then picked up his cell phone and called his mother. He needed to hear the voice of the one person in the world who unconditionally loved him and hadn't abandoned him. The name Lisa would show up on her screen, a fictional book club friend. If his father was around, she'd let it go to voicemail and call him back later.

"Hello, son. This isn't our usual day to talk. Is everything okay?"

"I was thinking about family and missing you." She worried about him as it was, so he wasn't going to tell her he was nursing a broken heart and give her more reason to be troubled on his account.

"I wish…"

"Yeah, me, too. But he's never going to change, Mama. I did get an interesting phone call. Do you know a Robert Sullivan?"

"If it's the same man, he's the Realtor your father used when he was looking for property in Savannah some years ago. I met him at dinner a few times when I went down there with your father. Nice man. Why are you asking?"

He remembered his parents going to Savannah to scout a location for a new pub back when he was in high school. "It's the same man. His daughter went missing, and he asked me to find her. Here's the shocker, though. He said Dad gave him my name, said that if anyone could find her, it was me."

There was a long silence, then, "Your father gave him your name? Actually said your name after swearing he never would again?"

"That's what Mr. Sullivan said."

"Oh, Liam. That's wonderful. It means there's hope he'll forgive you."

He crushed the anger heating his neck, swallowed the words she'd wash his mouth out with soap if he uttered them. This was his mother. "I did nothing wrong to be forgiven for, Mama. I'm doing good things, you know, like saving children. Why can't he see that?"

"I don't know, son. I've tried to talk to him about this, but the stubborn ass refuses to listen. I thought for sure he'd eventually come around."

He didn't have to see her to know that tears were running down her cheeks. "He's too hardheaded to back down. You know that. Once he takes a stand, that's it for him." He blew out a breath. "Listen, it's not your job to fix this. Only he can, so don't take this weight on your shoulders." Grayson came to the door. "I need to go. I'll call you on our usual day."

"Liam."

"Yeah?"

"I'm proud of you. I want you to believe that."

"Thanks, Mama. That means a lot to me. I love you."

"I love you, too, my precious boy."

"How's your mother?" Grayson asked after Liam disconnected the call.

"Missing her boy and wishing my father wasn't a stubborn ass." Both Grayson and Cooper knew he'd been declared dead by his father.

Grayson came in and took a seat in front of Liam's desk. "Think he'll ever come around?"

"No. If he was going to, he'd have done it by now."

"I say it's his loss. What was that between you and Quinn?"

"Hell if I know."

"As an objective observer, it seemed like you overreacted."

"I guess I really messed up. She insists we're nothing more than a fling."

"And you want more, I take it."

"Yeah. I think she's the one, Gray. Unfortunately for me, from her past experiences, she has it in her head that men want to control her life. I can't seem to get her to understand I'm not like those other men."

"Don't take this wrong because I'm on your side, but your reaction to learning she has a trip to Ukraine planned didn't help your case."

"I know. I didn't handle that well. She just caught me by surprise, and I reacted. Where is she? I'll go talk to her. See if I can repair the damage." It was going to be awkward with her staying with him if he couldn't, but she couldn't go home. Not yet. It still wasn't safe for her.

"Give her a few minutes to calm down. She called Harlow and asked if she'd come pick her up."

At least she would be safe with Harlow.

Chapter Thirty

Had she overreacted to Liam's reaction to learning about her trip? Maybe. Okay, she had, but his questioning her was a trigger from her time with Aiden. She'd learned to be defensive whenever Aiden started on her about her job and travels as if her career wasn't important. Even now, years later, those old wounds put her on the defensive, thus reacting the way she had.

Harlow would be here to pick her up in a few minutes, and Quinn decided to wait downstairs in the lobby to avoid talking to Liam. Pretty immature behavior on her part. He didn't deserve the way she'd treated him. Not that she'd changed her mind about their time together being more than a fling...maybe. The idea of a possible future with him if they could come to an understanding about her career had already been hovering in the edges of her mind.

She should've stayed and talked to him, and that thought had her returning to the elevator to go back up and do just that. He would understand when she explained that she'd heard Aiden's voice in her head telling her that her *pictures* weren't important. Just as she pushed the button, someone walked up behind her.

"We're going to quietly walk out of here, Miss Sullivan."

She gasped as she spun around, her eyes widening at seeing the man invading her space.

"One sound out of you, and it will be the last one you'll ever make." He turned his hand up, showing her the knife he held. "Don't for a minute think I won't cut you and leave your body for your boyfriend to find if you don't do exactly as I say."

Deputy Dog! She hadn't liked the vibes coming from him as he'd stared at her in the conference room. She should have paid attention to her instincts. "You'll regret this if you make me leave with you. Those men upstairs won't stop until they find me, and when they do, they'll make you sorry you came anywhere near me."

"Stop talking." He put his arm around her and pulled her next to him. "Feel that?"

"Yes." He was pushing the tip of the knife into her side hard enough to hurt. How could she get out of this?

"Start walking or I really will cut you."

"I'm not going anywhere with you."

He pushed the tip of the knife into her hard enough to pierce her skin. "Ow. That hurt."

"That's nothing compared to what I will do if you don't start walking."

Did she have a choice? It had been stupid of her to come down to the lobby by herself, but she'd thought she was safe as long as she stayed in the building, which she'd planned to do until Harlow arrived. She'd just been so angry at Liam that she hadn't been thinking about anything but getting away from him. It had been misplaced anger, and now she was paying the price for overreacting.

When Deputy Dog poked her again, she started walking. Maybe Harlow would drive up when they stepped outside. She wasn't that lucky. When they reached his car, he pulled her hands behind her back and handcuffed her. "Is that necessary?"

"Can't have you trying to jump out of a moving car." He pushed her onto the seat, then belted her in.

She wouldn't hesitate to jump out when she thought she could do it without killing herself, but now that she was handcuffed, she couldn't open the door. "Where are you taking me?" she asked as he drove away from the safety of The Phoenix Three.

"Someone wants to talk to you."

"Who?"

"Just someone." He glanced at her. "Why aren't you scared? You should be."

"Are you planning to kill me?"

"Me? No, but you should still be scared."

She wasn't because Liam would find her. He had before, and he would again. And knowing that, the truth stared right back at her. Liam wasn't Aiden. How many times had he told her he wasn't, but she hadn't been able to quite believe him. "My bad," she murmured.

"What did you say?"

"Just talking to myself, calling you vile names."

He laughed. "It's too bad we met under these circumstances, Quinn. I have a feeling you and I could've had some fun together."

In your dreams, Deputy Dog asshat. And really, not even then. What she could do was get information that would help them expose what the mill was doing. "So, is Sheriff Lamott involved in whatever this is?"

"That Boy Scout?" He snorted. "The good sheriff won't even take a free doughnut. What were you and your boyfriend doing in Hope Corner?"

"I assumed you rode down to Myrtle Beach with him,"

she said, ignoring his question. "Where does he think you are right now?"

"Obviously I didn't ride with him, and I had some time off due me, so I'm officially on a beach vacation."

"Could've fooled me, since it appears we're leaving the beach." If she had to guess, he was taking her back to Hope Corner. That was the first place Liam would look for her. Oh, how could she forget? He'd put a tracking app on her phone, so he'd easily find her…as long as Deputy Dog didn't take it away from her. What if someone called her? That would remind him to take it away from her. She was surprised he hadn't already. *Please, no one call me.*

"Are we going back to Hope Corner?"

Clearly losing his patience, he scowled at her. "Anyone ever tell you that you talk too much?"

"Nope, my friends love listening to me. So, who made that anonymous phone call about me to the sheriff? I bet it was you."

"How about you shut up."

"No problem. I don't like talking to you anyway." It was him, she just knew it. Why? So he could find her? That had to be it.

What she didn't understand was why they—whoever *they* were behind this—didn't think that if she did have the thumb drive, she wouldn't have made copies. Or shown it to someone. They had to have considered that, so why were they kidnapping her? What was their end game?

Chapter Thirty-One

"Is she planning to stay with you and Harlow tonight?" Liam asked. Would she need to get her things from his condo? He rubbed his hand over his chest, right where there was an ache in the vicinity of his heart. His place was going to feel empty without her in it. He didn't have to be there to already know that.

Grayson lifted from the chair. "I think so. Don't give up hope, Liam. Most relationships experience a bump along the way."

"Not fond of bumps." And he wasn't so sure this was a simple bump. Instead of hearing her, he'd closed his ears to what she'd said from the beginning, thinking he could change her mind. All he'd done was prove her point.

"Hey," Harlow said as she walked into his office.

She went straight to Grayson, and Liam glanced out the window when she lifted on her toes to give him a kiss. He'd never kiss Quinn again, never wake up next to her again. The sooner he accepted that... He didn't want to accept it. Maybe she just needed time, and with that time, maybe she'd miss him.

"Is Quinn ready to go?" Harlow asked.

"She's in the conference room," Grayson said.

"No, I just looked in there."

Liam frowned. "I saw her in there, too." He stood, telling himself not to panic. "She's around here somewhere." She had to be. He walked past Grayson and Harlow out into the hallway. "Quinn?" She didn't answer.

"I'll look in the bathroom," Harlow said.

"Where is she?" She wouldn't take off on her own, would she? Grayson disappeared into his office while Liam's search for her grew more frantic. She wasn't in the war room or any other room he checked.

"Liam, come here," Grayson said.

The urgency in Grayson's voice had Liam hurrying to his office. "You find her?"

"Unfortunately."

Liam's heart dropped to his stomach. What did *unfortunately* mean? "Where is she?"

"Come look at this."

He walked around Grayson's desk. The security camera feed from the lobby was frozen on the screen. "What are we looking at?"

Grayson hit Play, and they both watched as the elevator door opened into the lobby. Quinn stepped out, and it seemed she was deep in thought. A minute later, she turned back to the elevator and pushed the button. Was she coming back up? Hope beat in his heart that she hadn't been any happier than he with the way they'd left things, and she was coming back to talk.

"Who's that?" A man was walking up behind her, and Liam frowned when he recognized the face. "That's Lamott's deputy. I thought they left."

"Watch," Grayson said. "I've turned the volume up on the sound."

When they'd outfitted the building with security cameras, they'd included audio. The deputy stopped behind Quinn, crowding her body.

"We're going to quietly walk out of here, Miss Sullivan," he said, startling her. "One sound out of you, and it will be the last one you'll ever make." The deputy showed her the knife he held. "Don't for a minute think I won't cut you and leave your body for your boyfriend to find if you don't do exactly as I say."

Liam growled. "He's a dead man." He stared hard at the screen as the video continued. She should have been safe in their building, but they'd unknowingly invited the devil into their midst. They didn't have security personnel in the lobby, hadn't thought they needed it. That was going to change.

"Ow. That hurt," Quinn cried as she tried to pull away, but the man held on to her.

"The fucker cut her." When the deputy walked her out of the building, Liam wanted to punch his hands through the screen and snatch her back. "She has to be so scared. I was supposed to protect her, and I let my ego—"

"Stop right now," Grayson said. "That shit's not helping her." He pushed away from his desk.

"Yeah, okay. We need a plan." He was going to tear the deputy apart with his bare hands when he caught up with them.

"First we have to figure out where he's taking her."

"Back to Hope Corner?" Liam said. "We can't call her phone. If he hasn't thought to take it away from her, calling her will remind him to do that."

"Let's hope she still has it on her. She'll call you if she gets a chance to."

"She… Wait, I put a tracking app on her phone." With the shock of her being taken, he'd forgotten he'd done that.

Thank God he had. He logged into the app. "Looks like they're heading toward I-95. If they go north, then he probably is going back to Hope Corner. Let's go. I'll drive." He was halfway out of the room when Grayson stopped him.

"Hold up, O'Rourke. You were a Marine Raider. You wouldn't have gone on a mission with a half-cocked plan."

Liam fisted his hands as he turned to his friend. "And if it was Harlow in that car? Where would you be right now? I'll tell you where. Chasing them down, just like I'm going to do."

"True, and you would have stopped me, like I'm doing now. And I would thank you for it."

He was right. Liam knew it, but that didn't mean he liked hearing it. "They've got a good thirty-minute head start on us, and the longer we delay leaving, the bigger that lead is."

"So, we get our helicopter friends to pick us up. I'll call Brant and put them on standby so they're ready to go when we are. We need to get Coop in here, too."

"Let's hope they're available. I'll call Coop while you call Brant." Somewhat mollified that they'd be able to catch up with Quinn in a helicopter, he got Cooper on the line. "We need you here stat."

"On the way."

No question on Cooper's part as to why they wanted him here immediately. That was what it meant to be on a team, to be a band of brothers who would always have each other's backs no matter what.

"Bad news on the helo," Grayson said. "It's out on a charter. Brant said it'll be back in three hours, and he can have it refueled and ready to go thirty minutes after that."

Not what he wanted to hear. "Coop's on his way in." He checked the tracking app. "They're still heading toward I-95. Should reach it in about twenty minutes, then we'll know which way they go. We're only an hour behind them now. If we drive, we can make up some of that time, more than waiting three hours for a chopper."

"I still think the helo's our best option." Grayson headed for the door. "Let's go in the war room."

Liam followed him out. "We'll need transportation when we land if we take the helo. We drive, that problem's solved." He couldn't handle twiddling his thumbs while they waited for the helicopter to return. If they drove, they could leave as soon as Cooper arrived.

Grayson put an aerial view of Hope Corner on the large wall screen. They were studying the map for possible landing sites if they helicoptered in when Cooper arrived. "Sitrep?"

"Quinn's been taken." It was hard to even say that without putting his fist through the wall.

"Shit. How'd that happen?"

He brought Cooper up to date. "So, drive or wait for the helo?"

"Drive. We'll lose another three hours waiting for the helo, then add the time it'll take to fly us close to Hope Corner?"

Liam nodded. "We take the car, we're only an hour behind if we leave now."

"That's if they're going to Hope Corner," Grayson said. "If we take the helo, no matter where they go, we can…" He stared at the aerial view on the screen. "No, you're both right. We'll be too far behind taking the helo. We drive. Let's gear up."

"Good thing you put that tracker app on her phone," Cooper said as the three of them were putting enough weapons on their bodies and in their duffel bags to start a small war.

"I agree, because now I don't have to shoot myself for not doing it."

As they rode the elevator down, Grayson called Brant and canceled the helicopter. "He said if we need backup, they'll be on standby."

Brant and his partner, Zed, were former SEALs who'd served together before opting out of the Navy and starting their security company. They were good people, men who would always have a brother's back.

Grayson took the driver's seat, Liam the passenger's, and Cooper the back. The Range Rover's 626 horsepower twin-turbocharged V-8 was fast, with plenty of legroom for big men.

It was a car Grayson kept for missions like this. Liam pulled up the tracking app. "They're on I-95 North. Looks like Hope Corner is their destination.

"Do you think the sheriff's involved?" he asked.

Grayson passed three slower-moving cars. "I didn't get bad-guy vibes from him, but he could just be a good actor."

"I didn't get any either. The deputy, though, whole nother story."

"Yeah, I didn't like him either," Grayson said.

"When we catch up with them, the deputy's mine."

Chapter Thirty-Two

Quinn stared out the window at…pretty much nothing. I-95 was a boring highway. She'd given up trying to get information out of Deputy Dog since he'd stopped answering any of her questions. She was trying hard not to panic. Liam would find her, but until then, she had to be smart. She just needed to figure out how to do that.

So far, no one had tried to call her, so her phone hadn't chimed. That was a relief, but how long was that going to last? She'd talked to her father last night, so he wouldn't call. Liam hadn't called either, which was something of a surprise. Although, Liam was smart, and maybe he'd realized it was better not to.

"I need to stop for gas," Deputy Dog said as he exited the highway. "You try anything, you call out to anyone, I'll shoot you on the spot." He lifted the hem of his T-shirt to show her the gun in a holster strapped to his belt. "Then I'll shoot whoever you try to get help from. Understood?"

"Yes." He knew exactly what threat to use to keep her from trying to escape.

After he was out of the car, she managed to reach her purse and pull it behind her back. After a bit of fumbling, her fingers grasped her phone, and she felt around until she found the button to silence it. Instead of putting it back in her purse, she pushed it under the waistband of her jeans. Hopefully, no one would frisk her.

When they were back on the road, she tried again to find out where they were going. "I'm thirsty and have to go to the bathroom. How much longer before we get wherever we're going?"

"We'll get there when we get there."

"And there is where?" He ignored her. *Jerk.*

She was bored, her shoulders hurt, and her arms felt like a thousand needles were poking them. She was also scared. Why had she been kidnapped? Deputy Dog hadn't once asked about the thumb drive. Wasn't that what he, or whoever was involved in this, wanted? What were they going to do with her? Maybe she didn't want to know the answer to that question.

"There's the exit for Hope Corner." She frowned when he drove right past it.

She guessed they drove for another hour, and she was seeing mileage signs for Washington. "Are we going to DC?" Again, nothing. He was making her mad. If the capital was their destination, were they going to see Senator Hanson? She couldn't think of any other reason to go to DC.

He exited the highway some miles later. Before long, the four-lane road turned into a two-lane, and they were out in the country. The area was beautiful with big, sprawling homes on one-and two-acre lots. People with money lived out here, and that made her think she'd be meeting the senator soon. She didn't want to. Without ever having laid eyes on him, she had the sense he was a man she should be afraid of.

Deputy Dog pulled over to the side of the road. He reached into the console compartment and pulled out a sleeping mask and put it on her, covering her eyes. The car started moving, and she tried to ignore the panic rising up. Not being able to see, combined with her hands cuffed behind her back, made her feel like a caged animal. She focused on her breathing in an effort to calm her nerves. It didn't work.

After what seemed an eternity, but was probably twenty or thirty minutes, the car came to a stop. She heard his door open, and a moment later, hers. Deputy Dog roughly grabbed her arm, pulling her out of the car. She stumbled slightly, disoriented by the sudden change in movement.

"Where are we?" she demanded, the fear creeping into her voice despite her efforts to remain calm.

"Shut up and walk." He guided her with his hand on her elbow, and she'd only walked for a minute when he said, "Three steps up."

"This would be easier if you'd take off this damn mask."

"I said shut up."

Touchy. She tentatively lifted her foot, feeling for the first step, then did the same for the next two. It wasn't easy to keep her balance with her arms bound behind her back. Something creaked, and she thought it might be a door opening. When the temperature dropped, she knew they were inside an air-conditioned house. The strong smell of lemon oil permeated the air, telling her it was probably like one of the well-kept houses they'd passed before she was blindfolded. Deputy Dog pushed on her elbow, forcing her to keep walking.

"Can't you take these handcuffs off me? My hands and arms feel like someone's sticking a thousand needles in them. It's not like I'm going anywhere."

"Sit." She was pushed down on something soft, a sofa she guessed.

"Take the blindfold off," a man said.

He's someone who expects to be obeyed, she thought. Suddenly, she didn't want to see whoever it was. If she didn't see his face, he wouldn't have to kill her. "That's okay, you can leave the blindfold on, but I'd appreciate the cuffs coming off."

Despite her wishes, the blindfold was removed, and she blinked against the sunlight coming in through the window. Her gaze fell on the man sitting behind a chrome-and-glass desk. Behind him was a full wall of bookshelves, what looked like law books filling them. An attorney then? Was Senator Hanson a lawyer? She should've learned more about the man…if this was him.

The man wore a COVID-type face mask, only his eyes and hair visible. His hair was a dirty blond and expensively cut, and although she couldn't see his full face, from what she could see, she guessed him to be in his sixties. She had a photographer's eye for detail, and because she did, she noticed something about one of his, something most people wouldn't see. There was a gray ring around the pupil of his left eye but not the right one.

If she ever saw that eye again, she could point her finger at him and say, "He's the one who had me kidnapped." She made a mental note not to forget to tell the authorities about that gray ring. It would make a difference if she gave that description before she ever saw him again.

If she lived through this, that was.

"Where's her phone?" the man said.

Her gazed narrowed in on her purse that he was rummaging through. Not that there was much in there, since she hadn't replaced most of what used to be in her lost purse. "My phone was in my purse at the cabin, which I assume you people have. I'd sure love to have it back." She was getting mad, and she welcomed that anger because she wasn't quivering before this bully of a man.

"Frisk her," the masked man said.

Deputy Dog yanked her up, and when his hands slid over her, she gritted her teeth. As much as she'd wanted the cuffs off, she was glad they weren't for this. She was able to keep her bound hands over where she'd slid her phone to hide it. She almost sagged with relief when the deputy didn't find it.

"She's good."

"Uncuff her and then leave," the masked man said.

Okay, as much as she didn't like the deputy, she didn't want to be left alone with the man she was sure was the senator. Was that pity in Deputy Dog's eyes as he pulled her up to take the handcuffs off? Her stomach took a sickening roll when the door closed behind the deputy, leaving her alone with the man.

"Sit," he said in that intimidating voice.

As much as she wanted to refuse, to laugh in his face and tell him to go to hell, her legs decided sitting was a grand idea. Her body gracelessly crumpled in on itself. At least there was a sofa behind her to land on and she didn't end up a heap on the floor. Small favors.

Her hands and arms were tingling as if they were waking up from a long sleep, and she laced her fingers together and waited. When he did nothing but sit there and stare at her, she wanted to squirm. She managed not to.

When she couldn't take his staring with those cold eyes any longer, words she couldn't stop tumbled out of her mouth. "Who are you? What do you want from me? I—"

He held up a hand, palm out, and as if she was a puppet obeying the master, her mouth snapped closed.

"It matters not who I am. As for why you're here, it's

called damage control, Miss Sullivan. Who have you shown the thumb drive to? How many copies did you make? Where are they? You honestly answer those questions, and then we'll talk about how you get to live another day."

Okay, what was the next level of fear? Petrified? *Buy some time to think, Quinn.* "Your deputy kidnapped me hours ago and didn't let me have a restroom break. I really, really need to pee, so unless you want me to piddle on your sofa, you'll—"

A disgusted expression crossed his face. "Through there." He pointed to a door to the right of him.

His eyes stayed on her until she closed the bathroom door. That was just creepy. It was a powder room, only a toilet and sink. She did really need to pee, and she pulled her phone out and set it on the corner of the sink. After relieving herself, she washed her hands, and after drinking some, she splashed cold water on her face. She picked up her phone, intending to put it back in the same place, but what if… She checked the charge, finding it almost full. They'd already searched her, so they wouldn't do it again. Leaving it in silent mode, she hit Record, then stuffed it inside her bra.

It wasn't until she returned to the sofa that it occurred to her that she should've texted Liam when she had the chance. Disgusted with herself, she wanted to slap her head for not thinking smart. She folded her hands in her lap and waited for the man to speak.

Chapter Thirty-Three

"They passed the exit for Hope Corner without getting off," Liam said as he tracked Quinn's phone.

"How far behind are we?" Grayson asked.

"About eighty minutes." They'd lost more time when traffic came to a dead stop because of a wreck that closed both northbound lanes shortly after they got on I-95. Sitting still, unable to move, had been torture.

They were speeding and making up the lost time now, and he hoped they didn't get stopped. Considering the number of weapons in the car, it would take a lot of explaining. The Range Rover had a top-of-the-line built-in radar detector, so hopefully they'd have adequate warning to avoid getting stopped.

"Where the hell is he taking her?"

"You have considered the possibility that the deputy tossed the phone in the bed of a passing pickup truck, right?" Cooper said. "That we're on a wild-goose chase?"

Liam turned and glared at him. "Don't even go there. If that phone's not with her…" He couldn't let himself think that they had no clue where she was.

Cooper raised his hands. "Don't shoot the messenger, brother, but it's something we need to consider. What's

Plan B if we catch up with the phone and it's not with Quinn?"

"We could make a detour to Hope Corner and talk to the sheriff," Grayson said. "He might know where his deputy has a hidey-hole. That would also let us get a bead on Sheriff Lamott, determine if he's a part of this." Grayson glanced at him. "It's your call."

Liam closed his eyes and drew in a deep breath. It was an almost impossible decision to make. What was the right one? Was the phone still with her? What if it wasn't? He opened his mind to that place inside him that he'd learned to trust, that had kept him alive on dangerous operations. Every instinct he had said the phone was still with her.

"We follow the phone. Think about it. If the deputy had found it, he most likely would have destroyed it. That's what people tend to do." Although not a religious man, he sent a prayer to the Man above that he'd made the right decision. *And just keep her safe until I can get to her.*

"We'll find her," Grayson said as he pressed down on the gas pedal, picking up speed.

They would, but would it be in time?

"So, it's serious, you and Quinn," Cooper asked.

"On my part."

"Not on hers? Could've fooled me."

"How so?" Cooper hadn't been around the last few days, so he'd missed the blowup of any relationship Liam had hoped for with her. He was going to rescue her, and then he'd do as she wished and send her on her way. It was going to hurt to lose her, but he'd do it for her.

"The way she would look at you, like she had real feelings for you. What happened?"

"Based on prior experiences, she has it in her head that men and the career she loves don't mix."

"You have to show her it will be different with you."

If only.

"Move over, dude," Grayson grouched when a car in the passing lane stayed at the same speed as the car next to it. He flashed his lights, and the car finally moved into the right lane. "There's always hope, Liam. Look at me and Harlow. She was adamant that as soon as she had her son back it was over for us. She lasted a week, and now we're getting married."

"I guess anything could happen." But he didn't believe it. Harlow didn't have a career that took her all over the world, a career that she'd learned the hard way that men couldn't deal with. Quinn was wrong about that. He could, but she wasn't going to give him a chance to show her.

"What'd you do with Ruby?" Grayson asked Cooper.

"She's at your house, playing with Tyler and Einstein."

Grayson sighed. "Now Tyler's going to want a dog."

As the two of them talked about Cooper's new dog, Liam stared out the window, a battle brewing in him. He would respect Quinn's condition for their fling, but that wouldn't stop him from feeling angry that she refused to give them a chance.

"You still following Quinn's whereabouts?" Grayson asked.

Right. Get your mind on the mission, O'Rourke. He pulled up the tracking app and frowned. "They exited the highway about five minutes ago, now heading west. We've gained forty minutes on them." He gave Grayson the exit number. They were still forty minutes behind. Anything could happen in forty minutes. He pushed that thought out of his mind. Finding her safe and unharmed was the only acceptable ending to this operation.

He kept his gaze on the tracking app, following the moving dot that was Quinn's phone. "Looks like they're out in the country now." Where was he taking her? Twenty minutes later, the dot stopped moving. "Coop, pull up Google Maps." He held up his phone so Cooper could see the coordinates for where the phone was. "See what's there."

"Lakeside Estates. Stand by a minute. I'll do a search for that area."

"They're still not moving," Liam said as he watched his phone screen.

"Lakeside Estates is a community of million-dollar-and-up homes."

"What the hell are they doing there?" That didn't make any sense. Unless… "This is close to the capital. Do we know where Senator Hanson has a home?"

"Let me see if I can find out," Cooper said.

If anyone could, it was Cooper. He could tease information out of a computer that would make a hacker jealous. "They're still at the same location. We're thirty minutes from the exit, then about twenty from where her phone is." He refused to consider that the phone wasn't with her. If it wasn't, then he'd made a big mistake in insisting they drive instead of taking the helicopter.

"Got it," Cooper said. "Hanson has a condo in DC and a home in Lakeside Estates."

"Bingo. It is surprising that he'd risk bringing her to his home."

"I'm thinking he's arrogant enough to think no one will ever know she was there," Grayson said.

All he cared about was getting to her, and they'd just confirmed they weren't on a wild-goose chase. He blew out a relieved breath. "Does he think no one will come looking for her?"

"He's desperate to get that thumb drive," Cooper said.

Desperate enough to hurt her? They finally exited the highway and were soon on a two-lane country road. They'd be at the location in twenty minutes. *Hang in there, Quinn. We're almost there.*

Chapter Thirty-Four

"Here's what you need to understand, Quinn... May I call you Quinn?"

"I prefer Miss Sullivan." What was with all these people she didn't like wanting to get familiar and call her Quinn?

A beam of sunlight from the sun now low in the sky touched her face, and she turned toward it. The view outside the tall windows was beautiful. There weren't any buildings behind his house, and the word that came to mind as she took in the meadow of rich green grass, wildflowers, and rolling hills was *pastoral*. Behind a split rail fence, a herd of Arabian horses grazed. She wished she had her camera.

She wished Liam was here. He'd carry her away from this horrid man. Her gaze fell on a beautiful stark white horse. That was the one Liam would toss her on and then jump on behind her. She'd laugh with joy as they rode away, over those hills filled with wildflowers.

When he finally stopped the horse, he whispered in her ear, "This is my secret waterfall. I've never brought a woman here before." He lifted her from the horse, and they shed their clothes.

"Are you listening, Miss Sullivan?"

She reluctantly tore her gaze from the distant hill where

she was frolicking in the pool of the secret waterfall with Liam. "Not really."

"Well, you should if you care at all for your friends at The Phoenix Three."

He had her attention now.

"As I was saying, I want that thumb drive and any copies you've made. I want to know who you've told of its existence. I want your assurance that you'll convince the men helping you to forget anything to do with what's on that thumb drive."

"Or?" She really didn't want to know, but she needed him to say it for the recording. God, she hoped her phone was still recording.

"Or they'll lose their company and will be investigated nine ways to Sunday by every alphabet agency you can think of. And believe me, Miss Sullivan, I can make that happen. Do you want your friends ruined?"

"Who are you?" With that particular threat, she was certain now that it was the senator, but maybe he was one of the senator's minions.

"I'm someone you and your friends don't want to mess with."

She didn't doubt it, but not much she could do except keep denying, denying, denying. "I don't know what thumb drive you're talking about. All the Phoenix Three men have done for me is help me fight being accused of killing Jasper. I have a feeling you know for a fact that I didn't."

"Careful, Miss Sullivan. To imply I know anything about a murder doesn't please me."

She sighed. "Yes, I know, you're not a man I want to displease." She was poking the bear, but his threats toward the guys made her angry.

"Need I remind you that no one knows where you are?

There is no one coming to rescue you." He sat back in his chair and stared at her a moment before saying, "Your attitude needs improvement. I think a time-out for you to think about the situation you're in will do much to adjust your unfortunate attitude." He pressed a button on the landline on his desk. "Return," was all he said.

A minute later, Deputy Dog walked in. "Sir?"

"Take Miss Sullivan to spend time with our friend. Perhaps she'll rethink the wisdom of refusing to cooperate."

She didn't like the sound of that, and what friend? "I'm fine just sitting here. I promise I'll keep my mouth shut and not bother you."

Amusement filled his eyes, and she sensed that he was smiling behind that mask. "I'm beginning to be sorry we didn't meet under better circumstances, Miss Sullivan. I think we could have enjoyed each other's company."

When hell freezes over. Deputy Dog yanked her up, pulled her hands behind her back, and handcuffed her again. As he forced her to walk out of the room, she cast a glance over her shoulder at the horses, then lifted her gaze to the hills where Liam's secret waterfall was.

Tears filled her eyes that she wasn't truly playing in the water with him. If she had one wish, it would be to turn back the clock and not have ended things with him the way she had. What if he was mad enough at her to not search for her? That thought almost crushed her, but no, that wasn't Liam. No matter what he thought of her now, he was out there looking for her.

Deputy Dog blindfolded her again before taking her back to his car. "Where are we going?" she asked when they were on the road. He didn't answer her. The man was still ignoring her, and that made her want to snarl. "Aren't you worried about what's going to happen to you when this whole thing blows up? Like you'll be the one in handcuffs?" Still no response from him, but maybe she'd given him something to think about.

Her best guess was that they'd traveled twenty or so minutes before the car came to a stop. Deputy Dog opened her door, hooked his hand under her elbow, and pulled her out of the car. Rough gravel under her feet and the blindfold had her stumbling, and the deputy tightened his grip on her arm.

They stepped into a building, and she wrinkled her nose at the musty smell. He walked her deeper into the building before stopping her and removing the blindfold. "Enjoy your new home," he said, then walked out, closing the door behind him.

"You forgot to take off the handcuffs," she yelled.

"I doubt he forgot," a man said, the voice familiar.

She spun around and screamed at seeing a dead man. "Jasper?" she gasped. She fell back against the door. "You're dead." Well, obviously, he wasn't, but he sure looked like someone had tried to make him dead by beating him to a pulp. Both eyes were bruised black, his nose looked broken, and one arm hung limply by his side. He was sitting in a hard-back wooden chair, and blood stained his white T-shirt.

"As you can see, I'm still among the living."

He sounded like someone who had a very sore throat, rough and raspy. "Then who was the dead man in the cabin?"

"My cousin."

"Oh, I'm sorry." Well, she was sorry someone died, but everything that was happening was all on Jasper. She almost told him his cousin was dead, he was beat up, and she had been kidnapped because of his greed, but caught herself in time. She needed to continue to claim she knew nothing about the thumb drive, besides… She scanned the room, and yes, there was a blinking red light in a corner of the room. They were being recorded and listened to.

"How long have you been in here?"

"What do you care?"

Because they were being recorded, she needed to be careful about what she said. "Just because it didn't work between us doesn't mean I like seeing you like this. I have no idea why these people keep asking me about a thumb drive. Why would they think I have it? What's on it, do you know?"

"I know you took it, Quinn. All you have to do is turn it over to them, and we can walk away from this."

"Are you really that stupid that you think they'll just open the door and let us walk out of here as they tell us to have a nice day?"

"We can bargain with them. Give them the thumb drive and promise to keep our mouths shut. I know I will. These are powerful people, and they'll watch us to make sure we forget they exist, so I damn well know I'll wipe them from my memory."

He really was stupid if he thought he'd ever see the light of day again. "What powerful people?"

"You're better off not knowing." He gave her a sly look. "Unless you already know because you saw what's on the thumb drive. Why were you in Hope Corner, Quinn?"

"How many times do I have to tell you and these *powerful people* that I. Do. Not. Have. It? If I did, believe me, at this point, I'd gladly give it to them."

"You don't have to yell. I'm right here."

"If I want to yell, I will," she yelled. "I'm tired, I'm hungry, I'm very thirsty, and I'm in handcuffs. I think that gives me plenty of good reason to scream my bloody head off."

She glanced around. "Do they feed you or give you anything to drink at this resort?"

As if on cue, the door opened and Deputy Dog walked in, a bottle of water in his hand. "You want this?" He dangled it in front of her face. "Tell us where the thumb drive is, and it's all yours."

A low growl sounded behind her, and she yelped when Jasper barreled past her, his head lowered and aiming straight for Deputy Dog's stomach. The deputy dropped the bottle and brought his knee up, right into Jasper's groin. Jasper made a horrible sound of pain and fell to the floor in a fetal position. Deputy Dog landed on him, his fists pounding Jasper's face.

"You're going to kill him," she shrieked.

With her hands cuffed behind her back, she couldn't try to pull the deputy off Jasper, so she kicked his leg. "Stop it."

The deputy grabbed her ankle and pulled her foot out from under her. She hit the floor with a hard thud and pain ricocheted up her arm, bringing tears to her eyes. "I think you broke my hand."

"Roll over. I'm going to take the cuffs off you, so be a good girl or I'll put them back on."

After he removed them, he pushed her onto her back again, then fell on top of her. He aligned his body so that they were chest to chest and groin to groin.

Lust darkened his eyes as he stared down at her. "You want to play, little girl?"

Chapter Thirty-Five

Liam frowned when Quinn's phone was on the move again. She—or at least her phone—had been stationary for twenty-nine minutes. "Quinn's phone's traveling."

"Coming at us?" Grayson asked.

"No. The opposite direction. Do we stop at the senator's house or follow the phone? She could still be there and someone else has her phone."

Before Grayson or Cooper could respond, the car's Bluetooth announced an incoming call, and their FBI friend Sean Danvers's name appeared on the screen.

"Grayson here. I'm in the car with Liam and Cooper."

"Correct me if I'm wrong, but I have a feeling you'd rather I not ask where you're going. Am I right?"

"Why you're a good Fed," Liam said.

Sean chuckled. "Just try to stay out of trouble. I have some news for you boys. Turns out Jasper Garrison is not dead."

"Then who was the body in the cabin?" Liam didn't like this at all.

"Garrison's cousin, Joey Garrison. Coop, I'm sending you pics of both men. They could almost be twins. It was assumed it was Jasper because his wallet with his ID in it was found at the cabin. Fingerprints didn't match up, though."

"Where is Jasper if he's not dead?" Liam asked. He had a very bad feeling about this.

"In the wind. I wanted to give you a heads-up. If I hear anything more, I'll be in touch."

"Thanks for that," Grayson said.

"Anything you boys want to tell me?"

Liam shook his head as he shared a look with Grayson.

"Not at this time," Grayson said.

"I was afraid you'd say that. Listen, you're walking a fine line here. Don't cross so far over that I can't get you out of trouble."

"We'll do our best," Liam said, but he wasn't making any promises. He'd cross all the lines it took to keep Quinn safe, trouble or not.

Sean knew Garrison had kidnapped Quinn. They'd had to tell him that much to get him to keep an eye on the investigation into the murder. They hadn't shared with him that it appeared a powerful senator was involved or just what he was involved in. If he knew, the Feds would step in, and that would have put Quinn in even more danger.

"That doesn't reassure me, but I didn't expect a different answer. Stay safe." He disconnected.

"He's not going to be happy when he finds out what's going on," Grayson said.

"Don't care. You agreed that if we brought in the FBI before we were sure Quinn was safe that we wouldn't be able to protect her." She would've been their star witness and considering the people they were dealing with, that would have put a target on her back. An even bigger target.

"I did, and I still believe we did the right thing. Just saying, though."

"We'll just have to ask for forgiveness when it all goes

down. Hell, we'll be handing the FBI the case on a silver platter."

"Look at these pictures," Cooper said, holding out his iPad. "The cousins really do look like twins."

Liam studied the side-by-side photos of the two men. "I'm not sure I'd be able to tell them apart in person."

"The house is a half mile ahead," Grayson said, stopping on the edge of the road. "What's the plan?"

On an operation, Liam had a reputation in his Raider team for being able to sense things, especially danger. His teammates called it his Irish woo-woo. "Drive by the house slowly."

The house was a two-story, one of the biggest in the area. As they passed, he opened his mind, trying to feel Quinn. He got nothing. Didn't mean she wasn't there, but he was going to trust that he'd know if she was.

He tapped the screen of his phone, his eyes on the dot no longer moving. That was where she was. *You better be right, O'Rourke.* "Keep going. I'll tell you when to turn."

When they reached her phone's location, it was to find a boarded-up restaurant with no cars in the parking lot. "Let's check out the back," Grayson said as he drove around the building. "There's a car back here."

"That's the car the deputy drove away from our place." *She was here!* "I can feel her." His brothers didn't roll their eyes or question his sanity, and for that, he loved them.

Without a discussion between them, Grayson drove away. He found an empty house for sale and parked the Range Rover in the open carport. They slipped out of the SUV, moving swiftly and silently toward the restaurant. There was a dumpster at the back of the building, and they stopped behind it.

"It's your party," Grayson said. "How you want to do this?"

"We go in hot and heavy, we risk Quinn getting hurt, so we go in stealth mode." He leaned around the dumpster and scanned the door and windows. Although the windows were boarded up, the plywood didn't reach the top, leaving about a six-inch gap for light to enter. He glanced at Cooper, who was scanning the building with an infrared camera, which would pick up body heat. "What you got?"

"I'm seeing three bodies, all close together in the back left corner."

"Think the missing Jasper Garrison's one of them?" Grayson said.

Liam nodded. "Wouldn't surprise me."

"Weird," Cooper said. "All three are horizontal and low to the floor. One isn't moving, but two are…" Cooper hesitated, then lifted troubled eyes to Liam. "One of the larger bodies is on top of a smaller one, and it looks like they're fighting."

"Quinn's the smaller one," Liam said, knowing he was right. "We're going in hot and heavy." To hell with stealth. Quinn was in trouble. He took off running across the back parking lot, his brothers on his heels.

The back door was unlocked, and the first thing that hit him on entering was the moldy smell. The door opened into the kitchen, and a rat ran across his foot as he raced through the room. Fury burned through him that the deputy had brought Quinn to a place stinking of mold and home to rats.

Cooper had said she was in the back left corner of the building, so he raced to the left, running past bathrooms and down a hallway.

"Get off me!"

That was Quinn's voice, filled with raw panic. He reached the closed door at the end of the hall and kicked it so hard that the handle flew off and the wood splintered.

The sight that greeted him turned his blood to ice, and a red haze colored his vision. Rage like he'd never known exploded. Unleashed, the beast inside him had only one thought.

Kill him.

Chapter Thirty-Six

Quinn's heart hammered against her chest. Each breath a struggle. Her terror that she was going to be raped sent panic racing through her. She tried to scream but fear paralyzed her voice. The deputy wrapped one hand around her throat, squeezing his fingers, choking her. He reached down with his other hand, unbuttoned his jeans, and pulled his zipper down.

He rocked against her, and she could feel his erection pushing into her. No! She wasn't going to let him do this to her. When he put his fingers on the button of her jeans to snap it open, she spit in his face.

"You little bitch." He let go of her throat and put his hand over her mouth.

She bit his finger.

"You want it rough, bitch, I'll give you rough." He pushed her T-shirt up. "What the hell is this?" He grabbed her phone, pulling it out of her bra.

Oh, God. He'd found it. She couldn't let him destroy it. Not only would she lose the recording, but Liam wouldn't be able to find her. She fought him like a wild animal, beating her fists on every part of him she could reach. When she dug her nails into his cheek and scraped down, shredding his skin, he roared in anger and hit her on the side of her head. The pain in her ear was excruciating, and white stars danced behind her eyelids. Tears burned her eyes.

Taking him by surprise, she was able to snatch her phone out of his hand and toss it across the floor. It was safe for now, but unless she could somehow overpower him, he'd still destroy it. After he finished with her.

He laughed. "The more you fight me, the more I'm going to enjoy fucking you. So, go ahead. Do your best, bitch." He wrapped his hand around her throat again. "Every time you move, I'm going to squeeze harder." He reached between them and pushed his jeans and underwear down, exposing himself. Then he pulled the zipper of her jeans down.

"Get off me!" she screamed.

He laughed again. Then he crashed his mouth down on hers and forced his tongue into her mouth.

She tried to bite it off, tasted his blood. Felt victorious when he yanked his mouth away from hers. The fury in his eyes terrified her more than anything he'd done to her by now. He was going to seriously hurt her. He raised his fist, and she squeezed her eyes shut, anticipating the blow.

It never came.

His weight left her, and another voice roared out in rage. "I'm going to kill you."

Liam? Afraid she was hallucinating that he was here, she kept her eyes closed. She couldn't bear not seeing him if she opened them. Then the sound of fists hitting flesh and the deputy grunting in pain filled the room. She wasn't imagining Liam was here.

She opened her eyes, and for a woman who abhorred violence, she felt nothing but relief and gratitude at the sight of Liam battering the deputy with blow after blow, his fists connecting with the man's face with sickening thuds.

"Hey. You're going to be okay."

She tore her gaze from Liam at hearing the soft voice. Cooper was squatting down next to her, and when he gently pulled her T-shirt back down, covering her exposed breast, she was unable to stop the tears.

"Where are you hurt?"

"I—I'm o-okay." She tried to sit up.

"Just stay where you are for a minute. Let's make sure you really are okay."

"That's enough," a different voice said.

She turned her head back to Liam. Grayson was pulling him off the deputy, who was out cold. She looked at Cooper again. "You're all here."

He smiled. "Of course we are. You matter to Liam, so you matter to us. Did he…hmm—" His gaze slid down to her unbuttoned jeans.

"No, y'all got here in time."

"Really glad to hear that."

"He hit me on the side of my head, and my ear is ringing. My hand hurts a little where I fell on it. Other than that, I really am okay. He stuck his tongue in my mouth, and I tried to bite it off."

Cooper laughed. "You go, girl."

"He hit you?"

She turned her head to the other side to see the most beautiful face in the world. Her Liam. "Yes, but I think you paid him back for that. Hello."

"Hey. I was afraid we'd be too late."

"I knew you'd find me." The truth of those words hit her, and she lifted her hand to his face. "I'm sorry for the things I said. I know you're not like Aiden."

He put his hand over hers. "We have some talking to do, but right now, we have to take care of things here."

"My phone." She pointed to where it had landed against the wall. "There's some good stuff recorded on it. Help me sit up." He slipped his arm under her back, supporting her as she rose.

Grayson was putting the cuffs the deputy had taken off her on him. Once the man was secured, Grayson put his foot on the deputy's back. "Don't move."

"Is Jasper okay?" At Liam's narrowed eyes, she said, "I don't like him, but I don't want to see him dead."

Grayson leaned over Jasper. "He's fine, just out cold. What happened to him?"

"Deputy Dog happened."

Liam grinned. "Deputy Dog?"

"Fits him, don't you think?"

She looked at Liam, and they both laughed, which was amazing, really, after what had almost happened to her. "Thank you for coming for me," she whispered.

"I'll always come for you, Quinn."

Cooper handed her phone to her. "Guys, you have to listen to this." She opened her phone and played the recording. "Is that who I think it is?" she asked when it finished.

"Where did you get that?" Liam asked.

She told them about being taken to a house and about the man wearing a mask. "I just had the feeling it was Senator Hanson even though I couldn't see his face."

"It was his house you were at, so it was likely him," Liam said while Grayson called someone on his phone.

"You need to get down here ASAP, Sean. Bring a team with you…" Grayson eyed the two men on the floor. "And a few handcuffs." He gave whoever Sean was their location. "Trust me, you'll want to personally handle this one. We'll wait for you here."

Grayson slipped his phone back into his pocket. "He'll be here in two hours, so we have to hunker down until then."

"Who's Sean?" she asked him.

"The assistant director in charge of the FBI."

"Wow, go big or go home."

"I'm going to go get the car," Liam said. "Quinn will be more comfortable waiting in it than in here. It's filthy in here and it stinks."

She wanted to grab his hand and beg him not to leave her.

Cooper stood. "I'll get it. You stay with her." He glanced at her and winked.

While they waited, and although she'd told him she was okay, Liam had insisted she get checked out. Two EMTs had shown up and, after examining her, determined that she didn't have a concussion and her hand wasn't broken. The verdict was just to keep an eye on her, and if anything changed to take her to the hospital.

By that evening, she was exhausted and just wanted a shower to get the dirt off, and then she wanted to crawl into bed with Liam and have him curl around her and keep her safe while she slept. She'd been questioned by Sean—who she'd liked a lot—for two hours before he was satisfied that he had all he needed from her. He'd shown her a photo of Senator Hanson. She'd recognized his eyes and had positively identified him as the man who'd questioned her. She gave Sean proof that she was in his house by describing his office.

She was so tired that she only half listened as Sean outlined the plan to arrest Senator Hanson and the men who had destroyed her father's house. Jasper and Deputy Dog had already been taken away by two of his special agents. Honestly, she didn't really care anymore what happened from here on out. She'd done her job of bringing attention to the illegal dumping of chemicals into a lake children played in. The senator was going down, and that was all that mattered.

"Time to go home," Liam said, waking her up.

Sean had sat in the car to question her, and after he'd finished and left, she'd fallen asleep. "Yes, home please. Your home."

"Our home someday, I'm hoping."

She sleepily smiled. "Maybe."

He was still in the back seat with her when she heard the engine start. She noted that Cooper was driving. "Where's Grayson?"

"Staying behind with Sean," Liam said. "You've had a long day. Go to sleep."

"Okay." She toppled over onto Liam's lap and went to sleep.

The next morning, she awoke in Liam's bed with him curled around her just like she'd wished for. She didn't remember arriving home and barely remembered his taking her into the shower with him and gently washing her. She peeked under the covers to see that she had one of his T-shirts and her panties on. She smiled. Liam O'Rourke was a good man.

"Make me a promise," Liam's sleep-laced voice said from behind her.

"If I can."

"Don't go and get kidnapped again, okay? My heart can't take another one."

She rolled over to face him. "I'll do my best, but maybe I'm too much trouble."

He grinned. "You do have a way of making life interesting." His eyes turned serious. "Is it too soon to tell you that I love you, Quinn Sullivan?"

Well then. Her heart did a happy bounce, but she wasn't ready to say it back. Not yet. "Maybe a little too soon." She traced her thumb over his bottom lip. "Keep those words handy, though. I think I'll need to hear them before too long."

"They'll be on the tip of my tongue, ready to say them as soon as you're ready to hear them. Just say when."

"Speaking of tongues. Mine is missing yours."

"Is it now? Let's remedy that." He leaned in and captured her mouth in a soft, lingering kiss. Then his tongue found hers, and she sighed from the pure pleasure of being with Liam. And when he made love to her, softly and beautifully, she floated away on the feel of him, the taste of him, the scent of him.

Maybe she was in love.

Chapter Thirty-Seven

Two weeks had passed since the arrest of Senator Charles Hanson, and the attention to his arrest and the illegal dumping was finally dying down. It hadn't taken long for reporters to ferret out that Quinn was a major part of the story, and Liam had spent every minute of that time by her side, protecting her from the vultures who wanted an exclusive from her. They waited for her outside his condo, outside The Phoenix Three offices, followed her to the grocery store, and anywhere else she went, yelling their questions to her.

The one good thing to come out of all this, she'd postponed her trip to Ukraine, and it had been her idea, which was a relief. He hadn't had to be the bad guy and convince her she wasn't ready for that kind of trip.

She'd finally agreed to an interview with Felice Robertson, a reporter with a local Myrtle Beach television station. The big guys from the networks were mystified as to why she wouldn't talk to one of them over a reporter no one outside of Myrtle Beach had heard of.

That's my girl, he thought with considerable amusement when she announced her decision. Never doing what one expected of her. He stood out of sight of the cameras in the studio, listening to her answer Robertson's questions.

They'd been at it for twenty-five minutes now, and the interview was winding down. He could tell Quinn was exhausted, and he was close to walking onto the set, picking her up, and carrying her out of there.

She hadn't slept well since he'd brought her home, and he didn't like the dark circles under her eyes that had been covered with makeup for this interview. The first week, she'd had a nightmare every night, would wake up crying and struggling against the covers that were holding her prisoner. Sometimes it was Jasper in her nightmare, sometimes the deputy, and once it was Senator Hanson. The second week had been a little better. She'd only had two nightmares. She was talking to a therapist, and that was helping.

His girl was strong, and he knew she'd fight her way back to herself and do it surprisingly fast. She had not only him, but her father, along with Grayson and Cooper and Harlow in her corner, all of them there for her. His friends had welcomed her into their little family. She was laughing again, and that was great progress.

"A question many are asking," Robertson said, "is why would you risk your own life for people you don't know?"

Liam smiled, knowing what her answer would be.

"How could I not?" Quinn said. "Children were getting sick. What kind of person would I be if I turned my back on that? Whether I personally knew those children or not didn't matter. The EPA has identified the children in Hope Corner who are sick, and they are receiving treatment. That's what matters."

"You brought down a powerful senator, a possible future vice president," Robertson said. "That had to be—"

"He brought himself down. End of story."

Liam wished that was the end of the story. Hanson had a team of the best lawyers in the country working to get the charges dropped. Sean had told them there was no way that was going to happen, even with all of Hanson's expensive attorneys. Quinn's recording from when she was in his home was some of the Feds' best evidence that Hanson was not only aware of the illegal dumping but of the kidnappings and the murder of Garrison's cousin.

Quinn shook hands with the reporter, then headed his way, her eyes locked on his. He got the message. It was *get me out of here.* So he did.

"YOU WERE GREAT," Liam said after they finished watching Quinn's interview, which the station had aired as a special report.

"I'm just glad it's over."

He didn't tell her what they already knew. It wasn't over yet. There would be a trial, and she would be the star witness, but that was likely years down the road, so for now, she was right. It was over.

"I think we should turn off the TV, put on some love music, dim the lights, and let me show you how special you are." They sat in his recliner, her in front of him. He loved sitting like this, her back to his chest, his legs on the outside of hers. "Sound good?"

"Sounds like a perfect ending to this day."

"Great. Why don't you start with a bubble bath while I get everything ready, and then I'll join you. I'll bring you a glass of wine when I come."

She turned and straddled. "Or we could just get it on right here." She kissed him. "Right now."

"Tempting, but no. I'm going to romance you tonight." He patted her butt. "Go. I'll be there in a few minutes."

"Hurry." She was only a few steps from him when the doorbell rang. She stopped. "Are we expecting company?"

"Not that I know of. Probably a neighbor wanting to borrow something."

"Okay, I'll be waiting for you. Don't be long, or I might start without you." Knowing his eyes were on her backside, she slipped her shirt off and swung her hips as she walked away.

"You better not." He almost followed her, but the doorbell rang again. Whoever was on the other side was only going to get about ten seconds of his time, long enough for him to tell them to get lost.

"I'm busy right…" *Now.* "Mom?"

"Of course, I'm your mom. Who else would look like me?"

"I… I wasn't expecting you. What are you doing here? Does Dad know you're here?" She had a few gray hairs now, but she was as pretty as she was the last time he saw her, ten years ago.

"Are you going to invite me in or just stand there?"

He snapped out of the shock at seeing her at his door and pulled his mom into his arms. "You're really here." He couldn't wrap his mind around that. She'd wanted to meet secretly over the years, but he'd always been too afraid his father would find out and it wouldn't go well for her.

"I really am, and so is your father."

"What?" He leaned back and looked down at her. "Here now?" At her nod, Liam scanned the hallway but didn't see him.

"Yes, he's downstairs in the lobby. Your doorman is holding him hostage."

"Hostage?" Maybe he was dreaming his mother was here and his father was a hostage because that was the only thing that made sense.

"Your doorman, Wilson, wanted to call up and tell you

that you had guests, but I was afraid you would refuse to see us if you knew your father was here, too. So, I convinced him to let me come up if Patrick stayed with him until you gave permission for him to come up, too. Are you going to invite me in?"

"Of course. Sorry. This is just a surprise… A good one." He smiled at her. "Really good." He kept his arm around his mother as they walked inside.

"Do you need some money to buy furniture, son?" she said as she took in his living room and empty dining room.

He grinned. "I guess it looks like I might, but no. Quinn and I intend to go furniture shopping, but it's been a little hectic lately." They hadn't been in a big hurry because Quinn had been quite happy sharing the recliner with him.

"Where is she? I want to meet in person this woman who saved those poor children."

Right, Quinn was naked, waiting for him. "Let me tell her you're here, then I'll go down and rescue Dad." He needed to get to her before she came looking for him, wearing nothing but a towel…or not even that.

"There you are," she said when he came into the bathroom. "I thought you got lost."

"I kind of did. My parents are here."

Her eyes widened. "What?"

"You're no more surprised than I am. Mom's in the living room. I have to go downstairs and get my father."

"They're *here* here?" At his nod, she shot up and grabbed a towel. "I have to get dressed."

"Like you better naked, but that's probably a good idea." She grabbed his arm. "Are you okay, Liam?"

"I don't know. I feel like I'm in a weird dream. I better go downstairs. Come out when you're dressed."

When he returned to the living room, his mother had his

balcony door open and was looking out at the ocean. She turned and smiled when she heard him. "Who needs furniture when you have this view?"

"Yeah, it's pretty awesome. Be right back."

As he rode the elevator down, a hundred butterflies took flight in his stomach. The last words between him and his father had been bitter, and he'd walked away angry and heartbroken. He tried to think of what to say to his father for the first time in ten years, but nothing came to him. Not one word.

He reached the lobby and found his father leaning against Wilson's desk as they talked. Liam stopped and studied the man who'd said his son was dead to him. Patrick O'Rourke hadn't been an easy man to feel close to. He was opinionated, demanding, intimidating, and never wrong. But the man was his father, and in spite of the hurtful words hurled at him that day, Liam had missed him, had especially missed his mother, had missed being a part of a family. He'd always felt he was owed an apology, but did that even matter anymore?

No, it didn't, so he banished his hurt and approached the man who had the power to undead him. Would he? "Dad." Damn that quiver in his voice.

Patrick O'Rourke stilled, then turned. "Son."

Son. He hadn't been a son since he was eighteen years old. His father's gaze roamed over him, and Liam forced himself not to show that his nerves were a crackling live wire. He still didn't know what to say, so he didn't say anything more.

Patrick darted a glance at Wilson, then he lifted his chin toward the lobby seating. "Let's go over there and talk for a minute."

A minute? It was going to take longer than that to repair

the damage that had been done, but again, he stayed mute as he followed his father to the chairs. They sat facing each other, and Liam waited. What would his father say? Express more of his disappointment in his son? Make excuses for the years of silence?

"I...ah, I've been following the news about Quinn Sullivan's involvement in the arrest of Senator Hanson." His father frowned. "Knew there was something untrustworthy about that man."

"That's what you want to talk about? The senator?" He couldn't help the bitterness in his voice. He was expecting too much to think his father might apologize for the things he'd said.

"No." His gaze softened slightly, a flicker of regret passing through his eyes. "I wasn't an easy father, Liam. I know that. I pushed you because I believed in you, because I wanted you to be the best possible version of yourself. I had thought you would step into my shoes one day. Then when you said you were joining the military, well, I thought you were ruining your life. I was angry."

Not an easy father? That was an understatement. "The kidnapping changed me. I tried to talk to you about it, but you told me to just get over it. To man up."

"I did. But you were still a boy who'd gone through a terrible experience, and I was wrong. I've known that for some years now."

"Yet you didn't think to pick up the phone and call me? To ask to see me? I called your office once, told your assistant I was your son. I thought if I was the one to reach out, that it might be a step toward a reconciliation. You told her you didn't have a son. That was the day I gave up." Tears stung his eyes, and he glanced down at his feet to hide them from his father. His bare feet. He hadn't put shoes on.

"Pride got in my way, son. Would you look at me?"

Liam lifted his eyes to his father's. Let him see the tears swimming in his eyes. Let him see the hurt he'd lived with for ten years.

"I came here to say I'm sorry. I was wrong. Terribly wrong. I don't expect you to instantly forgive me, but I'm hoping that this is a chance to start over. That you'll give me a chance I know I don't deserve."

There were tears swimming in his father's eyes, too, and that was jarring. He'd never once seen Patrick O'Rourke humbled and even close to crying. A part of Liam wanted to refuse the chance his father was asking for. To get up and walk away. Let him see how it felt to be abandoned. But the bigger part of him had longed to have his father back in his life, to rebuild what had been broken.

"I'm a firm believer in second chances," he said, feeling the weight of years of hurt and resentment lift after saying those words.

"Thank you, son. You've grown into a man any father would be proud of."

He never thought he'd hear his father say those words, and to finally hear them, well, he was close to losing it, which would embarrass both of them. Before that happened, he stood. "Let's go upstairs so I can introduce you to Quinn."

"I want to meet the girl who took down a powerful senator. Your mother told me that the two of you are together now."

"So, you found out I secretly talk to her?"

His father chuckled. "I've always known, *Lisa*."

Well, damn. "And she thought she was so clever having a book club friend named Lisa."

He and his father looked at each other and shared the first laugh of what Liam hoped would be many more.

Later, as he and Quinn sat out on the deck with his parents, Liam leaned back in his chair and smiled at how Quinn had his father on the edge of his seat as she told him everything that had happened.

"Son, you've got an amazing woman here," his father said when she finished.

He had his family back, including one special addition, and he smiled at her. "Believe me, Dad, I know it."

Epilogue

One Year Later...

For the tenth time—probably even more—Liam eyed the board announcing arrivals. It hadn't changed since he'd checked it two minutes ago. Quinn's flight was still showing as late. Didn't the airline know she was on the plane and how much he needed to see her, to feel her in his arms again?

They'd talked almost every night that she was in Puerto Rico following a devastating hurricane, FaceTimed whenever possible, engaged in phone sex many of those times, which was hot but wasn't the same as being able to touch her. In—he glanced at the board again—twenty-one minutes her plane would land, and he would be hard-pressed not to go open the aircraft's exit door himself and dare anyone to move before he got to her.

He'd even bought a cheap ticket to fly from Myrtle Beach to Charlotte that he wouldn't use just so he could get past security and wait for her at the gate. He was a goner. He knew it and didn't care. When his brothers had teased him for doing that, he'd shrugged and said, "Bite me."

Keeping his mouth shut about her going on this particular trip, knowing she was pregnant, was the hardest thing he'd ever done, but he'd made a promise to himself that he'd never be *that guy*. The one who tried to control her or thought her job wasn't important. If he wished she would lie low until after the baby was born—and maybe a year or two after that—he was a smart man and would be keeping that thought to himself.

It felt like hours, but finally the board showed that her plane had landed. He laughed as he put his hand over his pounding heart. The woman would always send his heart racing, and he was grateful every day that he'd found her.

And there she was. Her eyes widened at seeing him at the gate, and then a big, beautiful smile greeted him. He wrapped his arms around her. "Welcome home."

"You bought a ticket, didn't you?"

"Guilty. Couldn't handle waiting in baggage for you to get down there. Couldn't wait that long to see you." He took her camera bag from her and slipped it over his shoulder, then he kissed her with all the longing of missing her the past two weeks.

"I love you, Liam."

"Love you more, Quinn."

"Nuh-uh."

"Uh-huh." It was a little game that they played every time she returned home. From the first time she'd finally said it to him, hearing those words from her mouth was a blessing he'd never take for granted.

"Let's go home where I can give you a proper welcome." Needing to touch her, he took her hand as they walked. When they reached baggage and were waiting for her suit-case, he put his hand on her stomach, and his breath caught. "You have a baby bump."

"Popped out overnight. Little bean's growing like a weed."

He pulled on her hand. "Let's go."

"What? I don't have my bag yet."

"Don't care. I'll come back for it. Right now, I need to see you naked. See this baby bump for myself." For the first time, it felt real, that his baby really was in there. There wasn't a happier man on this planet than him. He was sure of it.

The bell rang that luggage was coming out, and he sighed. His escape plan foiled, he impatiently waited for her suitcase. As soon as he saw it drop down, he went to get it. "Now can we go?"

She laughed. "Yes, Daddy, we can go."

Daddy! Hot damn, he loved the sound of that.

LIAM SAT ON the edge of their bed, his gaze on Quinn's stomach as she undressed. They hadn't planned for a baby so soon, but because of her travel schedule and constant time zone changes, she'd chosen an IUD over birth control pills. It rarely happened, but hers had dislodged and she hadn't realized it for a few days. Next thing they knew, they were having a baby.

"We need to look for a house," he said as he held his palm over the most beautiful thing he'd ever seen. Who knew a baby bump could bring tears to his eyes?

"We do?"

"Yeah, a condo's no place to bring up our little girl."

"How do you know it's not a little boy?"

"Because I want a little girl with red hair and green eyes who'll wrap me around her little finger."

"Maybe I want a little boy with blue eyes."

"Next time." He caressed that precious baby bump. Honestly, he didn't care whether it was a boy or girl, but he loved that she got salty every time he insisted their baby was a girl. "Why don't you go take a bath, get the travel grime off. By the time you get out, I'll have dinner ready. We're eating on the balcony."

"You really know how to treat a lady."

"Only this lady." He tapped her stomach. "Go."

While she bathed, he got everything ready. He'd had to use the discipline he'd learned as a Raider to not toss her on the bed—yes, she still loved for him to do that—and make love to her as soon as they walked in the door. It had been a close call, though, when she'd stood naked before him having been gone for two weeks and with her new baby bump. But tonight was the night, and when he made love to her, he wanted it to be with his ring on her finger.

He was nervous as hell. He surveyed his efforts. Her favorite pregnancy food and drink were a steak and peanut butter milkshake. Weird on the milkshake, but his lady had a craving for it, so that's what she'd get. Then the icing on the cake was…literally cake icing. He chuckled as he opened a can of the coconut pecan frosting she craved, stuck the *special* spoon in it, and carried it out to the balcony. He wondered how long it would take her to notice.

The grill was hot and ready for the steaks, and the asparagus were seasoned and wrapped in foil, ready to go on the grill. He paused to appreciate his efforts. He'd spread candles out on the balcony, scattered rose petals over the table—so far, the wind hadn't blown them away—and had soft music playing on the outside speakers he'd installed while she was gone.

"Perfect." Those romance novels he'd read on deployment had taught him much. Now he just needed the woman all this was intended for.

And there she was. He quickly stepped inside, stopping her in the kitchen. "Stay here a minute and close your eyes."

"Why?"

He laughed. "Always with the questions. That's an order, Little Marine, and good soldiers don't question their orders."

She saluted him. "Sir, yes, sir!"

Once her eyes were closed, he got her peanut butter milkshake from the refrigerator, and after taking it out to the balcony, he returned for her. He took a moment to just look at her. Her hair was down and wild, the way she knew he liked it. She'd put on one of his white dress shirts with the sleeves rolled up that she'd stolen from him and loved wearing. There was something about seeing her in his shirt that did it for him.

"I can feel you staring at me."

He loved that she was that attuned to him. "Can't help it. You take my breath away, baby." *Wait for it...*

"I'm not a baby."

"No, you're all woman." *My woman.* He didn't dare say that either.

"Can I open my eyes now?"

"Not yet." He took her hand. "We're walking out to the balcony. I'll tell you when you can open them." When he had her facing the table, he let go and stepped to her side so he could watch her face. "You can open them."

Her gaze took in the candles, the rose petals, and the table set with her mother's delicate china. "Liam," she whispered.

That was all he needed, to hear the wonderment in her voice and to see the pure pleasure in her eyes.

She stepped to the table and picked up the can of frosting. "What's this?"

Well, that didn't take long.

She pulled the spoon from the icing. "Is this..."

"A baby spoon."

"It's pink."

"Yep, for our little girl." *Wait for it...*

"Our little boy's not going to like eating out of a pink spoon."

Her attention returned to the spoon and what was tied on the end of it. "What's in this lace? Oh, it's… Liam?"

When she turned to him again, he was on a knee. "Quinn Sullivan, you are my heart, the reason for the smiles on my face. With all that I am, I love you and our baby girl…" He grinned. "Or boy. I promise to respect you, support you in all that matters to you, and to always protect you and the family we're creating. I—"

"Yes!" She fell to her knees in front of him. "Yes, yes, yes." She peppered kisses all over his smiling face. "I thought you'd never ask."

He laughed. "Well, technically, I haven't yet."

"Then for God's sake, get on with it. I want to put that ring on."

"Impatient little thing. I have a long speech I've been practicing, but I guess I'll just skip to the end. Quinn, will you marry me and make me the happiest man who ever lived?"

"If you missed it the first time, my answer is yes. A hundred times yes." She pulled the lace from the spoon and untied the ribbon holding it closed.

He took the ring. "With this ring, I promise to do everything in my power to make sure you're never sorry you love me." He slipped it on her finger. "If you don't like it, we can exchange it for one you do."

"Hush, you." She held her hand up. "It's beautiful."

"You're beautiful." He'd taken Harlow ring shopping with him, and when they'd seen the white gold two-carat emerald cut diamond engagement ring, they both said it was perfect for Quinn. Beautiful in its simplicity.

"I love you, Liam."

"Love you more."

"Nuh-uh."

"Uh-huh."

He stood, bringing her up with him. "How hungry are you?"

"Very… For you."

"Good answer." When she reached to set the frosting on the table, he shook his head. "I have some ideas for that. Bring it with us."

Her eyes lit up with delight. "You wicked boy."

"You have no idea." He carried his soon-to-be wife to their bedroom, where he showed her just how wicked he could be.

Later, after they'd gone back to the balcony and had their dinner, then a little more wickedness under the stars, he'd carried her back to bed. As she slept with him wrapped around her, he rested his hand on her baby bump.

"Hey, little girl," he quietly said. "Your daddy can't wait to meet you."

"Boy," Quinn mumbled.

He buried his smile against her neck. Liam had his family and knew he was a lucky man.

* * * * *

COMING SOON!

We really hope you enjoyed reading this book.
If you're looking for more romance
be sure to head to the shops when
new books are available on

Thursday 25th September

To see which titles are coming soon, please visit
millsandboon.co.uk/nextmonth

MILLS & BOON

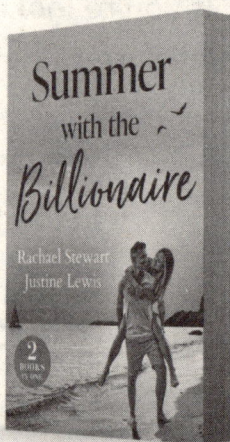